THE EDGE OF HONOR

"One heck of an exciting voyage . . . P. T. Deutermann ships a reader onto the bridge in that special place—where men go down to the sea in ships . . . a first-rate suspense novel."
—*Tampa Tribune and Times*

"*The Edge of Honor* is the rare book that addresses the complexities of war at the front and also at home. The author captures the Vietnam period and its confusion perfectly. Particularly interesting—and horrifying—is the culture depicted on the *Hood*, a real-life ship around which the novel is set."
—*The Baltimore Sun*

"*The Edge of Honor* . . . is headed up the bestseller list."
—*The Atlanta Journal-Constitution*

"Utterly convincing . . . Unlike many technothriller writers, he has a good grasp of what makes people tick as well as what makes a modern warship function. Deutermann's clear mission is to picture Navy life in a depth we have not seen before, and he succeeds brilliantly. His craftsmanship is amazing."
—*The San Diego Union-Tribune*

THE
FIREFLY

P. T. DEUTERMANN

St. Martin's Paperbacks

THE FIREFLY

Copyright © 2003 by P. T. Deutermann.

Photograph of the Washington Monument by Silvia Otte / Photonica.

Library of Congress Catalog Card Number: 2003008974

ISBN: 0-312-99481-8
EAN: 80312-99481-5

Printed in the United States of America

St. Martin's Press hardcover edition / December 2003
St. Martin's Paperbacks edition / December 2004

St. Martin's Paperbacks are published by St. Martin's Press, 175 Fifth Avenue, New York, NY 10010.

10 9 8 7 6 5 4 3 2 1

"A non-stop page-turner . . . [an] explosive tour de force . . . the author exceeds his near-perfect *Train Man* with this ripped-from-the-headlines plot pitting a middle-aged Rambo with a small but deadly arsenal of spy gadgets against spine-chilling villains, corrupt agency brass, and powerful political forces. Deutermann never sounds a wrong note."
—*Publishers Weekly* (starred review)

"The tale is loaded with political and bureaucratic skulldug-gery, and there are plenty of well-banked curves and clever twists. A solid read from an author whose own trade craft is every bit as good as that of his characters."
—*Booklist*

"You think you have read this before. Trust me. You haven't. And you should . . . a great read."
—*Tribune* (Greensburg, PA)

"One of the lasting conventions in thriller-writing involves putting the hero in a situation where the reader is forced to ask, 'How can he possibly get out of that?' . . . Deutermann . . . exploits that convention to the hilt in *Hunting Season*."
—*Houston Chronicle*

"Enough techno and black ops to satisfy Clancy fans, enough double-dealing, back-pedaling, internecine treach-ery to keep le Carré fans reading and enough plot turns and suspense to keep Crichton and Higgins Clark devotees guessing."
—*The Florida Times-Union*

"[Deutermann] returns in top form with this gripping tale . . . intensely plausible entertainment."

—*Kirkus Reviews*

SWEEPERS

"An explosive drama . . . Deutermann fans like myself will be thrilled to see that he keeps getting better."

—Nelson DeMille

"Deutermann's inside knowledge of the Navy and Pentagon politics, coupled with his likeable protagonists, make this a gripping new addition to his line of naval mysteries."

—*Publishers Weekly*

"A fine page-turner."

—*Library Journal*

OFFICIAL PRIVILEGE

"A tight story line . . . An attractive combination of murder mystery and naval politics."

—*The New York Times Book Review*

"P. T. Deutermann has become one of our best thriller writers . . . a keenly entertaining, fascinating mystery."

—*Observer* (Florida)

"Superb plotting and characterization are here, as is suspense and a clear awareness of the dangers and dalliances that can thrive in official Washington . . . *Official Privilege* is more than just a whodunit and a Navy story; it is a suspenseful indictment of power politics."

—*Florida Times-Union*

This book is dedicated to all the men and women in the departments of Defense, Homeland Security, and Central Intelligence who will be on the front lines, facing the barbarians, for a long time to come.

ACKNOWLEDGMENTS

I want to thank Don, Penny, and Laurie for their help with some of the technical aspects of this book, and my editor, George Witte, for his careful editing job. I also made extensive use of the public information Web sites of the U.S. Secret Service and the Department of Homeland Security and am grateful for the efforts put forth by these agencies, one of which is now part of the other, to help civilians understand what they do. I wish to also thank Dr. Marc A. Branham, Ph.D., creator of the Web site *The Firefly Files,* for letting me excerpt (loosely, from a technical standpoint) some of his fascinating material. That said, this book is entirely a work of fiction. Where real government agencies are depicted, the reader should understand that they are portrayed creatively and not necessarily in a factual manner. Any resemblance of the characters or incidents contained herein to actual persons, living or dead, is purely coincidental.

Fireflies 1

There are many species of firefly illuminating the common summer garden, and while their bioluminescent blinking appears to be completely random, it is not. Most of the blinks we see in the warm night are actually males in search of a mate, and each kind of firefly blinks out a specific code. The females watch. When they see the code of a male of their own species and it suits their purposes, they blink back the same code. The male then approaches for breeding.

Prologue

THE MAN WHO CALLS HIMSELF JÄGER HEISMANN AWAKES IN the dimly lighted recovery room of the private cosmetic surgery clinic in northwest Washington, D.C. He blinks rapidly to clear his sticky eyelids and then checks his watch. Almost midnight. Fire time. He closes his eyes for a few more minutes. His brain is not quite clear yet. He hears a nurse attendant come into the room, smooth his covers, check a monitoring panel, and leave. He does a mental situational-awareness check: He's just been through the last of the eighteen procedures of his year-and-a-half ordeal, this one relatively minor. His lower face and lips are numb and feel swollen to his touch. His lungs feel heavy and there is a soporific wave lapping at the edges of his brain, but otherwise he's in no pain. He concentrates on deep breathing to disgorge the last remnants of the anesthetic. The monitor behind him beeps encouragingly.

Sometime later, he opens his eyes and checks his watch again: midnight. His head is just about clear.

He sits up and swings his legs gingerly out of the bed, then waits for his balance to stabilize. He thinks about what he's about to do and summons the adrenaline necessary for the task. There's still a slight heaviness in the bottoms of his lungs, so he does some more deep breathing, shoulders back, focusing on extending his diaphragm. The monitor's beeping noise accelerates as he comes alive, so he reaches up and hits its power button and then removes all the probes and wire patches from his skin. There's no IV. He gets up, pulls on his street clothes, still doing the deep breathing and using a towel in his mouth to suppress the sounds of a sudden coughing fit. He goes over to the closet where he stashed his small duffel bag earlier, takes out the liquid Taser gun and its fluid pack, and carefully straps it on. He retrieves his jacket and slips it on loosely over the Taser gear.

He cracks open the door to the hallway and listens while he arms the Taser unit. He can hear the nurses cleaning up in the surgery, one door away, and the low murmur of the two doctors talking in their office, a door away in the opposite direction. The men first, he decides.

One more really deep breath. He detects the slight taste of something chemical at the back of his throat. Then he adjusts the portable tank pack and steps out into the hallway, the stubby Taser gun in hand, its fluid tube trailing around to the small of his back. He walks quietly down the hall and pushes the door to the doctors' private office fully open. They're still in their scrubs, drinking tea. The fat older Paki is dictating notes into a small machine. They both look up, surprised, although hardly alarmed. They never see the Taser in his hand. He points its boxy snout at the fat one, barely sees the charged stream arc out, and then the swarthy man is going over backward in his chair, flopping onto the carpeted floor like a pregnant fish. Heismann then turns and nails the other one, the young one, only two years out of Karachi, whose mouth is opening to protest. His whole body jumps and then pitches forward into a fetal position on the floor, one heel twitching audibly. Heismann waits a second and then hits each of them again, this time aiming directly for their exposed throats, sending them deep into a stunned stupor.

The equivalent of 400,000 volts. Nonlethal, they call it. Looks lethal to him. They're not dead—yet. He hefts the portable tank, tightens one strap, and then goes down the hall to the surgery.

Two women in green scrubs are loading the autoclave with trays of instruments. One of them sees him and smiles. "You're up," she says brightly.

"Ya," he mumbles, and drops her with a jolt to the throat. The tray of instruments crashes to the floor. The other, eyes widening, realizes something's terribly wrong and puts out her hand defensively. Heismann fires the stream right at it and she makes a sound like a turkey as her arm snaps back into her face. She stumbles against the autoclave, then folds to the floor, arm twitching. They both end up on their faces, so he fires a second stream at each one, hitting them in the back of the neck, hearing them grunt in turn. Then he turns off the unit and pockets the Taser. Mentally smiling at the memory of the instructor's careful warning about that sequence: "Unit off, *then* pocket it. Never the other way round." He grabs some plastic gloves out of a box and puts them on.

He drags the two semiconscious doctors down to the surgery and dumps them around the operating table. Then he drags the nurses over. The younger one has one unfocused eye partially open. She can see him. She groans, but she still can't move. He begins setting up for the fire, then pauses. If they'd all been working in here, one of them would have seen the fire and tried for the fire extinguisher. Right. He drags the middle-aged nurse by her heels over to the wall near the door, where there's a fire extinguisher. He puts it near her clenched hands. Then he pulls the pin and fires it in the direction of the operating table's curtain, covering the floor and lower wall in white powder, where the arson squad should find it. He can see her fingers twitching, but she still can't move her arms. Plenty of time, although he has the feeling he's missing something about the nurses.

Leaving the one nurse by the door, he repositions the remaining "victims" on the other side of the operating table. He glances again at his watch and then sets up the oxygen system for the fire. He's especially careful with the system lineup, ganging the two green service tanks together to ensure a plentiful supply. There are two spare nitrous-oxide tanks in a separate locker with a glass front panel. These are the ones he swapped out on Sunday, and they are fakes. What looks like metal valves and pressure gauges are instead heavy-gauge plastic, which shortly will melt.

Making sure the service valves are closed, he uses his cigarette lighter to burn through the oxygen-gas supply hose where it passes right over the wall receptacle. He takes an insulated screwdriver from his little bag and chooses the autoclave's three-pronged plug as the ignition source. He pulls one of the surgical curtains back to the wall, making sure it's in contact with the autoclave's cord. Then he pulls the plug partially out of the wall and touches the hot prong and the ground prong at the same time with the blade of the tool. There's a nasty snapping noise and a brief flash of arc light, but then the breaker trips down the hall, taking some of the surgery's lights with it. Dumb design, he thinks as he extracts the lighter again.

He checks to see that the blade prong has been physically cut by the arc, then ignites the hem of the surgical curtain. This, too, he had replaced on his 2:00 A.M. visit Sunday, substituting plain nylon for the fire-resistant Nomex curtain that had been there. This material flares nicely, first scorching, then *whoomping* into an ugly flame that quickly blackens the white ceiling tiles above it. He edges toward the door, watching the fire spread. Plenty of starting fuel in this room, with all that plastic ceiling tile, one entire wall of drapes, piles of surgical linens, the plastic laser-equipment cabinets. A dense, boiling cloud of noxious black smoke gathers rapidly along the ceiling like an angry octopus. He watches the sprinkler heads, but they do not fire. Good. Got them all. He opens the door of the locker containing the spare nitrous-oxide bottles, cracks the valves on the bottles, and then cuts on the main oxygen lines. He listens to make sure the hanging hose is hissing at full volume. Then he steps through the door and closes it behind him.

He figures he has about a minute before the flame-detector alarms go off. They're embedded in the building's security system, so he hadn't been able to cut them off. The sprinklers had been simpler—one maintenance valve. He takes one more thing out of his bag. It's a badly scorched folding steel clipboard. Inside is an equally scorched medical record, with the clinic's name and address printed on the forms. He removes the record, goes over to the water fountain on the wall, and soaks the cardboard jacket thoroughly. He puts it back into the metal clipboard and drops it into a metal record rack just outside of the surgery's door. He pats it once. He hopes it survives, because it's the key deception element—the bait, preburned to leave just the important bits legible.

He can hear the fire now, and the hallway walls are beginning to tremble. Fluorescent lights are starting to flare and dim, and the handle on the surgery door is hot to the touch. He listens at the vibrating door and smiles when he hears the familiar roar of an oxygen-fed fire. Getting really hot in there, he thinks, and it's going to get a whole lot hotter, especially when those altered nitrous-oxide bottles join the fun. The heavy plastic heads have been designed to melt through at only five hundred degrees and then release the flammable gas through a venturi nozzle that will feed the fire without exploding all at once. The bottles themselves have been designed to melt at one thousand degrees, which should happen about three to five minutes into the fire. By the time the fire department arrives, the humans in that room will have been reduced to carbonized goo. Something heavy goes down inside the burning surgery, so he grabs his bag, makes sure the doors to the office and records room are wide open, and then leaves through the clinic's back door. He walks around front, gets in his car, and drives off.

When he's two blocks away, he remembers what it was

about the nurses and mutters an audible curse in German. The third nurse: the sexy brunette. Thirtysomething, the *Ammies* would call her. She hadn't been there tonight. But of course she had seen him previously, several times. She knew what he looked like *before* those Paki doctors had done their magic. And wasn't she the record keeper? He slows and pulls over in front of an apartment building, stops the car, turns out the lights, and tries to think. He should have noticed before this. And now he has a big loose end to attend to. The record keeper. *Damn!*

He sits there in the car, forcing his still-muddied brain to remember her name. Wall. Something Wall. Catherine? No. He instinctively turns his head when he hears sirens approaching up Kalorama Road. He leans sideways down into the front seat as the big engine set goes bawling by, its red and white strobes lighting up the inside of his car. The engine is pursued by a fire chief's car, its red dome light flashing. Another engine comes up the avenue a minute later. He looks at his watch. Alarm-system call, probably. But plenty of time for the gas-oxygen mix to have done its job.

But now he must make an important detour. One woman. Shouldn't be too hard, but still . . . He has her address in his computer. Sunday wasn't the first time he'd made a nocturnal visit to the clinic, courtesy of the nurses' sloppy security procedures. Just like every office he'd ever been in. Access codes written down in phone books. Keys and even spare keys on plainly visible hooks. He could go back to his apartment, look up the address, go there tonight even.

Another fire engine comes up Kalorama, preceded this time by a police car. Second alarm. Excellent. Big *hot* fire. The surgery and certainly the upstairs rooms, all fully engaged. The floor sagging. Those spare bottles puddling into nondescript slag. He waits for the fire engine to go by, checks both ways for police, and then pulls out. He goes one full block before remembering to turn his headlights back on. Damned anesthesia.

No, he decides. Not tonight. Of course he needs her dead, like the others, but he remembers the old Army maxim: If you want something bad, you'll probably get it bad.

No. He has seven weeks until *der Tag*. The big day. Plenty of time to set up one final incidental kill. He will do this correctly. Go there, do a proper reconnaissance; see precisely where she lives, get inside, see about alarms, neighbors, dogs—the usual. She doesn't know anything that can point to what's coming, and she certainly doesn't have his name. Assuming the records room and all its contents are destroyed, the only name that should survive the fire is the one planted deep in the metal record holder, along with the tantalizing but fragmentary transcript.

He brakes hard as some idiot Washington driver runs a red light and nearly broadsides him. He automatically looks to see if there's a police car, officers who might have seen the criminal, but of course there isn't one.

Because they're busy just now, he remembers with an icy smile. And soon, very soon, they'll really be busy.

1

THE PRETTY YOUNG SECRETARY WAS STARING AT HIM OPEN-mouthed, so Swamp Morgan said it again. "Special Agents Morgan and White, United States Secret Service, to see Mr. Thompson."

"Um," she began, then stopped, apparently still at a loss for words. Swamp's face often had that effect.

"He is in, right?" Swamp asked, peering over her shoulder at the door of the corner office. A man could be heard inside talking on the phone. The polished brass sign on the door read C. FREER THOMPSON, DEPUTY ASSISTANT SECRETARY OF LABOR, PROCUREMENT POLICY. He rubbed his hands together and eyed the door as if anticipating smashing the thing in. He stopped when he saw the secretary getting truly alarmed.

"Yes, sir, he is," she said, "But he's on a teleconference call just now. I—uh—"

"Why don't you just pass him a note that we're here? That should do it. Okay? Special Agents Morgan and White, United States Secret Service, Department of Homeland Security."

"And do you have an appointment, sir?" she asked, speaking to Gary White this time, trying to reassert her position as gatekeeper to a deputy assistant secretary while pretending that Swamp was a disagreeable figment of her imagination.

"Will a federal warrant do it for you?" Swamp asked quietly, raising his eyebrows meaningfully.

She blinked, then reached for a telephone message pad to write down their names. She got up, went to the big oak door, knocked once, looked back at them, and went in, shutting it behind her.

"Warrant?" White murmured. He was a new agent, mostly along for the ride this morning, to see how the legendary Swamp Morgan did a closing. He'd been assigned to another agent in the Special Investigations Unit, the man who had actually worked up the Thompson case, but that agent had come down with kidney stones, so the case and probationer White had been handed over to Morgan for the closure interview.

"Didn't actually say I had one, did I?" Swamp murmured back. "Besides, that's the whole point of the closure interview. The idea is to excise the bad guy *before* we have to paper him."

The secretary had not returned. "What's she doing in there?" White asked.

"Probably nothing she hasn't done before," Swamp said with a crooked grin.

She reappeared and motioned them to go in. Morgan tipped his head for the younger agent to precede him. Gary White was an average-size man with a boyish face, which belied his six-year former experience as a civilian police detective. Swamp Morgan wanted to watch his quarry's reaction to his own face, especially when he saw White first. Swamp thought Gary looked to be about nineteen, so there was indeed some visible shock when C. Freer got a look at the adult member of the team. Swamp Morgan was tall, wide, and definitely not handsome.

Swamp's real name was Terry Lee Morgan. Born and raised in Harpers Ferry, West Virginia, Terry Lee had grown quickly into one of the biggest, and homeliest, kids in town. He got his size from his father, Henry Lee Morgan, who'd started life in the coal fields before moving to Harpers Ferry to escape subterranean slavery and the black lung that came with it. From the time he was ten, Terry Lee had had an oversized head, an unruly mop of black hair, and a face that faintly resembled that of a Neanderthal, complete with shelving brow, a huge jaw, large ears, and fierce dark brown eyes. From his mother, Terry Lee had inherited a gentle disposition, a sense of humor, and startling intelligence. It hadn't taken him long to discover that people made certain assumptions once they saw his face, and he'd been surprising people ever since, an attribute that was most useful in law enforcement. Rather than being sensitive or depressed about his appearance, Terry Lee had been having fun with his Neanderthal visage since he'd hit high school. He'd been a defensive guard both in high school and, later on, at Notre Dame, where he had often unnerved opposing quarterbacks by remaining outside the huddle, taking off his helmet, and then executing the threat display of a silverback gorilla, loping, jumping back and forth, all the while batting his own helmet back and forth rapidly between massive paws and staring pointedly at the quarterbacks' heads. This kind of behavior had tended to unsettle the front-line meat and thereby created frequent sacking opportunities.

He didn't acquire the nickname "Swamp" until he'd finished Notre Dame with a degree in financial management and then applied to the Federal Bureau of Investigation for a job as a special agent. During training at the FBI school down at Quantico, one of the training scenarios involved new agents setting up a sting operation by posing as a fence crew for stolen goods. The instructors posed as crooks. One of the instructors, a gorgeous redhead, took offense at the way Terry Lee was ogling her booty. She announced to the assembled crew that she would appreciate it if "Swamp Thing" over there would keep his eyes to himself. The entire cast of characters fell down on the floor laughing, including Terry Lee, who knew exactly what she was talking about. It had been "Swamp" Morgan ever since, but always with a smile, because no one wanted to offend a guy who was six three, weighed 245, and was reportedly a whole lot smarter than he looked. The name had carried over when he joined the Secret Service some years later.

The quarry today was C. Freer Thompson, Esquire, a plump double-chinned white man in his late fifties. His suit jacket was slung carelessly over the back of his executive chair, and he stood up behind an enormous mahogany desk as the agents came in. The executive office was spacious and well appointed, with floor-to-ceiling windows on the outside walls. There were two large upholstered chairs planted directly in front of the desk. Thompson's face was slightly flushed, and he was holding some papers in his hands, as if to emphasize the point that he was a busy man. The secretary remained standing in the open doorway, so Swamp pointedly asked her to shut the door behind her. Thompson started to say something but ended up clearing his throat instead. Swamp walked over to the desk, leaned across, and offered his hand. Thompson gave him a weak, somewhat moist handshake. Swamp sat down in one of the chairs. White, as previously instructed, remained standing.

"Mr. Thompson," Swamp began, "I'm Special Agent Lee Morgan, United States Secret Service. This is Special Agent Gary White. We're here to discuss your imminent resignation from government service."

Thompson blinked and then lowered himself slowly into his chair, as if not sure it would still hold him. "Resignation?" he asked. "What are you talking about?" There was a hint of defiance in his voice, but he was clearly alarmed. Swamp could see the beginnings of white knuckles.

"Why don't we keep this simple, Mr. Thompson?" Swamp said pleasantly. "I propose to talk, and I want you to listen carefully. I don't want you to say anything until I'm finished, and then I want to hear you say only one thing, and that is 'Okay, I'll resign.' Are we clear on that?"

"This is preposterous. Who *are* you? How *dare* you—"

Swamp interrupted. "Mr. Thompson?" He stared hard at the blustering bureaucrat, not blinking, moving his jaw as if disposing of one last bit of mastodon bone from breakfast, and widening his eyes to accentuate the glare. He noticed with satisfaction the sheen of perspiration appear on the fat man's face. "It really is in your best interest to hear everything I have to say, Mr. Thompson. All of it, okay? Because as best I can tell from reading federal sentencing guidelines, you're looking at right around thirty years. For someone your age, that means you'll die in prison, doesn't it? So, pay close attention and, above all, don't talk. Got it, Mr. Thompson?"

Thompson looked from Swamp to White and then back at Swamp.

"Good man," Swamp said before Thompson could open his mouth again. He then opened his briefcase and removed a fat file folder. He began thumbing through pages of material until he found his summary sheet. "The charges we have before a federal grand jury right now include multiple counts of embezzlement, contract fraud, tampering with a federal procurement-source selection board, tax evasion, racketeering, and money laundering. And that's the preliminary list." He looked over at Thompson. "We keep the prelim list short to expedite the grand jury process. There can and probably will be further charges. We like to layer things in these kinds of cases, in the event we get a picky judge. Clear so far?"

Thompson's face was pale now, and all he could manage was a tiny nod. Swamp saw sweat stains spreading under Thompson's armpits. Good, he thought. Attention achieved.

"All right," Swamp continued pleasantly. "Here's what we know." He then proceeded to describe in glowing detail how the deputy assistant secretary had been fixing Labor Department systems-analysis consulting-service contracts in order to steer a few million dollars a year to a so-called Section 8A small and minority-owned business owned secretly by Thompson's two sisters. How he'd been siphoning off two-thirds of the ensuing profits and depositing them in an offshore account, free of taxes. How he had manipulated the procurement-source selection process to cut out equally or better-qualified competing small businesses. How his special lady friend, who was not his wife, had been caught up in a Georgetown club drug sting and was ready to offer up some relevant quid on C. Freer in order to get the quo she needed to save her own admittedly delectable posterior. He casually recited a few names, dates, places, Freer's offshore bank, and Freer's mistress's apartment address just to focus things.

"Now, you asked earlier who I am," he concluded, putting the file folder back into his briefcase. "Admittedly, that's a bit complicated. I'm a recalled U.S. Secret Service agent, on secondment to the Special Investigations Unit in the Treasury Department."

Thompson frowned, apparently perplexed.

"Recalled," Swamp continued, "because I'm a *retired* U.S. Secret Service agent. That's right, retired. Twenty-six years, can you believe it? Careful how you answer that. Anyway, before I retired, I was a Senior Executive Service official, just like you, Mr. Thompson. SES. Well, maybe not just like you. For instance, I didn't commit federal crimes."

"I don't understand," Thompson croaked, looking to White as if the younger agent might enlighten him. Swamp saw White stare back at him, trying for a hard look but not quite managing it. Not with that baby face.

"Look at *me,* Mr. Thompson," Swamp said. "Here's how it works. The bad news is, we've caught you with your claws in the cookie jar. And the good news is, since we're both old hands here, well, you must know why I'm here, right?"

Thompson frowned again for a moment and then got it. "A deal?"

Swamp smiled broadly. "See how well our little system works, Mr. Thompson?" he said. He patted the back of the fat file folder in his briefcase. "Remember that I said the evidence I just summarized was *preliminary*? The sad truth is, I really don't want to work hard anymore, especially since I've already made it to retirement, so what we have here"— he patted the file again—"is just for openers. We can, of course, get more, lots more. We talk to people; they talk to other people. Hell, you know how it's done, right?"

Swamp saw Thompson wince and then look down at his hand. He'd managed to cut himself on the edge of one of the papers he had been compressing. When Thompson reached into a drawer for a Kleenex, White, God love him, slipped his hand inside his coat. Thompson totally missed it, which probably avoided a humiliating intestinal dysfunction on Thompson's part.

Swamp kept it going. He was close. He was sure of it.

"You see, Mr. Thompson, it's Treasury's position, and the Justice Department concurs, of course, that senior rotten apples like you give the whole government a bad name. And while we can and will happily prosecute your ass and lock you away in a federal penitentiary for years and years, sometimes, and especially when there's been no bodily injury, no violence against persons, it can be in the government's best interest to simply make you go 'away,' You getting this, Mr. Thompson? I can speak more slowly, use more one-syllable words, if you want me to."

Thompson looked back up, swallowed, and nodded again, all the while wrapping the Kleenex around and around the paper cut on his finger.

"Good. So here are the elements of the deal: You're going to have to make financial restitution. That means give it all back, okay? Your sisters are going to have to make financial restitution, and it'll be your job to explain that to them. I'm sure you'll want to do that, because it looks to us like they weren't really part of this. *Were they?* . . . No, we didn't think so. And, of course, you and the IRS are going to have some quality time together. You know how those guys are.

And finally, you're going to resign. As of *. . . well, let's see."
Swamp glanced at his watch. "Today's the ninth of January.
Happy New Year, by the way. I think you're going to resign
by close of business today, effective, let's say, on the fifteenth of this month. For personal reasons, of course. And
your resignation is absolutely going to be accepted. Did I
mention that I've already had a word with the Secretary of
Labor? . . . No? Well, I have. She's waiting for your paperwork as we speak."

He stopped to let Thompson absorb all this, or even to
say something, but the man was just staring down at his
desk now. Swamp couldn't tell if he was thinking or if he
was just in shock. Some of them went pretty much cata-
tonic at this juncture. He looked over at White, who nodded and then unbuttoned his suit jacket and extracted a
shiny pair of steel handcuffs. They positively glistened in
his hands.

"Or," Swamp said pointedly. White was holding the cuffs
in both hands, rubbing one against the other to make a small
scraping noise. Thompson looked at the cuffs, then back at
Swamp.

"Okay," he whispered. "I'll resign."

"There you go, Mr. Thompson. That wasn't hard, was it?
Now, we're almost there, so let's just nail it all down." He
reached into his briefcase and withdrew a much thinner file
folder. "Here's your resignation letter. Already typed out. On
Labor Department stationery, today's date, and everything. I
want you sign it and then date it under your signature." He
handed it over.

"Now?"

"Right now. That way, there won't be any of those pesky
second thoughts. Because we well and truly have you, Mr.
Thompson. And although your sisters think that this whole
sweet deal was within your legal prerogative, we can have
them, too. That piece of paper is the carrot, Mr. Thompson.
You watch the nightly news, don't you? So you know what

the stick looks like. So sign it. And, yes, right now. Madame
Secretary is waiting."

Thompson looked at the folder, then opened it as if expecting a snake to pop out. The resignation letter was a
grand total of two lines. As promised, it was on official Labor Department stationery, and all the appropriate titles
were in place. "Shouldn't I talk to my lawyer or something?"
Thompson asked.

Swamp leaned back in his chair, as if disappointed. "You
can certainly do that," he replied. "You can talk to lots of
lawyers if you want to. But if you don't sign that right now,
I'm going to take it back. Then we're all going to change
mode here."

Gary White rubbed the cuffs some more. "But," Thompson protested. "I mean, this is duress."

"Of course it is, Mr. Thompson," Swamp said, smiling.
"Absolutely. It's the epitome of duress. That's the whole
point of *my* being here. Although I have to say, if you think
this is duress, wait till you go into the system. Now *that's*
duress." White was nodding helpfully.

"The *system?*"

"Oh, c'mon, Mr. Thompson. The criminal justice system.
Federal court. Your arraignment. A starring role on the
nightly news for all your neighbors out there in Chevy Chase
to enjoy as you do the perp walk. And we will give the media
some advance notice. And then hordes of ravenously expensive lawyers. Then the IRS will pile on—remember them?
Think confiscation of all your assets—your home, your cars,
your bank accounts. Then more lawyers—financial guys this
time. A little bit of jail time, at first anyway. Then an expensive bail bond—they'll want ten percent in cash up front, assuming you have any left. Then a long, drawn-out trial, and
then real prison time, not jail anymore. Bad food, bad
clothes, really bad haircut. Big *horny* cellmates. A whole
new cultural horizon. Exciting, if perhaps initially painful,

adventures in your sexual education. You listening to me, Mr. Thompson? Am I coming through here?"

Thompson had the look now: Bambi out on Interstate 95, frozen in the median, about to make a really bad decision.

"Sign the damned letter, Mr. Thompson," Swamp ordered. "Before I conclude you're being defiant." He gave Thompson the look again. "Can you imagine how poorly I handle defiance?"

Thompson swallowed, took a deep breath, picked up a pen, dropped it, retrieved it, and signed the resignation letter. He closed the folder and pushed it back across the desk toward Swamp.

"Now what?" he said. He actually sounded relieved. That's the wonder of it, Swamp thought. They almost always sound relieved. Grateful even.

"We'll take this upstairs. In the meantime, Mr. Thompson, you go home now. Do not clear your desk. Do not *touch* your computer. Leave all your personal effects, and that Rolodex. The Labor Department IG's people are on call to do the housecleaning." He looked at his watch. "In fact, they should be outside right now. With security."

"Can I tell—"

"Tell your wife? Sure. But don't contact your sisters just yet—we have some other people who are on their way to talk to them. You can and should talk to your accountant, and your lawyer, if you have one. And you probably should have one. You can even have your lawyer call me if you'd like. Here's my card."

Thompson exhaled noisily. "I'm ruined."

"Financially, yes, you are, Mr. Thompson," Morgan said brightly. "But look at it this way: You won't end up a convicted felon, and you're not going to be living in some hot and sweaty federal penitentiary for the rest of your life. You're getting to walk out of here with a simple resignation letter. Truth is, you've just cut a smart deal, Mr. Thompson."

Thompson shook his head slowly. "Ruined," he murmured. "Just like that."

"Not 'just like that,' Mr. Thompson. You've been doing this shit for a long time. And, hell, Treasury's been assembling this case for five months. I'm just the closer, you understand."

Thompson got up, turned around, and stared out the windows. "I might as well shoot myself."

Swamp saw White frown. Swamp had actually been about to agree with Thompson; even without a trial, it would save a mountain of paperwork. On the other hand, all the new agents were reportedly getting sensitivity training, so Swamp relented. "You can do that, I suppose," he said, speaking sincerely, as if he truly cared. "Although, you realize, guns tend to make a real mess. Do it against a wall, you can never get the brain stains out, you know?"

He saw Gary blink, and Swamp knew he had to do better. "But really," he said, "I don't feel this situation is worth suicide. Look at me, Mr. Thompson."

Thompson was looking back at him but not seeing him.

"Compromise, Mr. Thompson," Swamp continued, gathering his papers. "Compromise is the very essence of good government, don't you think? You with me on this?"

With a small start, Thompson brought himself back to the discussion at hand and focused on Swamp's face. "What?" he said.

"Are you with me on this, Mr. Thompson?" Swamp said again. "That this isn't worth suicide or anything drastic like that? That you can think of it as a kind of career change?"

"*Career* change?" Thompson croaked.

"There you go, Mr. Thompson. You're getting the picture now." Then he laughed at the perspiring official. "Of course you are."

"And another one bites the dust," said Larry Daniels, director of the SISU at the Treasury Department, inviting Swamp into his less than spacious office. "Nice effing work there, Swamp."

"I appreciate your calling me," he told his ex-boss. "It was fun to do a closing again."

"You always were our best closer," Daniels said. "How's life at the Circus Maximus?"

"I'm up to my neck in alphabet soup. ILO in OSI at DHS. That's intelligence liaison officer to the Washington intel community within the Office of Special Investigations of the Department of Homeland Security."

"Aargh."

"Yeah. You try bringing all the intelligence lines in this town together in one place at the State Department from the seventy-three federal law-enforcement agencies and offices based in Washington. Talk about herding goddamned cats."

"Well, you get bored over in OSI, you're welcome back here. And I mean that. Gary White do okay?"

"Nice kid. Well, of course, he's not a kid. Just looks that way."

"I know, but that baby face allows him to sneak up on people sometimes, so it works both ways. Ex–Homicide detective with the Fairfax cops across the river. Look, he's about done with his probationary year. Reason I brought it up, I've been tagged to give back a cross-deck warm body for your outfit, Homeland Security. Want to take him on?"

"Sure, if he can get the clearances. I could use the help. I'm surprised DHS is still drafting people, though. It's been what—two years now since DHS stood up?"

"Press gang is more like it," Daniels grumbled. "I've lost track of who owns what anymore. But what the gestapo wants—"

"Right, the gestapo gets. If people only knew what a joke that was."

"What do I know?—I'm just a lowly Treasury cop. His

federal BI's almost done, so I'll go ahead and set it up. You get to tell him what Homeland Security actually does."

"If I ever find out," Swamp said. Both men laughed.

Swamp walked back to the Old Executive Office Building after a quick lunch in an L Street deli. It was a brisk eight blocks from the Secret Service offices on this breezy, cool January day, but Swamp appreciated the fresh air. He'd been with the Office of Homeland Security almost since its inception, having offered his services immediately after the September 11 disaster. It had been a frustrating slog since then, with the new cabinet-level department trying to define its mission, scope of authority, and bureaucratic power in a town that shared such commodities grudgingly. Compared to the almost military efficiency of the Secret Service, the start-up of the DHS had been an exercise in chaos management. And as a recalled annuitant, Swamp enjoyed none of the personal power he had exercised in his last active-duty assignment, as the deputy assistant director of the Secret Service's prestigious Intelligence Division. Still, he was grateful to be back in the national security game, able to do something to combat the cancer of international Muslim terrorism.

His office, or, more properly, cubicle, was on the third floor of the OEOB, as it was known throughout Washington. Many of the original Office of Homeland Security staffers had been shoved into cramped quarters in the graceful old mansion a block away from the White House, courtesy of a resentful National Security Council staff, which had had to give up the spaces. His boss, Tad McNamara, was the director of the Special Investigations Unit within the Homeland Security secretariat. Their charter had been drafted on the fly after September 11, 2001, and Swamp wasn't the only recalled agent working there.

There was a phone message, two hours old, on Swamp's

desk: "See Mr. McNamara." He called McNamara's secretary, Mary, who confirmed that the director was in and available.

Tad McNamara was a tall, hawk-faced man who had been the assistant director in charge of Intelligence Operations at the FBI when the Arabs attacked New York City. He and Swamp had worked together when Swamp was a deputy assistant director at Secret Service headquarters, and he had snapped up Swamp's offer to come back on active duty right after the attacks. Tad McNamara was a man who took most things seriously and looked the part.

"Mary said you had another project?" Swamp asked after being shown into McNamara's office.

The director was sitting behind his desk. He pointed Swamp to a chair and pulled out a case folder. "It's a firefly, I'm afraid," he said. "Came over from the Protective Research Unit, your old outfit. Came in routine, late last week. You're finished with that Labor guy, right?"

"Right. Closed him this morning. He walked the plank."

"Good. Larry Daniels said if anyone could close that guy, you could. Now this," he said, waving the file folder, "is probably going to be a lot less satisfying, but, unfortunately, we're probably going to see more of these, at least until we get through this goddamned inauguration."

"This is a good time *not* to be in the Secret Service," Swamp said. "It's what—eleven days from now? They start working up the security survey for an inauguration a year in advance, and right about now, everyone's hair is on fire."

McNamara nodded. "This thing is not strictly an intel matter, of course, but with your Secret Service background, you're the guy who can give me a quick evaluation."

"How'd we get it?"

"PRU is in overload. They're getting dozens of threats in every day and they simply can't handle the volume. If it even looks like a threat's a firefly, they're farming it out. Any outfit within DHS with the word *Investigation* in its title is getting tagged to help. Like I said, it's probably bullshit."

Swamp shrugged. "Bullshit 'R' Us," he said. "That's fine by me." And it was. A light load was the last thing he wanted these days. Busy, very busy—that's what he wanted. An endless string of twelve-hour days to make the nights' sleep come easier. "Need to keep in motion, boss," he said.

McNamara nodded sympathetically. Even though it had been almost four years since Swamp's retirement-day ceremony in the Secretary of the Treasury's office, everyone who knew him still remembered what had happened immediately afterward. It was one of the few things that could still seize him up, no matter how good a face he put on it.

"Okay," McNamara said briskly. "So, this thing. About six weeks ago, late November, I think, there was this bad fire up in northwest D.C. A plastic surgeon's private clinic. Four vics."

Swamp nodded, remembering. "Read about it. Something to do with the oxygen system."

"Right. Really hot fire. Got two docs, two nurses. All in the operating theater."

"And?"

"Some forensic problems. First, there apparently was no patient. At least that's what D.C. Arson thinks. Two docs, two nurses, why were they there in the operating room with no patient?"

"Getting set up? A training session?"

"Late at night? Plus, nurses do setup. Docs come in at the last moment, hands in the air, going, 'Scalpel, clamp, coffee.' . . . Anyway, that's one. And maybe there *was* a patient. Arson guys ended up calling in the Bureau lab people. You have to understand, ID of remains was problematic. Because of the oxygen."

"Serious toasts."

"Yeah. Carbon mounds on the floor kinda deal."

Swamp nodded. His uncle had been a professional gas

welder. Oxygen was what turned an acetylene torch into a steel cutter.

"And that was the second problem: D.C. Arson feels that there would not have been enough fuel in the OR to sustain such a hot fire. You know, big oxygen-fed flare-up when it starts, everything burns pretty quick, people inhale super-heated gas, flop and twitch, and then the whole thing dies down. This one didn't die down. Place looked like the inside of a blast furnace."

"An external fuel source?"

"Two of the four liquefied-gas bottles melted. Two did not. Something hinky there."

Swamp nodded thoughtfully. "So maybe a faked fire. Arson. Okay, homicide. What's this got to do with the Secret Service and protecting the president?"

"Well, D.C. Arson listed the case as open. Split decision: One guy says it was probably a deliberate fire, not an accident. Other inspector says no, insufficient evidence. Absence of a patient on the table doesn't prove shit, especially when the table's melted. So close it out."

"They got closure statistics, too, don't they?"

"Bingo. But still . . . This one guy's pretty adamant," he said, opening the file folder. "Let's see. Deputy Chief Inspector Carl Malone. I know these arson-investigation types. They get a sixth sense, and they're often right."

"And the connection to the president's protective detail?" Swamp prompted.

"Right. Last week, this case came up for automatic cold-case review. Malone's been taking a second look. First week in January, folks still out on leave, nobody else in the office, so time to actually think about a case. And now they have all the evidence boxes back from the Bureau labs. Malone finds something interesting in one of the boxes. Calls Secret Service at the White House. They shop it to PRU. It's a partially burned medical record."

"The missing patient?" Swamp asked, indicating the case

folder. He was suddenly impatient, ready to get into something new.

"This here is PRU's initial disposition report. The evidence in question is still with D.C. Arson. But apparently, the face-lifters were audiotaping their patients during anesthesia."

"You mean taping the OR? To catch errors? Good surgeons do that."

"That's usually videotape. This was strictly audio. Inspector Malone theorizes that these guys were into taping their *patients*. Apparently, people sometimes say some interesting shit under anesthesia."

"For what, blackmail? Their own patients?"

"Who knows? But go start with this Malone over in D.C. Arson. He says there's evidence of a threat to the president, but he's still got it. I'm assuming he laid it out for PRU, but you go see with a fresh set of eyeballs."

Swamp got up and took the case folder from McNamara. "Who's riding this one for the Secret Service?"

"It's on the route slip there. Actually, I don't recognize the name, although you might. And remember, they're classifying it as a firefly. Your mission is to confirm their judgment. On the other hand, you think it's real, write a point paper and I'll get it right back to PRU."

"Got it," Swamp said, definitely anxious to get going. McNamara wished him good luck and then he was out of there. Gary White was waiting for him when he got back to his office.

"That was quick," Swamp said.

"I managed to hand over the final report-writing job on the Thompson case to another probationer," White said with a sheepish grin. "But only because I had hurry-up, hurry-up orders to report immediately to OSI. Like right now. Today, even. Like I didn't want to piss you off. Sir."

Swamp grinned back. "Nice move. Don't try that one on me, however."

"Never happen," White said. Swamp told him to go see

Mary, Mr. McNamara's secretary, to get a cube assignment. "It'll take her at least the rest of the afternoon to pry some more space out of the NSC people. Meantime, you and I have a firefly to pursue."

White was clearly baffled, so Swamp explained the slang. "A firefly is a small insect that rises out of the nighttime grass and blinks its biolight right in your face. Everybody looks at it because it's kind of amazing that an insect can do that. Then somebody inevitably gets tired of the diversion and smacks its bioluminescent ass back down into grass."

The young agent was still perplexed. "Uh, and?"

Patience, Swamp reminded himself silently. You were a new agent once upon a time, too. "And all government agencies have lots and lots of issues on their plates. Nobody needs more work. Sometimes an issue pops up out of the bureaucratic noise level, which is sometimes called 'the grass.' It comes up looking really important, demanding immediate attention. Blink. Blink. Blink. People get excited; everybody starts to jump on it. Until some adult with supervisory experience takes a hard look at it and then smacks it back down into the grass because it really wasn't all that important. Or it wasn't true. Or it was some lord high pooh-bah's policy hobbyhorse. In other words, a firefly."

White nodded. "And 'grass'? Where did they come up with that word?"

"Old military expression. Comes from primitive radar sets, which were basically oscilloscopes. You look into an o-scope, you see what looks like a horizontal line of green grass all along the bottom axis—the signal you're analyzing sticks up above that 'grass' level. So when people say something's 'down in the grass,' they mean it's not significant."

Gary thought that one over. Swamp anticipated the next question.

"And now you're gonna ask me what an o-scope is," he said. White, relieved, brightened.

Swamp sighed. Hopeless, he thought. "It's time to go

back to work now," he declared. "Go find out where the District of Columbia Police Department's Arson Unit lives. If we're lucky and they're at police headquarters, we can take the Metro."

"Yes, sir. And can I use your phone?"

Deputy Chief Inspector Carl Malone welcomed them into his office on the second floor of the D.C. Police Department's headquarters building. He was a middle-aged black man, almost as big as Swamp Morgan. The three sat down at a conference table.

"I'm Mr. Minority on this case," Malone said, opening a large three-ring notebook with a case number stenciled on the front cover. "Our cold-case board wants to ree-tire this puppy."

"All I've seen was the Protective Research Unit's disposition report," Swamp said. "Can you review the facts of the case for us?"

"Certainly," Malone replied. He went through the two alarms, the discovery of four sets of human remains, the special nature of an oxygen-fed fire as it pertained to evidence and human victims, and then the almost archaeological investigation that followed.

"What got your attention?" Swamp asked when Malone had finished.

"Several things. First, one of the toa—um, victims, I mean, was found over by the door, an expended fire extinguisher near her hands, like she'd seen the fire and tried to get on it. Never happen in an explosive atmosphere. Goes too fast, and you can't move once the temp inside your lungs gets to twelve hundred."

Swamp grimaced at the thought. "And second?"

"Second was the fact that the fire kept going for so long. You know, people who build operating rooms are sensitive to fire danger. Plus, they use a lot of metal or hard plastic to make it easier to sanitize. So there shouldn't have been that much to burn, other than maybe ceiling tile. No carpets, no wood furniture. And yet this place looked like the inside of a blast furnace. Even melted a couple of the gas bottles."

"Meaning?"

"Meaning the oxygen supply and whatever the gas was stayed on."

"You said four victims: two docs, two nurses."

"That's the third thing. No patient. Or any instruments on the side tables. There were instruments on the floor."

"What could the building itself tell you?"

"Not that much, once you got away from the blast furnace. We were able to wet down the rest of the building and save most of it, except for what was smoke- or water-damaged. But the fire itself didn't spread much, except up— got to the roof."

"Their records?"

"We got partials. Their computers melted, but we've got several carbonized boxes of paper records. Did I mention that this was an interesting little plastic surgery practice? Because it surely was. For those records still readable, all the patient names were in numerical code. We never found the key. Both surgeons were Pakistani. One apparently the main man, the other one fresh out of medical school and then specialty training here in the States."

"Doing whom—wives of Washington VIPs?"

"No. Even though we don't have any names, all the surgery was apparently done on males. And at night. For this crew anyway."

" 'This crew'?"

"Yeah, another interesting bit. During the day, there was another set of docs, Americans, who did the normal stuff— tummy tucks and boob jobs. Totally separate from the night crew. Separate admin office, separate records, separate staff. Same OR. The American docs owned the building—bank held the mortgage—and they told us they subleased to the night docs."

"And knew nothing, saw nothing, heard nothing about the night crew?"

"Like those famous little monkeys, all in a row. All legal, by the way. Separate but current building permits and licenses. The senior day doc said that the night crew's clients wanted total privacy, which is why everything was done at night. He said these guys specialized in incremental physioplasty, which means doing what you do in small operations, so the patient 'has work,' but since it's done over a prolonged period of time, no one notices."

"Could you tell anything about the work?"

"Our medical guys say it consisted of two main categories: the standard cosmetic upgrades—facial work, hair implants, lipo work—and then more complicated procedures— facial-bone reconstruction, hair replacement, composite skin grafts on fingers and toes, iris coloration, even some retinal displacements, whatever those are. There's even a hint of a partial sex-change procedure. Remember now, we got mostly fragments."

"Skin grafts on fingers? You're talking identity changes."

"What I thought, too. I'm no doc, but the Bureau lab people picked right up on that, too."

"And all the night patients names are in code?"

"Yeah." Malone got up to refill his coffee cup. The two agents joined him at the coffee machine on the corner table. "Our Homicide people talked to the Bureau. The Feebs hinted that they had some information on the Paki docs, but they wouldn't share. You know how they can get."

Swamp nodded. The old feds-versus-locals problem. Washington's obsession with turf wars made it even worse than elsewhere in the country, despite the new cabinet department. "So what inspired you to send a report to the White House protective detail?" Swamp asked.

"One record," Malone said. "Lemme show you." He reached into an evidence box on the floor and withdrew a plastic evidence envelope with what looked like a steel clip-board inside. "This here's a medical-file board."

He opened the Ziploc bag and pulled out the file board. A faint odor of char seeped out of the bag. "I found this while I was getting ready for the cold-case board. It's a medical/sur-gical record. Evidence log said it was picked up out in the hallway, right near the OR." He flipped back the metal front cover.

"This thing was exposed to direct fire, because the front and back several pages are burned beyond legibility. The parts recovered from the crease of the file holder indicate the pages were standard post-op reports. Except for these three pages." He wedged open the clipboard and handed over three pieces of paper to Swamp. The edges were badly scorched, and the paper had that peculiar stiffness that comes when it's been wetted and then dried.

"The lab's done its thing, so they can be handled. These notes, or whatever they are, were all the way in the middle of the file. They appear to be typed transcript. Or maybe voice-recognition text. Hard to tell."

"Yeah, my boss said something about these quacks taping their patients when they were under anesthesia. Is there a name?"

"Nope. Still just the code number—two-oh-oh-three-four-one. We found other pieces of transcripts like this in some of the office records, although, like I said, we're talk-ing just fragments here. And lots of it was gibberish, of course. This one's no different, except for one block of text, which I highlighted."

A young woman stuck her head in and told Malone that the chief of detectives wanted to see him. "You'll have to ex-cuse me for a minute," he said, getting up. "But here's the thing: This guy, whoever he is, I think he's talking about bombing the Capitol on the night of the State of the Union address."

Swamp's head jerked up. "Whoa," he said.

"I should tell you that I'm the *only* one thinks this. Others disagree. It isn't exactly crystal-clear. Look for yourself. I'll be right back. Hopefully."

Gary White moved his chair so he could see. Swamp laid out the three charred pages of double-spaced typing. There were words and phrases in English and also, surprisingly, in German, although the typist had transcribed everything phonetically, misspelling many of the German words. The transcript had page breaks and dates, indicating the record had been assembled over the course of the last year. There was babbling about face-cutting, strange sounds in the patient's ears, painful breasts, what had sounded to the transcriber as some undecipherable names, then single words such as *rain* and *steel* and *oil.* A reference to a mountain of money, Faust, and two masters. Then more German words.

"That's German?" White asked.

"Yes," Swamp said. "Stream of *un*consciousness. Random words, sometimes associated, sometimes not. Like these names: Hitler, Heydrich, Himmler, Hess. Then something about '*H*'s.' . . . I see what Malone meant about it being obscure."

"What did he highlight?"

Swamp looked at the third page. The text was fractional. "Soon now . . . [undecipherable] . . . Head right off . . . right off! . . . Union *Staat* speech . . . *Sieg und Götterdamerung . . . Leichen regnen verden* . . . [undecipherable] Bomb . . . bomb . . . bomb . . . *Heil* [something]—Hitler? . . . Five *H*'s . . . [unintelligible German word] . . . [something] five . . . Hitler . . . Himmler . . . Heydrich . . . Hess . . . Heismann . . . Soon, very soon, *Ammie Schwein.*"

White shook his head. "I got the '*Heil Hitler*' bit; can you make out the rest?"

"Yeah. I did a year and a half in Germany during my exchange tour across the river; plus, I took German in college. The word *Staat* translates as 'state.' That could, as Malone thinks, refer to the State of the Union address. The word *Göt-*

terdamerung refers to the Twilight of the Gods. Think Valkyries going down in flames in a Wagnerian opera. A hugely dramatic finale. *Leichen regnen verden* means literally that it's gonna rain death or dead bodies. *Ammie* is pejorative German slang for Americans. *Schwein* means 'pig.' The 'Five *H*'s' beats me, other than the names that follow were the stars of the Nazi firmament. All except that last one—I don't recognize Heismann. But bottom line? I think Malone could be right: Somebody's babbling under the anesthesia about a bombing during the State of the Union speech."

Malone walked back in. "You get through the German stuff?"

"I speak some German," Swamp said. "This seems fairly provocative to me. This is what you sent over to the White House?"

"Right," Malone said, sitting down. "I remembered that the Secret Service does the security survey for the State of the Union address, too."

"Almost right. Actually it's the PRU. The White House protective detail is focused exclusively on protecting the president and his family, twenty-four/seven. This would have gone right to PRU—Protective Research Unit. They handle all the threat-analysis work."

Malone shrugged. "Whatever. They sent you."

Swamp smiled as he sat back in his chair. "After a fashion," he said. "And I now understand why they're treating it as a firefly. If I'm reading it right, the target's a year away."

"How so?"

"This is an inauguration year. There won't be a State of the Union speech until next year."

"Well now," Malone said, "technically, that's true, but there will be a presidential address to a joint session of Congress next month. I know that because we're already scheduling damn near a year's worth of overtime for that and the inauguration. Securitywise, it's just about the same thing. A foreigner might not know the difference."

Swamp nodded, acknowledging Malone's point. "Still," he said, "the Secret Service is totally absorbed right now in getting ready for the inauguration. My guess is that they shrugged this one off because they have more pressing threats. But still . . ."

"Yeah," Malone said. "I'm gonna keep my investigation open, see if we can explain that fire better. This other shit, that's officially over to you guys. We'll share any evidence, anything we find out, of course."

"Appreciate it," Swamp said. "As I remember, the papers said that one nurse survived this disaster—by not being there."

"Right," Malone said, reaching for another file. "A Ms. Connie Wall. Had the night off. We should have an interview record. Yeah, right here. She was at home when the deal went down. Horrified. Seemed genuinely shocked at what happened. Confirmed there were oh-two and nitrous-oxide tanks in the surgery. Didn't know who was being operated on that night. This is before we knew about the codes and shit. Interview terminated due to subject's becoming medium hysterical."

"I'd guess that the nurses never did know who was being operated on," Swamp said, tapping the metal file. "This one's coded in the name box, just like the other ones you mentioned. Okay. I'd like to do two things. One, go see the scene of the fire, preferably with you as guide. And two, talk to the nurse."

"No problem with the fire scene," Malone said, looking at his daybook. "How about four-thirty today? And as for the nurse, you're on your own."

Swamp looked at Gary. "Works for me," he said.

Heismann saw the pretty banker approaching from the direction of the L'Enfant Plaza Metro station. He moved casually from the middle of the park bench to the end. The Mall was moderately populated, it being lunchtime on this cloudy

January day. Three young bureaucrats in shirts and ties were gamely trying to throw a Frisbee while pretending it was warm outside. Heismann was wearing a suit and tie under his dark green loden overcoat, and a matching hat to keep his head warm in the cold January breeze. His square-rimmed oversized sunglasses covered most of his features. His beard appeared to be about three weeks old, even though it wasn't real.

He opened up a white deli lunch bag and began to root around in it. He tried not to smile when he saw the newspaper tucked under the princeling's arm. Amir—or was it Emir?—Mutaib abd Allah, managing director of the Royal Kingdom Bank, loved American and British spy movies and fancied himself thoroughly grounded in operational trade-craft. The *Wall Street Journal* was folded in thirds under his right arm. For identification, of course, as if Heismann wouldn't recognize him, even after eleven months. For his part, Heismann had been told to display a white bag. He mentally rolled his eyes as he remembered all this nonsense.

Mutaib sat down on the far end of Heismann's bench, nodded politely to him, and unfolded the newspaper. Staying in character, Heismann obligingly didn't look at him again. He spied the Coke in the bag. Shaken, not stirred, as he remembered. Best be careful opening it, then.

"The fire appears to have been rather a success," Mutaib said quietly from behind his newspaper. He was about the same size as Heismann, with light olive skin, a delicately hooked hose, dark eyes, and a sculpted black goatee. He affected a passable Oxbridge accent when he spoke English, even though he'd finished his English schooling at the public school stage. He looked exactly like what he was: a casually cosmopolitan Saudi Arabian businessman assigned here in Washington to the Royal Kingdom Bank. Heismann was convinced the Arab was also a flaming homosexual.

"Oxygen," Heismann muttered, pretending to watch the antics of the Frisbee threesome. Mutaib was technically his

field controller, so Heismann, who hated homosexuals, carefully erased all vestiges of contempt from his voice. He took
a bite out of his machine-stamped sandwich, made a face,
and returned the miserable thing to its wrappings. He then
cracked open the Coke. He despised American fast food, and
the pasty sandwich confirmed his worst expectations. The
Coke, at least, was drinkable.

"Well then. Any loose ends?" Mutaib asked.

That question was much too casual, Heismann thought.
The *Washington Post* had carried a detailed story of the fire
at the cosmetic surgery clinic weeks ago, but the story had
died out. So why the questions now? There had been a list of
the victims, plus the fact that one nurse, Ms. Connie Wall,
had not come in for work that night. Fortuitously, for both
her and the plan, as it turned out. "The nurse, of course," he
said.

"Ah, yes, the nurse," Mutaib replied, turning a page and
then grappling with the paper as a gust of wind tried to steal
it. Heismann shivered. Why couldn't we have done this over
the phone? he wondered. But then he remembered where
he was, in Washington, where one never knew who or what
was listening to your phone conversations. The city was
the headquarters of the FBI, CIA, ATF, DEA, the Secret
Service, DIA, NSA, and a host of lesser federal law-
enforcement and intelligence agencies, so anyone in the
game had to assume that the entire municipal phone system
was bugged and cross-bugged. Heismann did not own or
ever use a cell phone. He pushed the remains of his sandwich deeper into the white bag and opened a small bag of
chips.

"Does she need, um, attending to, then?" Mutaib asked.

"Not immediately," Heismann replied. They stopped
talking as three pretty young women came strolling by, con-
ducting a surprisingly frank anatomical commentary on the
Frisbee players.

"But ultimately, yes, hmm?"

Yes, dear, Heismann thought. Ultimately, all the loose ends had to be tied off. Including Emir Mutaib. "You forget," he replied, "that we can use her for stage two of the bait. Plus, if I terminate her now, the authorities will have separate deaths connected to the same incident. As things stand, it was a fire, with one lucky survivor. If she dies now, any investigator with half a brain would notice."

"Quite so," Mutaib said approvingly. Heismann thought that the Arab was also watching the three Frisbee players. Disgusting. "Will you require tracking assistance on her?"

Heismann sighed. "It is nothing. I have been into her house. She lives alone up near Rock Creek Park. It will be no problem. Do we know if the *Ammies* took the bait?"

"Bit too soon, I should think. One assumes the first indication will come from our contacts at Interpol. A sudden American interest in one Jäger Heismann. Then we'll know. Not before."

Heismann had told his Arab controller at the very beginning that he intended to wipe out the clinic when they had fulfilled their side of the contract. The Arabs hadn't seemed to care one way or the other. The Americans, however, might take a different view if they saw through the "accidental" nature of the fire. If they were competent, they would. "And you have no one inside the city police department?" he asked.

Mutaib made a dismissive gesture with his left hand. "The *Washington* Police Department? Whatever for? They are fools."

Heismann grunted. For the arson investigation, idiot. On the other hand, the real threat to his mission here would come from the federal police, not the city police. Especially *this* city's police.

"The bank will know at once," Mutaib said. "In the meantime, we have acquired the house."

Heismann sat up straighter and glanced around. This was important. "Ah, yes? Within range?"

"Absolutely. Well within range. A duplex row house behind Capitol Hill on Sixth Street, southeast, just above South
Carolina Avenue. Right on the edge of the so-called gentrifi-
cation area."

"Southeast?"

"Yes. Think of the Capitol being in the center of a gun
sight's crosshairs."

"Yes, precisely," Heismann said, nodding.

Mutaib suppressed a smile. "No, I mean for orientation
purposes. The Capitol is the city center. The crosshairs di-
vide the city into four quadrants, northwest, northeast,
southeast, southwest. All addresses in this city are given with
their quadrant."

"Ach, I understand. And duplex? This means two houses
together, ya?"

"Precisely, old boy. And mind that German idiom, if you
please. Duplex: two narrow two-story houses under one
common roof, with a common middle wall between them.
Brick construction in this case. There is an alley, where each
unit has a garage."

"So, there is a neighbor?"

"One occupant next door, a middle-aged white woman,
who works in the Library of Congress. Solitary sort, according to the estate agent."

"We will proceed with the cover story? That I am an
artist?"

"A sculptor, to be precise. That way, there can be lorries
bringing large, heavy objects from time to time. We'll actually have some marble blocks delivered."

"And the roof? Soft? Not slate, yes?"

Mutaib shot him a sideways glance. "Much better. Yes,
it's asphalt shingle, replaced two years ago. Plus, here's the
best part: There's a skylight."

"Truly?"

"Yes. It was a major selling point, as you might imagine.
The orientation is perfect. No large trees in the way."

"I will need to compute coordinates. Perhaps there is a survey map?"

"We have an appraisal company working on that right now. The bank is pretending to be interested in buying the duplex, so I asked them for a survey report, with coordinates in three different forms. I told them we needed precise locating data for a diplomatic satellite channel."

Heismann winced. "That could come back to bite," he said, scanning for unmarked vans among the cars parked along the cross street.

Mutaib shrugged. "I know, but we're not too worried. You'll burn it on your way out, correct?"

"It will burn," Heismann said. And so will you, princess, he thought. He looked forward to that part. All he had to do was figure out how.

"Very well, then," Mutaib said. "And the estate agents accepted the legend."

Heismann resisted the urge to laugh out loud. *The legend.* Really. "I am artist on commission to the bank for six months, yes?"

"For statuary art at the bank, that's correct. Which allows us to pay the bills, do the lease, and deflect with a whiff of diplomatic immunity any nosy questions from the authorities. We've even cobbled up a brochure on you, Erich Hodler, famous European sculptor, complete with photos of your 'work.' That's the name you wanted, correct?"

"Hodler is correct. Interpol should not have that one. Do you expect questions about me, the sculptor?"

"Not really. Besides, we paid full rate, in advance. When one pays what they ask, estate agents tend to move right along. They were politely interested, but nothing more. They did wonder about your not wanting a phone."

"If there is no telephone, there can be no wiretap," Heismann said. "Telephones are homing devices these days."

They both glanced over as a small motorcade growled its way up the Mall on the Constitution Avenue side, two Suburbans bracketing a pair of big black limos, three District police cars, the one in front with an impatient siren going, the other two at the back. As a new conscript in the East German army, Heismann had been a tank gunner. If they were serious, the dignitary would be in the lead Suburban, Heismann calculated as he mentally framed up that vehicle in some lovely Zeiss optics. Or maybe even in one of those seedy-looking police squad cars.

"Occupy it when, exactly?" he asked.

"This Thursday—that would be the twelfth. I've written the address down on this newspaper."

"The house is furnished?"

"The house is furnished, of course, but we've asked them to take all the furniture out of the master bedroom on the second floor—you know, for your 'studio.' They wanted to store it in the garage, but I insisted they take it away. You may need that garage. We will also get you a street parking permit for your van."

"It is close to a Metro station?"

"Yes indeed. One of our criteria, as you will remember. Eastern Market station."

Heismann nodded. The Arabs had surprised him with their thoroughness. They'd done exactly what he'd asked them to. "Very good," he said. "Then all I need is the weapon."

The Saudi didn't reply for a moment, and he buried his head in the newspaper, as if he'd found something truly interesting. Heismann wondered if he'd said something wrong.

"May we assume," Mutaib said finally, "that the fire at the clinic means you are finished with all your, um, medical procedures?"

And what is this? Heismann wondered. "That is correct."

"I wasn't sure I'd recognize you after all this time. That beard, for instance."

"But the coat and hat, yes? Loden is distinctive. And also the white bag."

"Yes, but, um, I can't see your face. And your voice. You sound . . . different."

"That is no accident," Heismann said. "From here forward, you do not want to see my face."

"They changed your nose; I can see that. Looks a bit like mine, actually. Your hair—they changed your hair?"

"They changed everything they could," Heismann said patiently. "That was the whole idea, remember?"

"Oh, quite," Mutaib said. "I completely understand."

No, you don't, Heismann thought. "It has been confirmed, then?" he asked. "You still wish me to execute this thing?"

"Absolutely," Mutaib said from behind his newspaper. "The weapon is en route. And given the results of this recent election, my, um, associates feel we have no choice. The Democrats have won the entire election. They have always been the war party. No matter how much they spin it otherwise."

Heismann had not followed the American election, other than to know that the Republican incumbent and his party in Congress had gone down to a surprising defeat and that the opposition party, the so-called Democrats, were now going to rule both on Capitol Hill and in the White House. He read the Washington papers diligently to keep up his English proficiency, and they seemed to make much of this "new" situation. In Europe, of course, the legislature and the executive branches were always controlled by the same party. Otherwise, how could anyone govern? One more example of America's idiotic politics. "It will be quite something," he predicted.

"Won't it just," Mutaib replied. "But we must strike first. Otherwise, we believe the Kingdom will simply disappear."

"And this bait business—I still wonder if that was wise."

"Deception is always necessary on something of this scale," Mutaib replied. "Especially these days. But do you really need to use the nurse?"

"No one was supposed to survive the fire. But since she has, once they find the file, they will question her. The file will establish the false time line. She may or may not be able to point them to the right name. If necessary, I will nudge her in the right direction. Then I will remove her."

Mutaib thought about that for a moment. "My, um, associates are concerned that she remains alive. We have discussed taking care of her ourselves, with our own assets here in the city."

"You doubt my abilities?"

"No, no, it's not that," Mutaib said, shifting his seat on the bench. "We agree that, if and when the bait surfaces, they will go to her, because she is the only one left. We don't know how much she knows about the clinic. Or if she can connect the clinic to the bank."

Heismann shrugged. "Then let me take care of it. If my doing that becomes a problem or interferes with the mission, she is yours."

"Very well. And if we do not see movement in Interpol channels, then we'll think of something else. A freight company will leave a message in the mailbox about delivery arrangements. For some Carrara marble blocks. One of the drivers on that delivery will leave behind instructions regarding the weapon container and *its* delivery."

Heismann nodded. "Excellent," he said. The deception plan had been their idea. He had never thought it necessary, but Mutaib had just made it his problem. Before he could say anything else, a man in a business suit and lightweight raincoat walked up, sat down on the bench across the way, and opened a newspaper.

Mutaib gave Heismann a theatrically significant glance from behind his own paper, folded it up, looked at his watch, dropped the paper on the bench, got up, and walked away. Heismann pulled the folded newspaper over and scanned the front section while finishing his potato chips. The address was not immediately visible, so he would have to take it with him, but for the moment, he decided just to sit there. The international pages spoke of the growing tensions between the Kingdom and the United States over oil: It described how the new Shiite clerical regime in Iraq, in alliance with the Shiite regime in Iran, had strong-armed the Kingdom into matching their own production cutbacks. How the Americans' unilateral decision to withdraw all its military forces from the Kingdom and Iraq had unleashed a huge upsurge in anti-American sentiment in the Gulf, to the point where the Iraqi *mullahs* had thrown all American reconstruction companies out of the country and replaced them with French and German contractors. The ruling faction, increasingly uneasy about the growing Shiite axis to the north and east, was preparing to open the oil spigots, but there was growing resistance within the Kingdom from some of the more powerful royal factions. Rumors of a royal Saudi coup were circulating in the bazaars. Gasoline, diesel, and home-heating oil at close to five dollars a gallon here in America had apparently had much to do with the outcome of the recent election. And equally much to do with why he was here.

These deluded Arabs, he thought. In his opinion, the Kingdom would most certainly disappear after this thing happened. Imagine. Playing medieval power games with the world's sole surviving superpower. Just like the ancient Jews, who, by intentionally provoking Rome back in the first century with their fervid dreams of religious and ethnic purity, had been flattened into the dust of history for their efforts. He had read that some prominent politicians in the newly victorious Democratic party wanted to do the very same thing to the Kingdom, given all that had happened since their so-called 9/11. No wonder the Arabs were worried. But what did they think was going to happen once they executed this incident? Once *he* executed this incident. Because there were absolutely going to be Saudi fingerprints all over it—he was going to make damned sure of that. It would be the only way he could buy time to effect his own disappearance. The *Ammies* would be far more interested in the bomber's masters than in the bomber himself.

The man across the walkway seemed to pay no attention to anything going on around him as he read his paper. Coincidence? Heismann wondered. He leaned back on the bench, tilted his face up to where the weak January sun should have been lurking, and rubbed his face, in the process pushing the big sunglasses higher up on his nose so he could just peek out through the two tiny clear spots in the lower lenses. He pretended to be napping but kept his eyes slitted open. The bridge of his now almost Semitic nose still twinged occasionally from the surgery. His Nazi grandfather would have gleefully broken that nose if he could have seen it. Grandpapa had also known a thing or two about fire.

He watched the man opposite and also scanned for signs of anyone following Mutaib as he strolled back across the wide expanse of dormant grass out on the Mall. Since no one seemed to be following Mutaib, he concentrated on the other man, whom he could not really see, hidden as he was behind the spread newspaper in his hands. In his perfectly still hands, he realized. When had the man last turned the page?

He focused harder on the man's hands. Black leather gloves. With his new, surgically altered eyes, Heismann's vision was now nearly perfect. Still the man didn't turn the page. Another foreigner trying to improve his American idiom by plowing through the *Washington Post*'s sometimes turgid prose? He stared hard at the man's gloved hands.

The wind gusted again, and the man's paper trembled. Something. There—the right hand. Yes. Yes. Yes! Right there. He felt his heart quicken. He could just make out a tiny black wire coming out of the glove on the man's right hand. The wire disappeared up inside the man's shirt cuff.

He wanted to shout. His tactical instincts were alive and well. This man was trying to photograph him. Through a tiny hole in the stupid newspaper, no doubt. Holding the paper very steady, despite the wind. Waiting for—what? Waiting for Heismann to take off the sunglasses and expose his face, of course. He closed his eyes and tried not to grin. Then he wondered how long the man could hold his arms out like that. That could get difficult after just a few minutes. He remembered watching the Soviet honor guard soldiers at the Battle of Berlin monument in East Berlin, when they would put their World War II rifles at right-shoulder arms and then, using only their wrist, bring the heavy piece up to a perfectly vertical position in their extended hand and hold it like that for twenty minutes. He'd tried it once, and his arm had collapsed after only sixty seconds. We shall see, he thought.

And the next question was, Who would want to take his picture? Some *Ammie* secret government agent? Except, as he remembered his own tradecraft, the *Ammies* preferred telephoto work.

No. Not the Americans. This was Mutaib's man. Some fat-joweled princes back in Saudi telling their point man, Emir Mutaib: you haven't seen this man for almost a year. He's had extensive cosmetic surgery. We need to know what he looks like now. You know, for afterward. Obtain a photograph. Meet him somewhere public. Put him at ease, and have someone get his photograph.

He could just hear Secret Agent Mutaib Bond speaking in code in that superior tone of his: We will be meeting on the Mall. Hidden in plain sight. He will be on the same bench with me. I will have a newspaper. He will have a white lunch bag. There will be secret signs. We need the new face. And the lackey replying, Right away, Your Highness.

And why would they need his picture? So when this thing was kaput, they could find him and kill him, of course. The management of loose ends.

The wind gusted again, and Heismann shivered despite the heavy loden coat. But he kept his head back and watched the other man hold steadfastly to his newspaper. He couldn't see the wire anymore. Had he imagined it? No, he had not. The wind died away, but the edges of the man's newspaper kept trembling. Ah. Any minute now.

Finally, the would-be photographer gave up, lowered the paper, and turned the page. Heismann stood up at once, yawned, picked up the newspaper, and walked away before the man could position the hidden lens again. He didn't bother to look at the man. Just another amateur. Fools.

But he had learned something important today. He had planned all along to do his own loose-end management by removing his delicate Arab controller, the one man who could tie him directly to what was coming. He'd been paid half the money in advance, as agreed, but he never expected to see the promised other half. He'd wanted only two things from them all along: the front money and the change in physical identity, something that would release him from his Stasi past forever.

Heismann had been surprised when he'd been approached by the Saudi moneyman two years ago in Hamburg. They had a big job for him to do, in the United States this time. They trusted him absolutely because he had killed for them and he was not an ideologue—he worked strictly for money. Plus, he had excellent English, American English, actually, and for that and the fact that he was not a major player in the world of professional terrorists, they were willing to pay a fortune. Heismann had no illusions, then or now, about his status as some kind of international terrorist operative. He was what he was—a journeyman criminal with a gift for languages and for physical violence. But he was getting older and tired of all this skulking around and working for the despised Arabs. And the Western nations' counterintelligence organizations were getting better at finding the players in the terrorist networks. Many of the major players were gone. People were disappearing and not coming back. Germans, too. Pretty soon, they'd concentrate on the midlevel operatives. So he'd named his terms: the money, plus a total change in physical identity. And total would mean total. That had been fine with them—they'd had two years to set the thing up. As was their custom, they'd allowed plenty of time.

Now he had half the money, the entire identity change, and the thing was running. Good enough in all respects. Since there had to be loose strings at each end of every rope, Heismann understood that he was Mutaib's loose end. So the photographer was really no surprise. He loved it when his opponents showed their hands this way. It made everything so much simpler.

He adjusted the big sunglasses as he walked across the nation's front lawn. He could almost feel the camera lens, hear the electric film winder grinding away as the man got some wonderful shots—of the back of his lovely green loden overcoat. And new ears. Well, yes, that would be something to report. Herr Heismann had new ears.

He laughed out loud.

Fools.

Swamp enjoyed the brisk walk up Connecticut Avenue from the Metro station. The afternoon traffic was already building toward rush hour, and he always felt better when he could walk faster than the cars could move. Gary White was keeping up with him, although Swamp detected an occasional puff when the young agent thought Swamp wasn't looking. He wondered if Gary was a smoker. Most Homicide cops he knew were.

"Only way to get around this benighted city's traffic," Swamp offered as they crossed Wyoming Avenue and passed

the embassies of Malta and Senegal. "By the time we get
there, all those cars out there will have moved two whole
blocks."

White muttered something in return, but his words were
whipped away by the January wind. Kid ought to learn to
wear a hat, Swamp thought, securing his own Borsalino on
his head. The fancy hat was an extravagance, but he loved
the contrast it made with his face. And besides, it wasn't as if
he had anything else to spend his money on these days.

The clinic itself was on the south side of Kalorama Road,
visible from a block away because of the yellow crime-scene
tape fluttering in the wind. Malone had driven over in a fire
department sedan and was parked partially up on the sidewalk, inside the tape. He got out when he saw Swamp and
Gary approaching.

The facade of the two-story clinic was brown brick,
blackened around the window frames. The windows had
been broken out. The front door was propped in place but no
longer on its hinges. Heavy smoke stains created a black
halo around the upper reaches of the doorway. Malone met
them on the steps.

"Sure you want to do this?" he asked.

Swamp blinked but nodded yes; he thought it was important to see the fire scene. "Nothing beats personal reconnaissance," he said. Malone gave him an "if you say so" look.

Malone then slid the heavy door to one side and they
stepped into a darkened hallway. The floor was littered with
debris and there was a strong stink of burned building, overlaid with just a whiff of cooked but now spoiling meat.
Swamp suppressed a gag reflex when he smelled that, and
White suddenly didn't look well.

"Sorry about that," Malone said. "That's why I asked.
That smell tends to linger. I've got some Vicks in the car,
you want some?"

White nodded emphatically, holding a handkerchief to

his face. Malone told him it was in the glove compartment, and White disappeared out front. Swamp examined the layout. Front door leading into a small reception area. Office area behind a counter to the right, doorway back to the clinic proper on the left. Walls, fixtures, furniture, countertop—all blackened. Carpet squishy with firefighting water. More interesting smells. Stairway going up to the next floor on the far right.

"Mixture of heat, smoke, and water damage out here," Malone said, shining a large flashlight around the reception area. "Office experienced severe heating. File cabinets jammed shut. Papers charred inside. Computer cases, hard drives—all melted."

White came back in and passed Swamp a small wad of the Vicks VapoRub, which he smeared beneath each nostril, blinking back tears at the strong camphor smell. Malone took them to the hallway door, which was off its hinges and propped up against the wall. "Back here, we have two examining rooms, two doctor's offices, what we think was a preop/postop staging and recovery room, the OR itself, a pharmaceutical closet, a full bathroom, and two utility closets back there."

"The fire began in the OR?" Swamp asked. Despite the Vicks, the battlefield corpse stench was still very much in evidence.

"Right. That's back this way. Watch your step—the ceiling came down all along here. Don't touch any wires. The power's off, but you never know about wires."

The area near the operating room was totally devastated, right down to the walls having been burned away. The fire department had erected temporary shoring timbers to ensure the roof didn't cave in all around, but the drooping ceiling gave a claustrophobic feel to the scene. A lone metal door frame stood detached from its surround.

"What's upstairs?" Swamp asked.

"Mirror image of what's down here, except for the OR. The daytime practice. Structurally intact, but trashed by heat, water, and smoke, of course. There's a completely separate entrance to the day clinic, around to the side, in the alley. That stairway over there connects. No fire doors, so that's why the day clinic took so much damage."

Swamp looked up at the large hole in the ceiling over what had been the operating room. Blackened fixtures, wiring, and piping drooped down into the hole from above. They could hear water dripping somewhere. They wandered around for a few minutes, then came back to stand next to the OR's empty door frame. In the middle of the room, the steel operating table, which had drooped down at both ends, was visible.

"What's down that hallway?"

"Couple of storage closets—cleaning gear, paper supplies. All pretty much black. No evidence of interest."

"How in the hell do you reconstruct from a mess like this?" Swamp asked.

"We do it all the time, Special Agent," Malone said. "I tell the new guys it's like archaeology—the evidence gets laid down in layers as the building comes down. You just reverse the process."

"Sounds simple, but I'll bet it isn't. Where were the bodies?"

"Right there," Malone said, pointing into the center of the wreckage that had been the operating theater. "Three by the table, plus one just inside this door frame. Lots more debris here when we first started looking, of course. About four feet deep, plus about a foot of water underneath. There's a basement, but it was empty—dirt floors, stone walls, remains of a coal furnace. No stairs down there that we could find. Partially flooded now."

"And no patient," Swamp said, shifting his feet to avoid something sticky under his shoes. He wondered if this smell was getting into his clothes, and he certainly didn't want to consider what might be sticking to his shoes.

"Well, that's the assumption we made. Ms. Wall said there would have been two women nurses, and two men, the docs, in here. She says if they were all in here, then there should have been a patient."

"Unless they all ran in to fight the fire—say *after* an operation," White offered. "I mean, it was close to midnight, according to the report. The patient's gone home. Nurses are cleaning up, fire starts, the docs come running, and then the oh-two mix gets right, lets go, gets them all."

Malone nodded thoughtfully. "That's certainly possible. We mapped, recovered, and inspected all the electrical plugs. Found one with a definite arc notch. According to Ms. Wall, that plug's map location would have put it near a big green curtain. But too much damage and heat here to determine point of origin. And some of the plugs were destroyed."

"Wouldn't an OR curtain like that be fireproof?"

"By code, supposed to fire-*resistant*," Malone said. "Only thing in this world that's fire*proof* is the damned ocean."

"Sprinklers?" Swamp asked.

"Turned off at the master valve."

"Why? I wonder," Swamp said.

"We find that more often than you'd think," Malone said. "Somebody does an inspection of the sprinkler system, then does maintenance on the heads or the valves, forgets to reactivate the system. There was a flame sensor tied to the office security system—that's what brought the department."

"And the bodies?"

Malone pointed down to the jumble of blackened wreckage, water, and melted globs of plastic littering what had been the OR floor. "Looked just like that stuff. We knew they were in here. Used steel-rod probes to find them underneath all this shit. Like getting a skewer through a hot dog on the grill. You feel for it, punch through; then your nose will tell you what you've found."

"I'm outta here," White said, his face an unpleasant gray in the light of Malone's flashlight.

Malone nodded, as if he had been expecting this. He led them back into the office reception area. White kept going right out of the building. Swamp smiled at Malone and then followed White, secretly relieved that the younger agent had been the first to break. He never thought he'd welcome the cutting January wind, but now he held his coat open to air out his clothes. Malone came next, pulling the front door closed, as much as he could.

"*That* was perfectly awful," Swamp told him. White was standing down on the sidewalk, puffing hard on a cigarette. Swamp had never smoked, but he wanted one now.

"You should've seen it right after the fire," Malone said. "That scene's actually been cleaned up—a lot. But you can see how bad that fire was."

"On a scale of one to ten, with ten being perfect, how good a reconstruction will you be able to do in there?"

"Three. Maybe."

"So proving that it was a deliberate fire?"

Malone shook his head. "We can speculate all day, but there's not much direct evidence of arson. No accelerants, other than the oh-two. First responders reported hearing the oxygen, or, technically, a gas roar, when they arrived. They used solid-stream, high-velocity fog, even tried foam, but none of that impresses a fire with its own fuel and unlimited oxidizer."

Swamp considered that for a moment. "Your report said two oxygen bottles melted?" he asked.

"Probably they were nitrous-oxide bottles. But yes, they melted, which I thought was a little weird. But we'd have to run tests to see what the specs were on those gas bottles."

"And nitrous-oxide is flammable? Or could the two that

melted have been filled with something else? Like, I don't know, ether?"

"We asked Ms. Wall that. She said nobody uses ether for anesthetic anymore. They were using a mixture of NO and oh-two. They were going to convert to Sevoflurane or something like that. She said they didn't sweat an OR fire from those gases, but that sometimes, under the right conditions, NO and oh-two can ignite in a patient's throat, if you can feature that shit."

"Yow. Anybody pull the string on the day docs? The owners?"

"I don't believe so, Special Agent. And at least for right now, this wasn't arson. Something went wrong in the operating room, and the sprinklers were shut off. Suspicious, maybe, but we've seen this scenario before. D.C. General had one, five, six years ago. Never did find out what set it off, but the presence of liquid-oxygen tanks did a number there, too."

There was considerably more traffic out on Kalorama Road now, and the late-afternoon sky was darkening fast. Most cars already had their lights on, but like most Washington evening traffic, they were getting nowhere fast.

"I would have thought that the oxygen bottles themselves would not be in the operating room. That there would be a supply line of some kind, with a safety valve that would cut off the oh-two if there was a leak or a sudden huge demand, like in a fire."

"That's how they do it in the big hospital operating rooms. But this was a private clinic. Maybe money was tight, or the docs were cheap."

"Was this place inspected?"

"We have just two guys who are qualified to inspect medical facilities for the whole city. You may have heard about our budget problems."

"Yes indeed. Plus, hospitals don't vote."

Malone gave an elaborate shrug. "We do what we can. Unlike firefighting, fire prevention isn't sexy."

"I really appreciate the tour," Swamp said. "And I *really* never want to do that again. My hat's off to you and your people. That must have been some tough sledding in there."

Malone accepted the compliment. "Fire is an impressive enemy," he said.

"We'll be in touch. Probably with more questions. And if you come up with something interesting, please call me." He gave Malone his card. The inspector asked if he could give them a ride, but Swamp thanked him and said they were using the Metro. "This time of day, we'll get back to our office before you get to yours, I suspect."

Heismann climbed through the damp winter underbrush, following a narrow but recognizable game trail. It was 2:30 P.M., and the January sun, while losing its battle with the bank of clouds over the western part of the city, was shooting yellow rays of light, which made it hard to see. He'd parked his car down in Rock Creek Park in one of the scenic-view lots and was now approaching the nurse's house on Quebec Street, which sat up on a bluff overlooking the park. He could just see the top of the house, a white Victorian surrounded by old oaks, their bare black limbs seeming to wrap the house in a votive web. Someone had planted a line of spiky cedars all along the bluff, and they'd propagated down the slope over the years. A dog was barking somewhere in the neighborhood, but he didn't think it had sensed him.

He paused when he got to the top of the bluff. He had spotted the evergreen slope on a previous reconnaissance. Now he was dressed accordingly in his loden hat and coat, with dark wool trousers and insulated boots. He turned around to survey the ground below and behind him to make sure there weren't any joggers down in the park watching him. His oversized sunglasses were polarized, or he wouldn't have been able to see much of anything in the yellow glare.

Two bicyclists were visible across a small ravine, whizzing down Tilden Road into the park. He planted his walking stick into the needle-covered ground, tipped his hat forward to hide his face, and watched and listened for five minutes. Standing still among the man-high cedars, dressed in dark green, he knew he'd be invisible until he moved. The sunglasses were the only reflective thing about him.

Connie Wall's antique car was parked up by the garage, but he thought she used the Metro system to get around town, based on the fact that he had seen her walking up the block one morning, the last time he'd come up here. He'd been into her house once before, and he knew from the calendar on the dining room table that she should be out at a job interview at the National Institutes of Health in Bethesda, Maryland, this afternoon. The Medical Center Metro stop served NIH, so that would be the easy way to do it.

He looked at his watch. Two-forty-five. Time to go.

He pushed on up through the last ten feet of cedar trees and stepped over a dilapidated waist-high split-rail fence at the top. A driveway led from the street on his right back to a single-car garage on his left, positioned partially behind the house. A large blue spruce tree at the edge of the driveway would block the view of anyone out on or across the street, but he didn't dally. He walked across the driveway, bearing left, aiming to get behind the house, and then went directly up a rear sidewalk and onto the steps leading to a screened back porch. The outer screen door was unlocked, so he let himself onto the porch. He went directly to the back door, which had a large window in the top half. He could see a pantry inside, and beyond that was the kitchen. There was a doorbell, which he pressed. The bell was in the kitchen and seemed to work just fine. He had no idea of what he'd do if she appeared at the door, but there was always the Walther in his coat pocket. He'd looked around for alarm-system decals or wires the last time but had seen nothing, and there'd been no signs out front, either. He propped his walking stick against the back wall, fished out the spare key he'd taken the last time, and, after wiping his boots on the mat, let himself in.

He went immediately through the kitchen, then down a central hallway to the front, where he looked out a side-panel window for little old ladies lurking on neighborhood watch. Those and dogs were the most dangerous threats to a burglar, and fortunately, Connie Wall did not have a dog. A cat, perhaps, but no damned dog. All was quiet out front. He checked his watch again and gave himself a five-minute stay time. Whenever he broke into a house or office, he always assumed that someone had seen him and called the police. The typical response time for a prowler call in Washington was fifteen minutes, so that was a satisfactory margin. Not likely in this sleepy little neighborhood, but still . . . Rules were rules.

Keeping his expensive leather gloves on, he went back to the kitchen and opened the refrigerator door. He found an opened half-gallon plastic container of skim milk. Perfect. He took it out, setting it on the kitchen table. He removed a steel cigar-shaped tube from his left-hand coat pocket, unscrewed the top, and pulled out the syringe. Then he unscrewed the milk container's cap and pressed the contents of the syringe into the milk. He sniffed the spout, but there was no discernible odor. He closed it back up, shook it gently to mix the contents, returned it to the refrigerator, and shut the door. Then he went over to the wall telephone, where he removed the receiver and then the cover and backed off one of the line wires. He then replaced the cover.

He went back to the front door and again scanned the front yard and street. Still nothing. He then went quickly up the stairs to her bedroom, which was just beyond the top of the landing. Up here, the house smelled faintly of old age, lavender, and mildew. She might be a surgical-team nurse, he thought, but she's no housekeeper. He pushed open her bedroom door and wrinkled his nose at the mess of clothes strewn about—dirty laundry piled in a hamper, clean laundry stacked in a chair. The bed was unmade. He went to the low bureau, whose top was covered with makeup bottles and jars. He found her lingerie drawer and began to paw through it. He found the items he needed, panties and a half-slip, closed that drawer, and then took an unopened pair of dark panty hose from the left-hand bottom drawer. He stuffed the underwear into his coat pocket and closed the drawers. The bottom one jammed an inch from fully closing, so he had to kick it shut. He made a quick survey of her clothes closet, but didn't see anything of use there.

He made a cursory check of the rug to see that he hadn't left footprints or dirt from his boots, found one piece of mud, and pocketed it. From the looks of the bedroom, he doubted this woman would ever notice a little dirt. He went back downstairs, checked out the front windows again, then let himself out the back door, making sure it locked behind him, and retrieved his stick. Ten minutes later, he emerged from the wooded slope down in the park and walked casually down the creekside path toward his car. Two joggers puffed by him, an older man with a much younger companion. For some reason, perhaps the way they were sticking close to each other, they looked like a couple to him. More queers, he thought. This fat country was full of degenerates. He'd resisted the urge to trip them both with his walking stick as they passed him.

He got into his car, a three-year-old minivan, and backed out of the lot. As he drove back up Tilden, he looked across the ravine toward the ugly white house at the end of the block on the other side for signs of blue police lights, but all was still quiet.

So, all the nosy old ladies had been taking their naps this time. Very good. He felt for the nylon underwear in his coat pocket. This was so much less embarrassing than going into some department store and buying it. He knew exactly what the clerks would think, and then he would feel obliged to do something about that. Plus, she wasn't going to need underwear once she had a nice glass of milk.

The light was red at the intersection of Tilden and Connecticut Avenue. He'd laced the milk container with ten cc's of a boiled concentrate solution of ant poison and water. The boiling had evaporated the foul smell the manufacturer put in to keep humans and animals from ingesting it. The poison would hit Connie Wall in minutes, rendering her helpless as she cramped into a retching, effluvial ball on the kitchen floor before she quite knew what had happened. Then she would stiffen into a paralytic stupor. Ant poison was a cholinesterase inhibitor, otherwise known as a nerve agent. The diluted paste he'd injected would float to the top of the milk, so she'd get the full dose. No smell, no taste. And if she did manage to crawl to the kitchen phone, well, it wasn't going to work.

Essentially, she was going to kill herself. Living alone like that, and with no coworkers or bosses to wonder where she was, it might even be days before anyone found her. By then, the milk would have spoiled entirely, and since the products of its decomposition would create acids that would in turn destroy the nerve agent in the ant poison, there would be no problem with loose ends. Messy, given what havoc a cholinesterase inhibitor wreaks on the central nervous system, but, at those concentrations, extremely effective.

He had told Mutaib that she would be useful to the deception plan, but after the princeling started talking about taking care of her with his own assets, Heismann had become suspicious. As Mutaib had observed, they could not be certain what she knew. Well, Heismann thought, that works both ways, does it not, Your Slipperiness? Better for me that she just goes away. Out of the equation altogether. That would leave him with one loose end instead of two. The light changed, and off he went, nodding to himself in satisfaction.

Connie Wall kept a polite expression plastered on her face while she controlled the urge to slap senseless this middle-aged Lothario wanna-be posing as an HR administrator. He'd spent the entire time he was supposedly interviewing her trying to get a better look up her skirt. The interview chair had been carefully positioned right in front of the desk, with him sitting to one side of the desk for a better viewing angle.

"And you live in the District itself, Ms. Wall?" he was asking. He was in his fifties, pasty-faced, with a potbelly and half a dozen gray hairs plastered back to front along the sides of his forehead to cover his bald spot. Birth-control glasses. Trousers too short, black nylon socks too short, revealing really yummy oyster white shins. As a bonus, there was even a red spot of what looked like catsup on his straining white shirt. At least six pens in his shirt pocket, and one of them was leaking. Mr. Perfect.

"Yes, I do," she said. "Close to the Metro, too. No commuting hassles."

"How nice for you," he murmured, looking over the top of the file folder. She turned almost sideways in the chair, trying to make it as obvious as she could that she was absolutely *not* flattered by his lecherous interest.

"It was my parents' house," she said. "Long before there was a Metro. Is there shift work involved in this position?"

"Normally not," he said, putting down the folder and straightening in his chair, apparently giving up on his periscope act for the moment. "You stated here that your last employer could not provide a reference because he was deceased. Do you have any performance evaluations from before that you can show us?"

She fished around in her briefcase, trying not to bend over too far. This guy might get really excited if he could see down her blouse as well as up her skirt. She pulled out a folder. "Right here," she said. "Those are copies, of course. The originals were lost in the fire."

"Fire?"

She explained what had happened at the surgery, and he said yes, he remembered that.

"Why at night?" he asked. "The paper seemed to indicate there were two sets of doctors using that clinic, one days, one nights."

"Our patients were all men," she said. "Important people, I think. My guess was that they did these procedures in the evenings for confidentiality purposes. The clientele during the daytime were mostly women. I occasionally worked for those doctors, too. Copies of their evaluations are also in that file, and they can give me references."

"Right, good. Well, look, you're technically qualified for the position. Maybe even overqualified. I'm going to forward your medical credentials to the department head. If Dr. Calvin wishes to proceed, I'll call you back for a second interview. That would be a technical discussion, you understand, with Calvin's people. And if *he* wishes to proceed with the hire, there will be a personal-background check. National agency screen. No problems there, I assume?"

"You assume correctly," she said. "Three traffic tickets in the past three years, but I drive a '68 Shelby GT." She shrugged. "Cops see one of those, they just assume you're speeding, you know?"

"I drive a ten-year-old diesel sedan," he said, pursing his lips, undoubtedly waiting to see if she would guess he had a Mercedes. "So, no, I wouldn't know. But I think this might work out just fine, Ms. Wall, subject to our internal checks, of course. I'll get your package over to Dr. Calvin this afternoon. When could you start?"

"Whenever you want," she said, gathering her things. "I prefer not to work weekends, as I like to go out of town on weekends. But otherwise . . ."

"That's fine," he said. "NIH is a government operation. We prefer not to work weekends, either. The due-diligence process takes about two weeks. Thank you for coming in."

What a complete el creepo, she thought five minutes later

as she descended the vertiginous escalator at the Medical Center Metro station. Hopefully, the surgeons will be humans, even if their Human Resources manager is a pencil-necked geek. The NIH deal did sound like a good chance for her to go back to work. She wasn't worried about the so-called technical interview. She had almost twenty years of work experience in operating rooms, and she also knew exactly how desperate most hospitals were for people with that much experience. Not that she was all that desperate herself—she could probably stop working now and live on the income from her investments, but she knew she'd go right out of her gourd just sitting around the house on Quebec Street.

She waited impatiently on the platform. The trains grew sparser when it wasn't rush hour, and the absence of anyone else waiting told her she'd just missed one. It had been six weeks since the fire. Everyone dying like that had freaked her out, and then the D.C. Arson cops with all their questions had actually made her feel guilty to have survived. She'd bailed out, finally, driving to the Valentine Hills ski resort, in West Virginia over the holidays just to get out of town.

Her elderly cat, Buster, was waiting for her on the kitchen doorstep when she got home. She let herself in, hung up her coat, and then gave the cat a dish of milk. She went upstairs to get out of her interview clothes and back into jeans and a sweater. When she came out of the bathroom, she noticed what looked like a long brown bug on the rug right by the bedroom door. She looked again and realized that it was a lump of dirt or mud, and she chided herself for not cleaning her shoes properly. The bedroom needed picking up and vacuuming anyway, so she left the lump of dirt, humped all the dirty laundry together to take it down to the washing machine, and went back downstairs to get the vacuum cleaner. While vacuuming, she found another small lump of wet dirt right by the bed. She frowned, wondering what she'd gotten into, and where. She engaged in a minor cleaning frenzy for the next forty-five minutes and then took the vacuum back downstairs. Then she went to the dining room table, where her computer was set up, and checked through her E-mail. There were two more requests for interviews, a dozen annoying messages from the Internet advertising world, and a cop joke forwarded from Cat Ballard, her good friend on the D.C. Homicide squad. It was now dark outside, so she went to turn on some lights in the kitchen. Which is when she found Buster.

Swamp Morgan was a list maker. He ended each day making up a short to-do list for the next day and leaving it taped to his office telephone. The first item on tomorrow's agenda was to make contact with the senior agent at PRU, the man who had reviewed the original file transcript and declared it a firefly. The second was to set up an interview with the nurse who had survived the terrible fire at the clinic. He had spent a great deal of his career in and around the world of intelligence. He knew that the firefly call might be based on information he did not or could not have. The Protective Research Unit would have a bigger picture than he did, especially now that he was a reactivated agent working *outside* of the Secret Service. The entire case might just die a natural death after he talked to PRU. As it should, if it was a firefly.

Gary White had already left for the day, and he would begin his day tomorrow doing new-guy transfer admin. But Swamp intended to make sure Gary went along when he went over to PRU. He liked the cut of Gary White's jib. He seemed to be levelheaded, intelligent, and able to focus on the task at hand. His experience in the Homicide Division wouldn't hurt, either, as those cops tended to view everything and everyone they encountered with immediate, unvarnished suspicion. He was glad to have the help, and more than willing to hold up his end of the new-agent bargain, namely to introduce White to the byzantine nature of federal law enforcement and to help him get ahead.

The office had quieted down now that the day was over. For Swamp, it was a familiar silence, with the noise of traffic outside on Pennsylvania Avenue competing with the hum of lowest-bidder fluorescent lighting in the office. He was hardly alone in the OEOB—the National Security Council staffers often worked until eight or nine o'clock, and longer during days of crisis. He had a one-bedroom furnished apartment over on the northern Virginia side, in a building right above a Metro station. It was a place to sleep during the week, but little more.

On the weekends, he took the train out to his hometown of Harpers Ferry and spent Saturdays and Sundays at the riverside inn his parents had run for many years. They'd maintained an owners' apartment at the back of the inn. It was on the third floor, facing the river, and he had taken this over when they'd given him the property and retired to Florida. Ben and Lila Hardee, longtime friends and next-door neighbors, had expressed an interest in running the place, so he'd let them take it on. They got to keep the income from the business, and he had a free and familiar weekend retreat for as long as he wanted it. He took the train back into town each Monday, and he did not even keep a car in town.

He pulled out the clean transcript file, the one retyped from the burned record, along with a legal pad. He went over the jumble of hallucinatory mutterings of patient number 200341. What kind of a clinic was this, identifying its patients with numbers? He made a note to touch base with the Bureau, see what they had and wouldn't share with local law on those two Paki doctors. And find out who had set up the docs in business and gotten them visas.

Then he wondered what *he* might reveal under anesthesia, when all inhibitions floated away in a cool stream of anesthetic. What he might say about Sherry, his former wife, and what she'd done to him on the day he retired from the Senior Executive Service. He could imagine his own stream of consciousness—or was it *un*consciousness in this situation?—where he'd mumble, "Thank you, Mr. Secretary," and then ramble on about cherry blossoms, the late afternoon on the Tidal Basin across from the Jefferson Memorial, and what his wife had said that day. "Let's sit down right here, Lee, because there's something I need to tell you. Which is that I'm leaving you, Lee. Yes, for Dr. Grant, my boss and my lover for the past five years, not that you ever noticed, did you? And no, there'll be no discussion, no negotiations or pleading, not that you would ever plead, would you? No, not you, not big bad Swamp Morgan. But there it is: I'm divorcing you, marrying him, and Bob's going to take care of everything from now on. We don't even have to go to court or discuss settlements, alimony, any of that, because you know what? I want nothing from you. Bob's going to take care of everything. He's already set up a fund for the kids' college, I'll have a new home in Chevy Chase, and we'll have our new life together.

"And why do you look so shocked, Lee Morgan? We haven't been really close for years, have we? Or rather, *I* haven't. Because we both know you've been a lot more married to the Secret Service than to me, haven't you? All those standard Secret Service five-to-nine days at the White House. Taking care of dear old POTUS. And then even more quality time at the office when you got to be deputy dog at headquarters. Well, I guess that's all noble enough, but my life's half over, Lee, just like yours, actually. Being an SES widow wasn't good enough for me. I want a loving and close relationship with a nice man for the rest of my life, and I don't think you can manage that anymore. So, yes, I stood up with you today, your very big, very important government gold watch day, but now I'm going away. Not very far away, actually, but a million figurative miles from you.

"Here are the papers; they're very simple, short, and sweet. Sign right by those little yellow arrows, mail them back, and you're a free man, Lee. I'm leaving you the house, the cars, everything, even my old clothes. Do what you want with all of it. Trust me, you'll be the envy of the divorced white male club, I promise you. And the kids? You know, they're totally on board with this. Surprised again? Quick now, can you tell me how old each is without thinking about it, Lee? Didn't think so. Look, you can see the kids whenever you want to, although they'll be away at college most of the time. And they may or may not want to see you—you'll have to work that out with them. They're effectively beyond custody questions now, so you do your best—I won't fight you, although seeing them may be tougher than you think. Besides, you've got a bigger problem. You have to figure out what you're going to do with the next half of your life, now that I'm no longer in the picture.

"No, no, don't say a word, Lee, not a word. Because you can't change my decision or how I feel about Bobby Grant. And you. One way or another, you're single. And once you switch your brain back on, you'll know this is as good a deal as any ex-husband ever gets. So don't even think about fighting this, Lee. There's nothing to win.

"Look at me, Lee.

"Say good-bye, Lee."

And then, before getting up and walking away, she'd smiled and patted the back of his hand, as if to say, No hard feelings, right? He didn't even have to close his eyes to still see her, a forthright, intelligent, physically attractive woman, her back straight and heels clicking purposefully through the carpet of fallen cherry blossoms blowing along the sidewalk. Who'd left him sitting there so shocked, he'd almost forgotten to breathe. So filled with astonishment, mixed with the growing recognition that he should have seen this coming, his hand clutching an envelope with engraved lawyer lettering in the top left-hand corner. And this less than an hour after his retirement and award ceremony in the office of the director of the Secret Service, with everyone he knew and valued, and even the Secretary of the Treasury in attendance, standing tall and beaming at him.

She'd done a perfect Pearl Harbor on him, and, like one of the doomed battleships on that terrible day, he'd felt his entire psyche rolling over and subsiding into the lagoon without a sound, trapping the memories of some twenty-one years of marriage inside dark submerging decks.

He blinked, gasped in a breath of air, and looked around the empty office. He dimly heard voices down the hall and the shrill sound of an encrypted telephone demanding to be picked up right now. He wondered how many other middle-aged men were staying late in the office just like he was, and for the same basic reason: They had nowhere else to go on a January night in Washington. What had happened next completed the Pearl Harbor analogy: Sherry a hundred feet away. The two black guys in full urban hoodlum costume—baggy pants, knit caps, huge sneakers—suddenly flanking her, one grabbing her hair and pulling her backward, the other tussling for her purse. His own instinctive reaction, bolting off the park bench and sprinting down the side of the Tidal Basin, screaming obscenities at the hoods, seeing them look back at him while he fumbled for the badge and the gun he no longer had, the gut-wrenching realization that he was no longer a federal cop, just another outraged middle-aged white guy, as the smaller of the two thugs flashed a knife, jabbed it twice into Sherry's throat, and then took off with his buddy with a triumphant shout, her purse in his bloody hand, while Sherry stepped one step sideways and then sagged onto the concrete as a clutch of tourists stared in disbelief from the other side of the Tidal Basin. He had never felt so helpless in his entire life—no gun, no badge, no radio, no authority, no backup, no nothing—as he knelt in the small lake of bright blood, trying to hold the big vein shut with slippery fingers, knowing, knowing . . .

He raised an open hand and brought it forcefully down on

the desk blotter with a loud smack to banish the black thoughts. He heard someone in the next office ask, "What was that?" He exhaled forcefully, then inhaled, exhaled again. Then he composed himself. He was strong and alive and there was that next half of his life, as Sherry had pointed out, still there to be lived. He'd been through the entire gamut of feelings endlessly—anger, bitterness, guilt, embarrassment and then, ultimately, resignation. He'd been amazed at the range of people's reactions, from the sympathy and quiet encouragement of his professional contemporaries to the drunk who'd told him that he was the luckiest divorced son of a bitch on the planet, because what Swamp had now was the perfect opportunity. "You ready for this, chief? You get to have seconds!" the bum had told him.

He took another deep breath, shook out his arms, and focused again on the transcript. His palm was stinging from hitting the desk. It almost felt good.

Sherry was gone. His own two kids, both in college now, not so discreetly blamed him for what had happened. "She wouldn't have been there if she hadn't had something to tell you, would she?" No answer for that one. Except maybe if she hadn't taken up with Dr. Bob, she wouldn't have been there, either. Several friends had told him after the funeral that the kids would either grow up and solve the problem on their own or they wouldn't, and that his best move was to let them work it out, and that was what he had elected to do.

But he was still here. He had an important job to do. There was a war on, and more than enough bad guys to chase. This day was drawing to a close. One day at a time. Litany complete. The text of the transcript slowly swam back into focus.

Tomorrow, he'd find out how far this firefly was going. Then on to the next one.

The elderly cat was stone-dead on the pantry threshold, curled into a grotesque ball and surrounded by copious

amounts of bodily fluids. His neck was twisted sideways and
his familiar old face was contorted in a rictus of agony, with
every one of his teeth showing and his angry eyes wide-
open.

"What the *hell* happened here?" Connie murmured,
aghast at the sight. The cat was clearly well beyond anything
a vet could do. She set about cleaning up the mess, bagging
the cat in a plastic kitchen trash bag, and setting the bag outside on the porch. The cat looked as if he'd been poisoned.
The milk? she wondered. Or had Buster gotten into something outside in his wanderings, some rat poison or something like that in one of her neighbors' yards?

She retrieved the milk container from the fridge and
smelled it. Nothing obvious there. The sell-by date was tomorrow, but it was skim, which kept well past the sell-by
date. She smelled it again. Milk. Even so, she poured it
down the sink and threw the plastic container into the
trash.

Poor damned cat, Connie thought as she splashed some
Clorox on the floor and sponge-mopped the entire area.
When she went to rinse the sponge, she found another lump
of that mud. This one was just like the others, rectilinear, as
if extruded by some tiny machine. She hefted the thing in
her hand. This mud had come from a boot, a boot with a really aggressive tread. She owned one pair of hiking boots,
but she hadn't had them on for three weeks. This mud was
fresh.

Mud here and in the bedroom. Fresh mud. Has someone
been in the house? she wondered.

She put the mop down and set the piece of mud on the
kitchen table, where it made a small damp stain. The other
pieces had already been eaten by the vacuum cleaner. She
checked the back door for signs of forced entry, but everything there was normal. She heard the winter wind stir the
big old trees in the backyard. The branches of some dormant
wisteria scratched at the windows along the park side of the

house. Suddenly, the old house felt wrong to her. She thought of Cat Ballard and decided to call him.

She went into the dining room and sat down. She tried the office and got the after-hours menu. She hung up, dialed his direct extension, and got a hit.

"Homicide, Lieutenant Ballard," he answered, sounding very official.

"It's me," she said.

"Yes, ma'am? How can I help you?"

She smiled. Very formal. The captain must be in listening range. "He's right there, huh?" she asked.

"Yes, ma'am?"

"I love it when you call me that," she said, "Makes me feel so . . . mature." She could just see the muscles in his face starting to twitch. "Actually," she continued, "I think someone's been in my house. And it wasn't a break-in, either. Can you come by on the way home?"

"You've got the wrong division, ma'am. You need to call burglary at extension four-one-two-three. They'll probably be there for another half hour or so."

"So I'll see you in forty-five, right?"

"Yes, ma'am."

"Thanks, Cat. Believe it or not, I'm a little scared. Thanks for doing this."

His tone softened just a bit. "You're very welcome, ma'am," he said, and hung up.

She put the phone down. She and Cat had met eight years ago at a cop promotion party. They'd dated for three years, then drifted apart, by mutual agreement. He'd met someone else, married her, and started a family, but occasionally he would call Connie just to talk. Two years ago, they'd met for lunch, ostensibly to celebrate his promotion to lieutenant, but with the help of one thing and another and more than a little nice wine, they'd ended up in her bedroom for a memorable few hours. He told her he was perfectly content with his marriage, and his wife had two little ones to keep her occupied. Unfortunately, neither of her babies had been a sixty-pounder, so there was now a lot more of Lynn than when they'd married. Which is when he remembered how much he had enjoyed time in bed with Connie Wall. She knew she should have been put off by his rather callous attitude, but actually the situation suited her. She had no intention of ever getting married, was increasingly leery of the singles scene with all its attendant health risks, and Cat more than adequately met her physical needs. It wasn't as if she expected him to leave Lynn and marry her.

An hour later, she heard his car pull into her driveway. She watched him drive all the way to the back of the driveway and stop behind her red vintage Shelby, which was parked right in front of the detached garage. The night was beginning to fog up, creating halos around the streetlights. He came around to the back door, as usual. She met him on the porch. He was just under six feet, and the closer he got, the bigger he seemed. He was three years older than she was, had sandy-gray hair, a usually smiling Irish face, and large, powerful hands.

"Hey, there, *ma'am*," he said with a disarming grin. He reached for her and she came into his arms gratefully, surprising herself. He kissed her and then drew back his head. "You *are* upset."

"Yeah, a little," she said, drawing him into the pantry and closing the back door.

"Shit, what's that smell—Clorox?"

She nodded and dropped into a chair at the kitchen table. She told him about the cat, and finding the mud bits. He peeled off his overcoat as he listened.

"This is what they looked like," she said, pointing to the bit of mud. He picked it up carefully.

"Boot tread," he said.

"Yeah. That's what the other pieces looked like, too. I

have some boots that could do that, but I haven't worn them in weeks."

"Where are they?" he asked. She pointed to the pantry area and he went out and retrieved them. He put one boot upside down on the table and tried to fit the piece of mud into the tread. "Not these boots," he said immediately. "Where are the other pieces?"

She got out the vacuum cleaner and then watched as he rousted out the bag and sliced it open, then went fishing among all the debris for the other two pieces of mud. Neither of them fit her boot tread. "This stuff is pretty fresh," he said. "I think you're right. Some mutt's been creepin' your house. Lemme go check the doors and windows. Put that mud in a plastic Baggie, and try to keep it intact."

He was back in ten minutes, shaking his head. "No signs of forced entry that I can see. You got a spare key?"

She retrieved it from the row of cup hooks mounted on the wall of the pantry. "Any more of these?" he asked. She'd considered giving him a key a long time ago but had held back.

"No," she said, then frowned. "Actually, yes. There were two, I think. Although I haven't used them for years." She went back to the pantry but couldn't find the second spare among the pile of mystery keys.

"You keep it hanging out here by the back door?"

"I think so, yes."

"People do the damnedest things," he snorted. "Lock the door, and then leave the keys in sight of the big glass window."

"So someone could have gotten in here, lifted one of the spare keys?" she said. "But nothing's been stolen or anything."

"You know that? You've looked at your jewelry? Your folks' silver service?"

She blinked. "No," she said. "So I guess I'd better go do that."

She checked the silver service, which was still in its box inside the buffet in the dining room. Then they went upstairs and she went over to her bureau. She kept her jewelry box in the lowest right-hand drawer. She hauled it out. She rarely wore jewelry, and the only nice things in the box had been her mother's. She shook her head.

"All here," she said, and put it back. "Wait," she added, still down on one knee.

"What?"

"This drawer," she said, pointing to the bottom left-hand drawer. "It's closed."

"So?"

"It won't close. It's always an inch open. And look, there's a scuff mark. Someone's kicked it closed."

"What's in there?"

"Stockings. Panty hose." She tugged at the drawer, but it wouldn't open. He reached down and pulled it open, but even he had to work at it. They knelt side by side.

"Anything missing?"

She looked into the drawer, but the stockings were in a jumble and she couldn't really tell. Then she opened the next one and pawed through it. There was a beige half-slip missing. And maybe some of her panties.

"Possibly," she said. "I'm not sure about the stockings, but I think some of my underwear is gone. And that drawer is never closed all the way. That I *know*."

"Was one of the mud bits right here?"

She looked over at him and nodded. "Right there."

"Close enough. Probably when he kicked the drawer. Shit."

They both got back up and she went over to the bed and sat down on the edge. "I hate this," she said softly. "Some pervert's got a key? And he's pawing through my underwear?"

Cat sat down beside her and took her hand. "I've always been interested in your underwear," he said. "Especially when you're in it. But look, this could be a neighborhood creep, you know. Some kid who's had a hard-on for you since he first found his pud. Or maybe a middle-aged peeper."

She shook her head. "This neighborhood is pretty geriatric. People here are contemporaries of my parents. Teenagers are extinct around here."

"Sounds nice. No young people at all?"

She shook her head. "The paperboy is a seventy-year-old Vietnamese guy. Goddamn it, Cat, I don't need this shit right now. What do I do?"

"First, change the locks; then call a security service. Get a system put in. Sure you're not wearing that underwear right now?"

She gave him an exasperated look and he grinned. "Worth a thought," he said. But then his face grew serious. "Lemme look outside, see what I can see. You got a flashlight?"

He was back at the door in five minutes. "Get a coat and come out here," he said. When she returned, he took her over to the side of the back steps. He went down on one knee and laid the flashlight flat on the ground, its beam pointing just over the tops of the wet grass in the direction of the park. She shivered in the cold evening mist. He motioned for her to get down so she could see along the beam of the flashlight as he swept it back and forth over the wet grass.

"See it?" he asked.

She could. The tips of the dormant grass were glistening with dew. But there was clearly a trail of tramped-down grass leading from the cedars beyond the driveway right over to the porch. He took her down to the cedars and they pushed their way into the densely packed trees, getting wet in the process. On the other side, which overlooked the darkness of Rock Creek Park, he knelt down again and fingered the dirt. Then he swept the light back and forth until he found the trail where Heismann had come up the slope.

There was at least one footprint where the tread was obvious.

"Not particularly careful about it, was he?" he said, shining the light down onto the boot prints. "He parks down there somewhere, comes up in broad daylight, walks to your back door, and lets himself in. Regular Cool Hand Luke."

"And takes underwear?"

He stood up, switching off the light. "And maybe poisons your milk?" he said softly.

Back in the kitchen, he put on some of her rubber cleaning gloves and retrieved the empty milk container and slipped it into a plastic trash bag. Then he peeled off the gloves and dropped them into the bag, too. He sat down at the kitchen table and got out his notebook. "Tell me everything you did once you came home."

She went through it, prompted from time to time by questions from Cat. He was specifically interested in the time interval between feeding Buster and finding him dead.

"I should have kept that milk, I suppose," she said.

"As long as you didn't rinse the container, the lab'll find out what was in it. From what you've described, it sounds more like food poisoning of some kind. As opposed to, say, arsenic or strychnine."

They made a joint tour of the house, looking at every room, the closets, the stairs, the pantry, and even the outside garage. While he looked for any more mud or other signs of intrusion, he asked her to tell him if anything was out of position or missing. But beyond what they'd already discovered, everything seemed to be in order. They went back into the kitchen and he made some more notes. She asked if he wanted coffee. Cat looked at his watch and told her he had to get home. Connie gave him a wan smile. She suddenly envied him his home life. He took her hand across the table.

"Look, Connie. I don't know what to make of all this, but I was serious about the locks and an alarm system."

She nodded. "I will," she promised. "Tomorrow."

He hesitated, then asked her one more question. "Could this have something to do with the clinic?"

"Don't start," she protested, "We've been through all that."

He was shaking his head. "No, we haven't. You clam right up every time I bring it up."

"That is—was—a private practice. By definition, the staff does not run its mouth about who the patients are or what procedures they had done."

He sat back in his chair and looked at his watch again. "I know," he said. "But that fire gave those people all the privacy they'll ever need. And you should know that the D.C. Arson guys think that whole deal was suspicious."

She stared down at the table. She'd read the newspaper reports about the four people she had worked with for years being roasted alive. But Cat was still a cop, and there were things she couldn't share with him.

"Cat," she began, but he waved her off and got up.

"Forget it," he said. "Lemme use your phone to call Lynn. New department regs—we can't use our cell phones to make personal calls."

He picked up the wall unit and punched in a number, waited, then listened. "This thing busted?"

"Wasn't this morning," she said.

"It is now," he told her. "Your phones are dead."

She shook her head. "I called you an hour or so ago." Then she realized she'd used the dining room table phone. Cat was ahead of her. He went into the dining room, listened to the phone, and then came back to take the wall phone apart. He popped the cover off with a penknife and then asked her for the flashlight. Then he gave her a sheepish smile, fished out a pair of reading glasses, and peered down into the guts of the phone. "Aha."

"Aha what?"

"One of the wires has been cut. No, not cut. Just bent back off the terminal. This little red one here." He fiddled with the wire, then listened to the handset. "Dial tone's back." He reassembled the cover and turned to look at her. "Whoever was here put some evil shit in your milk, then disabled the one phone you might reach when you did the macarena on the kitchen floor and tried to call nine-one-one. And you're telling me this has nothing to do with those night clinic guys?"

Connie bit her lip. "I can't see how," she said in a small voice. But of course she could. Everyone involved in the night clinic was dead except her. Because she hadn't been there. Cat just looked at her, as if he were waiting for her to get it.

"I can't talk about it, Cat," she said. "The whole premise of the clinic was secrecy. Hell, the patients' names were all in code on the records."

"Who's to care, Connie? Those guys are all toast."

"Don't remind me."

Cat gathered up his coat and the trash bag. "I'll get our lab to take a look at this," he said. "Don't know how quickly, though. We find out this is poison, then I'm back, officially this time. And you may want to rethink your position on this privacy bit, Connie. Arson people declare it S.O., it'll come to us. You still have that pocket gun?"

Cat had given her a small, .45-caliber derringer-style handgun back when they were dating full-time. It was taped to the back of the drawer in her night table. She nodded.

"Start carrying it," he said. "Load it and carry it. Leave it in the car when you're going to face metal detectors, but otherwise, carry it, Connie."

"I don't have a permit. And the District—"

"Carry it, Connie. Whoever's been screwing around in here won't sweat the District's gun laws."

Jäger Heismann stopped on the sidewalk in front of the U.S. Supreme Court just after 10:00 P.M. and pretended to gaze in awe at its magnificent facade. The temperature had dropped down into the high twenties, and he was wearing the loden overcoat, but with heavy black gloves and a homburg this time. He had changed his facial appearance with some extensive aging makeup, oversized tinted glasses, and a white wig. He had a thick rubber-tipped cane and had been affecting the labored steps of an old man ever since getting off at the Capitol South Metro station and walking up Capitol Hill on First Street. No fewer than four police cars had passed him along First Street, but none of the cops had given him a second glance. Even on a January night, old men took walks, and there were too many cops around the brightly lighted public monuments for night-time muggers.

Visually sweeping the empty street for more police cars, he turned around slowly and looked across First Street toward the Capitol. The manicured lawns, now dormant, and the curved approach roads were all studded with antivehicle barriers, and there were police walking patrols out on the grounds and standing next to each visible entrance. He wondered if there were sentinels stationed high up on the lofty parapets of the Capitol, armed with Stinger missiles, looking back at him through night-vision goggles. Probably, he thought, but one solitary old man shouldn't arouse much in the way of suspicion, even in terrorist-obsessed Washington. Unless he lingers too long or makes more than one pass along First Street.

He'd been taking periodic walks on Capitol Hill now for almost six months, both during the daytime and at night, often in different disguises, just to get a feel for the target area. Not that he'd be anywhere near the building on *der Tag*. Earlier this afternoon, he'd taken a walk by the house the bank had rented for him. He'd occupy the house in three days and then start his final planning for both the attack and his getaway. He thought that he had a fair chance of escaping the American government's security forces; Mutaib's people might be another problem, because they knew where he had to be on the day in question. But what he'd had done at the clinic over the past year could give him the crucial sixty seconds he'd need to get clear of the house.

He started back toward the Metro station, keeping to the opposite side of the street from the Capitol. It was a magnificent old pile, he had to admit, and such a perfect symbol of America. It amazed him that the professional lunatics of Al Qaeda hadn't already taken it out. He wasn't sure what his attack would do to the building itself, and he didn't care. Because his target wasn't the building. His target was the American government. Head right off!

He was somewhat surprised that the Arabs were going through with this and that it wasn't actually the usual suspects behind it. But maybe Mutaib's faction was a part of The Base. Everyone knew that their heart, mind, and all their banks lay in the Kingdom. And yet here he was, concealed in plain sight in America's capital, with an operational cover, a legal work visa, all the terms of his contract with the Arabs fulfilled as agreed, and proceeding with his time line. The loose end from the cosmetic surgery clinic had been snipped off, so now all he had to do was establish his artist cover story at the house not five blocks from here and wait for the weapon to be delivered. Then some home-remodeling work on the second floor, and the final arrangements for his swift and successful departure from the scene of the crime.

Another police car came by, slowed, and then resumed its patrol when they saw it was just him, obviously on his way home, and, more to the point, walking away from the sensitive areas around Capitol Hill. He wondered idly if those police officers would be on duty when it happened, and if they would survive. Probably not, he thought. But then, they were just policemen. Compared to everyone else he was going to obliterate that day, a pair of policemen would barely make a ripple on the casualty lists.

He smiled in the darkness and then winced. His face, among other parts of his body, hadn't quite settled in to its new look and shape. But he was confident that it would work just fine when the time came.

2

SWAMP MORGAN CALLED CONNIE WALL AT NINE O'CLOCK the following morning.

"Connie Wall," she said. A smoker and a drinker, Swamp thought when he heard her voice.

"Ms. Wall, this is Special Agent Lee Morgan, U.S. Secret Service, calling from the Department of Homeland Security. Good morning."

"I doubt that," she said.

Swamp smiled. "Ma'am?"

"Nobody in Washington getting a call from the American gestapo at nine A.M. on a Tuesday would anticipate a good morning, Special Agent."

Swamp laughed. "Oh, c'mon now. If we were those guys, we'd come at two in the morning and just kick your door in."

"Your department is still young," she said.

"Well, let me put your mind at ease, Ms. Wall. I'd like to talk to you, if I may. And preferably not on the telephone. It concerns that fire at your former place of employment, the Khandoor Cosmetic Surgery Clinic."

"Oh God," she said. "I've been trying to forget all that."

"I can imagine. Actually, I can't. I've never lost friends and colleagues that way."

"Nor do you ever want to," she said. "But what in the world does that fire have to do with Homeland Security?"

"I'll explain that when we talk, Ms. Wall. Now, I can invite you to come downtown to our offices here on L Street, or, if you prefer, I can go out there. I have your address, and you're near a Metro stop, correct?"

"Here would be fine."

"Ten-thirty work?" he asked.

"Sure. Although I can't imagine . . . I mean, I told those fire department investigators everything."

"Relax, Ms. Wall. Nobody's gunning for you. I need to pick your brains about that clinic and its operations."

There was a sudden silence on the line. He let it ride, interested to see what she'd say. "I signed an entire stack of confidentiality agreements," she said. "Plus, there are patient-doctor privilege rules. I mean . . ."

"Yes, I know all that and I understand," he said. "It'll be clearer when we can actually talk, face-to-face. I'll be bringing my assistant, Special Agent Gary White, with me. If you'd like to confirm that I am who I say I am, I'll give you a number you can call to verify our identities. And my name again is Special Agent Lee Morgan, and I'm from an office called OSI."

Connie put the phone down and stood there chewing on a fingernail. The Secret Service? Her immediate reaction was to call Cat Ballard, but of course that wouldn't work, because she'd have to listen to him bang on again about the damned clinic. Cat hadn't been the least bit interested in the clinic when she worked days, but the night duty had first interested and then bothered him. Her refusal to talk about any aspect of what she did there had only whetted his appetite. Then the fire, and the horror of four people with whom she'd worked for four years dying like that. And now, what he'd revealed last night, that there were still questions about the fire. And here comes the Secret goddamned Service to talk to me about—*ta-da*—the clinic. She shook her head and went to refill her coffee cup. Then she called that number, and a DHS government operator verified that there were indeed two special agents named Lee Morgan and Gary White. The operator did not have a physical description of Agent White but was able to tell her that Special Agent Morgan was a very large and somewhat scary-looking man. She gave Connie the last four numbers of each agent's credential serial numbers, told her it would be okay to ask them to verify those numbers when they showed up, and wished her a nice day.

Yeah right, I'm gonna have a nice day, Connie thought. Especially after a sleepless night. She'd gone around the house checking windows and doors, and then spent a few minutes of each hour thereafter imagining bogeymen in the bushes every time the wind blew. She had fished out the .45 derringer and now had it in her jeans pocket, where it created a heavy and fairly obvious bulge. Should she get rid of it before the agents showed up? Surely they'd know what that was, and then she'd be explaining why she was sporting a .45-caliber belly gun in her pocket. Concealed weapons in Washington were a definite no-no. On the other hand, it was her house.

And then there was the heart of the matter: How much should she say about the clinic? The D.C. Arson cops already knew that she had been more than just a shift nurse there. Christ, this wasn't about one of those damned transcripts, was it? She suddenly had a cold feeling that it was.

Heismann, decked out as a bird-watcher, stood on a knoll in Rock Creek Park, his ten-power Leica binoculars trained in the direction of the white house on the distant bluff. He carried an Audubon guide under one arm, and he occasionally pretended to enter notes into a bird-count notebook. From his vantage point, he could see both the front door and the top of the nurse's driveway. The day was gray, cold, and damp. The race car was still parked in the drive, its back window frosted from the night's condensation. That was a good sign. He was trying to make up his mind whether or not to go up there, see if she'd had a glass of milk lately. Preferably before she spoiled, so to speak.

Then, to his surprise, he saw two men in suits and coats, a bulky one whose face looked like that of a caveman, the other average size, walking down her street and turning up the sidewalk to her front door. With the sensitivity born of almost twenty years on the wrong side of the law, Heismann recognized them immediately as police. As far as he could tell, the entire city police force was black, so, since they were both white, they were probably government police. Improbably, the big one was wearing a gray Borsalino-style hat; with that face, he needed all the style he could get. The younger one waited at the foot of the steps while the big man rang the bell. When he realized the younger one was looking around, gazing out into the park, Heismann lowered his binoculars and pretended to scribble in the book. This would be the test: Would she come to the door? He saw movement in the distance and lifted the binocs again. And, damn her eyes, there she was, standing in the doorway, looking at something the big man had handed her. Credentials, not a badge. Government police. The big man turned to say something to the other man, and Heismann got a good look at his face this time. Late fifties. Heavy eyebrows, huge jaw. A fighter's face. Then she was letting them in, closing the door.

He swore out loud and began stuffing the binocs into their side case. Then he walked down the long slope of the knoll toward his vehicle, a homely gray minivan, whose most useful quality was that it was utterly forgettable. It was a good thing he hadn't gone skulking around up there. On the other hand, why were federal police visiting Wall now, weeks after the fire? Had the bait surfaced at last? He wondered if he should ask Mutaib for a bugging system, because it might be useful to know if that was why they were there. He stood there at the door to his minivan and turned to look back toward the house, but only the rooftops were visible. The timing was about right. About six weeks since the fire. The holidays were now over. Official Washington getting back to work, so, perhaps yes?

He needed to contact Mutaib. Today.

On second thought, no. He had told Mutaib that he would take care of the nurse problem. He had failed. Perhaps it was now time to do it the old-fashioned way. No more of this indirect shit. Heave a cinder block through a back window at two o'clock in the morning to make it look like a break-in, go in there and brain her with a tire iron. Take her purse, put the spare key back on its hook, and leave.

No, no, no. Not now, not like that. Not with government agents coming to see Connie Wall, the sole survivor of the night clinic. Who then turns up dead in her bed? Too much coincidence. No.

Think, he told himself. Adhere to discipline. Execute the plan. There is still plenty of time to take her off the board. If this visit was provoked by the bait, maybe he should go back to his original plan. Let her lead them to the name. When Mutaib's resources indicated that they were focusing on that name, *then* kill her.

He got into the minivan, put his keys in the ignition, then paused again. Or perhaps don't kill her at all. Terrorize her instead. Make her run. He didn't need her dead as much as he needed her *gone*. After the attack, what would he care what she knew or told anyone, because everything would be over and he would be long gone. What had been going on at that clinic would pale into total insignificance in light of what he was going to do to them.

So yes, terrorize her. Why not? You're a professional terrorist, aren't you? He smiled. Frighten her. If she bolted, it would only make the bait more believable. Except he had told Mutaib that he would take care of the problem.

Well, if she ran, that was removal, yes? He shook his head in frustration. He hated it when he didn't know what to do. That was always the big problem with loose ends. At the very least, he would have to watch her until he made up his mind. And keep the embarrassing fact that she was still alive away from Mutaib and his helpers.

Connie Wall led the agents back to the kitchen area. It was obvious to Swamp that she, like many single people, lived mostly in the kitchen and dining room, which he saw was set up as her personal home office. Gary White followed him in, looking around at everything, as if observing a crime scene. That's good, Swamp thought. White would focus on the house, which would allow him to focus on the woman walking in front of him. She was about forty, he guessed. Dark-haired, fit, an attractive, if slightly wary, face, even without makeup. She was wearing old jeans, slippers, and an oversized sweatshirt, which did not disguise a bounteous figure. She offered coffee and he accepted for both of them. When she reached up to pull some mugs down from a cupboard, he thought he saw what looked like a derringer outlined in her jeans pocket. He glanced at Gary, who nodded slightly to confirm he had also seen it.

"January in Washington," Swamp said, making conversation. "Cold, dark, and wet."

"I expected an unmarked car with antennas all over it," she said, pouring out coffee.

"I never use a car if the Metro can get me close," Swamp said, taking off his coat and hat and draping them over a kitchen chair. "Our offices are airless cubicles. It's good to get outside, even in January."

She passed over the mugs of coffee and sat down on the other side of the kitchen table. "So," she said in a businesslike tone of voice. One that went with the gun in her pocket, he thought. "You called."

"So I did," Swamp said. "Let me begin by saying we're here to talk about the cosmetic surgery clinic where you worked. The one that was burned."

"Was 'burned'? As in deliberate fire?"

"I think so, yes," he said. "At least that's a distinct possibility."

Her complexion lost a little color, as if she had just realized something. "Am I a suspect or anything like that?"

"No. Nor are we aware of any criminal enterprise at that clinic. We've come to see you basically because you're the only survivor."

"Have you talked to the owners of the building? The American doctors?"

"Yes. Or rather, the District police have. They explained the nature of the leasing arrangement, and that the night doctors, as they called them, specialized in patients who demanded absolute discretion. They also made it clear that these were two entirely separate operations."

Connie Wall nodded at that. Swamp thought that she seemed to be loosening up a bit. "I worked for them, too," she said. "Initially, full-time. Then when the other group showed up, they offered almost twice the money. So then I worked nights, but I occasionally did fill-in work in the day clinic."

"Let me get right to it, Ms. Wall: What kind of procedures were they doing in the night clinic?"

She shrugged. "The usual, except they treated only male patients. These men wanted to get work done, but gradually. A little here, a little there. Minimum bruising and bandaging. A lot of special timing if it was going to be something significant. Very little visible evidence they were having work done, but a steady cosmetic improvement. Multiple procedures."

"These were prominent people?"

"They may have been," she said, looking right at him. She had clear hazel eyes, and he could see that, under the right circumstances, he'd find her very attractive. But right now, her expression revealed nothing. She was a surgical nurse, which meant that there was a good brain under there, so that completely neutral expression was worrisome. "But *we* were never told who they were," she went on. "The records didn't have names, just patient numbers."

So she knew about the codes. "Who would have known who the patients were?"

"Dr. Khandoor, the boss. He acted as his own patient coordinator."

"Did you handle patient records?"

He thought he saw her tense up a bit as she fiddled with her coffee cup for a couple of seconds. "I did admin work in both clinics," she said. "Putting medical charts and case history records together. Postop documentation. Mary and Karen did admin work, too. But reservations, patient interviews, billing, that was strictly Dr. Khandoor."

"Did the doctors record what they were doing during operations? You know, speak into a microphone while they did the operation, so that there'd be a record of the procedures?"

"Yes," she said, but she did not elaborate. She had folded her hands in her lap, out of sight beneath the edge of the table. A certain stillness settled over her. Careful here, Swamp thought.

"Were these notes transcribed after the operations?"

No blink at the mention of transcripts. No reaction at all. But she did not look at him when she answered. "No," she said. "We simply kept the tapes as part of the patient's record. We wouldn't need them unless a problem came up, so there was no point in transcribing them." Swamp saw her look over at Gary White as if to say, Where is your partner here going with this?

"Were there ever problems? Complaints?"

"Not that I was aware of. Both doctors were very good at what they did. Dr. Khandoor especially—he was amazing."

"Better than the American doctors?"

"Much better. He was nearly sixty, so I think he'd been cutting for a while."

"Do you know who set them up in this country? As foreign nationals, I mean."

"That was sort of vague," she said, patting a few stray hairs back into place. "There was something about a foreign bank, but, really, I never knew."

"Did they ever work on foreigners?"

"Yes, I think so, based on some of the accents I heard. Dr. Khandoor said that they were people from the Washington diplomatic corps. He said he had an international reputation, and I believed it. Like I said, he was very good."

Swamp had been writing in a notebook as she answered his questions. So had Gary White. He took a moment to review his notes, even though Gary had a voice-activated tape recorder turning silently in his suit pocket. Swamp had already decided that he was going to reinterview her later, after they learned more about Dr. Khandoor, but right now he needed to focus the interview.

"You said they offered you twice the money. Why was that, do you suppose?"

She shrugged again. "Well, for one, I was ready-made, I guess. I knew that OR and also the computerized office-management system. I'm a very experienced surgical nurse. I have a Master's degree, in fact. It was all going to be night-shift work. They wouldn't even have to advertise."

"Why was that last bit important?"

"Like I said, I got the impression that privacy and staff discretion meant everything to them."

"The other two nurses?"

"They came with Dr. Naziri, who was Dr. Khandoor's assistant."

"Did the docs ever hand out bonuses?"

She hesitated. "Bonuses? Yes, they did. Christmastime, usually. I think they made a ton of money."

Swamp made a note to check with IRS on her tax returns. "More than the day doctors?"

"I don't *know* that. The day clinic handled more patients. But yes, I think so. It was a different clientele altogether. Lots of limos and drivers."

"I'm going to ask you to do something for us, Ms. Wall. Can you generate a list of the types of procedures performed at your clinic? The District Arson squad has recovered some records from the fire, but they're badly damaged. Can you do that?"

"*Arson* squad? So this fire *was* deliberately set?"

"Well, they haven't called it yet," he said. She was definitely upset now. Fair enough. She'd lost friends and coworkers in that fire. "But that's all I can tell you right now. Officially, the investigation's ongoing."

"So why are you here, Special Agent?" she asked suddenly, cocking her head to one side.

"Um, I thought I explained that the—"

"No, I mean, why are *you* here? You said Secret Service. What did our clinic have to do with protecting the president?"

Swamp sat back in his chair and sipped some coffee, which was getting cold. Gary White was studying his own notes now, fully aware of Swamp's discomfort. Swamp decided that the truth wouldn't hurt.

"Okay, Ms. Wall," he said. "As I'm sure you're aware, there's a war on. The D.C. Arson squad removed a lot of evidentiary debris from that clinic. The patients' records, at least the paper ones, made better debris than evidence, but there were some indications that your clinic was performing changes in physical identity. As you might imagine, that's an activity of interest to the Department of Homeland Security these days."

"Is that illegal?" she asked. He could see her forearms moving slightly beneath the edge of the table. Was she wringing her hands? Her tone of voice was still very carefully neutral. A pulse was now visible in the veins of her throat, something that hadn't been there before. She was definitely on edge.

"Changing one's physical appearance wouldn't be illegal per se. Using that new physical identity to commit fraud or other crimes would be illegal. And if a resident alien gets his or her physical identity changed, that moves into the realm of '*interesting*,' depending on who that person is. Within the context of our intelligence efforts against the terror networks, that is."

She appeared perplexed. He decided to elaborate. "We're not working for the presidential protective detail right now, Ms. Wall," he said. "In fact, I'm actually a *retired* Secret Service agent, called back to active duty within the office of Special Investigations of the Department of Homeland Security."

"Retired?"

"Quick source of trained and experienced manpower, Ms. Wall. This is a people-intensive war we're in."

"Well," she said. "I'm not sure I can help you. I mean, I could list procedures, but I can't tie procedures to individual patients. That's what you want, isn't it?"

Definitely a good brain under there, Swamp thought as he nodded. She knows what this is about.

She hiked her chair closer to the table. "The problem is, we all worked different nights, and with different patients."

"And you don't remember any of them as unique, or special?"

"I wouldn't tell a patient this, Mr. Morgan, but as surgical assistants, we didn't see these patients as people. I mean, by the time they got into the OR, they were medium mummies scheduled for one of a hundred different 'plasty' procedures. By the time I saw them, they had become just part of a surgical procedure, requiring specific knowledge on our part, standard sets of instruments, specific draping, lights, anesthesia."

"Do you remember a sex-change operation—say in the past year?"

Her eyebrows rose, but she nodded. "One partial SRS, yes."

"SRS?"

"Sexual-reassignment surgery. That's really specialized stuff. This one was a male to female mammopexy, with prosthesis implantation. It was interesting because the patient wanted to be able to, um, inflate them, as it were."

"Inflate them? As in breasts on demand?"

"I guess. Instead of straight implants, he had his breast tissue loosened, the musculature rearranged, and specially adapted saline sacs implanted. He could then use a pump syringe, attached to a tiny stoma in his nipples, to pump them up with saline solution."

Swamp shook his head in amazement.

"Yeah," she said. "I use the word *guy* advisedly. Straight for his day job. TS-TV for his night games? Who knows, huh?"

Swamp smiled, but he didn't say what he was thinking, which was that any man who wanted to be a woman didn't know much about the "joys" of female physiology. "I can't imagine," he said truthfully. Then he got to the question he'd come there to ask. "Tell me, Ms. Wall, do people under anesthesia ever talk? Like people who talk in their sleep?"

She frowned, and appeared to choose her words carefully. "Ye-e-s, people sometimes do that, Mr. Morgan. But it's usually not intelligible. More like a bunch of slurred words. Gibberish, interspersed occasionally with moments of perfect clarity. It often sounds like a word-association game. Although most surgical patients just burble like a baby."

"Ever hear anything interesting?"

She laughed. "Yeah, once. A guy goes, 'Ow, that fucking hurts.' Now *that* got everybody's attention."

Both Swamp and Gary White laughed out loud. "What did you do?"

"Got a new anesthesia tech. But if you're asking if people admit to killing their wives, no. Besides, the patient usually had a mask over his mouth and nose and one or more tubes hanging out of the sides of his mouth. Not conducive to speech."

That makes sense, Swamp thought. "You said earlier that the docs would dictate the procedure into a taping machine. Would that machine be able to pick up anything the patient said?"

She shook her head emphatically. Too emphatically? Swamp wondered. "No. The surgeon had a lip mike attached to his headgear. And he was speaking right into it, so anything the patient might have been mumbling would just have been background noise."

She'd neatly shut off his line of questions about transcripts. He closed his notebook and stood up. "Okay. Thanks for your time this morning, Ms. Wall. We'll let you know if we need to talk to you again. Maybe if we can determine who the patients were, we might be back to see if we can put patient and procedure together."

"I doubt it, Mr. Morgan," she said, also getting up. "But I'll be glad to help out any way I can. Right now, I'm busy looking for another job."

She walked them to the front door. "This is a nice house," Swamp said, slipping on his coat.

"It was my parents' home," she said. "A little big for one person, but the price was right, you know?"

"And overlooking Rock Creek Park, too," he said, thinking of what a house with a big yard in that location might be worth in today's market. To his surprise, he saw a flicker of apprehension in her eyes.

"The park's a mixed blessing, Special Agent," she said.

"Call me if you think I can help. I lost two good friends in that fire."

Gary discreetly checked the tape recorder as they walked up the block toward Connecticut Avenue. It had done its job. "Did we get what we needed back there?" he asked.

"Maybe," Swamp said. "I think she tried to disabuse me of the notion that anything interesting was ever revealed by people under anesthesia."

"Did you catch what she said at the door? About losing *two* good friends?"

"Meaning the doctors were not friends?"

"Yes, sir. They paid these nurses double the going rate. The women had to suspect some of this shit was a little bit out there."

They got to Connecticut and turned left down toward the Zoo Metro station. "I'm wondering if those tapes were made *after* an operation," Swamp said. "You know, while the patient was still under—say in the recovery room—but starting to surface."

"And no longer wearing the mask and tubes. That might make more sense."

A blast of wind shrank them into their overcoats, and they stopped talking until they were down inside the Metro station. "What I need here is a way to put that transcript together with a specific patient. I need a name, not a code number."

"We'd need to find the code list somewhere in all that wreckage. How much time do we have?"

"Good point. My tasking was to evaluate this as a firefly or not. You're right. We need something a lot quicker."

"Maybe interview her again, show her the transcript this time? She said she did admin. Go ahead and brace her up? You had a possible terrorist on the table and you changed his looks. Who the hell was it, missy?"

The tunnel to their right began to glow as the next train

approached. "She could plead total ignorance about the transcripts," Swamp countered. "Maybe one of the other nurses did that. You know, one of the dead ones. And it's not likely those docs would have let the nurses see the code list."

"If she did admin, she might know where the code lists were kept—that would be something the docs would have had backed up off-site, like their medical records."

The train roared into the station, once again making conversation impossible. They boarded and rode it back downtown; meanwhile, Swamp tried to think of a way to prove the transcript, one way or the other.

"Bomb, bomb, bomb. Union Staat." Put a bomb in the Capitol? Which was getting the security scrubbing of a lifetime in preparation for the inauguration? Besides, the Capitol was a big building. That would require a big bomb.

But after that? After all the pomp and circumstance of the inauguration, the Capitol security people would naturally relax a little, stand down the surge effort. Tactically, that speech to the joint session would be a better window to try something. Maybe the right answer here was to go back to PRU right now. Tell them to keep going full bore on inauguration preps, and then sustain that for the month between the inauguration and that first presidential speech to a joint session of Congress.

After they got by that, if some nutcase wanted to bomb Congress, he might actually do the nation a favor. Seeing Gary White looking at him, he realized he'd been smiling to himself. And that he would definitely not be explaining the reason to his new ace assistant. He wondered, not for the first time, if he'd been doing this stuff too long.

Connie desperately wanted to talk to somebody after the agents had left, but she couldn't think of anyone except Cat Ballard. And after his pointed comments of the night before about the clinic, Cat would be less than sympathetic. She knew exactly what the problem was: Those Secret Service guys had a transcript in their hands. They couldn't *know* that she was the one who'd transcribed the recovery room tapes, but they'd come to her because she was the only one of the night crew left alive.

She paced her dining room, trying to remember if there was anything in the transcripts, or any other documentation, that could prove she'd written them up. She didn't think so. Dr. Khandoor had made it clear that he wanted only the patient's code number on the transcripts. No other information, not the procedure or even a date. Just what the patient actually said. She'd type them up from the tapes, print one copy, and then delete the computer file. Dr. Khandoor would get the only copy. She had no idea where he'd kept them, but she'd never found any sign of them or the master code list in the clinic. All their medical records had been kept both as traditional paper records and as scanned and then encrypted computer-graphics files. Once a month she'd run a master backup routine on all the computerized records and then given the backup CD to Dr. Khandoor.

Dr. Khandoor had done the paperwork on patient workups. He would hand over a folder for each new patient; it contained all the forms that would apply to whatever work was going to be done. Reportedly, everyone paid cash, so she had never had to do any perambulations through the medical insurance swamp, which was a major blessing in itself. In every name blank would be that patient's assigned code number, handwritten by Dr. Khandoor. Postsurgery, she would scan all the forms into an Adobe PDF file to create the backup. There was never a name, especially on the recovery room transcripts. She hadn't been kidding about the patients being just part of a surgical procedure—the first time the nurses ever saw the patient was at the first procedure.

With a few interesting exceptions, most of the transcripts

had been a hodgepodge of mumbles. That said, she was willing to bet which one the feds had their hands on. "Bomb, bomb, bomb." And a bunch of German words she hadn't understood. She remembered bringing that one to Dr. Khandoor's attention, and he had told her he'd take care of it immediately, whatever that meant. In these uneasy times, any foreigner talking about bombs should be fed right to the nearest police precinct, as far as she was concerned. But is that what the good doctor had done? The transcripts were supposed to be insurance against trouble down the line, but she'd always wondered if he and Naziri hadn't been making some extra money on what some of these people revealed. One congressman, whom the whole crew had recognized, had come in for a series of facial procedures. On one occasion, as he lay in the recovery room, he'd babbled into the microphone about how much he loved his pretty little boys. Connie had dutifully recorded it, while carefully blocking out any troubling thoughts of blackmail when she handed it in.

But now there were feds coming around, asking questions about patients getting identity changes, and confirming what Cat had been saying about arson. Damn it.

She'd known all along that place was on the fringes of medical ethics. Two slick Pakistani doctors, setting up an off-the-books practice in the capital? They had to have had an important sponsor. And a rich one. The money had been so-o-o good. And you just wouldn't face it, would you, Connie? Not with that big fat paycheck. And, of course, the bonuses. The little one for the IRS, and the much better one, the cash bonus. The Secret Service used to work for the Treasury Department. As did the IRS. She just knew that guy was going to pull her tax returns. Her brokerage submitted 1099 forms, just like the clinic turned in W-2 slips. If they did one of those reality audits, they'd see right away that she had invested more income than she'd reported.

She gnawed a fingernail as she sat down at her computer

and powered it up. She spied Buster's bed in a corner of the dining room and remembered that Cat Ballard had taken the milk container.

Her stomach sank. Someone had been in her house. He'd passed up valuable stuff but taken some of her underwear. That smacked of neighborhood pervert. But what if the container did show up traces of poison? Had that been the real objective of his being in her house?

A chill went through her. Everyone else from the clinic's night crew was dead. Who would have burned down the clinic? The day docs? For the insurance money? No way— that place had to have been a cash cow for them, too. So, a disgruntled patient? Maybe someone the docs had tried to blackmail?

Or had that fire been aimed at the crew, not the clinic? The cosmetic surgery crew, who might know too much.

"Bomb, bomb, bomb." You know which one said that, she thought. The foreign-looking guy with the inflatable boobs, not to mention all the rest of the work. Identity changes, Special Agent? Well, yes, you might say that. Shit! Had he been the torch? The night she'd done that transcript was the night she first confessed her doubts about the clinic to Cat Ballard. No details, of course, but a deepening suspicion that she was getting in over her head with these guys. Cat had been as direct as ever: "They're Muslims, Connie. All this terrorist shit's being done by Muslims. Get your ass out of there. Because if one of your patients does something weird, something big and bad, the government will do one of those root-canal investigations and then they'll grind you up. Turn you over to the grieving widows."

But of course it hadn't been that simple, nor that easy to cut and run. She was single and forty years old. She knew she wasn't the marrying type and never would be. Which meant that the quality of her old age was entirely up to her. She'd worked hard her entire professional life. She'd done the additional training, gotten her master's, and invested well. She'd been able to ride the nineties boom to the point that she just about had her screw-you money. Plus, she hadn't been doing anything wrong. Just her job as a surgical and administrative assistant. The docs had been pulling in the big bucks, not the staff. Identity change wasn't illegal—even that big Secret Service agent with the Neanderthal face had agreed with that. Or mostly, he had.

She nearly jumped out of her skin when the phone rang. She glanced at her caller ID box. A 998 number, which she didn't recognize. She picked it up and said, "Hello?" She heard three coins dropping into a call box. Okay, a phone booth. Then a whispering voice said, "Everyone's dead. Except you." Then a click and the dial tone.

She lowered the phone back onto its cradle slowly, as if afraid of breaking it. She jumped when something moved past a side window, just out of her line of vision. She reached down for the derringer, then realized she'd only seen the bushes bending back and forth in the January wind. The house was still, the dining room a mix of shadows and light streamers from the midmorning sun. Her mind went blank, and for a moment she felt frozen in the chair.

Everyone's dead. Except you.

English, but English with an accent. A man's voice.

Everyone's dead. Except me.

That certainly clarifies things.

After lunch, Swamp met with Gary White to brainstorm about their next move. They needed to put some meat on the transcript's bones, something that would allow them to both evaluate it and sell it to PRU as evidence of a real threat.

"Okay, so we need the code list," Swamp said. "Ideally, we want to put a name on this guy, and, again ideally, a history of what procedures he had done at that clinic."

"If there are names," Gary pointed out. "These docs may

have run the whole thing on a code basis—no names, cash only, code only. We won't ask, and you won't tell us who you are. Money up front, we'll do exactly what you want, Mr. Two-oh-oh-three-four-one."

Swamp nodded. "Yeah, but they were bugging the recovery room. My guess is that it was both insurance and a shot at a little extortion. For that, they had to know who it was they were working on."

"Yes, sir, they may have known, but if it were me, I'd never write that down. I'd give the guy a code number, show him that's what I was doing in the records, and keep the name to myself. Or in some secure off-site storage place."

"Off-site, yeah. Okay. Here's what I want you to do: go back to the D.C. Arson evidence locker and go through those records. You're looking for anything that could tie the docs, either one of them, to an off-site storage system. Like those companies on the Web that will store all your files as backup? I'm going to go get paper to search their homes, any PCs they may have had at home."

"Got it," Gary said. "But those records . . ." he shook his head.

"Yeah, I know. They looked like the Dead Sea Scrolls. But spend an afternoon. See what you can find. Anything that might lead us to the code list. Any other transcripts that could lead us to a name. We need a way into this hair ball."

Gary left ten minutes later, after making the arrangements with Carl Malone. Swamp then began the paperwork to get a warrant for searching the homes and personal property of the two deceased doctors. He retrieved their names and addresses from the D.C. Arson files, then generated the forms for a search warrant. This was a process that could take weeks in a routine case, but these were not routine times, and he was able to use his position in the Department of Homeland Security, plus some connections at the Justice

Department, to get the package together in an afternoon. He had it couriered over to the Washington federal district court after making sure his morning calender for the next day was clear for the hearing. He then called Carl Malone and asked him to be available for a possible probable-cause hearing in the morning. There'd been some bitching from the clerk's office until Swamp invoked the standard Secret Service mantra about presidential security. Everything smoothed right out after that, and Swamp went back to studying the case file Malone had given him.

Gary White came back into the office just before six o'clock, looking tired. Swamp was asking Malone some questions on the phone. Gary dropped his briefcase on his desk and went to get some coffee. Swamp wrapped it up with Malone and joined Gary at the coffee machine.

"I did find a partial duty roster, the one that lists which nurses worked which nights. It confirmed Connie Wall was off that night. Here's the good news: The roster also had the code numbers for the patients who'd be worked on. From that, I found that patient two-oh-oh-three-four-one was up for a one-hour procedure on the night of the fire."

"And?"

"The patient code number on the "bomb, bomb, bomb" transcript was two-oh-oh-three-four-one. That would put our transcript firefly in the clinic the night of the fire, assuming the roster is correct."

"Nice. Very nice, and also significant. What do you make of those numbers?"

"Calender year 2003, patient number forty-one?"

"Yeah, that works. But 2003? He'd been going there for a year?"

"It gets better. I found a partial invoice from an on-line file-storage service called NetZDocustorage.com. It's a site where companies can store their backup stuff. There was a single account number on the invoice, which I'm assuming was the clinic. If you've got a warrant coming down . . ."

"Absolutely, I'll work up an amendment tonight. Maybe that damned code list will be in there. Hopefully, that company will have a password-recovery system."

"Even without the code list, maybe we'll get lucky and see what kind of work patient forty-one had. Although I'm not sure how that helps."

"It helps if it looks like a total identity change," Swamp said. "That plus the German plus talking up bombs and the State of the Union makes this whole deal look less and less like a firefly. And it'll help at the hearing."

"But with just a number, how do we find his ass?"

"First things first. Let's get our warrants, do the searches. I also want to know lots more about the head doc, that Khandoor guy, before I go back to PRU. See if he's connected to anybody of interest."

"Read me his card again," Cat Ballard told her. "I want to make sure I got the right guy."

Connie picked it up and read off Swamp Morgan's business card: Special Agent T. Lee Morgan, United States Secret Service, retired, Office of Special Investigations, United States Department of Homeland Security. She had to turn on a light because it was getting dark outside. She had just finished cleaning up after the security system people when Cat finally called her back.

"Yeah, that's him. Our deputy chief for intel knows him. Big, sorta ugly guy, right? Supposedly played front line at Notre Dame. Something of a legend around federal law enforcement."

"Is that good news or bad news for me?" Connie asked. She had told Cat about the agents' visit, that they were investigating the clinic fire, but that was all. She hadn't mentioned the cryptic phone call from the man with the foreign accent.

"Morgan's been around, Connie. He's a senior G-man with a reputation for playing ball with local law whenever he could, the kind of guy who banked and returned a lot of markers. Secret Service, but he knows people on both sides of the river. Intelligence guy, as opposed to a street cop. Did an exchange tour with the CIA; did a tour over in Germany back when it was still East and West. A player, in other words."

"And the answer is?"

Cat exhaled audibly. "The answer is, Connie, that this Morgan is a high-level, very experienced, very connected fed. If he's looking at you, pay attention. And a guy like this? He doesn't investigate fires."

She didn't say anything.

"So," Cat said, "you ready to tell me what the *fuck* was going on at that plastic surgery clinic that's got a daddy spook coming out to your house for coffee?"

"He said he was retired."

"They brought back a whole grunch of senior people after nine eleven. Don't let that retired bit fool you. I talked to Inspector Malone in Arson. Morgan's the real deal, and he said not to let the Neanderthal face fool you—the guy's got his brain switched in. So what's going on, Connie?"

"Cat, he told me not to talk about it to anybody. I don't think they're after me—I just happen to be the lone survivor. Me and several boxes of badly burned records. I worked admin, remember?"

"Actually, I don't remember that, Connie."

She couldn't think of an answer to that, and the silence grew uncomfortable. "Did you get anything back on that milk container?" she asked.

"Not yet. I couldn't give it a high-pri number. There's no active homicide case. Is there a hurry?"

She took a deep breath and then told him about the phone call, and he became very quiet. "Say the exact words again," he ordered. She did.

"Did you buy a security system?"

"Yes. ADT. They said it would take a week. I told them I'd pay extra if they'd set it up today. As in this afternoon. They did."

"Okay—don't go out of the house. I'm coming over."

"Cat? Should I be scared?"

"Yes. You're sitting in too many crosshairs. Let me make a coupla calls; then I'll come over. But you're gonna have to talk to me, Connie, or I can't help you. Think about that between now and then."

"Cat . . ."

"Or you can call that Morgan guy. Hell, now that I think of it, you probably should call him."

"I'll wait for you," she said, and then hung up.

Heismann shifted his position in the garage behind the nurse's house so that he could see both the driveway and the back windows of the house. She was downstairs, in the dining room. She'd been talking on the phone; then she'd left the room for a few minutes, turned lights on and off throughout the house, and now was back in the dining room. He'd slipped into the yard just after dusk, coming up the hill from the park again. He'd spotted the ADT decals on the back door immediately, but there were none on the windows, so he'd have to do some snooping before trying any more break-ins.

The garage was a dusty, spidery place, filled with old furniture, boxes, yard tools, boards in the rafters, and one ancient riding mower that reeked of gasoline. There were single windows on either side, but they were so covered in dust, grime, and webs as to be useless. Down one side was a workbench with a row of power tools—drill press, a large band saw, a radial-arm saw, all draped in deep cobwebs. There probably hadn't been room for a car in here for years, and hers was parked in the driveway, where it had been the last time. But there was room for him, right up at the front, where the two big side-hinged doors came together, a two-inch crack between them. He'd pulled two boxes over to the crack, blown most of the dust off, and sat down to watch.

He hadn't made up his mind as to what he was going to do tonight, but he was going to do something. The day after tomorrow he had to occupy the house on Capitol Hill. After that, he would be busy putting the cover story in place and preparing the house for the weapon's arrival. This woman was still a loose end. How important a loose end depended on who those men in suits were and what they wanted from her.

The *Ammies* could always get lucky. If you could believe the papers these days, the FBI, CIA, and a host of other law-enforcement bureaus and agencies were actually talking to one another. But as best he could tell, the American government, supposedly at war with terrorism, was still making the most basic error of military planning: They were hell-bent on determining their enemy's intentions, when every good planner knew that you focused on the enemy's *capabilities*. That's what made the fanatics in Al Qaeda, the Base, so dangerous—they did target surveillance for as long as two years, but they never set a date for action. They built up their capabilities to act, developed opportunities and only when they saw such an opportunity would they seize it, which is what rendered the *Ammie* predilection for focusing on plans useless.

Headlights flared in the driveway. He ducked back from the big crack between the doors. Peering through a smaller crack between two boards, he saw the nurse's car silhouetted for an instant by a car behind it, and then its lights went off. He moved back to the larger crack and watched as a tallish white man got out of the new arrival and walked up the drive to the back porch. He was wearing a suit under an open trench coat. He looked to be about her age, early forties. Handsome, well built, in shape. He watched her come to the door and let him in. Then he saw them exchange a quick kiss. Okay, her lover. For a moment, he couldn't see them anymore, until they both appeared in the brightly lighted dining room, to the left of the kitchen, whose windows gave on to the backyard.

He pulled a pair of minibinoculars from his pocket and studied the man's face. A hard, serious face, skeptical eyes. Policeman perhaps? Another federal agent? This damned nurse seemed to be a magnet for police. He put the binoculars back in his coat pocket and sat down, tapping his fingers impatiently. He'd wait until they were busy doing something and then slip down to check the car. Maybe they'd go upstairs. That would make things a lot easier.

Then he had a bad thought: If this man was a policeman, he might be here because of that menacing phone call he'd made earlier. In which case, he might have to take action much sooner than he'd wanted to, perhaps tonight. He had hoped she would just bolt and solve his problem, but now he cursed his impetuousness. Here was a prime example of his not doing his homework. He should have known about the boyfriend. Now he might have *two* loose ends. He swore out loud in the darkness, startling some rodent in the furniture into skittering flight across the concrete floor.

"You get the whole enchilada here with this ADT system, or just doors?" Cat asked.

"Doors. Now I just have to remember another damned password, a system number, and a name for when I accidentally set the thing off and have to call them. It's off right now, until I reread the instructions."

He grunted. "Those signs on the doors are the best part of the system," he said. "Your average burglar sees that, he'll just go creep the house next door, one that doesn't have a system. Got any coffee?"

"I thought you were cutting back on caffeine?" she said as she went back out to the kitchen to make a fresh pot. She was wearing jeans and a sweatshirt, and she'd taken a moment to run a brush through her hair. Then she remembered

that the caffeine bit had been Lynn's idea. She found it
amusing that Cat's wife, who was at least fifty pounds over-
weight, would be hectoring lean and mean Cat Ballard about
his diet. But wives did that, she supposed.

"I tried," he was saying from the dining room. "Found
myself falling asleep at my desk by four. Having withdrawal
headaches. Just like some damn hype. Recognized my jones
when I saw it, gave up that decaf plan for Lent." He came to
the kitchen doorway. "Listen, I can't stay long. Bobby's
birthday—we're going to something called Chunky
Cheese."

"*Chuck E.* Cheese," she said. "Kids love it. You're probably gonna hate it."

"It's a place for some 'quality time,' as she calls it." He
sighed. "So, we gonna talk or what?"

She brought his cup of coffee in and sat down at the opposite side of the dining room table. She raised an eyebrow.
"'Or what'?"

"C'mon."

"The clinic?" she asked.

"Yeah, Con, the fucking clinic."

Game's over, she thought. She collected her thoughts for
a moment. "There was this one patient," she said. "A European guy. Medium-medium. They did the full Monty on him
over the course of the last year or so." She told him that
she'd assisted at several of his procedures, and that this guy
had paid to change out damn near everything. A new face,
taken, as she remembered, from a picture of someone else.
Subdermal smoothing grafts on fingertips and toes. Tonal
changes to his vocal cords. Altered eye color. Reshaped ears.
Permanent dye job on his hair—*all* his hair. A dentist in
three separate times to alter his teeth. If they could have
swapped out his DNA, he'd probably have wanted that done,
too.

And then there was the SRS angle: the inflatable boobs.
He'd kept the rest of his equipment, with the exception of

having a pouch opened up in his groin that would allow him
to bind his genitals practically out of sight. But from the
waist up, he would damn well startle the good folks in
church if he ever lifted his shirt. Then, switching gears, she
told him about the taping system, and the transcripts. That
had been her job, for which she was paid extra. Except for
her, only Dr. Khandoor had handled the tapes. And finally,
she told him that there had been one tape—she didn't know
who it was—of a guy talking about bombs and shit.

Cat just listened, staring at her, his coffee long forgotten.
"Bombs? You tell the feds all this?" His voice was rising.
"You tell this to the Secret Service?"

"I played ignorant," she said. "But I think that Morgan
guy was being coy. Asked if people talked in their sleep. I
sloughed it off. Tried to change the subject. But . . ."

"But?"

"He looks like a big dumb . . . caveman. There's no other
word for it. But he isn't. You can see it when he gives you
that goofy smile. I felt like he was looking right through
me."

Cat rubbed his chin. "You think they maybe retrieved
some of this shit from the fire scene?"

"Something tells me they might have that one transcript.
Heaven knows how, but I think that's why it's Secret Service
coming around."

"You know who it was that actually said that shit about
bombs?"

"No. Khandoor wouldn't give me a tape until it was full.
He ran the machines, dictated the code numbers before each
procedure. My job was to type up what I heard on the tape. It
would be *his* voice saying the code number, then the patient's voice in the recovery room. Sometimes there wasn't
anything, and I'd type the code number and then 'nothing
spoken.' "

"But this one guy?"

"Whoever it was, he kept saying 'bomb, bomb, bomb,'

and then some shit in German—'*Heil Hitler,*' Nazi stuff. If *that* guy, whoever, *whatever* he is, found out about the tapes and somehow knows I did the transcripts, then that's why he's been in my house." She raised her eyebrows at him. "Cat?"

"What?"

"I think I need to get out of here."

He nodded distractedly, then suddenly shook his head, as if coming to his senses. "No, hell no, you can't just rabbit. There'd be red rockets all over town, you go disappearing."

"I haven't done anything wrong, Cat," she said, almost shouting. "I just worked there, okay? I typed those damned things. The doctors were the ones recording their own patients."

"Doesn't matter, Con. I think you need to call that guy Morgan back and lay this all out for them—the Secret Service, I mean. Hell, the inauguration's in what—ten days? The whole police department is jumping through its ass for that. Did you know they're gonna lock down the whole downtown government area starting next week?"

"I read the papers," she said. "But how can I spill my guts to federal agents without getting into trouble, Cat? I didn't do anything but my job—you know, ace surgical assistant. But you know how it's gonna look. Identity changes on foreigners?"

He eyed her across the table, suddenly looking every inch the Homicide cop now. "This guy talking about bombs—he get an identity change?"

Shit, she thought. "I don't *know*! Like I said, we had no way of knowing. Each tape had several patients on it. I just fucking typed."

But Cat was shaking his head. "Some lunatic gets an identity change, talks about bombs? Suppose this *is* the same asshole who's creeping around your house, making death threats, killing your cat because you gave him the milk instead of putting it in your coffee?"

"But why me? I don't know who *any* of those people were!"

"Maybe it's just like this fuck told you on the phone, Con: Everyone's dead except you. He doesn't know what you know or don't know, but everyone else at that clinic is dead. Except you. That would do it for me."

"You just don't understand. Most of it, all the transcript shit, was pure babble. Disconnected words. Like those famous monkeys at the typewriters. It's probably meaningless."

"Okay, Con," he said, clearly exasperated. "So you tell me what all this is about, then, if not the clinic. Some guy in your house, your cat poisoned, threats on the phone? You been borrowing money from the wrong people or something?"

She didn't know what to say. He slapped a hand down on the dining room table, making her jump. "Listen to me, Connie. Something bad happens, and it comes back to this guy, or anybody at that clinic with the Muslim doctors? The whole country will want to crucify you, you don't bring it in. Right now. Tonight. You listening to me? You need to tell that Morgan guy what you know."

"But—"

"Yeah, yeah, I know you don't know who or even what it's all about. But this might be the final link in some deal the Secret Service has been wrestling with for a year or two. There's no telling what might be going down. You have to call that guy."

Heismann, watching them argue, decided to go check out that car. Keeping low, he opened the big wooden door wide enough to slip out. Staying bent over, he went right, away from the back porch light, and then down the driveway to where her car was. He crouched beside it on the side away from the house, then crept over to the driver's side of the man's car. The engine was still making ticking noises as it cooled in the night air. It was a large four-door sedan. He checked the house, but the front windows were still dark. He looked inside the car and saw a radio handset and a small console below the dashboard. He looked through the back window and could see the radio antenna embedded in the glass, but there was another one, a stubby wire antenna sticking up out of the trunk. He slipped behind the car and checked the plate. District plate, but no sign of government decals. He examined the taillights and saw the extra lens for a white or blue strobe light.

Very well, then. Police.

He went up to the grille to confirm that, ran his fingers along the warm plastic louvers, where he found another pair of recessed strobe lights. Definitely police.

Talking to the nurse about what? Their sex life? Or that doctored medical file he'd left behind at the clinic?

If this was about the bait, what would the policeman do? Demand that she come in, tell all she knew about the clinic, the patients, especially the patient in that record? Federal agents, now police. Weeks after the fire. Surely they did not suspect her of starting the fire. So this had to be about something else. Something that would concern the sole survivor.

It had to be the bait.

He took a deep breath of cold night air, stood up, and then began moving back to the garage. It was too soon. Much too soon. The deception plan had been designed to play out in two stages. The first was to drop an indication that a patient at the clinic, whose name was unknown, was planning to bomb the Union State speech. That had been the point of leaving the fake record behind at the clinic, in such a way as to ensure that it would survive the fire. By mentioning the Union State speech, they had established the wrong target, and, more important, the wrong time line. As long as everyone in the night crew died in the fire, stage one would initially be all they had. But for whatever reason, this nurse had survived. His reaction to that unexpected development had been to drop the second critical piece of information into the investigation, but Mutaib had scotched that idea. Told him to kill her.

Now federal police, and even a city policeman, were talking to her all of a sudden, weeks after the fire. The nurse might inadvertently compromise the timing of the second stage of the deception, which involved getting the *Ammies* to focus on that last name in the transcript's Nazi pantheon, Heismann. They'd need a description, and Interpol, which had a file on Heismann, would give them one. The trick was that his Interpol description no longer pertained, not after a year of cosmetic surgery. At the beginning of their search, they wouldn't know that. And they would also think they had some time, because stage one had pointed them at the Union State speech.

But everything depended on their being unaware, at least for a while, that he had a totally new physical identity. With all these policemen suddenly converging on his loose end, there was now a distinct chance that this damned woman could reveal that one crucial bit of information much too soon.

Mutaib was right. And he had already failed once to do what he had promised to do.

He would have to take her now. Tonight. Direct action. No more delay.

He'd tested the car's doors, but they had been locked. A security light had been blinking out its warning on the dashboard. Besides, he'd brought no tools, other than a small flashlight, the minibinocs, and his trusty Walther. So improvise. Do something to bring the policeman out into the backyard. But what? Shoot him? No. Too drastic. The hue and cry would be tremendous. Something else. He had to disable the policeman, not kill him. Unless, of course, the policeman himself forced the issue. But the policeman wasn't the objective; it was that damned woman he needed to silence.

He scuttled back up the driveway and into the garage

again, swinging the big doors almost shut behind him. Looking through the crack, he could see that they were still in the dining room, talking, faces frowning, the policeman up now, walking around, agitated, although not shouting. Not an argument, more like a serious discussion. He needed to get that man out into the backyard, away from the woman. Disable the policeman, then disable and grab the woman, take her down the hill, drown her in the creek, and stuff her body under a rock. "Disappear her," as the Argentine secret police liked to say. *Desaparecidos.* Wonderful expression, that. Those Argies were German-trained, too. By real Germans. Back when Germany commanded some respect in the world. Not like now.

He looked around the garage for something to use to set up a trap. A wire of some kind. Something that would ensnare the policeman if he came running out. He spotted the band saw. It gave him an idea.

He checked back to see where they were. They were still visible in the window and still talking. He moved to the band saw and used a bench brush to wipe off all the cobwebs. He felt the band blade—a flexible steel ribbon of serrated teeth one-quarter of an inch wide and about two and a half feet long. Times two: The band would be almost five feet. That would do. He unscrewed the wing nuts that held the housing cover and pulled it off, revealing the pulley wheels and the tensioning latch. He rotated the latch and the band sagged off the steel pulleys. He undid the bottom cover and removed the entire band. The teeth were still sharp and spiked his hands, even through his gloves. He lay the band on the workbench and searched for metal cutters, which he found on a Peg-Board wall. He cut the band, ducking his head when it snapped back into one flat ribbon of teeth and then flipped like a live thing down onto the floor.

He went back to the crack and looked out. She was still sitting there, head in hands now, while a shadow was visible moving around the kitchen. He went back and retrieved the glistening band, then spotted a miter box, its short, hard-backed, fine-toothed saw gathering webs on the bench. Perfect. Now all he needed was something large to throw through that dining room window. He looked around and spotted the vise.

"How much money we talking about?" Cat asked from the kitchen, where he was refilling his coffee cup.

"They paid eighty, base pay," she replied. "Plus overtime for day work, and benefits. The bonus I reported was five grand; the cash bonus was twenty." She was getting tired of this. She was suddenly ready for him to leave, go see his goddamned kid.

"Wow. And you invested all that?"

"Most of it. My broker, God bless her, pulled me out in early 2001, and we slapped it all in grade A, six and a half percent tax-exempt munis. Everything."

"Those guys must have been making a fortune," he said. "And you've got what—a couple hundred large working for you, tax-free? Nice."

She had a lot more than that, but he didn't need to know. Not now. "The IRS probably won't think so," she said. "Another reason I don't want to go front and center with the government."

He sat back down at the table. "I'll tell you what, Con. I think with the right shyster, you could get immunity from all that tax shit if you were willing to lay it out, everything that was going on at that clinic. You might have to pay some back taxes, but that would be negotiable. Your info is too valuable. Foreigners getting ID changes right here in Washington? Shit. Those DHS people would go nuts for that."

"And what if they lock me up?" she said, chewing a nail. "After nine eleven, they rounded up a shitload of people, and some of them are still in jail, no charges filed, no bond, no lawyers. Hitler would feel at home here these days."

He laughed. "No way. Hitler kept it simple—just the

gestapo. We've still got eighty-odd law-enforcement outfits here in D.C. alone, the DHS notwithstanding. It's like this Morgan guy—him and his Office of Special Investigations. That should be Bureau work."

"How's about I do an anonymous tip? Write something up, drop it into the system. Or I can give it to you—you can say you developed it from a confidential informant as part of this arson investigation."

He grunted sympathetically. "Like they wouldn't know who that was? With one person surviving the fire? C'mon, Con."

She screamed as something large crashed through the dining room window, landed on the table, and knocked her computer monitor right onto the floor, where its glass face exploded in a puff of arcing white smoke. Still frozen to her chair, she stared at the billowing curtains, stunned to see a face, a horrible face, pop up into view for a split second and then disappear. She heard Cat yell, "Hey!" and then he was running into the kitchen, trying to snag his gun out of his hip holster. She willed herself to get up, to get out of that room, trying not to step on all the glass or breathe the noxious cloud of phosphorous smoke hovering above the ruined monitor. That face—something about it. It had been all eyes and teeth, as if illuminated from below. How was that possible? She heard the back screen door open and then bang shut. And then came a strange strangling noise and then a huge thump as something—Cat?—went down in a heap on the back steps.

She snatched up the phone and dialed 911 as she backed into the living room, feeling almost naked in the light, those curtains blowing in and that ominous silence outside. The phone rang and rang and rang, but no operator picked up. Goddamned District of Columbia! She hung it up and redialed, this time getting a busy signal. She swore out loud and redialed one more time, the cord stretching all the way out now. Ringing. Then she heard footsteps coming toward the back of the house. Cat? Or that face? She was terrified to go out there, but then she remembered the derringer in her pocket. The operator came on just as she pulled the heavy little gun out of her jeans, nearly dropping the phone.

"Nine-one-one. What is your emergency?"

She froze again. What *was* her emergency? The footsteps were still coming, and they didn't sound like Cat's.

"*Murder!*" she said, blurting out the one word that ought to move their asses right along. "Help me, please." And then she dropped the phone and backed into the living room, where the lights were off, as the footsteps came up onto the back porch and she heard the screen door open slowly, then bump closed. She could just hear the 911 operator saying hello several times from the handset down on the floor. They would have caller ID, and that would give them the address. But right now, she had bigger problems, for she saw the lights in the kitchen switch off, followed by those in the dining room. Definitely not Cat.

She shuffled as quietly as she could backward across the living room carpet until she felt the couch behind her legs. Realizing she was silhouetted against the dim light coming in through the front window drapes from the street, she slipped behind an upholstered chair and squatted down. The house was silent except for the noises of the wind moving the front bushes around. She held the derringer in both hands, then remembered it wasn't cocked. The two diminutive side-by-side hammers were still down on the receiver. She heard a sound in the dining room, then another.

He was coming.

His shoes were crunching through the bits of glass from the monitor. And where the hell was Cat? She folded the derringer into her belly to mask the sound and thumbed back the two hammers. She sat fully down on the floor, her back against the wall radiator, and brought the gun up. She froze, barely breathing. Let him find me. Cat had told her the effective range of the derringer was arm's length. Okay, that's where I've got it, she thought.

She heard a small noise and what sounded like a grunt of effort, and then one of the table lamps came flying over the chair and into the front window, breaking out the glass and dropping heavily on her right shoulder. She nearly dropped the gun and had to bite her lip to keep from crying out. Where are the fucking cops? She wondered. Where is Cat? And then the man was right there, pulling the chair away, towering over her, that same face, a familiar face, something in his hand, a hammer coming down in a wicked strike at her head.

She rolled to the left, toward the hallway, aimed upward, and pulled both triggers on the derringer. Two rapid-fire blasts banged the palm of her hand and she heard him yell and stumble backward, colliding with some piece of furniture. She didn't hesitate. She scrambled away from the overturned chair, rolled into the front hall, got up, and ran as fast as she could straight out the back door, where she promptly tripped over the inert form of Cat Ballard, who groaned when she hit him. Her arms windmilling, she whacked her shoulder as she hit the railing on the back porch and slipped in something wet. She sat down abruptly on the top step, then went bumping right down the steps on her backside and hit the cold concrete of the sidewalk on all fours, her hands covered in—blood?

Cat's blood?

She heard footsteps again, this time from inside the house, thumping heavily down the front hall toward the kitchen, sounding like a drunk trying to run. She saw Cat's gun lying at the bottom of the steps and reached forward to grab it as a form filled the kitchen doorway, just inside the screen.

She raised the gun and tried to pull the trigger, but her

bloody, trembling hands slipped on the butt and she dropped the gun. As she lunged to retrieve it, she heard the man laugh, and then the screen door was opening and he was silhouetted in the kitchen light, shooting at her, stars of red flame blossoming in the doorway as steel hornets slashed the air by her cheeks. She screamed and began rolling across the yard, barely conscious of bullets hammering the concrete and tearing up chunks of dead grass all around her as she kept rolling, rolling, and then she was into the cedars, Cat's bloody gun still clutched in her hand. She tumbled through the dense green branches, got up, and ran straight down the hill, bushes and branches whipping her face. She was falling forward as much as she was running, caroming off small tree trunks in the darkness, until she twisted an ankle when she finally reached flat ground. She went down with a yelp, then stopped to listen.

She got up, hopping on one leg, rubbing the throbbing ankle, trying to hush her screaming lungs, her heart pounding so hard in her ears that he *had* to be able to hear it. She listened for signs of somebody coming down the hill after her, and then she could hear sirens, so she slumped back against a tree and tried not to cry. The creek was right below her, and, even in the cold, she thought about sliding down the huge boulders into that black water, if only to get that sticky mess off her hands.

He lunged out of the darkness and tackled her, sweeping her sideways and down, grabbing for her mouth with one hand while she fought, twisted, bit, and tried to shout, but he was too strong, one iron arm encircling her chest and squeezing the breath right out of her. She thought she felt Cat's gun under her knee, but she couldn't reach it. Then he lost his balance for an instant and came lunging over the top of her, giving her one glorious free shot at his crotch, which she took, kicking out with every ounce of her strength. And then he was off of her, curling into a retching ball that went sliding down the stone banks of the creek and into the water. She patted the ground for Cat's gun, found it, and crawled to the edge of the rocks, looking down, determined now, waiting for him to surface, ready to kill him, to empty that thing at him in the water. But he didn't surface. There was only the sound of the creek, running high in winter, rushing over all the rocks. Rock Creek, that's why they called it that, she thought as her adrenaline began to crash and she slowly lowered the gun.

She heard voices shouting above her on the bluff and saw blue lights flickering through the cedars. Walking backward up the hill, she kept the gun pointed down the slope, waiting for him to show himself again. She trudged back up the slope the way she'd come, step by step, the backs of her shoes filling with bits of soft dirt and mud. When she neared the top, she stopped, out of breath, her ankle pounding, her ribs sore from grappling with her attacker. She could hear men shouting, doors banging, other vehicles arriving. Then she heard an authoritative voice shouting, "What've we got, Larry?" And another man—Larry, she guessed—answered in an excited voice: "You're not gonna believe this, but it looks like Cat's punch cut his throat and then shagged ass. That's his car, and that's her car. We need some fucking dogs back here."

She froze in the cedars. Cut his throat? Sweet Jesus! And they thought *she* did it? She started to push forward, out of the cedars, determined to clear that shit right up, but then stopped in her tracks. She didn't recognize any of those voices, and she knew most of the guys on the District Homicide squad. Could she clear this up? She felt the sticky mess on her hands, Cat's blood. She hefted Cat's gun. What would that look like to a bunch of cops who were cranking up a cop-killer frenzy out there? And the guy who'd busted into her house? Where was he?

Instinctively, she backed down the hill again, watching the bluffs this time, waiting to see if someone would come through the trees, or turn loose a pack of tracking dogs. Surely the evidence in the house would reveal—what, exactly? Two broken windows. Overturned furniture. A struggle in the living room. She thought she had hit him with the .45, but then he'd come right back after her. So there'd be bullet holes in the ceiling, right? Proof that she had—what? *They'd* had a lovers' quarrel, which had escalated into a *shooting*? The derringer was still up there, with her prints all over it.

God! She needed time to think, and also time for them to go through the house, see the evidence, put it together. She knew cops. In this situation, if one of them spotted her right now, he'd probably start shooting.

And Cat: The bastard had cut his throat? Shit, shit, *shit*! Poor Cat. And now their private thing would erupt into public view. Lynn and the kids would be dragged into a media circus when the truth came out. What had that cop Larry just called her—Cat's *punch*? These cops were strangers, and they *knew*?

She reached the bottom again, backed into a tree, and stopped, aware now that she was back in Injun country. Had that bastard climbed back out of the creek? Was he out there in the woods now, ahead of her, waiting for her again? She shivered, both from the cold and the memory of how he'd come out of the bushes like some blood-crazed bear. She tried to remember his face, but there hadn't really been one. She began to make her way slowly north, paralleling the creek as she went upstream as quietly as she could, keeping just out of sight of the water, conscious of the rising commotion up on the bluffs: more cars, more lights, radios on external vehicle speakers.

She needed time to think. Which meant she had to get away, at least for tonight. But she had no car, no purse, no ID, no money, and no coat. And it wasn't like she could go back to the house just now, not with dogs coming. She was reasonably at home in the woods, but she had always been afraid of dogs. Especially in packs. She squeezed her sticky fingers together. Dogs would find her, too, no sweat.

The evergreen undergrowth closed around her in the darkness, but she kept going, pushing pungent pine branches out of her face while trying to make no noise, half-expecting to see that lunging form again each time she pushed a branch aside. She held Cat's gun in her right hand, and the butt was sticking to her palm now. Peering ahead, she saw a flare of headlights through the underbrush as a car came down Tilden Road and rumbled across the stone bridge at the base of the hill before disappearing into the park.

She needed to get the hell out of here. She had to go to ground somewhere, somehow. No: She had to get a car.

Think, she told herself again as she arrived at the edge of Tilden Road. There were no streetlights down here at the bottom of the hill, and the water rushing under the old bridge was shiny black in the moonlight. Right or left, she wondered as she caught her breath. She had no goddamn idea of what to do next, but she was out of the underbrush now, so she'd see him if he came at her again. She checked the gun, a stainless-steel Taurus Millenium Special .45. She peeled back the slide to verify that there was one up the spout. Her older brother had taught her about guns a long time ago, and Cat had done the same thing when they had first been dating, taking handguns along when they went together on one of her photography expeditions. If that lunatic came out of the bushes, it wouldn't be hand-to-gland anymore. Unless, of course, he used his own gun. She shook her head, then went down on one knee by the side of the creek and washed her hands, keeping an eye on the edge of the woods. More headlights at the top of the hill. Maybe she ought to just wait there until the first patrol car came blasting down, give herself up. Had to be warmer than this. She washed the gun butt and dried her hands on her jeans. The lights grew brighter, so she moved closer to the road.

But it wasn't a cop car. It was a United Parcel Service truck, and the driver slowed when he saw her kneeling by the side of the road. She had stuffed the gun into the small of her back by the time he pulled abreast, but she stayed down on one knee. The driver got out of his seat, leaving the engine running, and slid open the door on the passenger side.

"You okay, lady?" he called.

"No," she said. "Someone's chasing me. I need out of here."

He was a young black man, wearing the standard UPS brown uniform. "Uh, I'm not supposed to pick up passengers, ever. Lemme call dispatch. They can call the cops. I'll stay here with you until someone shows up."

He had the door open, which was all she needed. She wasn't about to add kidnapping to her up-and-coming wanted poster, but hijacking? She stood up and produced the gun. "Step down," she said. "I need your ride."

His eyes widened in surprise, and she repeated her order, yelling it this time, waving the gun at his face. He popped right out of the truck with his hands up, looking ridiculous as he danced around, trying to keep his balance with his hands still in the air.

"Put your wallet in the truck," she ordered. "And then get under the bridge. *Do it!* Now! Don't make me hurt you!"

Speechless, he extracted his wallet and threw it into the truck. Then he scuttled past her, never taking his eyes off the gun, and slipped down into the bushes beneath the bridge. She leaned over the stone railing. "The whacko chasing me has a machete," she called down into the darkness. "He cuts people's heads off. I wouldn't go making a lot of noise right now."

Then she climbed into the truck, scooped up the wallet, and closed the side door. Sitting down in the driver's seat, she looked at the gearshift diagram for a second, then banged noisily into first and took off. Her first car had been a manual, so jamming gears was nothing new to her. The truck left the bridge behind in a rattling cloud of diesel smoke.

She went straight until she cut Piney Branch, then left

over to Sixteenth Street, and right on down to New Hampshire Avenue and over to Dupont Circle. Going into town, against traffic, it didn't take fifteen minutes. She went completely around Dupont twice and into the first side street on the north side big enough to admit the truck. She found an alley next to a liquor store, pulled in, and shut it down. She cut off the lights and looked around. Nobody seemed to be taking any special interest in a UPS truck, even at this hour. UPS trucks were everywhere these days, which made them practically invisible.

With the gun stuck between her thighs and one eye on the alley, she looked through the guy's wallet and extracted a grand total of seventy-three dollars. But it was cash, and cash could buy a Metro ticket, and the Metro could get her out of the area faster than anything else. They shouldn't have her description out yet for taking the truck, not until the UPS driver got to the cops and reported a hijacking. The cops might have a BOLO out, though, so she had to hurry, because the Metro system was fully covered by surveillance cameras, especially after all the terrorist threats.

She threw the guy's wallet and the truck keys over the top of the heavy mesh door that led to the package compartment, which was still locked. Then she put the gun into her waistband, pushing it down in the small of her back, pulled her sweatshirt down over it, and got out. It was really cold outside. She spied the driver's brown jacket on a hook in the truck, grabbed that, and slid the door closed. She realized her hands were still sticky with Cat's blood, so she looked around for a spigot, found one on the liquor store's side wall, and cleaned her hands again. Two men walked by out on the sidewalk and glanced at her curiously, but neither of them even broke stride. City-dwellers, she thought. They never get involved.

She walked the three blocks to the Dupont Circle Metro station and went down the escalator, keeping an eye out for security people and metal detectors. Feeling conspicuous in the entirely recognizable UPS jacket, she bought a five-dollar Metro card and went through to the platform for downtown and northern Virginia. She waited back along the sloping walls of the station, leaning against the steel railing as she tried to lift the gun back out of her underwear. Then a train came roaring into the station, opened its welcoming doors, and she was gone.

It was almost midnight by the time Swamp Morgan made it out to the nurse's house in Cleveland Park, courtesy of a Secret Service driver. It had been Carl Malone who'd called him via the Homeland Security duty office when word got out about the incident. There were still several police cars parked along Quebec Street, some of them with their blue strobe lights still winking silently into the winter night. He had to show his credentials three times in order to get up to the house, where he was logged in by the crime-scene coordinator, a patrol cop who looked half-frozen despite his bulky coat. Carl Malone came out the front door and waved him through the tape.

"How's the lieutenant?" Swamp asked, buttoning up his overcoat against the cold. He wished he'd worn a hat.

"Touch'n go," Malone said, waggling his hand. "Lost a boatload of blood, but he's still alive. It's a real mess back there."

"They piece it together yet?"

"Split opinions right now," Malone said, his breath condensing in front of his face. "Homicide guys. You work with 'em for years, they still don't share so good. Couple of 'em wondering out loud what the hell I'm doing here."

"Appreciate the call," Swamp said. "I was planning to reinterview her tomorrow. I guess that's today." They both looked at their watches.

"Anyway," Malone said, "the primary now thinks the nurse *didn't* do it. There were two coffee cups in the dining room, and it looks like somebody outside threw a workshop vise through the window. Knocked shit all over the place in the dining room. They think Ballard went after him, ran through the kitchen, out the back door, and right into a truly wicked trap. You'll want to see this."

Swamp wasn't sure he did want to see this; he hadn't been kidding when he told Gary White that murder and its attendant gore unsettled him probably more than most cops. They walked around the driveway side of the house to avoid the crime-scene efforts going on inside. They stopped to one side of the back porch, where there was more tape and four large crime-scene floodlights illuminating practically the entire backyard. Swamp heard police dogs barking from inside a K-9 van parked on the grass.

"Look up at the top of the stairs," Malone said. "See that fucking thing?"

Swamp squinted into the bright white light and saw the serrated ribbon of bloody steel stretched tightly across the top of the steps, about throat-high.

"That's the blade from a band saw," Malone said. "Somebody cut two horizontal notches in the support posts either side of the steps, just deep enough to fit the blade flat into the notches so the teeth faced the back door. Neck-high."

"Christ on a crutch," Swamp said quietly. "He'd never have seen that."

"Got that right. Especially if he was coming through the door after some wacko pitched a table vise through the window at them. They got the perp's footprints over there by the window, and some more over there, front of the garage. That's where we found the band saw."

"How bad is Ballard, really?"

Malone shook his head. "Really bad, according to one of the medics. I didn't get out here until an hour or so after it all went down. Heard about it in the hallway as I was headed home, didn't put it together with the nurse until they mentioned *her* name. Had no idea that she and Ballard were an item."

"They were?" Swamp said, although he didn't see why anyone would care particularly, and then he saw the expression on Malone's face.

"Ah," he said.

"Yeah," Malone said. "His own Homicide crew apparently all knew, at least the senior people. His wife and two kids did not know. Now they will."

"Oh dear," Swamp said, mindful of things he hadn't paid much attention to as recently as a few years back.

"The nurse managed to call nine-one-one. All she got out was 'Murder' and 'Help me.' Nothing after that. The nine-one-one ops people called in the address to the street cops, and they also put a code into Homicide. Street cops found Ballard, called that in, and then, of course, the whole Homicide crew rode out on it."

"And the nurse? Where is she?"

"Some kind of struggle went down in the living room. Derringer .45 tracks in the ceiling. Front window broken. She apparently beat feet. Left everything—car, keys, purse, money, apparently just shagged ass into the night. A neighbor heard gunfire from the backyard, and the dogs found a trail down into Rock Creek Park. Perp tracks, too. Signs of another struggle down there. Get this: She makes it out to the road—that's Tilden, across that ravine over there—and hijacks herself a UPS truck. Driver stopped to be a Good Samaritan. They think she has Ballard's gun."

"This gets better and better."

"Oh yeah. Driver was a new kid. Sees this white woman down on one knee by the side of the road. Looked to be in trouble, so he stops the truck to help. She waves this cannon at him, takes the truck, and his wallet, by the way, goes downtown with it to Dupont Circle, and then disappears."

"Right into the Dupont Circle Metro station," Swamp said.

"Probably. UPS reported the truck missing; patrol cops found it in an alley off of Dupont. Keys and the guy's wallet still in it. We're holding the UPS angle back from the media. We've got Metro reviewing security tapes as we speak. But, you know, tail end of rush hour . . ."

"Yeah, she could be anywhere in the system. Or the suburbs. Damn. So what's it all about, Sherlock Holmes?"

Malone took his hat off and rubbed his head. "I keep coming back to that fire. There were five people worked at that after-hours clinic. Four are dead in a not so righteous fire. Now we get this mess at the home of the fifth, and last, member of the night crew. Who calls for help but then boogies."

"Was this Ballard guy on the up-and-up?"

"Outside of his love life? Yeah. Reputation as a stand-up guy. Eighteen years on the force. Made lieutenant the long way, but with style. Came around asking about you, by the way."

"Oh yeah? When?"

"Would you believe earlier this afternoon?"

Swamp nodded. "That figures. I interviewed Ms. Wall this morning, along with Gary White. She spooks, calls her boyfriend, the Homicide detective. I guess I need to talk to Ballard."

Malone made a face and shook his head. "No time soon, Special Agent. If ever."

Swamp kicked some grass around with the point of his shoe. There were several cops over by the garage now, smoking cigarettes and stamping their feet in the cold. Some of them were eyeing him suspiciously. "Well, I was slated to get a warrant to search the dead doctors' homes and bank accounts this morning," he said. "But I guess now we'd better do a full court press on finding Ms. Wall."

" 'We'?" Malone asked quietly. He turned so the Homicide cops couldn't hear what he was saying. "Secret Service gonna take this mess federal?"

Swamp eyed the older man, hearing the concern in his voice. "You've got some advice on that for me?"

Malone puffed out his cheeks. "Man, now that's a god-damn first."

Swamp smiled, shoving his hands deeper into his pockets. He'd forgotten gloves, too. It must have been in the twenties out here in the suburbs. "Remember, Carl, I'm just a retired pogue these days," he said. "Left all my rice bowls and turf shoes at the front desk the day they sent me home. I'm not listed in any government phone books. Don't have a code next to my name on anybody's spaghetti chart. No axes to grind, no hobby horses to ride."

Malone nodded. "You telling me you can work an investigation back-channel? All the way?"

"Exactly. DHS is still coming together, bureaucratically speaking. Lots of slippery cracks in the org chart. Plus, I'm intel. So what's the advice?"

Malone tilted his head imperceptibly toward the group of Homicide cops. "They're ready to rumble on this—find the fucker who laid out that blade and bring his ass in for some pointed questions, while fervently hoping he does something stupid, like resisting arrest, okay? Feds come barging in, take all that fun stuff away, be hell to pay downtown."

"Got it," Swamp said quietly. "Lemme suggest this: I want the nurse more than I want the guy who cut up Lieutenant Ballard. I'm working a potentially much bigger deal, remember? A fuse you lit with your call to the White House detail. And then again, maybe it isn't. The point is, right now, nobody knows. I do think the nurse was shining us on a little this morning."

"They'll want the nurse, too," Malone said. "She's the one can tell 'em what the fuck happened here. Brother Ballard sure as hell can't."

"So we both look," Swamp said. "I'll turn on what federal assets I can to find the runaway nurse. We find her, I'll make sure the District cops get first shot at her, too, so to speak."

"Then she needs to stop her rabbit act. Some of these guys still like her for the cutting."

"I understand. And no federal extradition bullshit, no unnecessary paperwork. They find her, I'd appreciate the same courtesy. And our side of it stays off the case-books."

"She's at least a material witness to this deal," Malone said. "They're gonna want physical custody."

"I've got no problem with that."

Malone nodded thoughtfully. "Okay," he said. "I can sell that deal. You want me to talk to them?" Two more detectives came out of the back of the house, arguing, their breath visible in the floodlights. Swamp could see them stepping carefully around the mess on the back porch.

"You're Arson," Swamp said. "No dog in this fight. How about being the honest broker? Like I said, we can keep our action all back-channel."

Malone gave him a skeptical look. "Your bosses cool with that?"

"Oh, yes. Especially since I'm the intel liaison wienie in OSI."

Malone grunted. "Okay. I'll go talk to those boys." He looked over at the group of cops, who were moving around the way hornets do when their nest has been disturbed—standing up, sitting down, looking around for something to fly at. "But probably not tonight. Later in the morning. Right now, I do believe they got their blood up, you know what I'm saying?"

Swamp agreed, said he'd be in touch, and went to find his Secret Service car. He didn't need to see any more of this scene. As he slipped into the front seat with the driver, he realized he did not *want* to see any more of the scene. He ratcheted the car's bucket seat back, strapped in, and closed his eyes.

The next twenty-four hours would be critical. Right now, she was apparently on the run, with no clothes except what she had on her back, no money, no car, and no ID or other plastic with her. If she'd been scared enough to hijack a UPS truck, there was no telling what else she might do to get away, but the longer she was out there, the more likely she'd think of something. She had to be desperately afraid.

He tried to put it all together. If the transcript fragment was real, then somebody at that clinic, some patient, had been talking about a possible terrorist attack. Was the patient after Connie Wall? His brain was stalling. He made a mental note to call PRU in the morning, ask them to let him talk to the agent supervising the security survey for the presidential address to a joint session of Congress. Let him know they were still pulling strings. And now he'd have to delay the searches on the Pakistani doctors' homes, which meant turning off the hurry-up push on getting those warrants. He'd tell Gary to get the warrants.

But the main thing was that he no longer thought the transcript fragment was entirely a firefly. The good news was that they had some time to work it. That joint-session speech was literally weeks away.

Heismann stared at the ceiling in his bathroom, unable to close his eyes and sleep. He lay in the bathtub, in cool water up to his chest, an ice pack pressed to his groin where she'd kicked him. As long as he didn't breathe too deeply or try to lift his legs, he could stand the pain. He ignored the scrapes, bruises, and scratches he'd sustained in his slide down into the creek, the flash burns on his right cheek from that belly gun going off in his face, and the swelling in his left knee from hitting a submerged boulder. He'd barely been able to get to his van and clear out of the park before the world at the top of the bluff flared up with blue strobe lights.

And the bitch nurse had gotten away. Again.

This was real trouble, for now she was fully alerted. She had to know.

First, he must ensure that Mutaib didn't find out. There would be reams of news coverage, a policeman getting killed like that. He must be dead, of course, with all that blood, although the first news reports had been vague on that point. His own socks and shoes, soaked in all that blood, were now safely in a plastic bag down in the apartment building's Dumpster. But he would have to communicate with Mutaib by telephone from now on. Absolutely no more face-to-face meetings, not until he could walk normally again. He eased from one buttock to the other and grunted when the pain lanced up his belly, calling forth the waves of nausea. If it hadn't been for the groin pouch, he would have been paralyzed for days. *Bitch!*

For some reason, she had decided to run from the police. She'd had plenty of opportunity to go back up there while he was floundering in that damned creek, but she hadn't. The television news reporting the incident said that the police were looking for a nurse named Connie Wall. Well, he would have a totally different version for the banker: I took her, killed her, and stuffed her in a hole in the banks of Rock Creek. That's why they can't find her. That would be his official line.

Back in the fall, when he was nearing completion of his course of identity-change procedures, he had begun his preparations to destroy the clinic and everyone in it. He'd come back late at night and let himself in with a stolen key and the filched code for the security system. He had gone through some of the records there and discovered that they were using code numbers instead of names. He had never found the code list that might turn numbers into names, but after an extended search, he had understood that the crooked bastards were dabbling in a little blackmail by recording the recovery-room babble of their patients. One of the transcripts had had a question annotated in the margin, and the question had been addressed to C.W., so it was a safe bet that Connie Wall was the trusted transcriber. He had mentioned the transcripts to Mutaib, and it had been Mutaib's idea to use a fake one as part of the deception plan.

If federal agents had taken the bait, that would explain the morning visit, but it wasn't likely that they knew she had been the transcriber. They were probably talking to her simply because she was the last one left alive from the clinic. But if one of them had let slip something about transcripts while interviewing her, that might explain why she was now running from the police, instead of seeking refuge with them. That and the attack. She was fleeing for her life. Especially after his last little phone call.

The question now was, Where would she go? He knew nothing about her family, relatives, place of origin. The phone call had been rash. He'd had no time to do his usual research, and this was the embarrassing result. The only good news was that she had had no time to take a purse, identification, her car keys. He had seen all these things in her kitchen. So at this moment, she was effectively homeless.

He wouldn't wait to entertain Mutaib's anxious inquiries. First thing in the morning, he would ask Mutaib to use the resources of the bank to get details on the woman. He would say that he was just sweeping up, making sure there wouldn't be anxious relatives appearing out of nowhere to search for her or talk to the press. Banks, even foreign banks, could find out anything about an individual in America—account information, medical history, insurance records, credit histories, mortgages. He would ask Mutaib to put surveillance on all that—to make sure no one was tapping into the dead woman's accounts, he would say. And if they were, find who they were. And *where* they were. That way, if *she* accessed anything, it would give him a place to look. He must absolutely convince the princeling, and his factional masters back in the Kingdom, that she was dead and buried. They must have no doubts as to the efficiency of their hired gun. His reputation in Hamburg among the Arab fanatics was one of amoral ruthlessness: He would do anything or anyone for money, and without blinking an eye. That's why they'd hired him in the first place.

He'd watched enough *Ammie* television to know that the

Washington city police would be in an uproar, searching for
the perpetrator, even if the policeman didn't die right away.
All points bulletin. Cop killer. BOLO. Full court press.
Lockdown on the streets. Scumbags up against the wall. He
knew all the police idioms. But being police, they would
concentrate on the easy route—they'd be looking for her, not
him. They'd know there'd been a third party to that little
mess. The dining room window broken from the outside.
Mud and dirt in the front rooms. Glass from the front windows outside as well as inside. But he'd left no fingerprints,
and the footprints could no longer be traced to his shoes, because by morning, they would be on their way to the landfill.
They wouldn't have a clue as to his identity.

Unless.

He tried deep breathing again to stabilize his feverish
brain. He knew he was thinking in circles again. The bolus
of pain in his groin was making him forget something important. There might be *two* sets of police looking for Connie Wall, local and state police. No, not state. Wrong word.
Here, they called it federal. *Geheim Stadt Polizei*. Gestapo.
State secret police. No, still not right: Secret Service, yes,
that was correct. His mind was drifting badly. He figured it
must be the painkillers he'd taken.

Two sets of police hunting the nurse. The federals: What
if *they* caught her? Would that help him or hurt him? She
couldn't really describe him. He'd deliberately put the flashlight under his chin when he'd shown himself through the
window; she would remember only the monster's face. There
was a slim chance she might remember his face from the
clinic, but the light should have distorted it beyond recognition. Plus, she had been visibly shocked by the vise coming
through the window. No, she could not make the connection.

But the bait might.

He forced himself to concentrate, despite the waves of
pain that were keeping perfect time with his pulse. Line by

line, do the logic, one more time. If the *Ammies* had taken the bait, they would need Wall to lead them to the *name* of the patient whose transcript he had faked in that record. Because that was the key to the deception: First aim them at the wrong date; all right, they'd done that. Then set them in pursuit of the wrong face. Which did exist, oh my, yes, it did, even though they'd have to look hard for details, all the way back to the Stasi files. The trick was that he no longer looked anything like Jäger Heismann, nor was Heismann even his real name. That was the whole idea behind the bait: Give them something to chew on, but tie them up in knots, focus them on the wrong target and the wrong man, make them spin their wheels hunting for code lists, patient records, anything that could identify the mad bomber. Waste their time. Tease them with a threat, but the wrong threat.

But with the woman on the run, it would now be up to him to initiate stage two. It was still a bit early, but there was probably no avoiding it now. Besides, soon he would need to concentrate on other things. Like setting up the weapon.

He leaned his head back against the cool tile. So, go forward. After calming Mutaib, he would activate the second stage of the deception. Without the woman, he would need a new channel. All right, how?

He had no idea. He shifted position in the tub and instantly regretted it as his brain was overwhelmed by new lances of pain. He couldn't think like this. His testicles were killing him. He took a long, very careful breath. His bones ached with the pain of it. *Bitch!*

It was already Wednesday. Tomorrow, Thursday, he was supposed to occupy the house and begin his technical preparations. He needed to be physically operational again in twenty-four hours. He rubbed his cheek and felt the stinging powder-burn specks. His brain was spinning slowly, like some great galaxy. The deception plan—had it really been necessary?

Focus. Back to the woman. He still needed to kill her. The house would occupy his days. But nights? Nights would be for hunting, injured or not. If she stayed in the Washington area, and did anything electronic, the bank would detect it. Assuming the *Ammies* thought they had a real transcript, *his* transcript, then they should be searching hard for the doctors' code list. If they found it, they'd be off after their terrorist prime suspect, Herr Jäger Heismann. They'd query Interpol. The bank would be informed. And then he wouldn't need her. If, after a few days, there was no indication of that, he'd find a way to prompt them. So either way, the nurse was now fully expendable. This time, once he found her, he'd cut her fucking head right off.

Circles again. You just went through all of this, he told himself. God in heaven! Focus, idiot.

He desperately needed to sleep, to rest. To make this pain stop. He reached for the bottle of pills sitting on the toilet lid and took two more pills. His stomach almost rebelled, but the thought of puking froze his senses. The pain would be unbearable. He drifted, trying the deep-breathing technique again. After awhile, he felt a little bit better.

And then he realized how he could do it. After tonight, the police would be all over that house. And they would most certainly monitor her telephone. Why not leave her a telephone message at the appropriate moment? Assuming all this propaganda were true, that the local and the federal police were fully integrated these days, that might get them to work on the matter of Jäger Heismann. Put Mutaib's stupid little plan behind him once and for all, and get ready for the big event.

At 11:30 P.M., Connie Wall crept out of the ladies' lounge in Lord & Taylor and into the bed and bath department. She had heard the cleaning crew come through this area an hour ago, and she had spent some anxious moments hidden behind the couch while two Hispanic ladies vacuumed the lounge and cleaned the bathroom itself. Listening at the door, she could still hear big vacuum cleaners running somewhere on the floor, so there shouldn't be motion detectors waiting for her if she left the rest room area. She figured she had thirty minutes before the crews were done and the store went on to its nighttime security system.

Keeping low to the floor to avoid cameras, she headed for a display area called Arabian Nights, which had freestanding columns, silk curtains, Persian carpets, and a half a dozen exotic-looking bed arrangements. Some delirious decorator overdid his special mushrooms, she thought as she slipped between the billowing curtains, checking continuously to make sure there wasn't a brace of rent-a-cops headed her way. On the other hand, the display provided a perfect area to hole up for the night. Assuming they didn't have Dobermans wandering around after they turned the lights off, she should be able to hide there until morning, when she'd get herself back into the ladies' room and wait for the store to open.

She'd taken the Yellow line all the way to Springfield, in northern Virginia, and then decamped into the sprawling Springfield Mall. The giant shopping center had been crowded with people. The whole place was heated, and it sported three food courts, where she could get something hot to eat and then hang out under one of the all-news TVs and keep an eye on what was happening. Once in the food court, she'd taken off the UPS jacket and turned it inside out, not wanting to display the one bit of clothing they might know she'd be wearing. But two teenage girls recognized it, and one offered to trade her brand-new L. L. Bean parka for the way cool UPS jacket. Connie took her up on it, then moved to a different food court in the next wing of the mall.

She knew she didn't have enough money for a Washington-area motel, not even one of the curry palaces down on Route 1. She'd remembered the story of the woman who had lived and even delivered a baby in a Wal-Mart store, and she began doing some reconnaissance of the various stores. The Lord & Taylor store looked like the best bet, so she had gone to ground in the rest room about fifteen minutes before the closing announcements began to purr through the cavernous store.

Now she made herself a nest behind a pile of huge cushions, pulling an entire rug over her hidey-hole in case there were security people patrolling after hours. She nestled Cat's gun under her right armpit. Right now, she was warm, secure in a locked building, and completely out of sight. She wondered if Cat Ballard was still alive. He'd been gravely injured, given the way those cops had been reacting up there in her yard. She had washed her hands several times after getting into the mall, but they still felt sticky to her. Surely by now the cops would have put the scene together and know she hadn't done that to Cat. If they'd brought in dogs, they'd have found her trail down the bluff and into the creek area, and signs of the man who'd pursued her into the park. If she was really lucky, they had him in custody. But if not, then he was out there somewhere. She had visions of him prowling the mall parking lots in a sinister-looking car, like some predator hunkering down outside its prey's burrow.

She knew that was ridiculous, but this was all new territory for her. At the very least, the District cops wanted to talk to her, and they would have her high on the suspect list when they did. The guy with the monster face was looking for her, and those two federal agents would add their own pressure as soon as they found out she was on the run.

She was pretty sure that big guy hadn't been fooled by her deflections on the transcripts. The store had gone quiet, but she had to assume the entire place was now being swept by motion and heat sensors, along with video surveillance. She was thirsty, and she wished she'd bought a bottle of water, even at the mall's exorbitant prices. But she couldn't move now. Not until she heard signs of the staff arriving in the morning. And then what? She still had no money, clothes, ID, or transportation. She could try going back to her house, but surely there'd still be cops all over it.

No, she had to get right out of town. If the clinic had not been destroyed, she could have hidden there.

The clinic. Well, part of it was still there. The daytime doctors' half. Yes, there'd been smoke damage, and the owners were probably going for a declaration of total loss, but the upstairs was physically still intact. The premises were shut down, of course, while the docs and their lawyers haggled with the insurance company and its lawyers. But the building was still there. The upstairs office. The upstairs recovery room, with its beds. And then she remembered something. The night docs had a small safe in the back of the clinic, in the cleaning closet, where they kept the petty cash. And she, as the senior administrative assistant, had the combination. She opened her eyes. Had the investigators found that safe? There was never much money in there, perhaps five hundred to one thousand dollars, except for those odd occasions when one of the clients paid in cash at night, which Dr. Khandoor would always get deposited the next morning without fail.

But if they hadn't found it, and she could get to it, a thousand dollars could get her on a Greyhound bus for parts unknown. Then maybe she'd contact the cops and begin a process of long-distance negotiation. Tell her side of the story, but from a safe distance, not from the depths of a holding cell in the notorious D.C. jail.

When to do it? Quickly. First thing in the morning. During rush hour, where she'd be one face in a crowd of thousands. Walk up Connecticut in broad daylight? Yes. Walk right up to the building and go inside. Like she belonged there. See if the money was there, and then hide out until darkness and the evening rush hour, when the Metro would again be full of people, and then get away. There were too many people chasing her right now. She wanted some distance, and then she'd sort it out—on her terms. I haven't done anything wrong, damn it, she told herself.

She revisited that terrible moment when she had tripped over Cat's body. She had a terrible feeling that all of this was **her fault.** And if he did survive, he would still have some problems to face. Especially at home. She wept at the thought of her predicament, and his.

3

CARLTON HALLORY OF THE SECRET SERVICE PROTECTIVE
Research Unit looked like a worried man when Swamp finally was ushered in to see him. He was in his early fifties.
Of medium height and slightly overweight, he had a round
face, a receding hairline, dun pouches under his eyes, and
the midwinter pallor of a professional bureaucrat. Hallory
was the supervisory special agent in charge of the security
survey for the upcoming inauguration, and, from what
Swamp could see, there were obviously not enough hours in
the day or days in the week to get all the bases covered.
There had been a steady stream of agents coming and going
while Swamp waited in the PRU's small conference room.
Every extension light on the conference room's phone had
been on continuously, and there was an air of barely controlled panic in the offices along the hallway.

Swamp had known Hallory in his previous life as a director in the Secret Service, when Hallory had been an up-and-coming headquarters staffer. He had a reputation for being
smart and thorough, if not overly imaginative. More than a
plodder, but not someone Swamp would have put in charge
of an extremely dynamic situation. He was surprised at how
much Hallory had aged over the intervening years, and he
almost felt like apologizing for intruding.

"I can give you three minutes," Hallory said, looking

pointedly at his watch. "Hopefully, you're gonna tell me this Nazi thing is a firefly."

"Actually," Swamp began, sitting down, but Hallory cut him off, waving a piece of paper at him.

"C'mon, for Chrissakes, Mr. Morgan, I've seen this so-called transcript. Sounds like some kind of drug addict coming down off bad dope. *Heil Hitler*? This is a nutcase, not a terrorist."

"Mr. Hallory? You read the papers this morning? See the story about that Homicide lieutenant getting his throat cut last night?"

Hallory stopped his protestations. "Yeah?" he said warily.

"This is going to take more than three minutes," Swamp said. "And, no, I don't think it's a firefly."

Hallory just looked at him for a moment, then picked up his telephone, punched the intercom button, and waited for a couple seconds. "Find Lucy," he ordered. "Get her in here ASAP."

"Who's Lucy?" Swamp asked, a little surprised at Hallory's hostile tone.

Hallory ignored the question. "You're a retiree recall, right, Mr. Morgan? Headquarters DAD for intel before you left?"

Swamp nodded. As if you didn't know that, he thought.

"No offense intended here, but I have to tell you, I don't think this recall program's such a great idea. In my experience, retired guys who get recalled try too hard. Especially senior guys. See shit that isn't there to justify being back in the game. With all due respect, sometimes it gets a little pathetic."

Swamp took a mental deep breath and composed the expression on his face. "If the active-duty guys could handle the job, then I don't suppose anyone would be recalled," he said calmly. "As it was, they called me."

"Yeah, I believe that," Hallory said, either missing or ignoring Swamp's barb. "But that was all nine-eleven panicsville. Over three years ago. We've got things a little better organized these days."

An argument broke out in the next office, the voices carrying over into the hallway through the thin partitions. Somebody banged something on a desktop to make his point. "I suppose," Swamp said. "But listening to this place for the past half hour, I have to wonder."

As Hallory's face reddened, the door to his office opened and a tall blond woman stepped in. "Yes, sir?" she asked. She appeared to be in her mid-forties, with bright blue eyes in a distinctly Nordic face. Her erect posture emphasized her trim figure.

Hallory kept staring at Swamp, but then he answered her. "Mr. Morgan here has himself a theory. About a firefly. Unfortunately, he says he can't summarize it quickly for me, so I want you to take him down to the conference room and let him . . . expound. Then maybe you can summarize it for me. Assuming it makes any sense. Okay, Lucy? Mr. Morgan?" He passed her the piece of paper he'd been waving at Swamp.

Swamp gave him a broad smile and followed the woman out of the office. She led him back to the conference room. The argument was still noisily going on, so she pushed the door partially shut and sat down at the head of the table. She was wearing a tailored gray business suit and round gold-rimmed glasses. Her ash-blond hair was done up in an elaborately woven bun, confined by a gold clasp. Swamp offered his hand. "Swamp Morgan, OSI," he said.

"Lucy VanMetre," she replied, taking his hand briefly. Her fingers were as cool as her expression. "What did you say to provoke that interesting color?"

Swamp smiled and sat down. "I was the deputy assistant director for intel a few years back," he said. "Before I retired. Got recalled into Homeland Security, Office of Special Investigations, after nine eleven. Mr. Hallory apparently doesn't care much for recalled annuitants."

"Secret Service?" she asked, cocking her head to one side.

"Yup."

"Right," she said. "You're *that* Morgan. Well, well. It's a pleasure to meet you, sir. I was doing an exchange tour across the river when you were DAD intel. You were very well known over in Langley."

"You mean notorious, probably, but thanks for the compliment. And don't call me 'sir'—I'm just an anonymous working stiff these days. Serving very much at the pleasure of—hell, I'm not sure anymore. Somebody important, I suppose."

"And apparently chasing fireflies?"

"For my sins," he said. "PRU's been farming out some of the weirder stuff to federal LE offices all over town, what with the inauguration looming in just over a week."

The argument down the hall reached a climax of sorts and then went quiet.

"I do appreciate the strain everybody's under here," Swamp continued. "But this one, I'm afraid, may have some legs. The good news is that it's aimed at the president's address to a joint session of Congress, so there's time to work it."

"Based on Mr. Hallory's expression, working it may or may not be an option. Walk me through it?"

Swamp did, beginning with the initial report from D.C. Arson all the way up to the events at Connie Wall's house the previous night. She did not take notes, but she listened carefully, and he had the impression that under all that spun platinum hair, there was a big brain soaking up every word he said.

"On balance," he concluded, "I think there's something going on. By all rights, that woman shouldn't have bolted like that, not once the cops got there. But she did. And this unknown individual apparently pursued her down the hill."

"And your theory is that this individual was a patient at

the clinic, who's now trying to erase everyone who laid eyes on him?"

"Yes," he said, getting up to stretch his legs. The only government furniture that had ever been big enough for his bulky frame had been his executive chair when he was a supergrade. And those days were gone forever, as the choleric Mr. Hallory had so kindly pointed out. Standing, he realized he was towering over her, so he sat back down.

"Evidence?" she asked.

"Damned little, and some of that's in code. Or in German."

"Yes, I see that," she said, glancing at the paper. "'It will rain dead people.' That's fairly specific."

Smart, and reads German, Swamp thought. Maybe not Scandinavian. "My next step, of course, is to identify which patient made that little speech. We can't know that it's the guy in the bushes out there in Cleveland Park until we get our claws on that nurse again. But if we can get an ID, we might be able to tap some databases."

"*We*," she said, raising her eyebrows at him.

"Well, I've been tasked to pull the string on this," he said. "By *my* boss, who's supposedly doing your boss a favor. My unofficial title is intel liaison."

"Which translates into doing whatever OSI wants to shove your way," she said.

"Precisely," Swamp replied. "And PRU, as well, right? What's your background?"

"Math and linguistics at Columbia," she said. "Started out as an Agency analyst, Eastern European division. Got tired of research, so I did a lateral into the Secret Service. Did my probationary tour in New York, then the protective detail, an exchange with the DDO at Langley. Then here. What exactly did you want from Mr. Hallory this morning?"

"Normally, fireflies die in the grass. When they're not fireflies, they come back to PRU for threat analysis. I was bringing it back to PRU."

"Where it bounced, from the looks of it," she said, frowning. "Everyone's under a lot of pressure just now, as you observed. Please don't take it personally."

"I never do," Swamp said. "Especially from people who are in over their heads."

"You think?" she asked, tilting her head again. It was somehow a charming move, but there was a glint of anger in her eyes.

"How many days until the big event?"

"Too few."

"Well then, a properly aimed security survey would have been locked down by now and everyone would be in the 'polish the weapons' mode at this juncture—in my opinion, that is."

"In your opinion."

"Yes. Sounds to me like you're still stuffing snakes back into the box."

As if to make his point, a second argument erupted next door, followed by a slamming door and then a strained silence. Lucy VanMetre looked down at the table for a moment.

"I guess what I'm asking now," Swamp said, "is for PRU to leave this one open for the moment. Won't cost you anything to have OSI gnaw on it some more. We find the hole in my theory, there's lots of other work to do back over at OSI."

"Is that what you want me to tell Mr. Hallory?"

He paused for a moment. He still didn't know what her job was here at PRU, nor had she told him. She might be Hallory's executive assistant, or even his deputy, for all he knew, trotted out in all her splendor to humor the old guy.

"Why don't you tell him that you just . . . took care of it? Then don't do anything. Don't shitcan it, but don't push it, either. I'll give it another week. Trust me, I've chased enough fireflies to know one when I see one."

She nodded and folded the piece of paper in half, then in half again, making sharp-edged creases. She stood up and fished a business card out of her jacket pocket. "Call me if you develop anything, Mr. Morgan," she said with a professional smile. "And it's been a pleasure to meet you finally."

"Me, too," Swamp said, suddenly feeling awkward, while at the same time fully conscious that he was being dismissed. He didn't bother to give her one of his cards.

She escorted him back to the security desk for that floor, signed in his visitor's badge, shook hands politely, and sent him on his way. He kept seeing her face as he rode down the elevator. Now that, he told himself, is one smooth operator. He carefully slipped her card into his own card holder.

As he walked down K Street toward the Old Executive Office Building, he wondered again if he'd simply been given a semipolite brush-off by Hallory and his Slinky. But in a way, it didn't matter. He'd come in to alert PRU officially that there was something out there in the woods bigger than a phosphorescent insect. If they chose to ignore it, well, shit on them if it blew up on them later. He made a mental note to back-brief his boss on Hallory's reaction, give him a quick memorandum of the conversation. Do it in writing, just for the record. Then he grinned. Once a bureaucrat, always a bureaucrat.

He'd given himself a week back there. There was, of course, always the possibility that Hallory's instincts were right and that his were wrong.

"Nah," he said out loud, startling a woman who was walking past him on the street.

Connie Wall began to get cold feet, literally, the closer she got to the clinic building. Suppose the cops had it under surveillance? Suppose the District Arson people were there right now, probing through the ruins? Wouldn't that be an inconvenient surprise! She turned down Kalorama Road and slowed her pace, almost not wanting to cover the three remaining blocks. The morning was gray and blustery, and she was very grateful she'd been able to trade off that UPS jacket. She imagined that the entire city was looking for a woman on foot, wearing one of those distinctive brown jackets. But her legs were cold and her feet were freezing.

Two blocks from the clinic, a police car came down Kalorama. She turned into the railing in front of an apartment building and pretended to tie her shoe, but the cop car went right on by, the officer in the shotgun seat busy with some paperwork. Once it was out of sight, she resumed her approach to the burned-out building, only to stop at the final corner. She could see the building, which was still decorated with fluttering yellow tape all over the front entrance. Two men in suits and overcoats were standing on the front steps, going through some papers. She immediately turned around and retraced her steps back up Kalorama. So much for that plan, she thought. She had no idea of who the men were—insurance adjusters, arson investigators, Secret Service. But she wasn't planning to find out.

So now what, Einstein? The wind hit her full in the face as she went back up Kalorama Road. Her toes were beginning to get numb and she knew she had to get somewhere inside before she developed hypothermia. It was going on noon, and she needed a public place that was warm, dry, and, most of all, free. A movie theater? Nothing open at this hour, and definitely not free. Go back downtown to one of the Mall museums? But that would mean being on her feet, and right now, her feet weren't working so well. Then she spotted the public library, right across the street. Hallelujah! Warm, dry, and free. With chairs and a bathroom. Perfect. Stay there until closing time, rush hour again, dusk. Then go back to the clinic. Where there had better be some petty cash left in that safe, or she was going to be in real trouble. She thought about jaywalking but then hurried to the corner to cross the street. This was no time to attract cops. There'd be newspapers in there. Maybe she could find out about Cat. From what she'd seen of the back porch, she wasn't sure she really wanted to know.

Upon returning to the office, Swamp reviewed procedures with Gary White on how to turn on the federal fugitive machinery, which was done primarily through the FBI headquarters. Then he had Gary call the District police to get a status on their search for the missing nurse and anything else he could find out about the incident the previous night. While Gary was dialing through that maze, Swamp called an old friend, Bertram Walker. He'd been surprised to run into Bertie at Caruso's, Swamp's usual dinner spot, only a week ago. Swamp learned that Bertie had been detailed secretly to the campaign staff of the new president when the Agency's Director read the tea leaves and decided the Democrats were going to win this one. He'd been on the road with the presidential campaign for months, and his wife had tired of it, so now he was recently divorced and just beginning to find his way around the solitary dining scene in northern Virginia. Since he was still on active duty in the counterintelligence operations directorate over at the CIA, Bertie was a natural contact for Swamp to pull the string on Lucy VanMetre.

"Hey, Swamp, it's been a week. OSI hasn't fired you yet? Sent you off to work at the Social Security Administration?"

"Up yours, Bertie. Although OSI, SSA? Sometimes hard to tell the difference."

"Well, if it's any comfort, I feel my homeland is a lot more secure with you riding herd on all that fervor and industry. What's up?"

"Tell me what you know about a lady named Lucy VanMetre. Used to work for you guys?"

"Ah, yes. Currently at nine-five-oh H Street, your old headquarters, if I'm not mistaken. Where they call her 'La Mamba.'"

"La who?"

"La Mamba. As in black mamba, the very dangerous African serpent."

"She's hardly black, Bertie."

"Technically, neither is a black mamba, Swamp. But that's inconsequential when one rises up in front of you on the jungle path and you find out that its front half is taller than you are."

"Yeah, I guess I got a little of that, although I think you're being a bit extreme. She told me she started her government service over there."

"That she did. I met her back then, and she was *formidable* right out of the gate. Came here with a Ph.D. in math from Columbia, said she'd been recruited by NSA but thought the Agency would be more 'suitable.' I think that's the word she used."

"I can't feature her as a street agent."

"Which means she could probably surprise you. But basically, she's never been street. This is one blonde who gets hired for what's above her neck, not below it. So what's shakin' that you're consorting with dangerous creatures like our Lucy?"

Swamp explained the firefly he was chasing, the aspects of the fire at the night clinic that had his attention, and the tie-in with the story in this morning's newspaper.

Bertie was suddenly serious. "Full-scope identity changes? Let's go secure."

Swamp switched his phone, waited for the electronic handshake to subside, and then Bertie was back. "You been to the Bureau with this?" Bertie asked.

"No, I'm staying in Secret Service and OSI channels for the moment. Keeping it in DHS. Our tasking came from PRU. They're up to their hairlines with inauguration preps, and they've been farming out everything they think might be a firefly. I went back there this morning to tell them this one wasn't. Guy named Hallory's running security for the inauguration. He sloughed it off, and I got the Lucy treatment for my troubles."

"What's she do there, exactly?"

"Don't know. Hallory's deputy or EA, maybe?"

"Carlton Hallory? He's been giving us daily gas pains with that inauguration security task force. He and I have some history, not all of it pleasant."

"Well, he basically didn't want to hear it when I said his firefly was refusing to go gracefully into the night. And, of course, I can't prove shit right now, so suddenly Lucy appears to make me feel better while easing my ass smartly along to the ee-gress."

"Yeah, maybe. But listen: Lucy VanMetre is always running her own agenda, no matter where she goes. You think this is for real, you call her back when you get something solid. Despite some of the career casualties bobbing in her wake, she's first and foremost a cryogenic brain. You convince Lucy, she'll get it in front of the director."

"Yours, theirs, or ours?"

"Whatever's best for Lucy, pal. Listen, can I ask that you keep me in the loop on this one? I mean, if it solidifies? I trust your instincts a lot more than some poor sweaty bastard up to his neck in the inauguration security swamp."

"Why, Bertie, I'm flattered. I told you I'm just a recalled annuitant, right? Not SES, not even technically in the Secret Service anymore?"

"Yes, you did. And we all understand that OSI is DHS's version of an intel op. So, please? This might relate to something we've been sniffing."

"Which you cannot share, I presume?"

"For the moment, that's correct, my friend. All I can say is that you might be right."

Swamp shook his head. Agency guys always did this whenever information was traded. Some cardinal rule over in Langley said that the Agency always had to appear to know just a little bit more than anyone else. About everything. You could always tell you were there because they broke into clichés. "Some of those famous straws in the wind, huh?" he said.

"More like burning embers in the wind, Swamp."

"A fire up the canyon?"

"Truly disturbing portents," Bertie said solemnly, going with it. "The real possibility of tectonic shifts in—"

"Bertie."

"Yeah, okay. But saying please here?"

"Okay, Bertie, of course. Can I trust this Lucy La Mamba?"

"To a point. She's a professional, flint-hearted bureaucrat, like the rest of us, so if it ever comes down to you or her, Lucy will save Lucy."

"Well, thanks for that, Bertie. And I'll let you know what shakes out with my firefly."

He hung up the phone and stared at nothing for a minute. So Lucy VanMetre was a player. La Mamba. Bit over the top, that, he thought. But then, he didn't know her and Bertie presumably did. She'd been professional and perfectly pleasant, as well as positively radiating intelligence. Gary White came walking over, a grim expression on his face.

"Been on the horn with the District," he said. "That lieutenant didn't make it. Stroked out early this morning. Too much blood loss."

"Whoa boy." Swamp sighed. "And I suppose the hunt is on in earnest now?"

"Yes, sir. They're out there tearing up Rock Creek Park again, now that it's daylight. Definitely looking for two people: the nurse as a material wit, and the bad guy, the one who probably laid the blade."

"This in the papers yet?"

"Yes, sir."

"They're hoping she'll read it and come in?"

"Right."

"Did they release that the lieutenant died?"

"Negative."

Swamp nodded. If she thought he was still alive, she might be more willing to surface into their loving arms. "The hive pretty stirred up?"

Gary nodded. Swamp remembered Gary had been a Homicide cop over in Fairfax County. He would absolutely relate to a cop-killer frenzy. He decided he needed to talk to Carl Malone as soon as possible.

Connie had to wait nearly two hours before she could get her hands on the current edition of the *Washington Post*. Apparently in this branch, the staff got to read the day's papers before the patrons. She had spent the time cleaning up in the ladies' room and then wandering the stacks between sessions of magazine reading in a lounge area. At least she was warm. When one of the staff finally brought the day's papers out to the rabble, Connie covered her face with a recent *Time* magazine until the woman left, then grabbed the morning paper.

The story was featured on the front page of the "Metro" section, along with two pictures: one of Lieutenant Ballard, who was reported in guarded condition at Walter Reed Army Medical Center; the other one of her, taken from her driver's license.

She stared at it in shock, then looked around to see who might be watching. There were two men in the lounge now, older gentlemen, who were pawing through the *New York Times* and the *Wall Street Journal*. Probably looking for the *Post*, she thought, so she moved to the far corner of the lounge with the paper, sitting down with her back to the main room.

She examined the picture and tried to think of what she could do to alter her appearance now so that it wouldn't be such a damned good resemblance. Not much, other than go blond in a bathroom somewhere. She felt like putting on the sunglasses, but it would look very strange here in the library reading lounge. Then she felt a presence behind her.

"That today's *Post*?" one of the old men asked.

"Yes," she said without turning around. Like I'm reading it here, bub.

"If you're done with the front section, can I have it?" he asked.

She casually folded the "Metro" section over and then handed the front section back over her shoulder without turning around. She felt him take it and leave. Some people, she thought. But she was in no position to make a scene or step on the guy's feelings.

So now what? Why not just call the cops and turn herself in? According to the paper, they no longer thought she'd harmed Cat Ballard, and right now, without money, transportation, shelter, or ID, she was as good as homeless. She might find some money at the clinic, but that wasn't really going to solve her problem. But suppose the District cops took her statement, held her for a while, and then handed her over to the Secret Service or the FBI? What had happened to Cat was serious enough, but she could visualize being taken to some CIA farmhouse over in Virginia and worked over by big guys with rubber hoses regarding the goings-on at the clinic.

She felt someone behind her again; now it was the other old guy, probably after the sports page. She turned to snap at him, whereupon she discovered two large men in suits and two uniformed police officers standing behind her. The staff librarian was standing triumphantly behind them, holding a copy of the *Washington Post* "Metro" section in her hand.

"Want to come along with us, please, Ms. Wall?" one of the plainclothes cops said, stepping forward with a set of plastic cuffs in his hand.

"They just apprehended the nurse," Malone said. "Found her holed up in a branch library down near where the clinic is."

"Good news," Swamp said, indicating to Gary White, who was sitting nearby, surrounded by the boxes of records from the clinic, that he should pick up the phone. "I've got Gary White on with me. They gonna hold her?"

"Oh yes," Malone said. "They're interviewing her right now. Some of the guys are talking charges for the hijacking, felony with a gun, taking the guy's wallet, evading, et cetera, but of course what they really want to know is who set that blade. And why."

"She probably doesn't know," Swamp said. "But if that clinic fire was deliberately set to kill all those people, the arsonist may be the same guy who iced the lieutenant. She talking at all?"

"Word is, she got her Miranda and took it literally. They're getting her a public defender. The Homicide crew is less than pleased."

"I'll bet. Any chance I can get in line for some table time with her?"

"Right now? I'd cool it, I were you. I talked to the chief of detectives this morning, right after we got the word that Ballard died. The timing wasn't wonderful."

"I understand," Swamp said. "Still, now that she's invoked her rights, I'd like to swing by. Maybe you can tell your people that I've got an angle, and that I'll share?"

"Lemme bird-dog that," Malone said. "I've got your number."

"I'll be here," Swamp said, and hung up.

"They have her on the peripheral charges," Gary said. "She did hijack the UPS truck. And use a gun in the commission of a felony. Big deal in the District."

Swamp rubbed the sides of his face and nodded. "Yeah, but they really want the cutter. She could always say she was fleeing for her life, and they've probably got corroborating evidence that the guy chased her."

"But why did she stay gone?"

"Doesn't want to talk about that clinic," Swamp said.

"She's going to have to."

"And there's the rub, I think. She might be more afraid of this guy who attacked them than she is of some prosecutor. We know absolutely nothing about the attacker."

"We know he was a patient at that clinic. And was German."

"No, we don't. *Know* that, I mean. We've been assuming all that. In any event, we've got a much bigger problem. The District's got a dead cop. *We've* got a transcript indicating a possible terrorist attack, a code number indicating that a patient at the clinic made the threats, and absolutely no way to ID that patient."

"I've been through every box of this shit," Gary said, indicating the cartons of scorched papers littering the conference room. "Sampling, admittedly, but Malone was right—they're just fragments. Take months to put this all together."

"We need that code list," Swamp said, standing up. "If it's not here in this collection of burned papers, then it might still be at the clinic. So call Carl Malone, get permission for us to reenter his fire scene, and we'll go back to the source."

Gary looked at him and made a face. "The clinic?"

"Yes, the clinic. Let's go get lunch and then we'll go back out there."

"Let's not and say we did," Gary replied, a worried look on his face. "Lunch, I'm talking about."

Connie Wall sat at the conference table in the interview room, her hands folded in her lap and her eyes looking straight ahead. A policewoman sat at the other end of the table, watching Connie intently. There was a video camera mounted near the ceiling, covering both of them. There were no windows or two-way mirrors in the room, just a bank of fluorescent lights overhead and the single door. Connie understood the matron's hostile expression: The word was out in the hallways that they had someone in custody for the assault on one of their own. At least she had her own clothes back. The forensics people had taken them for two hours after bringing her to the police headquarters.

The door opened, and two detectives in suits came in, one black, one white. She recognized the white man, Jake Cullen, whom she'd met socially before. Jake had known her older brother, and it was actually Jake who had introduced her to Cat Ballard. She didn't know the young black man with him. The matron got up and walked out without a word. The younger detective sat down directly across from Connie, while Jake Cullen sat at the head of the small table. Jake introduced himself as Detective Cullen and the other man as Detective Howell. He stated that the interview they were about to conduct was being videotaped. Connie saw the tiny red light come on under the camera as Cullen was speaking. Jake then read out her Miranda rights and pushed a file folder with the written Miranda warning in it down the table for her to sign. Connie took a moment to read it, just to make sure she wasn't signing a confession or something, but it was identical to the one she had already signed. She scribbled her name on the form and pushed it back. Howell, sitting across from her, just stared at her as if she were an ax murderer.

"Ms. Wall, do you know why you're here?" Cullen asked, making no indication that he knew Connie personally. She played along.

"I presume you want to find out what happened at my house last night," she said.

"That's correct, Ms. Wall."

"What's my status here?" she asked.

"Status?"

"Am I a suspect in a crime?"

"Yes, you are," Cullen said calmly. "Several crimes, as a matter of fact."

Connie nodded. She'd made up her mind about this when she'd first been arrested, and this was not the time to waver.

"Then I choose to exercise my rights," she said.

"Meaning what, exactly?" Howell asked. They didn't appear to be playing any good cop/bad cop games with her. They both seemed professionally calm.

"Meaning I intend to remain silent and that I request a lawyer."

Both detectives just looked at her for a moment. Howell pushed back his chair, but Cullen put up his hand. "Do you have your own attorney?" he asked.

Connie shook her head.

"Will you cooperate and give us a statement, tell us what happened last night, once your attorney is present?"

"Probably," she said. "Unless he advises me not to."

Cullen gave Howell a sign and they both stood up. The light went off under the camera. Howell went out into the hallway first, looking angry now, and Jake followed, but then he stopped and turned in the doorway. He cocked his head to one side. "Connie, did you kill Cat Ballard?" he asked in a soft voice.

Connie was shocked. *Kill?* Cat was *dead*? Cullen saw the expression on her face. "I'm sorry," he said. "He died this morning at Walter Reed. Did you do that, Connie?"

"Jesus, no," she whispered, unable to find her voice.

Jake was nodding. "We don't think so, either," he said. "But we're not going to be able to catch the bastard who did this unless you help us. We'll get you someone in from the public defender's office. It'll probably take a few hours. You want some coffee?"

Numb, hand to her mouth, she could only nod. She was still trying to get her mind around the idea that Cat Ballard was gone. Poor Cat, she thought. And poor Lynn, the kids. Great God! Lynn would really hate her now.

Jake Cullen left, and five minutes later, the matron came back in, set a paper cup of black coffee down on the table, and sat down at the other end. The little red light on the television camera came back on. Connie smeared a single tear off her face. Cat? Dead?

When Swamp came back from getting a sandwich, Gary White told him that he needed to call Carl Malone. "Said it was urgent."

"Problem with us going back to the clinic?"

"No, sir. Unfortunately. But I think this is about the nurse."

Swamp called Malone's office.

"They interviewed the nurse," Malone began. "Got zip. She's not talking until the public defender shows up."

"What's her attitude?"

"Jake Cullen has the lead on it. Said she didn't know Ballard was dead. He knows her, by the way. He introduced the two of them way back when. Can you believe it?"

"Really."

"She comes from a cop family. Her old man, her brother. Anyway, I just sat in on a meeting. Told the Chief of D's and the case officers about your involvement, and the possible terrorist angle in this case. The chief was a little more receptive this time. Mixed feelings in the room about who does what, who knows what, but he's willing to let you talk to her, long as their guys can sit in."

"You able to get him offstage for a minute, tell him how we want to play it?"

"Yeah. He's cool with that. But time is of the essence. The Homicide crew wants somebody's skin for this. Ms. Wall is the skin in hand, if you follow me."

"We'll be right over," Swamp said, and hung up.

He told Gary White to get them a car and then went in to brief McNamara on what they were up to. Fifteen minutes later, they were signing in at the District police headquarters building. Carl Malone came down to reception to escort them upstairs.

"Got a lawyer for her yet?"

Malone, obviously frustrated, shook his head as they waited for the elevator. "Waiting for a judge to assign one out of the pool. Judge not back from lunch yet—he's giving a speech somewhere. You know how that shit goes."

"Oh yeah," Swamp said. Sometimes he felt he'd spent a lifetime waiting for lawyers and judges. The elevator finally arrived and they got in. Malone pushed a button for the third floor. "So what now?" Swamp asked. "Your guys want me to go in, talk to her now, or wait for the lawyer?"

"Chief said for you to go on in. Detective Jake Cullen will go in with you—he's the lead."

"Do I need to meet with the chief before I see her?" Swamp asked.

Malone shook his head. "Chief said he wants to keep at arm's length on any federal involvement. That way—"

Swamp understood. "That way, something goes wrong, he can deny that he knew anything about any deals," Swamp said. "That's fine with me."

"Probably why he's the chief," Malone said.

Malone took them into the Homicide Unit's office area, through yet another sign-in desk, where they got visitors' badges, and then down a hallway to the office next door to the interview room, where Detective Sergeants Cullen and Howell met them and everyone made introductions.

"Here's what I propose to do," Swamp said without preamble. "I'll go in there and just say my piece. Lay out what I think's going on, and why she should open up and cooperate with you guys."

"She flat said she wasn't going to say anything," Cullen said. "Legally, we have to wait now for the shyster."

"You do if you want to question her," Swamp replied. "I'm not going to question her, at least not directly."

"Huh?" Howell said.

"Just go with me here, Detective Sergeant. Worst that can

happen is that she remains silent, which is where you are now. Right?"

There were nods all around. "And in the process, I'll try to elicit some body-language responses—you know, 'Isn't that right, Ms. Wall?' after I lay something out. She nods, you have that on videotape. Not admissible, I know, but you can show her the tape later, maybe expand the dialogue. Like that, okay?"

More shrugs and nods. Then they went into the interview room. The matron got up and took the remains of a vending-machine sandwich and the coffee cup out with her. Cullen, Gary White, Howell, and Swamp all sat down around one end of the table.

"Ms. Wall," Swamp began. "I'm Special Agent Morgan, U.S. Secret Service. You remember me?"

"Yes," she said. Swamp thought she looked depressed, which was appropriate, assuming she'd had some genuine feelings for Lieutenant Ballard.

"I'm sorry for your loss," he said, and that seemed to surprise her. "I'm talking about Lieutenant Ballard. I've been to your home. Whoever set that trap wasn't fooling around."

She stared down at the table but said nothing. Swamp kept it going, as if this were nothing more than a casual conversation between friends after lunch. "I understand you've elected to remain silent until you get an attorney. That's an intelligent thing to do. I've been told they're waiting for a judge to make the appointment."

She sighed but still didn't say anything.

"I'm not here to question you, Ms. Wall. The District police, Detectives Cullen and Howell here, they have the primary jurisdiction over the incident at your home last night. There'll be no questioning until your lawyer shows up. I'm just here to share my thinking with you. I'll be frank: I hope to convince you to talk to these people. You remember what

we talked about yesterday morning? The business about people talking under anesthesia?"

"Yes," she said. Good, Swamp thought. She's engaged.

"You told me then that it was implausible, for technical
reasons, but in fact, I have what looks very much like a transcript that was recovered from the ashes of the clinic."

She gave him a wary look but again said nothing. He
paused for a few seconds before going on.

"The thing is, this transcript seems to be the record of
someone whose mind was adrift, like, say, in the recovery
room, as opposed to being on the operating table with all
those tubes you talked about."

No visible reaction. She's listening, though, Swamp
thought. "And this guy's talking about bombs. And rambling
away in German. Our problem is, the transcript doesn't have
a patient's name on it, but it does have a code number on it.
And we've found that same code number on the clinic
schedule, which indicates that this guy was in the clinic the
night of the fire. For some kind of lip procedure?"

She was paying very close attention now.

"As the detectives have told you, Ms. Wall," he said, "I'm
not here to question you, and you don't have to say anything
to me until your lawyer shows up. But let me tell you what I
think. I think that Lieutenant Ballard was simply in the
wrong place at the wrong time last night. I'm beginning to
think that the guy talking about bombs had something to do
with that fire, which the District police here think was of
suspicious origin."

He paused to let that sink in. "I believe *you* were the target last night, Ms. Wall," he said, and saw her blink. "That's
right, you. Not Lieutenant Ballard. He was a . . . friend?"

No reaction.

"You called him after we came to see you yesterday,
right?" He smiled as he slipped the question in, and after a
second, she nodded.

"Perfectly understandable," he said. "A visit from the Secret Service can be unsettling. But here's the thing: Everyone in law enforcement in this city is nervous these days, what with all these terrorist threats, fanatical Arabs flapping around the world, plotting the destruction of our country, nine eleven. We all still remember nine eleven, right?"

Another nod. "Of course we do. I'm beginning to think that this guy who talked about bombs and the end of the world found out that the docs in that clinic were secretly taping their patients, not during anesthesia, but afterward, in the recovery room. And if that's true, then that might explain a motive for that fire. And everybody dying that night. Except you."

He was surprised at her reaction to the last words he'd just said. She put a hand to her mouth and was just staring at him. "What?" he asked gently.

She just shook her head, still staring at him, as if he knew something very important. He wished to hell he knew what it was, but he couldn't stop now.

"The thing is," he continued, "both the District police here and the Secret Service want to catch this guy. They want him for killing Lieutenant Ballard. We want him because we think he may be planning some kind of terrorist act. You're the only one left alive from the clinic. You're the only one who might be able to ID this guy, assuming we can break those codes somehow. That's where we are with this thing. You with me so far?"

She was regaining her composure as she nodded again.

"Now, you're worried you're going to be swept up into some tangle with federal and municipal police authorities over what was going on at that clinic. Perfectly understandable. Let me be frank: There are going to be some hard questions asked, and for that, you definitely want an attorney."

Swamp saw Cullen frown, but he pressed on. "So here's my advice: You talk to your public defender. Lay out the corner you think you're in. You were a surgical assistant at the clinic, correct? A surgical nurse?"

"Yes."

"And I'm willing to bet that those doctors were making money hand over fist. Unlike the staff."

She didn't say anything.

"Point is, Ms. Wall, if the government wanted to nail somebody for doing improper things at that clinic, like secretly taping their own patients, they'd want to nail the doctors, the people who took home all the profit. Not the staff. In fact, they'd use the staff to nail the doctors. That's how prosecutors do things these days. You know that, right? I mean, it's in the papers, every day. Use the little fish to roll up the big fish?"

She started to say something but then stopped. Swamp anticipated what she was going to say. "I know. Neither you nor anyone else on staff at the clinic ever knew what the names were, did you, Ms. Wall?"

"No," she said.

"That's what it looked like to us when we went back through all the records that we could still read. All those coded patient files. No names. Look, the doctors are both dead. I've got search warrants being worked up that will allow me to search their homes, interview their survivors, their families, if they had families, and look at their bank records, their tax returns, their off-site storage, the whole deal. But even with all that, I'm not optimistic. What I really want is that code list. I know you don't have it, right?"

She barely nodded, but he thought it was enough for the cameras. He leaned in closer, almost like a co-conspirator. You and me, Ms. Wall. Working together here.

"The government needs your help, Ms. Wall. If you ran from the police, hijacked that truck, took the driver's money, all because you were in fear for your life, then that changes things. A lot. But you'll have to tell the police here that, and also tell them the details of what happened last night that resulted in Lieutenant Ballard getting killed. Details they can corroborate with forensics. Details that will absolutely clear you of any suspicion regarding this homicide. You come from a police family. You know how this works, right?"

Another nod.

"Good. And then the Secret Service is going to try to put some things together, using what's been retrieved from the clinic records, that will lead to a name."

She didn't say anything, just stared straight ahead, as if she knew something that made what he was saying meaningless. Then a thought occurred to him, and now he knew what had been bothering him about getting all those search warrants. Gary had found a surgical schedule that put the transcript guy at the clinic the night of the fire. Which, of course, meant he'd been getting some work done. So even if they did break the code, got a name, ran it, got a description, would that description still fit their guy? Holy shit!

"Mr. Morgan?" Detective Cullen prompted.

Swamp blinked and then went on. "Right. So there it is, Ms. Wall. I know you're scared. I'm sure you're shocked by what happened to Lieutenant Ballard. We all are. But please, help the police out here. I don't think you caused Lieutenant Ballard's death last night, other than that you may have been the real target. If that's true, those other things you did will be cast in a totally different light. Okay?"

A nod.

"Now, you wait for your lawyer, take all the time you need with him, and tell him what I said. Tell him that the government isn't after you for anything except your help. And then you do what you think is right, okay?"

She swallowed and nodded again. Swamp got up and they all went out into the hallway, where the matron was waiting to go back in. Once she closed the door, Cullen confirmed that they had videotaped the entire session.

"This all sounds like you guys are way ahead of us on this deal," Cullen said.

"Not on the Ballard killing," Swamp said. "I meant what I said—Ballard was in the wrong place at the wrong time. But we might know what's behind it. Emphasis on the word *might*. Problem is, she really doesn't know who this guy is, either."

"She probably saw him," Howell said. "Something happened down there in that park."

"Maybe. But it was dark, right? In the woods, in the park, with no streetlights?"

"Yeah, okay."

"Okay. But I meant what I said in there. The G's not interested in prosecuting her for anything. That transcript is what has our attention. Was this some guy with a midlife crisis fantasizing, or is there a real badass out there with bombs and a mission? You know what I'd do, I was you?"

"What's that?" Howell asked skeptically.

"Get what you can from her once she gets her lawyer. Focus on the incident, she'll probably talk to you. Forget the UPS truck and all that. Stay off the clinic. Then cut her loose."

"Bullshit," Howell said immediately.

"No, not bullshit. Neither you nor we have any idea of *who* this guy is, or what he looks like. Nothing. But if he's after her, you cut her loose and keep her under surveillance? He'll be back."

"Why?"

"Because he's serious. He's so serious, he was willing to kill a cop. And probably all those people at that clinic fire. For some reason, he *needs* her dead. So he'll be back. You be there, and you'll get your shot. Your only shot, as best I see it."

"If you're going to use a civilian as bait for a killer, you'd better get her permission," Gary pointed out.

Nobody had a reply for that comment, and then Detective

Cullen thanked Swamp for the little session back there with Connie Wall. "That was smooth," he said. "You questioned her without really doing it. Where'd you go there, right at the end?"

Swamp hesitated, but then he realized the District cops had been more than accommodating. "We'd been focusing on breaking that code list, getting a name, then a description, then doing our federal manhunt thing. But if he was at that clinic as a patient . . ."

Cullen got it. "He may not look like that anymore. Right. *That's* why you wanted to do this little show this afternoon, wasn't it? You *need* us to cut her loose."

Swamp grinned. Would that he had been so prescient. "Just so, Sergeant," he said, tipping an imaginary hat. "They said you were smart."

"Now that," Cullen said, "*is* bullshit." But he was grinning anyway.

"Is anything she said in there admissible?" Gary asked as they headed back to the office. Swamp had decided to walk back to OEOB, to let the brisk January air clear his brain.

"I guess a judge would have to decide," Swamp said. "Part of the Miranda is that anything you do say can be held against you. But she'd also requested to remain silent, wait for her lawyer, so my guess is no. Doesn't matter, though— those guys don't want her for the murder of their lieutenant."

Gary had to hustle to stay up with Swamp as he strode down the sidewalks along Constitution Avenue. There weren't that many pedestrians out, even as rush hour approached, but those who saw Swamp coming managed to step aside. "So what do we do next?" Gary asked.

"I'm thinking of giving up on the code list. What we need to do now is go back through those frigging record fragments again. Only this time, see if we can find that code number and tie it to specific surgical procedures. See how much work this guy had done. If it was just that one procedure, then finding the code list can still help us."

"Just because that code number was scheduled for the night of the fire doesn't prove he set the fire," Gary pointed out. "Remember, the body count didn't include a patient. Guy could have come and gone, and then the torch shows up."

Swamp was waiting for a pedestrian crossing signal, well aware that anyone who jaywalked across Constitution Avenue at rush hour had a death wish. "You're absolutely right," he said. "We just assumed that the guy in the transcript would have a motive to whack everybody there. But maybe not."

"Or, there're two of them," Gary said. The light turned and they hurried to cross the street before the impatient phalanx of commuters executed a Le Mans start on their heels.

"Now that's helpful," Swamp said, and they both grinned. "Let's go see where we are on the warrants, and then we'll go toss that clinic one more time."

"It'll be dark," Gary said hopefully.

"That's why God invented Mag-Lites," Swamp said. "You can actually see things better in the beam of a good flashlight."

"We're looking for one file? A list of the codes and names?" Gary's skepticism was evident.

"Yup." Three cars got into a horn-honking match abreast of them, causing Swamp to hold his ears. "I got Malone's permission to go back in there."

"I would think that if those docs did keep it there, it wouldn't just be lying around in some file cabinet," Gary said. "That had to be some precious information."

"There was that connecting stairway between the night clinic and the day clinic, remember? I wanted to hide something like that, I'd stash it upstairs in the day doctors' area, without their knowledge. In plain sight, if possible. Let's roll."

Forty-five minutes later, they stood in the upstairs clinic, flashlights on, both trying to pretend they couldn't smell the hideous vapors that were still seeping up from the ruins of the operating room below. The upstairs offices were intact but coated in soot, and there was evidence of the intense heat of the fire in the furniture, electronics, and file cabinets. The floor felt uneven, and the carpets had been reduced to carbonized Brillo pads. Swamp swung his flashlight around the walls and realized that what was missing was color. Everything was gray or black. Gary waited patiently for Swamp to start the search, but Swamp was quickly coming to the conclusion that this was hopeless. Finding one piece of paper?

"Okay," he announced. "This was a dumb idea. This won't work. Not for one piece of paper. Let's get out of here."

"Fine by me," Gary said quietly.

They found a wine bar three blocks down Connecticut Avenue and Swamp suggested they stop in for a drink. Gary stopped just inside the door and looked around at the half dozen or so all-male couples in the bar.

"Uh," he began, but Swamp chuckled and slapped him lightly on the back.

"C'mon now, where's your sense of adventure, Special Agent?" he asked, and headed for a table. Gary followed reluctantly, trying not to look at the other patrons, who were all looking at them. A middle-aged waiter, dressed in an 1890s costume, complete with an elaborate mustache, came over to take their order.

"I don't spend a lot of time in gay bars," Swamp said quietly. "If that's what you're wondering. But I gotta tell you: I've never had to dodge a bar fight in one of these places, and they're usually a lot cleaner than most straight bars."

"I don't mind being in one," Gary said. "I just don't want to be seen in one."

"Tell me this," Swamp said. "If you were working this case as a homicide investigation back in Fairfax County, what would you do right now?"

The waiter brought their drinks, and Gary waited until he was gone before he answered. "Hand it over to the Bureau?" he said promptly. But then he grew more serious. "Our original tasking was to see if this transcript thing was a firefly. Was it something the Service needed to get into, as a matter of urgency?"

"Correct."

"Based on the transcript alone, I'd say dump it. But with what's happened out at that nurse's house, a cop getting killed, the nurse obviously holding back something? We've got an arson fire where almost the whole night crew was killed, and then this deal at the lone survivor's house? I think somebody's cleaning up after himself."

Swamp nodded. "So what do we do next?"

Swamp knew that Gary understood that he was being tested, and he liked the fact that the younger man was thinking about the questions instead of just popping up with the first thing that came to mind.

"We need help," Gary said. "To really go through all those evidence boxes Malone sent us. To get everything out of that upstairs office, go through all that, too. I was serious about the Bureau: I'd get a team of Bureau forensics people into it. They give terrific fine-toothed comb."

"Looking for?"

"The code list would be nice," Gary said. "A name, address, and phone number would be nice. If we could somehow get a basic physical description of the guy who corresponds to the code number on that transcript, there are people who could reconstruct what he ought to look like now, based on the operations performed."

"Yeah," Swamp said. "Plastic surgeons who can generate a three-D picture model of what your new nose is gonna look like—only in reverse this time."

"But the key is the start point, and for that, we need to lean on that nurse. Maybe fold her into the process."

Swamp was nodding. "She's scared, though. She didn't ice the lieutenant, but she ran anyway."

"Do we give a shit about prosecuting her, or do we want what's inside her head?"

"Right. Maybe I'd better call the District Homicide office before they take me up on my other bright idea."

Gary was nodding. "If it was me, I'd get an assistant deputy AG from Main Justice in a thousand-dollar suit to go talk to the District cops, set up some kind of immunity deal. Then get her together with the Bureau people, let her inform the search. Put together a composite—whatever we can get—get the best description we can, and *then* go hunt this bad boy down. We have a month, right?"

"In theory," Swamp said. "But first I have to convince PRU. Any DHS request for Bureau assets is going to have to come from the Secret Service. I keep saying I'm Secret Service, but I'm really not. The PRU won't make that request just on my say-so." He thought about Hallory's demeanor at their meeting. "Or ever, perhaps."

"Didn't they call you?"

Swamp smiled. "Yes, they did," he said. "But they didn't seem very impressed with what I brought them. The DHS bureaucracy is a lot more convoluted than what you were dealing with over in Fairfax County. Everybody being oh so careful not to step on anybody's toes. A committee-of-equals theory. A couple dozen scorpions in a fog-filled bottle is closer to the truth."

"What does PRU care if the Bureau works it? Everybody knows those guys are really good at that kind of shit."

"If we surface an actual conspiracy, PRU'd want the credit. The FBI would never allow that."

"Credit? Who gives a shit about credit?"

"Anyone trying to turn an organizational reputation into federal budget dollars."

Gary shrugged, and then Swamp saw one of the patrons giving Gary a not so subtle once-over. Gary saw it, too.

"Let it go, now," Swamp said calmly. "Remember, you're a married man."

Gary turned back to stare hard at Swamp for a second, then started laughing. They finished their drinks and left to go make their phone calls.

Connie Wall couldn't believe that she was being freed. She'd finally gotten to talk to a lawyer, an extremely young-looking black man from the District public defender's office. She'd begun to tell him the background of what was going on, but he had stopped her right away.

"They're gonna cut you loose," he had announced. "Surprised me, too, when I heard the original beef. But I went in, asked the usual questions about charges. Senior Homicide dude just says, 'No charges. We're gonna ask her for a statement; then she walks.' Wanted me to come in here, just so they can say you got your lawyer, because you did ask for one."

She hadn't known what to say to that, and it was obvious that the lawyer thought his time had been wasted. He'd told her she didn't have to give a statement, that all the cops wanted was a sequence of events from the night before. Her side of the story, in other words. She'd told him that she would do that, but not answer any questions beyond that. The lawyer left and then returned with Jake Cullen and the other Homicide detective. They'd put down a tape recorder, opened the interview, and then let Connie tell it. She was done in ten minutes.

"I know you said no questions, Ms. Wall," Jake Cullen said. "But I'd like to ask a couple. You can answer or not, and we'll go with it, either way."

"What kind of questions?"

"Like did you get a look at the guy's face? Good enough so's you could ID him, you saw him again?"

"No," she said. "He did one of those Halloween numbers—you know, flashlight under his chin? All I could see were teeth and eyes. And, no, I don't think I could ID him."

"When you struggled down in the park, did you get the impression he's a real big guy? Really strong?"

She had to think about that. It had happened so fast. "It was dark. I was fighting to get away, and I'm in pretty good shape, but he was able to hold me down with one arm. I got lucky with that one kick, and then he was all done."

"Big, then?"

"No-o. Probably my height. But strong. Very strong."

"What did he smell like?" Howell asked.

"Smell?" She had to think about that.

"You know, stink like some homeless guy, or was he wearing aftershave? Garlic breath? Curry breath? Beer breath? Smoker? Any smells you can remember?"

She shook her head. "It was a fight. My adrenaline was pumping. I smelled and tasted mostly metal. But, no, nothing sticks out."

"He wearing gloves?"

"Yes. I felt leather against my cheek."

Cullen sat back in his chair and punched the recorder off. "Connie, here's one you may not want to answer, but hear me out. As you know, Cat Ballard and I went way back. I went to his wedding, but I also introduced the two of you at that party. I knew he was seeing you. That was Cat's business, none of mine, or ours, for that matter. Okay so far?"

She just looked at him.

"Here's the question: Did Cat come out there last night to socialize, or was he there for some other reason? Had you called him?"

"I'll answer that, as long as you promise that it won't get him in trouble. I mean, I know he's dead, but—"

Cullen put up a hand. "Lemme explain," he said. "If he was there because something had happened, as in he was there as a cop, then there's a way into a line-of-duty finding. You know how this stuff works, right? You follow me here?"

Connie absolutely understood. If Cat had been there for a late nooner, then he was on personal time. But if he'd been there because she'd called him fearing a threat to her life, then he had died in the line of duty, protecting a citizen that he'd also happened to know. It could have a bearing on his estate, and, just maybe they could sell that story to the grieving widow. She nodded. He turned the recorder back on.

"Ms. Wall," he said. "Was Lieutenant Ballard there on official business?"

"Yes, he was. I'd called him."

"Why?"

She went through the sequence of events, including their suspicions that someone had been in the house and left poison of some kind in the milk container. Detective Howell was writing in his notebook. Connie continued. "He said he was going to give the milk container to your lab. Anyway, on Tuesday, I got an anonymous phone call. A man's voice whispering, 'Everyone's dead. Except you.' I got scared, called Cat again. That's why he was there that night."

"This clinic—is that what the Secret Service guy was talking about?"

"Partly. But that's why Cat was there. Actually, we were arguing. He wanted me to come in, make a statement to the government security people. I was . . . reluctant to do that. Then when the guy threw that thing through the window, that's . . ."

She didn't finish the sentence, and nobody said anything. She nodded at the tape recorder, and Cullen shut it off.

"That's when Cat went out the door, after the guy."

"And ran into that saw blade."

She nodded. "Now I've got one, Jake."

Cullen blinked and said, "Go ahead."

"I want to go home, pack some shit, get in my car, and get

out of town. Just hit the road, get away from Washington. You guys have any problem with my doing that?"

They looked at each other; then Cullen shook his head. "We'd prefer that you hang around."

"But do I have to?"

He raised his hands in a gesture of defeat. "I guess we could tag you as a material witness, get a judge to make you stay in the area. Or we could keep you in custody. But here's the real deal: We can't catch this guy because we don't have the first clue as to what he looks like. All we know is that he's after you."

He stopped and waited for her to get it, which she did. "No way," she said immediately. "You want me to be the *bait*? To go home, wait by the window for him to do it again? Or to push me under a Metro train one day?"

"Not in those exact words, Connie, but yeah, we do. And let me tell you why you should do it: Until we catch him, your life's gonna be hell. Every stranger you see walking toward you on the sidewalk, every knock on the door, every phone call, you're gonna be asking yourself, Is this *him*? The guy standing behind you on the Metro platform. The guy who's going the same direction you're going in the grocery store parking lot. Like that."

"Not if I leave town."

"You *know* that? A guy wants you bad enough to ice a cop? And what if he follows you? And what happens when he finds you? All alone now."

She closed her eyes. "And I suppose you'd have people around to protect me?"

He nodded. "Right."

"Twenty-four/seven?"

"It wouldn't appear that way, but yes. We need him to think he's got a shot."

"Great choice of words there, Jake." He sighed, but then she smiled, and some of the tension drained out of the room.

"Look," she said. "I'm a lone wolf. Cat Ballard was probably my best friend. We go back, too, guys. To *before* he got married, just for the record, okay? So yes, I'll help you. But listen to me: I didn't do anything wrong at that clinic, except maybe take some easy money."

"And?"

"And the government's looking into what those doctors were doing. I'll take my chances with them. But if I help you, I want your promise that you won't do anything to put me under the government's wheels. Can you make that promise?"

The detectives exchanged glances. "I can," Cullen said. "We're after a cop killer, and between you and me, we're kind of ambivalent as to whether or not his ass survives the arrest. We don't know what the government wants; we never do. But since it sounds like they want this mutt, too, you should be safe from the G. After that, though, it's anybody's guess."

She thought about that for a minute. It sounded like the truth. "All right," she said. "I'll help. Can someone go with me tonight, make sure there're no snakes in my house?"

"Tonight, we'll put you in a hotel," Cullen said. "Give us time to clear the house, make it look like we're all done there. Set up the surveillance operation. Tap the phone. Some other technical stuff. Then tomorrow, we'll announce you've been released but told to stay in town."

"So he'll know."

Cullen nodded. "If he's still around, he'll know."

"Okay," she said. They settled a few other logistics issues, asked her to wait there in the counsel room, and left. Her lawyer got up.

"What do you think about all this?" she asked.

He glanced up at the video camera to make sure it was off. "Florida's nice this time of year," he said as he closed his briefcase.

"You know what I meant," she said. "About being bait."

"Bait gets bitten before the hook gets set," he said. "Me? I'd go to Florida."

Jake Cullen came back into the room as the lawyer left. Detective Howell was not with him.

"How's . . . how's Lynn coping with all this, Jake?" she asked.

Cullen started to answer but then shook his head. "Her husband's dead. She hasn't asked the hard questions yet." His pager went off. He looked at it and swore. "I'll be right back."

As the door closed again, she mentally kicked herself for asking that question. Then she wondered if she was doing the right thing.

Why start now? she thought.

It was 7:30 when Gary came back into Swamp's cubicle. "Too late, they've let her go."

"Shit. Another one of my bright ideas bites me in the ass."

"Well, I talked to Carl Malone. He says they have her in a hotel for the night, and then they're gonna set up a watch box and see if the guy tries again. He said we needed to talk to Detective Howell in the morning, because he's the one setting up the box."

Swamp looked at his watch and shook his head. Time flew while you were having real fun. "Tomorrow's another day," he said. "I guess we wait. I have to talk to Tad McNamara first thing in the morning. Bring him up to speed, see if he'll go along with folding the Bureau in."

"He'll make it dependent on PRU's read?"

"Probably. Carl say how big a surveillance op they're going to set up on the nurse?"

"He said a rough-and-smooth. They don't have all the assets in the world right now. Or any extra overtime money."

Swamp nodded thoughtfully. "Better than nothing. I hope PRU goes along."

"They work late? Maybe call that dragon lady you were talking about. Telegraph the punch."

Gary had a point. PRU would indeed be working late this close to the inauguration. He nodded. "Good idea. In the meantime, why don't you—"

"Right," Gary said. "Take the rest of the day off."

"Something like that. What's your wife think about your new posting?"

"I'm in the Secret Service. She's still waiting for the White House tour."

After Gary left, Swamp fished out the card Lucy Van-Metre had given him earlier and placed the call. He expected a secretary, but then he remembered what time it was. An agent working late in PRU answered, said he thought she was still there, and put him on hold. She came on the line a minute later.

"Developments so soon, Mr. Morgan?" Her voice was cool, a little impatient.

"Can we go secure?"

The telephones did their thing, and then she was back. He told her what had transpired since they'd last talked. "Now I'd like to enlist the help of Mr. Hoover's finest—to do an evidentiary screen of all the medical records in that clinic."

"Why the Bureau and not our own resources?"

"You've got some bodies to spare, Lucy? A week before the big day? And besides, the Bureau's better at this kind of thing than we are. They've got all those specialists."

"That would take the intervention of our director," she said. "To bring in assets from another agency. For what might be a firefly."

"I understand. I suppose I could just run this up to the fusion committee, and they could order the Bureau directly into it. Or order your director to sign off on Bureau involvement."

"The fusion committee? As easy as that, Mr. Morgan? I'm impressed."

He laughed. "I would be, too, if I could swing it. That may have been an attempt at crude bureaucratic strong-arming. You're supposed to be quailing in terror at this point."

He heard her laugh. "The truth is," he said, "I would have to convince my boss to expend political capital with his boss, and then we'd have to gen up a briefing for the fusion committee, probably staff it around OSI, and so on."

"Which is why you want PRU to make the request."

"To sign off at least. But there's a better reason: Wouldn't PRU rather control this investigation?"

"I thought PRU did control what you're doing—PRU tasked OSI, which tasked you. And as I recall, it was fairly limited tasking: Is it a firefly, and if so, say so. If not, report back to PRU, which will handle it from there."

"My problem is that I think Hallory's gonna tank it. Based in no small part on what he had to say this morning. 'Pathetic' as that might sound."

"Handling potential threats to presidential security is PRU's job, Mr. Morgan. You were in the Service. You know how it works. The detail handles the crazies who pop out of the crowd with guns; PRU handles the plotters and schemers, hopefully before they get into the crowd. If Mr. Hallory thinks it's a firefly, then that's his call. It's his to make."

He tried again. "The District cops are going to troll the nurse, in hopes that the bad guy will make another play. If they catch him, the Service can always step in and wave White House security at them, especially since it's the Service that started this ball rolling in the first place. But not if the Bureau has been turned on by somebody else. Then all bets are off."

"Somebody else?" she said.

"We all work for the secretary of DHS. If it escalates to that level, PRU and the Service won't have a pit to hiss in."

"You obviously think that the guy who killed the lieutenant and who's after the nurse is the same guy who did the Nazi rant."

"I don't *know* that. But I can't find out, either, unless we all take this thing seriously."

"Yes," she said. Then a moment of silence. "Well, it's late, isn't it, Mr. Morgan? I'll see what I can do."

"Bypass Hallory, Lucy. If he doesn't ask, don't tell. If he does, tell him you're handling it."

"Oh right. Cut my boss out of the loop. Is that how you got to SES, Mr. Morgan?"

He took a deep breath. They were going to punt it. He just knew it. "I got to SES by tuning my instincts, Lucy. By being able to tell the fireflies from the firestorms. In advance."

"That was then, Mr. Morgan. Admittedly, you were famous for it. But now I think it's Mr. Hallory's turn."

Swamp hesitated before asking the question that had just popped into his mind. But he had to know. "Do you have the authority to be telling me this, Lucy?"

"I'm Mr. Hallory's deputy, so, yes, I think I do."

Suspicions confirmed. Not an assistant, but the number two at PRU. He should have guessed, if only from her demeanor. "Okay, Lucy. Thanks for taking the call. Let me know something tomorrow morning if you can."

He hung up and sighed audibly. PRU was going to pull it back. We asked you to look at a firefly. You did. You reported. We disagreed. Thank you very much for your interest in national defense and good fucking bye. And if Hallory was really clever, he'd ice the cake with some sympathetic noises to Swamp's boss, Tad McNamara, about how heartwarming it was that the old guys always wanted to get back in the game. We appreciate it, we really do, but, you know, things have changed a lot. We have different sources and methods now. It's too hard to bring the recalled guys back up to speed, what with the press of everything that's going on. You know how it is . . . and nothing from our web makes a connection between presidential security and a fire in D.C., or some cop getting his throat cut. A married cop, who was visiting his main squeeze, as we understand it. We don't want the Service involved in tawdry shit like that. You see where we're coming from, right?

But if nothing else, Swamp thought, a cop did get his throat cut. While trying to protect a woman who might have indirect knowledge of a plot to bomb the Capitol when most of the government would be present in the building. That *was* sufficient reason to pull the string. He thought about calling McNamara at home, then got up and went into McNamara's office to look at his calendar for Thursday. Annual physical exam.

Shit. He'd probably be gone all day.

On the other hand . . . he'd probably be gone all day. Time enough to maybe start the process of getting some help from the Bureau. He still had some friends over there. If PRU wouldn't investigate it, then OSI would. He'd do some "liaison" work. Right, he thought with a grin. Liaison—that's my job description, isn't it?

One of the building's night security guards stuck his head into Swamp's office and asked how late he'd be staying. Swamp told him fifteen minutes, and the guard withdrew with a two-finger salute.

Swamp looked at his watch. Eight o'clock. He checked his coffee cup, which was a quarter full of what looked like asphalt. He tilted the cup, but nothing happened. He sighed. It *was* asphalt, solidified after another standard five-to-eight day at the office. At least the guys over at PRU had an excuse. He, on the other hand, had a reason. The longer he stayed in the office, the less time he had to spend at the apartment over in Ballston.

He called Caruso's and told them he'd want his usual single in thirty minutes. That would give him a pleasant hour to hour and a half in the company of familiar waiters and Chef Ricci's excellent food. By then, with the day's edges worn

down by a couple of glasses of Sicilian red, he could walk
the one block to his apartment building and face the stark,
silent apartment with some vestige of equanimity. Then
when the black dog of depression came around, he would at
least be ready.

Who are you feeling sorry for? his conscience whispered.
For you or for her? For *us*, he wanted to shout, but he knew
that wasn't true. Which was precisely why they'd been down
on the Tidal Basin that day in the first place.

"Mr. Morgan, sir?" It was the night guard again. "Fifteen
minutes?"

4

CONNIE STOPPED ON THE WALK UP TO THE FRONT OF HER
house and tried to decide whether to use the front door or the
back. She'd taken the Metro just as soon as the cops told her
she could leave the hotel, turning down their offer of breakfast and a ride out to the house. Jake Cullen had shown up as
she was leaving and had returned her purse and keys, telling
her he'd be out to check on her later in the morning. Warned
her to lock herself in and said that the technical people
would be calling to check the phone-tap system. Now, as she
stood in front of the familiar facade, seeing the bare trees
and the sloping, sleeping lawns almost as if for the first time,
she wondered if it had been wise to come out here without
an escort. Suppose he was already in the house? Waiting for
her to unlock the door and step right into his—

Oh for God's sakes, she chided herself. It's a Thursday
morning in January, and there are cops watching somewhere
nearby while you dither like some schoolgirl in a Hitchcock
movie. And you want the front door because you don't want
to see the back porch just yet. So just do it.

She walked up to the front door and unlocked it, then remembered the security system—was it set? She hadn't set it,
but had the cops? No, because they didn't know the code.
Right. She stepped through the door and locked it behind

her. Then she turned on the hallway light. Everything looked
familiar: the stairs rising to the second floor on her left, the
living room to the right, the dining room beyond that, toward
the back of the house, and the kitchen straight ahead. The
furniture in the living room was right side up now, not like
she'd left it after her struggle with—She stood there for a
moment, her eyes closed, and tried to visualize her attacker.
The monster face in the wedge of flashlight at the window.
The smell of him—she remembered the cops asking about
that. Wet wool. Sweat. Adrenaline, a scent with which she
was all too familiar. And something else. She focused.
Something medicinal. She held her breath, trying to force
the thing into definition.

Ointment.

She opened her eyes. Yes! She'd recognized it. An anti-
septic ointment they used at the clinic. That's what it was.
They gave it to their patients to put on exposed skin surfaces
for six weeks after surgery.

Son of a bitch.

The big Secret Service guy had been right.

This *was* about the clinic.

She'd have to tell Jake. Or should she tell the government
guys? Or should she keep her mouth shut for a change?

She shook off the moment, walked down the hall into the
kitchen area, and turned on the light. She put her purse, keys,
and coat on the kitchen table. Her purse had been searched,
but everything seemed to be there. Just to be sure, she emptied it all out onto the kitchen table and then rearranged
everything back the way she'd had it. Even the three-pack of
condoms. She could just imagine the cop comments. Three.
Damn. Woman's got some great expectations.

The back kitchen door was closed, and beyond that . . .
well, she still wasn't quite ready for that yet. She went into
the dining room, where her computer monitor was sitting on
the table, disconnected, the glass screen looking like some
gaping maw. There was a piece of plywood covering the

window. Whatever had come through the window was gone, and the floor had been vacuumed. Someone had been through the piles of paperwork on the table, but it didn't look like anything had been taken. There were smudges of what she assumed was fingerprint powder here and there, but otherwise, the cops had cleaned up after themselves. She could smell stale coffee in the sink, where there were half a dozen coffee mugs stacked. Well, almost cleaned up after themselves.

She made herself go through the pantry area to the back door and look out the window. Everything looked different in the daylight, totally familiar, except for the black stains all over the back porch. And those two horizontal slots in the porch support posts. She thought she could smell Clorox, and sure enough, there were two bottles of it perched next to the back door. Nice try, fellas, she thought, but that stain's never coming out. Or out of my sight. Those boards are going to have to come up.

Poor damn Cat. Poor Lynn. Poor kids. Maybe literally so.

Then the phone rang. She picked up the kitchen extension. "Hello?" she said.

"Is this Ms. Wall?"

She frowned. Who the hell was this? The police? Jake said they would be calling. "Yes, it is," she said. "Who's calling?"

"I am with the Washington police," the voice said. "I have a telephone number for you to call. Are you ready to write it down?"

"Wait a minute," she said automatically, looking for the pad of paper she kept near the phone. It was gone. She slid a blank envelope over, then had to hunt for a pen. The man was speaking with an accent, his W's sounding like V's— "Ms. Vall . . . Vashington police." She picked up the pen and said to go ahead. He rattled off a phone number and she started to write it down, then stopped, a chill blooming in her stomach. It was the phone number for the clinic.

"You call that number, Ms. Wall," the voice said, dropping now to the whisper she'd heard before. "Or better yet, come down here. Where your friends are. Or bits of them anyway. Only this time, I will take your head right off. Right off! And soon, very soon, Connie Wall."

The dial tone came on and she replaced the handset on the wall mount. She jumped when it rang again, hesitated before answering. She didn't want to hear any more of that shit. But the phone kept ringing, insistent, again and again. She took a deep breath and picked it up but didn't say anything.

"Ms. Wall, this is Sergeant Stafford, District police technical operations. Please don't hang up—we overheard that last phone call, and that was not, I repeat, *not* us."

"No shit," she said, finding her voice at last.

"Yes, ma'am. But the tap was on. We got a phone number, and we have units en route to the trace point. It's downtown, so you should be in no immediate physical danger. But please lock yourself in, and we'll have a patrol unit out there ASAP. Don't let anyone in unless he's a uniformed police officer, okay?"

She nodded, then realized she hadn't said anything. "Got it," she said. "Should I answer the phone?"

"Yes, ma'am, if you don't mind. I mean I know that's some scary shit that guy's talking, but the more he talks, the better shot we have of nailing him. So, yes, if you don't mind . . ."

"Okay. I need to go lock up now." And use the damn bathroom, she thought.

"Yes, ma'am. A black-and-white will be out front shortly."

She hung up and then checked all the doors and windows on the ground floor. She got out the instruction booklet for the alarm system and set that. She turned on lights in every ground-floor room, then answered a suddenly urgent call of nature.

The patrol cops showed up ten minutes later, as she was making some coffee. They identified themselves, did a walk-through of the entire house, then the grounds. They came up to the door on the back porch, apparently oblivious of the dark stains all over the floorboards, and told her the place seemed secure but to stay in the house until the detectives called. She offered them some coffee, which they declined. Then she thanked them and locked herself in again. She fixed herself a cup and sat down at the kitchen table. She wondered if she ought to go down to the pound and get a dog.

There were three message slips on Swamp's desk from Hallory's office at Secret Service headquarters when he got to work. He noted the receipt times, which had begun half an hour ago. Gary White was talking on the phone in his cubicle; he waved as Swamp parked his coffee mug, sat down at his desk, and called Hallory. An assistant put him on hold, then came back and said Hallory would call him back in fifteen minutes. Swamp sighed, said he'd be there, and went over to Gary's cubicle.

"That was the District," Gary said. "They have the nurse's phone tapped and they've intercepted a death threat. Guy apparently posing as someone from the police told her he was gonna cut her head off. And soon."

"Lovely," Swamp said. "So he's still here in town?"

"Yeah, or at least he was. Phone booth at Union Station. Maybe he took the train."

"Right. They faxing us a written copy of what they got?"

"Yes, sir. What did Mr. Hallory want?"

"Still waiting to connect," Swamp said. Then he told Gary about his conversation with Lucy VanMetre late last night.

"They're gonna dump it? Really?"

"I think that's what he's—hang on." The office intercom light was blinking on Swamp's desk. The secretary announced a Mr. Hallory on line four. Swamp picked up at Gary's desk. "Morgan," he said.

"Yeah, this is Carlton Hallory, PRU. You keeping banker's hours these days, Mr. Morgan?"

"Pathetic, isn't it?" Swamp said.

"Touché," Hallory said. "Lucy says you want to bring the Bureau into your firefly."

"That's correct. I need an evidentiary response team. They're the best in that business. I want them to—"

Hallory interrupted. "No deal, Mr. Morgan. It's a firefly, and I'm calling it that officially as of now. No further assets. We thank you for your investigation. But as of now, PRU does not consider that transcript to be indication and warning of a viable threat to presidential security. That clear enough for you, Mr. Morgan?"

"Clear as a bell, Mr. Hallory."

"And if you want to run it up to the fusion committee, come at the DAD level, because that's the pay grade you'll be up against from our side of the table, okay?"

"Not a problem, Mr. Hallory," Swamp said. "I'll see your DAD and raise you an undersecretary."

"In your dreams, Mr. Morgan. But then, that's what retirement's all about, isn't it, happy dreams on the front porch?"

"Are you going to put this in writing, Mr. Hallory?"

"Do I have to?"

"Well, it would be nice to have, if the Capitol goes boom in about a month."

"I'll bet you'd like that. Yeah, I'll put this in writing. Lucy here will send something over. E-mail good enough, or you need it signed in blood at midnight?"

"Since I definitely think it's going to come back to haunt us, I'd prefer a memo."

The bantering tone went out of Hallory's voice, "CYA forever, huh?"

"I get that way whenever I encounter tunnel vision, Mr. Hallory. This is the same old hidebound attitude I used to run into when I was DAD Intel."

"*Was* is the operative word, Mr. Morgan. And, you might call it hidebound—I call it focus."

"You can't even admit this is possible? That there's more here than meets the eye, rather than automatically less?"

Hallory sighed. "You're the one with tunnel vision, Mr. Morgan. And since you're outside the main show here, you're becoming a distraction. I don't need distractions right now."

"Then let *us* work it."

"No, Mr. Morgan, because I know what'll happen. 'Us' means you. Your reputation precedes you. You'll grab this thing like some damned terrier and shake it and shake it until a head comes off, somewhere. Enough. You'll get your memo. Nice doing business with you. Happy trails and all that over there in OSI land."

Swamp put the phone down, shaking his head. "What a mule," he said. He summarized the conversation for Gary, who whistled in surprise.

"He came at you personally?" Gary asked. "Talking about your reputation?"

"There were times," Swamp said with a rueful smile, "when I tended to get up some senior noses. But it was always about business, not my career."

The secretary from the front office came in to deliver a fax folder. It contained the transcript of the threatening phone call to Connie Wall, courtesy of Detective Jake Cullen. They both scanned it, and then Swamp told Gary to read it out loud.

"Sir?"

Swamp went back to his desk, fished around in the stack of papers, and pulled out the copy of the original clinic transcript.

"Read that aloud, slowly."

Gary shrugged and began reading. When he got to the phrase "Head right off . . . right off!" Swamp repeated it out loud. And the same with "Soon, very soon." Gary stopped reading.

"We've heard this before, Gary," Swamp said. "The phraseology is identical. The guy calling Ms. Wall is the guy in the bomb transcript."

Gary looked at the words again. "I guess that's . . . possible," he said. "You going to call Hallory back with this?"

"Hell with him. He had his chance. We'll take it from here. But I do want you to follow up on that memo. Hallory will drag his feet on that."

Gary had a frown on his face. "What?" Swamp asked.

"Uh, I'm new here, but if the boss initiating a case calls it off, then, in my experience that's it. I mean, how do we keep working it?"

"Technically, you're right. But OSI can generate a case, too. As soon as Tad McNamara gets back, I'll brief him, and I'm sure he'll let us run with it."

"Even if the Secret Service is dropping it? The guys who asked us to look at it in the first place?"

But Swamp was staring down at the transcript. "You know what? We may not need Bureau assets after all. I think I know this guy's name."

Gary's skeptical expression spoke volumes, but Swamp was shaking his head again. "No, look, I think it's right here. In the original transcript. The five *H*'s: Hitler, Heydrich, Himmler, Hess, all the superstars of the Third Reich. And then the one we didn't recognize—Heismann. I think this guy's name is Heismann. He's hallucinating under the anesthetic about becoming part of the Nazi pantheon."

"Um . . ."

"Yeah, I know, but it's at least plausible."

Gary politely erased the skeptical expression on his face. "So what do we do next?"

"We run the name Heismann on NCIC. And if that comes up empty, we go to Interpol. We need to listen to the tape of that phone call, see if there's an accent. And I'll call some folks I know across the river, see if the Agency CI folks have anything on a Heismann."

"Fax here says there was an accent—*V*'s becoming *W*'s, and vice versa."

"That's German. So is Heismann."

"And you don't want to take this back to Mr. Hallory?"

"No—you heard the way he was being this morning."

"Actually, I didn't."

Swamp blinked. "Right, you didn't. Suffice it to say, he was sarcastic. Resentful of the fact that I'm even in the picture. Seems to have forgotten they called us, not the other way around."

"Yes, sir, but, with all due respect, if we do get a solid line on this Heismann guy, I think it needs to go back to PRU. Insist they look at it. If it's true, security for the speech before the joint session is a Secret Service responsibility."

Swamp smiled. "You're absolutely correct. But first I want that memo from Hallory, declaring the original transcript a nonissue. If this Heismann thing turns up empty, we're done. If he turns out to be real, then I'll definitely go back to the Service, but probably not to Mr. Hallory."

"And if it solidifies," Gary said, "you've got that memo."

"And?"

"Which would mean you've got Hallory."

Swamp beamed. "You're catching on there, young man. Now, let's run that name through the system. You start with NCIC. I'll take care of the Agency query."

Jäger Heismann stood in the front parlor of the brownstone town house. Actually, he didn't stand as much as lean on the armrest of a truly ugly upholstered chair. Doing the walk-through with the real estate agent had been painful and tiring, especially going up and down those steep stairs. But now it was done and he was officially "in possession." The agent had talked about activating the telephone, but Heismann had demurred. He had no intention of having a telephone in this house.

He looked around at the small room, eyeing the motes of dust revealed by the sunlight streaming through the side windows. The layout was simple: The front doors of the duplex were side by side in the middle of the building, three steps up from the sidewalk, with no front yard. There was a tiny front hall, stairs up to the left, living room to the right. Straight ahead, a short hallway to the kitchen, with the dining room behind the living room. Upstairs were three bedrooms. One, the master, was at the back, over the dining room and kitchen; it had a skylight, bath en suite, and two windows overlooking the backyard and the alley. The other two bedrooms were much smaller and side by side across the front, with a shared bathroom between them.

The other half of the duplex was presumably the mirror image of his. They shared a backyard, divided right down the middle and enclosed across the back and sides by a six-foot-high wooden privacy fence. A two-car garage intruded into both yards an equal distance, and there was an alley behind the back fence. Across the alley was another row of almost identical brick houses and garages. There were small fireplaces in all the major rooms, but the agent had taken great pains to point out that none of them worked except the one in the living room, and it was strictly a gas-log affair. There was a tiny covered back porch, with steps down to the winter-bare yard. All the rooms except the master bedroom were furnished. The master bedroom remained bare floor from wall to wall, ostensibly for use as his sculpting studio.

There was a basement, but it was only partially floored in concrete, the area where the heating, hot water, laundry, and air-conditioning machinery were installed. The rest of the floor was hard-packed dirt, with two tiny windows at street level, one of which had been the coal chute in days gone by.

There was a trapdoor to an attic, but Heismann had told the agent he wasn't interested in the attic. If the skylight in the master bedroom did not work out, he might have to get into the attic, but certainly not in his present condition. He moved in front of the chair and gingerly sat down, still wearing his heavy overcoat, homburg, and those oversized sunglasses. Anyone looking in from the street would have seen the makings of a Magritte painting.

Mutaib had been surprisingly calm when Heismann had called him earlier from a pay phone in a Metro station. Interestingly, he'd taken the position that the killing of the police lieutenant would only give legs to the deception plan, and ensured that the government would take the bait seriously, especially once Heismann connected the dots for them. Heismann had given the Arab no inkling of his own injuries, and he had told him to be alert for Interpol queries after today, when he dropped the second piece of the bait into the game. Mutaib had assured him their man was watching. He had also told him that "the package" was in the United States and would clear customs in Baltimore harbor by the end of the week. Delivery of the sculptor's tools and other special equipment Heismann had requested was to be made this afternoon, just before dark. The first marble delivery was scheduled for next Monday, and the "package" itself would be delivered on Tuesday, the seventeenth, right before the downtown area around Capitol Hill was slated to be shut down for the inauguration. Details on the delivery would be sent to him the day before. So far, everything was going smoothly. The security preparations for the target were conveniently being reported publicly in gratifying detail, but nothing they did would have any bearing whatsoever on what Heismann had planned for them.

In the meantime, he had work to do, beginning with a detailed walking reconnaissance of the neighborhood, so that he could plan two, possibly even three escape routes. He had to prepare the house to receive the weapon, especially the roof and the floor of the master bedroom. He had to create a reasonable facsimile of a sculptor's studio in the master bedroom, and for that he would need some tools, building materials, and probably a ladder. And finally, he wanted to get a sense of how often the local police patrolled this specific neighborhood. As much as he wanted to finish the problem with the nurse, that was probably secondary now that the weapon was in the country and the time was drawing near.

He longed to get out of the heavy disguise business—the wigs, the beard, the glasses, and all the bulky clothes. But he needed to stay in character until the neighbors had seen him, learned that he was a reclusive artist, and then forgotten about him. His groin still ached, and there were fiery nerves he'd never known about connecting his bruised testicles to points deep within his abdomen. He wondered if a kick to a woman's groin would have the same effect. With any luck, maybe he'd get to find out. He began the deep-breathing technique again, willing the pain to subside.

Bertie called back at just after four o'clock. Swamp took the call on his secure phone. Bertie began with a question. "Did you get any hits on this Heismann in the national database?"

"Negative," Swamp said. "We got some hits, but none of them sounded like our guy. As I told you this morning, I think he's a European national. Possibly German."

"He is indeed, if this is him. I'll send you a secure fax with the details, but we've come up with a possible. Heismann, Jäger. Low-level Stasi operative at the time the Berlin Wall came down. Went back into the Rodina with some of his Soviet masters right after that, then surfaced again in Western Europe as a low-level enforcer for the FSB."

"FSB. Who are they?"

"Russian federal security service. You know, the successor to the KGB. His job was chasing down Russian businessmen turned émigrés, the ones who were slipping out of the motherland with real cash money."

"A player?"

"No, not really. One of those guys who dances around the fire but never risks the actual flames. When the Ivans ran out of money, he migrated to the Muslim underground back in Hamburg. They, of course, did have money. Supposedly did more enforcement work, screening out plants and informers, but never doing anything so egregious as to get any of the European CI outfits spun up. Speaks colloquial English."

"How so?"

"Orphan. Taken in by an American air force sergeant at an early age in Frankfurt. Can probably speak English like an American. The Muslim fanatics would really like that angle. Ran away as a teenager to Berlin, drifted east. The Russians and the East Germans would have loved the American connection and his language ability."

"They know *where* he is?"

"Not at the moment, which is only mildly intriguing. Emphasis on the midlevel aspect of this guy, Swamp—he's no heavy hitter, no Carlos the Jackal. I talked to a German BND source earlier this afternoon. Their BVS directorate has Heismann as a Nazi sympathizer. Longing for the good old days of yesteryear, when Germans were Germans and the world was afraid. Trusted outside man for the Islamic fanatics, but never gonna be the guy who drives the truck bomb into the embassy compound. He reportedly has a stash of Nazi memorabilia somewhere, but even their neo-Nazi CI people say Heismann's a guy who's never done anything significant. A talker, waiting for the one big score."

Swamp thought about the four names. "Sometimes," he said, "those guys are the most dangerous. They conclude one day they have to prove themselves, make their mark. Then they come out of nowhere and do serious damage. Think Lee Harvey Oswald. The OK City bombers. Who'd ever heard of them?"

"Granted. He the guy who did the nurse's boyfriend?"

"We think, which is not to say we have any really impressive evidence. I think he's also the guy in that original transcript." Swamp reviewed what had happened in that case since they last spoke.

"'Bomb, bomb, bomb,'" Swamp chanted. "I think maybe he's on a mission for somebody with money."

"The State of the Union? Or I guess it's the speech to the joint session this year, isn't it?"

"Yeah."

"Hell, why not the inauguration?" Bertie said. "I mean, if he's going to make his grandstand play, why not do it right? Get both the old government and the new government in one fell swoop? Talk about a decapitation strike."

"Because the inauguration is probably the most heavily protected event on the planet," Swamp said patiently. "Much too hard. But the speech to the joint session? Just a month later? When maybe the security people have let their guard down a little? Sneaky, but feasible."

"And Hallory and his people at PRU insist this thing's still a firefly?"

"They might not yet know about Heismann, or that we've made a connection here with the original transcript, flimsy as it is."

"We could have the wrong guy, Swamp," Bertie cautioned. "I mean, this guy's a pretty low-level thug to be trying something like what you're suggesting."

"What are you saying?"

"If it's him, then he has to have some serious money behind him," Bertie said. "And we all know who's behind most of the serious money going into attacking America these days."

"And?"

"I'm just suggesting you need to look for some connection between the Arabs and this guy to make your theory more convincing. You gonna let the D.C. cops know you have a name?"

"They've been really cooperative, so yes. Unlike my one-time brethren in the Service."

"Yeah, well, you play that as you will. But keep me in the loop, okay?"

"Will do, Bertie, and thanks again for the lead."

Swamp hung up, called Gary over to his desk, and back-briefed him on what Bertie had revealed. "There should be a secure fax coming through on this. Oh, and any sign of that memo from Hallory?"

"No, sir, but that VanMetre woman called and says she wants a meeting."

"Really. What about? And when?"

"This evening. And she wasn't sharing as to the subject."

"Okay, I'll call her," Swamp said.

"What do we do if we surface this guy Heismann?"

"We turn the whole package over to the Justice Department."

"We wouldn't build the case? Take it to prosecution?"

Swamp shook his head. "Negative. Old Secret Service rule. We want to catch these animals. You always want somebody else to clean them."

Heismann finally felt well enough to get in his van and drive uptown. He'd waited until after the rush-hour traffic had flushed itself out of the city's broad avenues, and then he spent an hour changing his disguise. Now he wore a white wig, wispy white eyebrows, Coke-bottle eyeglasses with a tiny clear central area for normal vision, a dark overcoat and gloves, and a floppy French beret. He carried a cane. And the liquid Taser pack was strapped to his body under that roomy overcoat. He drove the van up Connecticut Avenue, then went right and down into Rock Creek Park on Tilden, then right on Porter and all the way back to Connecticut. There was just enough residual traffic so that his van shouldn't stand out, although it was fully dark by now. He'd been able to catch a glimpse of her house from the top of Tilden, but he had seen no evident police activity. He watched for signs of police surveillance as he drove down into the park and again as he passed the entrance to the nurse's street, Quebec Street. He saw nothing obvious. All right, so they aren't being blatant about it, he thought as he went left this time into Ordway Street and found a parking space in front of an apartment building.

If they did it German-style, there'd be one openly visible surveillance unit and one or more covert units. A police car parked in front of her house, or along the street. Obvious, out there in the open for anyone to see. And then a second unit, probably an unmarked car or perhaps a van, parked in someone's driveway. Definitely not the old television show standby, the telephone company van. Perhaps even some individuals on the ground or in the house itself. It was cold, though, and the *Ammies* loved their vehicles. He was betting on a second vehicle of some kind. Maybe hidden in the yard, or even that garage. Or in the driveway of one of the adjacent houses.

He paused to think. He'd made the threat. The papers said she had been released on her own recognizance but had been ordered to stay in the city. They would have her under police protection. She was either a suspect in what had happened to the policeman or the next victim—she couldn't be both. If suspect, she'd still be in custody. So now she was bait, ya? Very well. He'd tickled their web with that phone call. If she was still in the house, then it meant they wanted to play.

He'd told Mutaib that the police were running a deception of their own, because he, Heismann, knew precisely under which rock in the park the nurse was buried. Mutaib seemed to believe him, and he even warned Heismann to stay away from what was obviously a trap. Heismann had played that same warning back to him: Mutaib needed to keep his people away from the nurse's house, as well. The

Arab had agreed immediately. Heismann smiled in the darkness. Check.

So now he would take a walk. A white-haired old man, complete with three-toed cane, would take a tottering walk down Quebec Street, see what he could see. He made some adjustments to the Taser pack, then switched the charging unit on. He put his Walther in his outside coat pocket, checking it once more to ensure there was a round chambered. He took two Levolor cords rigged with locking clamps out of the bag on the right front seat and put them in the other pocket. If he did this right, he could leave the nurse an unambiguous message. He'd never scare off the police, but he might be able to make the nurse doubt their capacity to protect her. And *then* she might run. He needed her to run, for two reasons: to give the *Ammies* somebody to chase besides himself and to get her out from under police protection. If she went far, she was out of the game. If not too far, he might still find her and end the problem once and for all.

Five minutes later, he turned into Quebec Street, on the side opposite the nurse's house. The sidewalks were uneven, heaved up by the roots of huge trees that lined the street. The houses on either side were substantial but old, dating probably from the 1940s or even earlier. There were picket fences, nice lawns, established shrubbery, and wall-to-wall cars parked along the street and in driveways. Every house seemed to have a detached garage, and each house was lighted and clearly occupied. There were streetlights only at street intersections, so most of the light on the street came from the homes themselves.

He took his time, trying to make it look right, not tapping the cane but leaning on it and carefully navigating the humped sections of concrete. He hoped no dogs would come roaring out to devil him, but he had a cure for that, too, a canister of pepper spray embedded in the top handle of the cane. One quick twist and the handle would come out of the cane, ready for business. Back in the old days, in Berlin, it had been a can of something a lot more permanent than pepper spray. But those days were gone forever, unfortunately.

He got to the small bend to the right in Quebec Street before he finally saw the police car. It was parked on his side of the street, and he could just make out two heads outlined against some internal greenish light in the black-and-white cruiser. Probably a computer screen. He stopped behind the bulk of a large tree trunk and watched for a few minutes. He saw the flare of a cigarette lighter, and then a puff of smoke streamed out the window on the passenger side into the cold night air. All right, this one was totally obvious. The question now was, Where was the covert unit? He continued on down the sidewalk, getting closer to the police car. The other unit should be in visual contact with this unit, while still being able to watch the house. He could see the front and right side of the nurse's house now, but her driveway was empty. The stand of cedars was clearly visible, and she had her front porch light on. He stopped again. That porch light would blind anyone in the cedars themselves. So, the second unit—farther up the driveway? But then they would be out of visual contact with this unit. Or they were in one of the nearby driveways.

He looked around while pretending to rest, scanning all the driveways as best he could through the shrubbery. They could also be inside any of these houses. That would be the best spot. No visible vehicle, but in visual contact with the cruiser. Watching him even now. He felt a chill rise along his neck, imagined telescopic crosshairs or even one of those laser dots playing across his back. Was he making a big mistake here? Had he indeed walked right into a trap?

He shook off those thoughts and started walking forward again. The Washington police? Not to worry. He was fifty feet back from the patrol car, and the puffs of smoke were coming regularly out of that window, almost as if the smoker was sending smoke signals. The glow from the computer screen in the front dashboard was more visible now. Definitely two occupants, no more. The one in the driver's seat was slumped lower than the one in the passenger seat. No hats. Windows cracked all around. The emergency light set mounted on the top was glistening with dew. He shifted the cane into his left hand and closed his right hand around the Taser. He slid the arming tab forward, imagining that he felt the boxy little thing begin to quiver with lethal energy.

Twenty feet. No face visible in the left side-view mirror. He could hear a radio muttering inside the car, see the shotgun strapped into its rack. The driver—sleeping? The other one smoking furiously, puff after puff. He could smell it now, the pungent tang of tobacco hanging on the still night air. A lot of hair on the smoker's head—a woman? Oh, he hoped so. That would make it even better. He kept a peripheral sweep going, looking for any signs of a car that didn't fit, but they were all covered in dew. The nearest houses all had blinds or shades.

He finally drew abreast of the police car, looking sideways through the hideous glasses, stooping now, and making his movements more painful-looking. Yes, the driver was napping. A black man, with double chins bulging against his chest. The other one was indeed a woman, also black. She was reading a paperback book by the light of the computer screen. He stopped alongside the car, but incredibly, neither of them noticed him. He withdrew the Taser, held it down alongside his coat pocket, and then banged the cane forcefully on the hood of the car.

The driver's head snapped up as the woman dropped her book, and they both gaped at him.

"Communists?" he asked in his best imitation of a querulous old man's voice. "You watching for the damned Communists?"

The driver, still blinking himself awake, glanced over at his partner, who was relaxing, taking her hand off her service revolver. Heismann tapped on the car again, and the driver lowered his window all the way.

"Say what?" he asked

"Communists!" Heismann said. "They're everywhere. Everywhere! You stay on guard. They are devils! They're coming, you know. Soon."

The driver glanced again at his partner, who was now trying to control her amusement, first at how badly surprised the driver had been, and now at this bat-blind geezer ranting on about Communists.

"Yes, sir, okay," the driver said. He was a young man under all that flesh, but his uniform was visibly straining its buttons. "We got it covered, sir," he said reassuringly. "You go on home now. We'll catch the bastards."

Heismann straightened up, nodding approval. "Good," he said. "Very good! We cannot be too careful. The Communists are everywhere, you know." He made a great show of looking carefully up and down the street for Communists, glancing around one last time as he did so to see if he could spot the other surveillance unit. But none of the nearby vehicles seemed to be reacting to his small theater. So he bent down again, pointed the Taser behind the driver's neck, and fired once at the woman, sending the needle-thin stream into the side of her throat, which caused her to slam sideways against the right front door, then back against the seat, her head bucking upward and back into the headrest with an audible thump. Before the fat driver could react, Heismann backed away and fired again, hitting him in the left temple, barely missing his own hand with the back spray. The policeman's arms and legs spasmed wildly, his body looking like a puppet whose master has fallen off his stool behind the curtain as he made a gagging sound and slumped sideways against the left front door.

Heismann maintained his position, bent down by the driver's side window, as if he were still talking to the two cops inside, while looking around again slowly, deliberately, half-expecting cops to come boiling out of the bushes or to hear excited yells over the radio. But there was absolutely no re- action. The policewoman seemed to be having trouble breathing. Her jaw was working, although no sounds came out. Heismann reached into the car and hit the master door locks, then opened the rear door behind the driver and got in. Just like in German police cars, the automatic dome light had been disabled.

Keeping the door partially open, he sat down in the back- seat behind the driver. There was a wire-mesh screen be- tween the front and back seats, with Plexiglas inserts directly behind where the policemen would normally be sit- ting. He pulled out the two Levolor cords and then threaded one end of each cord through the center of the screen. He got back out, leaned into the front seat, found the power switch for the computer, and shut it off, darkening the interior of the cruiser. Then he fashioned quick nooses, slipping one over each policeman's head, settling them under their chins and then pulling them tight, but not too tight. Then he slid the locking clamp up the right-hand side of the loop until it held the noose tight enough to dent the flesh of their necks just barely. Then he pushed the other end of the cords back through the screen, got back in the rear seat, and tied them off on the headrest support brackets.

The man was out of it, but the woman was aware of what he was doing, and her eyes widened in fear. That's right, Fraulein copper, he thought, I could strangle the both of you if I wanted to, and you could do absolutely nothing about it. But then there would be much too much commotion. I don't need that just now. One dead policeman is enough. But do not struggle, *hein*?

Checking once more to make sure no one was coming, he fished out their cuffs, made a chain through the steering wheel, and locked the man's right hand to the woman's left hand, effectively imprisoning them in the car. They had keys, of course, but the Taser's effects would make it very difficult for them to manage even such a simple task as putting a key into a lock. He thought briefly about starting a fire in the car to see if their survival instincts could overcome their paralysis. He smiled to himself. That was something his uncle Karl, a real German, would have done. But he had one more thing to do, and a fire might arouse the neighborhood. Definitely second class *Polizei*, he thought contemptuously. If there was a second surveillance unit, they were obviously asleep.

He got out and closed the door. He bent down again, pretending to talk to them in case anyone inside a house *was* watching, then waved good-bye and walked back up the street marginally faster than he had come. A car came down the street but turned into a driveway before reaching him. He walked right on past that house as the people got out of the car. They did not appear to have seen him.

When he reached the dogleg turn in Quebec Street, he turned around. He could still see the top half of the nurse's house. Two windows showed lights upstairs. Bedroom and bathroom, if he remembered correctly. That would do. He stepped off the sidewalk and stood in front of a large SUV, which was in the shadow of a big tree. He waited for a long minute, looking around and listening carefully for signs that someone had discovered the situation in the police cruiser, but the neighborhood remained quiet. He could hear the background hum of traffic up on Connecticut Avenue, and what sounded like the audio from a television set in a nearby house. Good enough, he thought.

He pulled out the Walther and rested it on the driver's side mirror and aimed carefully down the street at the nurse's second-story windows. Bedroom or bathroom? Bathroom. More glass in there. It was a very long shot for a pistol, of course, but all he really wanted to achieve was to hit the house. There was no wind, so he looked around one more time to make sure no one was standing in their doorway looking at him, and then he lined up the bathroom window in his gun sight, elevated the barrel about an inch, and carefully fired two rounds. Then he pocketed the Walther and began walking quickly up Quebec Street toward Connecticut, abandoning all pretense at lame old age, the cane under his arm now like a drill sergeant's baton. He was aware of some front porch lights coming on behind him down in Quebec Street, but he was across Connecticut Avenue at the light in the next minute, then back in his van two minutes after that.

A joke, he told himself as he drove away. The Washington police were just what all his sources said they were: a total joke. And now that nurse would know it, too, once they found the two patrol officers. If he'd had a telephone, he would have been tempted to call her and ask her if she was all right.

They met in the Oyster Bar of the Old Ebbitt Grill on Fifteenth Street, a block from the White House. Swamp, who knew the maître d', had asked for a table for two in the bar for a twenty-minute meeting, with the understanding they'd give up the table whenever the maître d' needed it after that. Lucy, elegant in a gray silk suit, caused a small stir when she came through the restaurant, heading toward the bar at the back of the rapidly filling dining area. Swamp had arrived five minutes earlier and had a glass of wine going. Lucy told the waiter she'd have a vodka rocks with a twist. When the waiter left, she produced a franked government envelope.

"Your memo," she said, passing it to him.

The envelope wasn't sealed, so Swamp opened it and read the action paragraph in the memorandum, Hallory writing in the bureaucratic third person. "It has been decided that the original transcript does not indicate a credible threat to presidential security, and that the Secret Service requires no further action or assistance from the Office of Special Investigations (OSI) on this matter." That was it. The memo was signed out, however, by Lucy VanMetre, by direction. Swamp smiled. By having her sign it, Hallory was protecting himself. If this thing ever coiled back to bite him, Hallory could always say he didn't know anything about the memo and thereby blame Lucy. He looked at her and she smiled back at him, acknowledging the game.

"Thanks for bringing this," he said, pocketing it. "Old habits are hard to break."

"Perfectly understandable," she replied. The waiter brought her drink. "Do you really intend to go to the fusion committee with this problem?"

"If I have to," he said. The room was noisy enough that they could speak privately even in such a public place.

"Then perhaps you have more information than you gave Mr. Hallory this morning?"

He nodded. "Since Hallory refused to get an FBI forensics team into it," he said, "I tapped a few sources from a prior life. In fact, I think I now have a name and a tentative face to put to that transcript."

"Really," she said, her eyebrows rising. Her ice blue eyes were all business. Swamp remembered Bertie's comment about La Mamba, and that Bertie had told him he could trust Lucy to be working her own agenda, even as Hallory's deputy. She had signed the memo. If Swamp had new and more substantial information, she was definitely interested in hearing it.

"Yep," he said. "Still no solid evidence, but we've made a connection between the original transcript and a voice message left on that nurse's answering machine—*after* the lieutenant got killed. The District cops had her phone tapped, with her permission. We think the guy's a German national."

She sipped some of her drink. "They're using her as bait to try to catch the lieutenant's killer?"

"Yes."

"Do you have any details on this German?"

He nodded. "I can send you a secure fax in the morning.

Then you'll have what we have. The next step, of course, is to find him. We'll have an Interpol picture, but of course if he was at that clinic, he's had cosmetic surgery. But at least we're going to take a shot at finding him."

She put her drink down and looked away for a moment. In profile, her face was all lines and angles. Highly defined facial bones. Straight, sculpted nose. Lips full, although not too full. Her hands were elegantly long, with delicately shaped fingers and polished neutral-colored nails. No rings or jewelry of any sort, he noticed. Not even a watch. Her hair was amazing, and he found himself wanting to touch it.

"Has your superior in OSI authorized an investigation?" she asked. "Beyond the first phase?"

"That's Tad McNamara," he said. "And no, not yet." He wondered where she was going with this.

"So, you're sharing information with me. Why? Ah, so you can tell him that you are keeping the Service in the loop, even though Mr. Hallory has, in fact, turned it off. And thereby you maintain control of what happens to it in OSI, yes?"

He tipped his glass at her. Full marks.

She nodded. "That's intelligent," she said. "Would you be willing to interface with me directly? In return for which, I'll do two things: One, I'll make the requisite responses to any queries from your Mr. McNamara. And, two, at the appropriate time, I will approach Mr. Hallory to argue that perhaps further assets should be deployed. Assuming you produce tangible evidence, of course."

"Deal," he said immediately. "And please understand, I'm not so rabid about this that I can't admit I'm wrong. If it crumbles, I'll trash it myself."

"Very good, Mr. Morgan. I was told you were someone with whom one could do business."

By whom? Swamp wondered. "Why is Hallory so hard-over on this issue?" he asked.

"Well, first, he's totally absorbed by the inauguration

problem," she said, finishing her drink. "Which, as you might remember, is a security nightmare."

"A target-rich environment, as the Army likes to say."

"Indeed. From our perspective, we want to limit access, while everyone who's anyone in Washington is trying to get in."

He shook his head. "Better thee than me-e," he intoned. "The good news for me is that I've got some time with this one. That speech to the joint session is almost a month away. Not like your problem."

She swirled the ice in her glass for a moment. "I've heard some stories about you, Mr. Morgan," she said, looking away again. "One in particular. About the day you retired from active duty with the Service."

Swamp didn't say anything. Again, he just waited.

"Did that really happen?" she asked. "That your wife went with you to your retirement ceremony and then announced she was leaving you?"

Swamp simply nodded, not trusting himself to speak. No one had ever come right out and said such a thing to his face.

"And then . . ."

"Yes."

She blinked and didn't say anything for a few seconds. Then she leaned forward. "I don't mean to pull emotional scabs, Mr. Morgan. It's just that some people think Mr. Hallory is a jerk. He's not. Overfaced by his job right now, perhaps, but he's not an incompetent or indifferent boss."

"I remember him when he was an up-and-coming staff officer at headquarters. I don't think he's a jerk."

"Well, you should understand that he truly believes that your zeal on this transcript matter stems at least in part from the fact that you came back to government service because your life was otherwise empty. And that what happened that day has perhaps clouded your judgment."

Well, bully for him, Swamp thought. "In what way, specifically?" he asked.

"In the sense that you might attach disproportionate significance to an issue like this just to stay in the game."

"He send you to tell me this, Ms. VanMetre?"

"No," she said immediately. "No. This meeting was my idea. Just so you know that there's no conspiracy to marginalize you or what you're doing. There's no turf fight here. We're all too busy for that kind of thing."

"All right," he said, anxious to get back on firmer ground. "Glad to hear that. I'll keep you informed, one way or another. Like I said, if it's a firefly, I'll swat it myself."

"All right, good."

"And my emotional gyros are pretty stable these days, Ms. VanMetre. I admit that I don't date or otherwise socialize with anyone. My kids, who are both grown, think that I am responsible for what happened to my wife. She wouldn't have been there if I'd been a better husband, and so forth. So now we don't communicate anymore. In effect, I've lost my entire family."

He paused for a few seconds to let that sink in. "And it's absolutely true," he continued, "that I'm still working because that's all I know how to do, which also happens to be the point Sherry was making that day. But that fact hasn't clouded my judgment."

"That's all?" she asked quietly. Swamp almost didn't hear her.

"What?" he asked.

"That's all? I mean, no affairs, alcoholism, abusive behavior—she left you because you worked too much?"

"That's right," he said. "I was married more to the job than I was to her. Those were her words."

She sighed. "I'm German by ethnic heritage, Mr. Morgan," she said. "A reasonable woman does not divorce a man who works too hard."

She obviously meant that. He smiled, surprisingly relieved. "Well, those are the facts, Ms. VanMetre. I'm not nuts, or no more so than any of us in federal LE. If I'd still had my badge and my gun that day, maybe some things would be different. Maybe not. I'll never know. I don't feel guilty anymore, just sad."

She gazed across the table at him for what seemed a long time. A man could get lost in those blue eyes, he thought, if she ever softened them. "I believe you, Mr. Morgan," she said, finally. "And I hope things get better for you soon."

"So do I," Swamp said, and then he spotted the maître d' pointing a finger at their table. "Our time's up, I'm afraid," he said. "Thanks for meeting me."

She smiled, and for the first time he caught just a glimpse of the woman who might live behind the silvery mask. "Stay in touch, Mr. Morgan," she said as she got up and slipped her coat back on. "And please, I preferred it when you called me Lucy."

He followed her across the dining room area. The maître d' passed them with a young couple and two menus, giving Swamp a conspiratorial man-to-man wink as he went by. As if, Swamp thought wearily. By the time he got his coat and made it to the front door, Lucy was already gone. As he stepped out onto the sidewalk, his cell phone vibrated in his suit pocket.

"Morgan," he said, turning his face out of the cold wind blowing along Fifteenth Street.

"Sir. This is Gary. You need to come back to the office."

Fifteen minutes later, Swamp sat on the edge of his desk while Gary told him about what had happened in Quebec Street earlier that evening.

"He shot at the *house*?"

"Two rounds. One went through the bathroom window; the other hit the window frame. She was in the bathroom. Some kind of medium-caliber pistol. Too long a range to have been a serious attempt to hit anyone inside."

"That's probably a distinction without a difference to Ms. Wall," Swamp said. "Judas Priest! Where was the covert team?"

"Parked out back by the garage, so they could watch the

approaches from the park. That's how he'd come twice before, apparently, but they were beyond line of sight on the overt unit. Never even heard the shots. Didn't know squat until the nurse came running out of the house with her hair on fire, figuratively speaking. Then they found their buddies trussed up like Sunday chickens. Carl said it's a regular Lebanese goat grab out there right now."

Swamp couldn't suppress a grin. "I can believe that. But in a way, this is good news for us. He's still trying for the nurse, which means he's still in town."

He got up and walked around the tiny office, the fumes of Chardonnay and Lucy's subtle perfume still rising in his nose. "And it reinforces my sense that Connie Wall knows more than she's told us."

"About?"

"About some bastard bombing the Capitol."

"Is it possible she knows but doesn't know that she knows?"

"Maybe," Swamp said. "Or it's possible she does know what he looks like but can't surface it."

"She ought to remember some big balls," Gary said. "First, he whacks a cop, just to get him out of his way, and then two nights later, he comes strolling down the street right in front of two surveillance units and disables two more cops. Making it clear he could have killed them, too. All over this nurse."

"*He* certainly thinks she knows something."

Gary perched a hip on the edge of Swamp's desk. "With all this heat, if I had a mission to bomb the Capitol, I'd be laying low. Letting things subside, so I could do the job, whatever it is. Not go throwing gasoline on the fire like this."

"Correct," Swamp said. "So there's a reason for all this. I think we need to go back to interview Ms. Wall. Before her role as bait gets her dead."

"On the other hand, the bait idea worked," Gary said. "He did make a move."

"We might not like his next move," Swamp said. "Hell, I'm ready to go out there tonight."

But Gary was shaking his head. "Carl thought you might say that. He says tomorrow is a much better idea. Let the hornet swarm subside a little."

"As in they're embarrassed. No time for feds to show up. They'd assume we were gloating."

"Yes, sir."

Swamp, disappointed, nodded. Carl was probably right. He wondered if he ought to inform his newfound ally over in PR, but decided against it. Wait until you have the facts, he thought. *All* the facts. Evidence, even. Admissible evidence, even better. "Okay, tomorrow it is. I'll need to bring McNamara up to speed first thing; then we'll try to get some face time with Ms. Wall. Assuming she doesn't bolt first."

Heismann cleaned the Walther in the kitchen sink and then reassembled it, wiping each component with an oiled rag before fitting it back in place. He replaced the two spent rounds, but not before first emptying the entire clip and oiling the spring. He could just hear the sounds of a television from the duplex next door. It was one of those stupid *Ammie* shows where the television laughed all by itself, whether what was being said was funny or not. He needed to get a television set, as none had been provided with the furnishings. He didn't want to rely entirely on newspapers for news of the city, especially when he'd been out making some of that news. He would need one on *der Tag*.

The television switched to a loud automobile advertisement, complete with some brute yelling about zero something. He put the gun down on the table, resisting the temptation to start shooting through the wall until the brute shut up. Time to have a better look at his neighbor, he thought. He turned out his own kitchen light and looked out the window to verify that her kitchen lights were on. Based on the wedge of white light spilling out onto their shared back porch, they were. He went to find the mini-binoculars, then put on a jacket and his loden hat. He went out the back door as quietly as he could, down the steps, and walked quietly to the garage at the back of the yard, not looking back until he was at the garage's side door. He could see her through her back kitchen window; she was washing something in the sink. Short dark hair, plain face with a short, pointed nose. Indeterminate age. Late forties, early fifties. Glasses. He couldn't see anything of her fig-ure, but, based on that face, she was probably not over-weight.

He stepped into the garage and closed the side door be-hind him. He had to squeeze past the left front of the van, as the garage had been built a long time ago, when cars were not as wide and high as they were now. There was a tiny dirty window at the yard end of the garage, and he wiped off some grime so he could examine her through the glasses. Yes, late forties. The oyster complexion of an office worker. He could see the television behind her, colors flickering silently now that he was in the garage. He felt the contour of his nose and looked at her face again. Similar enough. He raised the glasses once more and studied that face as an idea solidified in his mind.

With the right wig, and that nose . . . yes. He lowered the glasses. He was probably much thinner than she was. He'd have to get into her house when she was at work. Check the sizes of her clothes. Find some pictures with her face in them so he could begin the study of her makeup, eyebrows, lip colors. He'd also have to see about relatives, children. But if she was a solitary individual, what he had in mind would work on *der Tag*. When all was in chaos and there were police scrambling all over the neighborhood. It only had to work for sixty seconds at most, and that within one minute of the attack itself. He wouldn't have much time to fix his own face, but the essentials would take only about thirty seconds, with practice.

He'd have to get her out of the way, of course. Not now, but perhaps the day just before. He raised the glasses again, waiting for her to turn in profile. The nose was the key. He ran his finger along the curving contours of his own brand-new nose, the one Mutaib had said looked like his. And so it did. Never mind that it was a total betrayal of his Aryan heritage. He had wanted a physical change, and he had succeeded beyond his expectations.

She turned to reach for a dish towel. Yes, indeed. This would work. He lowered the glasses and leaned back on the front grille of the minivan as he began to go through the list of things he would need to acquire in the next seven days. Another vehicle, one that could pass for a police unit. A television. A GPS navigation device—he'd need to find a boating-supply store for that. The woman moved away from the kitchen window and then turned off the light and the television. A minute later, her bedroom light came on upstairs. He moved back to the window and raised the glasses again. He could see her shadow moving around the room. There were sheer curtains in place in the window, but the tiny binoculars allowed him to see through them fairly well. She passed into his field of vision briefly, visible from the waist up, wearing what looked like a slip. Full-breasted, with just the beginnings of a belly. Too full? Her bra size would tell him.

She would do for the day in question. Do very nicely.

Seven days. He shivered, both from the cold and the thrill of what was coming.

5

SWAMP GOT IN TO SEE MCNAMARA AT TEN O'CLOCK ON FRI-
day morning. He took Gary White with him, and together
they briefed McNamara on the clinic transcript and the
status of the case. When they were finished, McNamara said
he had three questions.

"First, the conclusion that the guy on the clinic transcript
and the one whose phone call was taped are one and the
same is based strictly on the language, right?"

"Yes, sir."

"Any other evidence of that?"

"No, sir."

"And the leap from that to the guy's name, this Heismann, is it? That's based on what again?"

"In the original transcript, it's the one name that's not notorious. Hitler, Heydrich, Hess, Himmler, all Nazi superstars, and—Heismann? I've looked up the history of the
Third Reich and can't find anyone prominent with that
name, civilian or military. I think he has this secret dream to
join the Nazi pantheon."

McNamara just looked at him. "I know," Swamp said.
"It's a reach, except that we've put a face to that name, as I
told you. A German, and this guy was ranting in German on
the transcript. '*Heil Hitler* . . . raining dead people,' among
other things."

"And you got the profile from whom?"

"Across the river," Swamp said. McNamara knew exactly what that meant, and Swamp did not expect him to push for specifics. He didn't.

The boss picked up a piece of paper. "And the third question is, Have you seen this memo?"

Swamp took it. It was a copy of the one Lucy had given him last night, but then, he'd been interested in what it said. He hadn't noticed to whom it was addressed—namely, McNamara. Now he'd have to come clean about his arrangement with Lucy.

"Yes, sir, I have." He described his meeting last night with Lucy VanMetre, and their deal.

"And you trust this woman? Who I'm told is Carlton Hallory's deputy in PRU?"

"Until she does me dirty," Swamp said. "Besides, they have nothing to lose."

"Well, let's verify that she wasn't sandbagging you, shall we?" He checked his Rolodex, placed a call to PRU, and asked to speak to Ms. VanMetre. When she came on, he asked her to confirm that PRU had no objections to OSI continuing to probe the transcript case, as long as any pertinent information that surfaced was shared with PRU. He listened for a moment, thanked her, and then hung up.

"Good to go," he announced. "Okay, so now you get together with the D.C. cops. Find out what they're doing to find this guy who's been embarrassing them. Did your source give you a picture?"

"An old one from Interpol," Swamp said. "That's what he *used* to look like. If we're correct on this string of assumptions, then we think he's changed his physical appearance. That picture might be useless."

"Then how the hell will you find him? And if you do, how will you know it's him if somebody happens to take him into custody?"

"That's a very good question," Swamp said. "Right now our only hope is to keep building our house of cards."

"Meaning?"

"Meaning more assumptions, unfortunately. If we assume that Heismann is our guy, then we can put the patient code number we found for the night of the fire together with Heismann. Then we screen all the record fragments the District cops retrieved and see if we can put together a list of cosmetic surgery procedures done on the patient with that code number. Then—"

"Yeah, I get it. Is a month enough time to do all that?"

"Funny you should mention that, boss," Swamp said. "I was thinking of getting some Bureau help to go through the clinic's record wreckage. One of their evidentiary analysis teams."

McNamara nodded thoughtfully. "Outside DHS. I'd have to go to the fusion committee for that. Unless . . ."

"That's a big paper drill. Takes time we don't have. Don't you know anybody?"

"Yeah, I do. And she owes me a big favor. But you know what they'll probably give us, don't you?"

"Let's see," Swamp mused. "This is the Bureau we're talking about. So we'll get one guy, probably. Some poor bastard who pissed off his supervisor so bad that they'll be dying to cross-deck him to OSI for what they see as the ultimate shit detail?"

McNamara was laughing. "Pay attention, Agent White. This is Swamp Morgan in oracle mode."

"Yeah, well, I still think it's worth doing. Grunt-level police work. But sometimes—"

"Got that right. More often than we ever wanted to admit when I was in the Bureau. In the meantime, start building a dossier. Trace his movements for the past two years. Check in over at the Justice Department with the Foreign Terrorist Tracking Task Force. Get a profiler down in Quantico going on this guy."

"Right."

"And I'll call in an IOU or two."

Connie Wall stood in her bedroom and surveyed the empty suitcase, photo-equipment bag, and her backpack. She'd awakened this morning with the decision crystallized in her mind: Connie Wall was going to get the hell out of Dodge City. Cops or no cops, creepy terrorists, secret agents, and all their plots notwithstanding. The three cop cars parked around her neighborhood had instructions to keep bad guys out, but, supposedly, not keep her in. She hoped. Either way, she was going to pack up some stuff, stop by the bank, and head west to the hills of West Virginia, where she'd been doing her wildlife photography expeditions for the past seven years. Once you got outside of the major towns in West Virginia, damn near everybody at least looked like a domestic terrorist of some kind. Any foreign variety who came up there after her probably wouldn't come back.

She started putting things in the suitcase while making a mental inventory of what she'd need in the way of outdoor gear. It was January, so the West Virginia hill country would be cold, snowy, and barren. Ironically, winter photography was often the most spectacular, if only because there was so little cover. Fall and spring were gorgeous, but the background competed with the animals. She made a mental note to call one motel in particular so that she'd have a reservation for the first leg of her trip. She didn't think the cops would actually chase her, as she was under no legal restrictions. She'd call Jake Cullen once she was out of town and tell him generally where she'd be.

Then she remembered that the Shelby's brake job was scheduled for Monday at Steve's Vintage Motors down on Wisconsin. She'd waited three months for that appointment, and they'd called just last week to say they had found all the parts and were ready to do the deed. But Monday was too late. She wanted to go now. Even with two cops sitting at her kitchen table last night, she hadn't slept very well, dreaming of guns and crashing mirrors.

She went downstairs to her phone book and then gave the shop a call. Asked for Steve himself and went into her best begging-damsel mode. She asked if she could bring the Shelby in this afternoon instead of Monday. Pick it up Saturday morning if that made things easier, but she *had* to have the car this weekend. Had to have it. Steve, a burly ex-Marine, who'd given her more personal attention than many of his customers, wavered. She offered to do phone sex, gave him a little intro work until he started laughing. "Pretty please?" she said. Steve relented. Said to get it in by two, she could get it back at six. An hour's job, but with a '68, they always allowed time to fit parts, in case something had to go up on the lathe.

She was halfway up the stairs when the phone rang. She came back down into the dining room and looked at the caller ID, thinking it might be Steve. But it was one of those 998 numbers. Phone booth. The cops had told her to answer the phone if she was there, no matter what. And to keep the bastard talking if at all possible. To be cool, unruffled. But when she thought about those two bullets zinging through the bathroom like that, she felt a flush of anger. I'll show you unruffled. She picked up the phone.

"Listen, asshole," she hissed, "I don't know what your act is, but why don't you just come on up here and I'll meet you out in the street? You bring your little popgun and I'll bring my ten-gauge. Compare some notes."

"Um, I guess we could do that," a familiar voice replied. Then she recognized it: the big Secret Service agent. "But I think the local cops might get upset. You know, District gun laws and all that."

"Oh shit," she said, suddenly remembering that the police were taping all this.

"Actually, we need to talk," he said. "You free for lunch?"

"I guess so," she said. "What's up?"

"Now's when I say something elliptical—like 'We have developments.' Fact is, we don't. We're stuck in first gear. I just want to pick your brains on the record systems at that clinic—how they were organized, how much of the medical procedures were recorded, like that."

"Sounds like a pretty dry lunch," she said, peering out at the street, where one of the District cop cars was still parked. She wondered where they did their listening.

"Well, we could cover other ground, I suppose."

She frowned, but then she understood. What he was saying: Your phone's tapped. Why don't I tell you what I really want once we get there?

"O-kay, right," she said. "What time, and how dressy?"

"It's a business-lunch spot. Gucci Gulch clientele. The ladies will be in their power skins. I'll pick you up at twelve. Tell your minders I'll have you back by two at the latest."

"Twelve it is," she said, "Oh, wait. I have to drop off my Shelby at a shop down on Wisconsin Avenue on the way. It's right across from that mega Chevy dealership."

"Something broke?"

"Nah. It needs a brake job, but it's taken awhile to find the parts. You can follow me down there, if you don't mind."

"No problem. We'll probably have an escort, though."

"The more the merrier," she said, and hung up the phone. She went upstairs to resume packing. She wasn't going to tell the cops what she planned, and she wasn't going to tell the Secret Service, either. And after the fiasco last night, she had diminishing confidence in her so-called police protection. Now all she had to do was figure out a way to get her bags into the Shelby without the watchers seeing them. They did a shift change every eight hours. Left the car in her driveway and walked down to a police van out in the street. Do it then. Tomorrow morning, she'd get one of the cop cars to take her down there to the shop, and then get Steve to let her out the back doors. Give her two blocks' lead and she'd be down the road and gone.

Heismann dutifully allowed the babbling car salesman to show him another brand-new Suburban, this one smaller than the last one. He was wearing his heavy overcoat and a hat, and the oversized square sunglasses. He sported a bedraggled goatee, and he'd thickened his eyebrows with some makeup. His appearance was entirely different from what he'd exposed last night. He'd already spotted the vehicle he wanted, after taking a walk earlier through their used-car lot: a dark-colored ten-series Suburban with oversized tires, lightly tinted windows, and a luggage rack on the roof. Three years old, 58,000 miles, standard interior, and missing the third-row seats. Perfect. He thanked the car salesman for his time and then walked back across the lot towards the used cars—or, as they called them with a perfectly straight face, "previously owned."

He was amazed at how easy it was for a foreigner to purchase a vehicle here in the United States. Once Heismann had told him what he needed, Mutaib had set the whole thing up with the dealership manager from his office in the Royal Kingdom Bank. He'd messengered over a preauthorized bank draft for up to twenty thousand dollars. Heismann had a temporary foreign-national District of Columbia driver's license, good for six more months, and the proper visa on a German passport in the name of Erich Hodler. Title and registration were to be sent to the Royal Kingdom Bank. The price scrawled on the vehicle's windshield was $15,900. So presumably, all he had to do now was— He stopped.

The nurse's fire engine red race car was turning right in front of the dealership's entrance on Wisconsin Avenue and pulling into the chain-link-fenced lot of a commercial garage on the opposite corner. The sign read STEVE'S VINTAGE MOTORS. There was a District police car right behind her, and another vehicle that looked like an unmarked police car right behind the black-and-white. All three vehicles pulled into Steve's parking lot.

"And how can I help you today, sir?" an enthusiastically friendly voice asked from behind him.

"What is that place—over there, that Steve's?" he asked without turning around.

"Classic-car garage."

" 'Classic'? What is this?"

"As in old," the salesman said. "Like that '68 Mustang that just pulled in there. See those cop cars? Probably has a dozen unpaid speeding tickets on it."

"Nineteen sixty-eight? That's quite old for such a car, yes?" In Germany, a car that old would have been ordered off the roads a long time ago.

The salesman shrugged. "That's a Shelby GT five hundred KR. Classic muscle car. Four twenty-eight CobraJet engine, three sixty ponies, clean. Probably run a flat fourteen seconds on the quarter mile."

Muscle car? Did that mean race car? None of these terms meant anything to Heismann. "So," he said, "very fast, yes?"

The salesman grinned. "You might say that, pardner. Most guys'd give their left nut to drive one just once. And how about you, sir? We've got some fine vee-hicles of our own right here on the lot."

Heismann looked over the salesman's shoulder in time to see the nurse, this time riding in the right front seat of the unmarked car, leaving Steve's and heading back up Wisconsin Avenue. The District police car followed them, but not so closely this time.

"That one—Suburban is it called?" he said, pointing with his chin. "Right over there? May I see that one, please?"

Swamp took Connie to a twelve-table bistro just off of Wisconsin and two blocks from the back entrance to the Naval Observatory. He'd booked a table in the back for one o'clock. And for a change, there was no waiting. Connie wore a dark green suit with a knee-length skirt, and she'd obviously taken some time with her hair and makeup. Swamp was always amazed what a difference it made when a woman took some time and effort in the powder and paint department. She was actually quite attractive, and he told her so. She smiled at the compliment and asked him what he recommended from the menu. He took a quick look and told her the prix fixe lunch looked pretty good, and that's what they both ordered. Connie had a glass of Chardonnay, and Swamp settled for mineral water. He asked her about the Mustang, and she walked through some of the technical specs.

"Where can you run something like that? Surely not here in D.C."

"Not anymore. My avocation is wildlife photography. I usually go up into the hill country west of here. West Virginia, western Maryland."

"I grew up in West Virginia," he said. "Harpers Ferry, to be precise. My folks were innkeepers. When they passed on, I inherited the inn, but I was already away in the Secret Service. Got a local couple to run the place. Eventually, we made a business arrangement. I go out there on weekends now. I own the property, but it's basically their show and their livelihood."

"I've been to Harpers Ferry," she said. "You're not talking about the Jackson Inn?"

"Right."

She shook her head. "I've stayed there. Going after eagles along the Potomac palisades, right below the junction with the Shenandoah. And you own that?"

"I own the property. They own the business." He paused while the waiter put down their main courses and topped off Swamp's water. Then Swamp switched direction abruptly and got down to business. "We gave up on finding the code list. Gary ran down the two doctors' home addresses, but both families had already decamped back to Pakistan. Along with some fairly substantial bank deposits."

"And the off-site storage?"

"Closed down. By the family, apparently. Wiped clean."

"Can't Pakistan produce those people?"

"I'm sure they could, but we felt it would be pointless now. Why would they keep the code list? They got out of America with lots of money, which is why they were here in the first place. The clinic is history."

"I believe it about the bank deposits," she said. "But I never knew anything about their personal lives. They'd speak in Pakistani, or whatever it's called, among themselves. But for us, it was just doctors giving orders and nurses doing what they were told to do. Professional, businesslike—no booze, no drugs, nobody patting anyone on the ass, and absolute control of each patient's true identity."

"Sounds like they knew what they were doing."

She nodded.

He withdrew a picture from the pocket of his suit jacket and passed it across the table. She put her fork down and examined it. "Yes," she said. "He was in for some major work. Photo transference, if I remember."

"What's that mean?"

"Guy comes in with a picture, says, 'Make me look like this.' If his facial structure can stand it, the docs can do it. I remember him because we did the nose first. It was major."

"What's 'major'?"

"Not for discussion at lunch," she said. "But totally different from that. I think we had to harvest some cartilage to get what he wanted."

" 'Harvest'?"

"Like I said, not for lunch."

"Oka-a-y. Was everything done on this guy 'major'?"

She looked across the table at him. "Where we going with this, Secret Agent?"

"Special agent," he said, trying to disarm her with a smile. "We know who this man is. We think he's the bad guy who burned the clinic, who killed Lieutenant Ballard, and who's after you. Because you're the last survivor from the clinic. What we don't know is what he looks like *now*. Do you?"

She shook her head immediately. "*Can't* know," she said. "See, it's not like I took him through every procedure, all the changes. I was undoubtedly there for some of it, but, like I said, if they were working on hands, only the prep nurse would have seen his face. I'd see the hands. There were at least two operations a night, sometimes three. We saw body parts."

A laser-eyed woman sitting close by flinched when Connie mentioned body parts. Swamp gave her a look that encouraged her to quit eavesdropping.

"Look," she said. "I want to help. I have a personal stake here, too, right? But I can't give you something I don't know. I can tell you this: Some of our patients came out looking very, *very* different from when they started. One Italian-looking guy came in and had himself turned into an Arab, for God's sake. Hair transplants, eye color, nose job, everything."

"And did he have anything else done?"

She threw up her hands. "Yes?" she said. "No? Who knows? I think he was an actor. Wanted to have a permanent face for the chance to do character parts—playing Arabs in terrorist and war movies. But only the docs had the full picture."

"So if we go through the medical records, searching by the code for one patient, and then summarize all the procedures done on that person, we'd have the full picture?"

"If you got them all, yes," she said. "But if you missed one, because it's gone, you might miss the fact that 'he' became a 'she.'"

"Shit," he said.

"Sorry," Connie said, pushing her plate away. The waiter appeared to clear the table and then brought their salads.

"Well, we're going to try," he said. "In the meantime, the cops are going to watch you like a hawk."

"One with two eyes this time?"

"Yeah, we heard. That was pretty ballsy, walking right down the street and up to a cop car like that. He does that again, I think the cops are gonna grab his ass. He embarrassed them."

"I should hope so," she said. "But what if he decides just to wait? Like until the cops run out of overtime hours?"

"Then we'll take over," he said, mentally chiding himself for making a promise he wasn't sure he could keep. "We think the guy's real and is planning some kind of shit."

"Oh, he's real all right," she said. "But how do you know my bad guy is your bad guy?"

"Well, right now, we're working on a daisy chain of assumptions. Plus the fact that the name we're working on is tied to Muslim networks in Germany."

"Then why don't you federal guys take over now?" she asked.

Good question, he thought. "Two reasons. One, all he sees right now are D.C. cops. Made him confident enough to do what he did last night."

"And two?"

"Two, not everyone on the federal side of the fence agrees that he's a real threat to national security."

"Too many assumptions?"

"Yeah. But we're all talking to one another, for a change. And we're trying to build a picture. Profilers, forensics experts."

"And the District cops?"

"They're looking to stage a really dramatic arrest, if you follow me, when he tries again."

"Oh, yeah, I know about those. Where the bad guy resists to the point where he gets dead."

"In a way, that would solve everyone's problem."

She smiled. "My, how things have changed," she said. "And you said 'when'? Not if?"

"Unfortunately, you're still our best hope for catching

him. Because, like you pointed out, there's a big hole in our plan to screen the records."

"Got a plan C?" she asked. The expression on her face indicated that having a plan C would be a really good idea.

"We need one, Ms. Wall?"

"Look," she said. "I'll do this bait gig for a while, Special Agent. But not for ever and ever. I'm a girl who likes to keep things moving, you know?"

"We're grateful you're even giving us the time of day, Ms. Wall. For Lieutenant Ballard, if nothing else."

She gave him an arch look. "Oh, right," she said. "For Lieutenant Ballard."

Heismann stepped into the office of Steve's Vintage Motors and approached the counter. The sounds of a busy auto-repair shop came banging through a large metal door behind the counter. A pretty young woman with an enormous hairdo asked how she could help him.

"I was across the street, looking at autos. I saw this race car—the red one, out front? I saw it come here. Can you tell me what that is?"

"Sure," she said. "That's not really a race car, though. That's a 1968 Ford Mustang Shelby GT five hundred KR."

"Ah," he said, as if those details meant something to him, which they still did not. "And how much is it, please?"

She smiled. "This isn't a car dealership, Mr. . . ."

"Hodler. Erich Hodler. I am visiting from Germany, you see."

"Ri-i-ght, okay. This is a car shop. We work on classic cars. Some of them are really old, like that Shelby out there. People own a car like that, they can't take it just anywhere, put any old parts in it. To keep the value, they have to keep it authentic. You with me?"

"Yes, yes," he said, trying not to show how baffled he was. "And who owns that car?"

"She wouldn't sell it, Mr. Hoffler," the girl said. "She just brought it in for a brake job, and she'll come get it first thing in the morning, when we open. Nine o'clock sharp."

"Ah," he said wistfully, grateful for the error on his name. "There is no possibility the owner would sell it, then?"

"No, she actually drives it. Like, she's cutting out to West Virginia in the morning. Some place called Garrison Cap. Already got her stuff in the trunk." She leaned forward, lowered her voice. "Didn't want all those cops to know. Gonna hit the road right from here. She's a big-time wildlife photographer, you know."

"Ah, I am also photographer, too. She is a good one?"

"Oh yeah. She's won some prizes and everything. Cool lady."

"And how does she come to drive such a car?"

"It was her brother's. He was a D.C. cop, got killed several years ago. That's why she'd never sell it. No way, no day."

"Ah, so it is valuable, then?"

"Oh yeah. We'll pull her into the shop tonight before we close, and that's where she'll stay."

He clucked his disappointment. "It would be really something, to drive such an old auto in Germany. All we have is Mercedes, boring Mercedes, everywhere."

"We don't work Mercedes at this shop," she said. "Strictly Dee-troit iron. American cars. You want to work classic Mercedes, you have to go to Georgetown."

"I am so bored with Mercedes," he said, looking again at the Shelby, memorizing the shape and color of it.

"You get really bored with yours, I'd be happy to take it off your hands," the girl said brightly.

But Heismann wasn't listening. He was making plans.

Swamp Morgan found a window seat on the train and settled in, his *Washington Post* folded in his lap. Like many Washington commuters, reading the city newspaper was a luxury reserved for lunch at the desk or the ride home. A duffel bag with the week's laundry was perched in the overhead rack.

The bulk of the rush hour was over, but this was the last train running via Baltimore out to Harpers Ferry, so it was filling right up. He had been surprised at how many people commuted this way from so far out in the country, but it took only one attempt at driving it on a workday to make him a believer. Now he took the train home on Friday evenings and back in on Monday morning, staying in his sparsely furnished one-bedroom box over in Ballston for the other four nights of the week. In the rush to get talent back into the anti-terrorist game right after the attacks in 2001, the government had thrown in a housing allowance to entice retirees back into harness, so the bulk of his in-town living expense was covered.

The train lurched uncertainly out of the station, through some short tunnels, and then began the run to Baltimore through the drab northeast corridor of Washington, D.C. He stared out through grit-scratched windows at the grubby rail yards and thought about his weekend routine. He'd be in his room at the Jackson Inn by 7:30, dinner downstairs in the weekend restaurant at 8:30, when the dining room began to thin out. Then, weather permitting, a night walk along the Shenandoah River Civil War ruins, followed by a cognac in the river bar with Ben and Lila Hardee, proprietors of the inn. His rooms were on the third floor of the house. There was a small bedroom, which adjoined the much larger room created by the Victorian-era round tower, whose major asset was a spectacular view of the Potomac River palisades, overlooking the junction with the Shenandoah. The rest of the third floor was, for all practical purposes, attic storage space, but the bedroom had a working gas fireplace, air conditioning in the summer, and its own bathroom. He'd made a study-library out of the round room, with its conical ceiling and wavy-glass French doors. He paid no rent and generally stayed out of the way of the paying customers on the ground and second floors. He would help Ben with repairs and maintenance if he had nothing else to do, which was often these days, and there was always something that needed fixing in a vintage 1870s wooden house.

Because of his intense schedule when he had been on active duty in the Secret Service, weekends had been frenetic, although often fun, because that's when the family got to operate together, even if it was often on a semi-chaotic basis. But then he'd risen to supergrade, the Senior Executive Service—deputy assistant director. And more often than not, Saturday mornings had been spent at headquarters. It wasn't so much the workload as the fact that the director started coming in on Saturdays. If the director was in, then the senior principals felt they also had to be in. By Saturday afternoon, the kids' activities were already in full motion, and he'd missed more and more of the family's activities.

He shook himself out of this familiar introspection. Those chapters of his life were over. Done. Finished. His kids weren't kids anymore, and they had written him off when Sherry died on the sidewalk while he stood there helpless. Sherry had told them what she was going to say that day, and the fact that neither of them had called to warn him spoke volumes about relationships long squandered. "She wouldn't have been there to talk to you if you had been there for us those past five years; this was on you, Dad," his son had told him bitterly during their last conversation. Thanks a heap, Billy. What was that old saying about a child's ingratitude being sharper than a serpent's tooth? He'd made no effort since then to reach out to his son, although he wondered from time to time who'd be the first to make an overture—if ever. Kenny was young. Eventually, he'd get over it, or he wouldn't. Swamp didn't have to get over it. He was in it.

"This seat taken?" a woman asked from above his left shoulder. He didn't even bother to look up.

"All yours," he said looking out the window at a rapidly blurring vista of row houses along the right-of-way, lights on here and there, interspersed with bare winter-blackened trees. He switched on the reading light and picked up his paper.

Heismann maneuvered the Suburban into the garage and winced when the can of tennis balls he'd stood upright on the luggage rack came tumbling off. The light bar would have maybe an inch of top clearance to spare, if that. He had to pull the vehicle toward the right wall just to leave himself enough room to open the door on the driver's side. Tight, very tight. He shut it down, got out, squeezed back along the left side, and tried to pull the two garage doors closed. The Suburban was just too long, so he found some string and tied them as close to shut as he could. He'd moved the minivan to the front street, where each resident was allowed to park one vehicle, after having obtained a color-coded permit.

Buying the vehicle had been a quick transaction, especially since he'd met their price. The paperwork was done in a half hour, and he was given the keys and a half a tank of gas. If it had been a new car, the salesman explained, he'd have received a full tank of gas. Heismann could fully understand that logic. He'd driven the vehicle to a gas station, filled it up, and then found an auto-parts store on Wisconsin, where he'd purchased some whip antennas for CB radios, maps of the states surrounding Washington, and an emergency flasher bar with red and white lights. For fifty dollars in cash, he got one of the kids at the counter to wire the lights for him out behind the parts store. The antennas were only going to be for show. He had the kid put the switch for the lights into the ashtray's lighter fixture.

The nurse was supposedly going to pick her race car up at nine o'clock in the morning, and then leave town. Without the knowledge of the police, apparently. His plan was simple: He would wait on the street in his new Suburban, then follow her when she left town. The salesman had assured him that the big Suburban could go plenty fast enough on the highway to keep up with any car except a police car with an interceptor package. "Pass everything but a gas station," the salesman had said, smiling.

In the time he'd been in this country, he'd learned that American highways weren't anything like Germany's autobahns—there were speed limits, and there were many police out there enforcing them. So he did not anticipate any high-speed chases, just a discreet tailing job, made easier because he knew the nurse's destination. Garrison Cap, West Virginia, the girl at Steve's had said. Then all he would have to do was pick his time, place, and the correct weapon. Without her watchers, she would be easy prey.

6

CONNIE WALL THANKED THE POLICE OFFICER WHO'D DRIVEN her down to Steve's. She told him it might take a few minutes to retrieve her car, especially if they'd run into any parts problems. He told her he literally had all day. She smiled at him, closed the door, and went inside.

"Hey, Dorie," she said to the girl behind the desk. "Got Baby ready?"

"You bet, Connie. Steve took her out for a test drive an hour ago, before there was any traffic. He said she's balanced up and ready to rumble."

Connie paid the bill, got the keys, and then asked if she could talk to Steve for a minute. Dorie eyed the cop car parked out front, grinned, and went to find Steve. No secrets here, she thought, and then remembered she'd been the one running her mouth yesterday. Oh well. The night had been uneventful, except that the inside cops had used up all her coffee. Guys must be total addicts, she thought. She'd walked down to the Riggs Bank branch on Connecticut Avenue late yesterday afternoon to draw out a thousand in cash. One of the cops, who was not overweight but was a heavy smoker, had gone with her, visibly not thrilled with the prospect of walking twenty blocks up and back in the January air. With the cop puffing alongside, she'd felt pretty secure, even with all that cash on board. But her gear was already packed in the trunk of the Shelby, and all she had to do now was get the car on the street and out of sight of her shadows out there, both good and bad.

"Steve's elbow-deep in a Nova tranny," Dorie announced from the door leading into the shop. "He said to come on through."

Dorie took her over to one of the work bays, where Steve and one of the mechanics were indeed elbow-deep in the bowels of a Chevy Nova. It was cold in the shop, and Steve's breath was condensing on his work. A portable heater was radiating noisily but not very effectively at the two of them.

"She's ready to go, Ms. Wall," he told Connie. "And Dorie here says you maybe want to ease out the back, get yourself over to the Virginia side?"

"Sure would," she said. The Shelby was already positioned at the back of the open bay, sitting in front of an industrial garage door. Bless their hearts, they'd washed it.

"That there's gonna let you out onto Thirty-third Street. Take a left, go downtown to Reservoir Road, and then out to Chain Bridge. This time of day, you'll be on the GW in ten minutes, max."

"You think he might hear me, even from in here?" she asked.

"Mike'll rev up the engine on that Vette over there. We've got the mufflers out. Dorie will watch to see that he's not coming in or anything."

"That guy's here for *my* protection," she said. "He might get pissed."

"But not at us," Steve pointed out. "You told us there'd be less traffic on Thirty-third Street. So's you could get over to the Whitehurst Freeway, go downtown to New York Avenue, and out to Fifty and the Beltway. For your trip to Annapolis?"

She smiled. "I appreciate that, but you guys don't need to get into trouble. They haven't told me to stay in town or anything. I just need some space. Too much weird stuff going down over the past few days."

Steve grinned, his mouth a white half-moon against all the grime on his face. Nobody in a muscle-car shop loved the police. "Happy trails," he said. "Dorie honey, go make sure that cop's still out there in his ride."

Connie thanked him again and headed for the Shelby. The garage door began clanking upward at about the same time as one of the other mechanics revved the Corvette's unmuffled engine. The racket was terrific, but it effectively masked the deep rumble of the Shelby's heavy eight coming to life. She drove straight out the door, looked both ways to make sure there wasn't a second cop car lurking out back, turned left into Thirty-third Street, and drove as quietly as she could toward Reservoir Road, M Street, and Chain Bridge. M Street in Georgetown was its usual snarled mess, but she was making all right turns, so it was simply a matter of plugging through it. She didn't even notice the Suburban running three cars behind her until she was already over on the Virginia side on the George Washington Parkway, headed upriver toward the Capital Beltway. But when she did see it, she noticed it had red and white lights on its roof, not blue, and so she dismissed it. Red and white was the fire department, not the cops. No biggie.

The posted speed limit on the parkway was fifty, but she was being passed by everybody, so she notched it up just to sixty-five to join the flow. Once she hit the Beltway, she would take the Dulles toll roads all the way out to Leesburg, where she could pick up westbound Route 7. That would avoid the crush of Saturday-morning traffic around Tyson's Corner. Besides, there was a gun shop she needed to visit out there along Route 7, right where it crossed the Blue Ridge. She'd lost the derringer in the house fight, and the cops had relieved her of Cat Ballard's .45. Nobody with half a brain went into the hills of West Virginia without a gun.

Heismann backed the Suburban carefully up the roadside fire lane until he had a clear view of Route 7 where it de-

scended the western flank of the Blue Ridge and snaked
down toward the Shenandoah River. The woman had turned
into a driveway about a mile back. There'd been a sign advertising gun repairs. Heismann had driven right on past, in
case she was checking for a tail, but there was nothing but a
cloud of dust hovering above the dirt road leading north into
some hardwoods beyond the sign. Assuming she would continue west, he'd taken a right onto a county fire lane and then
stopped to wait.

He'd had no trouble keeping up, even as he stayed a mile
or so behind her. The road west had been rising steadily as it
left Leesburg and approached the eastern side of the Blue
Ridge, and even with periods when he couldn't see her, he
knew they hadn't yet reached the state of West Virginia. That
idiot girl at that garage had said Garrison Cap in West Virginia. A search of the index on his West Virginia map had
produced a Garrison Gap, not Cap. Based on the map, he es-
timated that they had another half hour or so to go to the
state line between Virginia and West Virginia, depending on
which way she went once reaching the Shenandoah Valley.
Fortunately, the American maps were excellent, and he
could stay well behind her, even lose her, as long as she went
to that town. Then he would simply search parking lots for
that unusual car.

His plan was to track her to Garrison Gap and then finish
this annoying business. And he must finish it soon, because
he had more pressing priorities looming on the horizon: re-
inforcing the second-story floor to receive the marble deliveries, refining and practicing the escape routes, verifying the
geographical coordinates, practicing the changes to his appearance, and dealing with the neighbor. Assuming he could
squash this woman tonight, he could be back in the city by
Sunday afternoon. That would give him four days to complete his preparations.

A large hawk slid by the Suburban's side windows, slant-

ing down a thermal as it disappeared into a meadow below
his line of sight. He could see the occasional roofline among
the trees ascending the slope, evidence that others had figured out what a stupendous view was to be had up here.
Across the highway was Mount Weather, according to the
map. This was where the supposedly secret government
bunkers for nuclear war were located. Well, war was coming, but it wasn't going to be nuclear. And it was not going to
drop out of the earth's atmosphere at nine times the speed of
sound. No. This war would come into the city in one of those
boxy brown trucks one saw everywhere, followed by some
very special delivery.

A flash of red down on the highway brought him back to
the task at hand. He put the Suburban in gear and started
down the firebreak road as her car disappeared down the
mountain. So now she probably had a gun. So what?

What Connie had sitting on the seat beside her was a World
War II flare pistol. Made of steel, with rubber grips, it was a
twelve-gauge gun. It broke down just like a shotgun did, allowing one flare round at a time. It was large and bulky but
had only an eight-inch barrel. "Hold it out beyond your
knees," the gunsmith had warned her. "Bend your elbows a
little to absorb the kick, grip it tight, and pull the trigger
hard. Nothing sophisticated about this gun. No careful
squeezing of the trigger, establishing a sight line, none of
that, because this was never meant as a weapon in the first
place." He'd given her a box of handmade cut-down shells
with game load, since the old flare gun's chamber could not
accept a standard shotgun shell of 2.75 inches or longer.
"You'll get one shot," the guy had said, "and you'll want
maximum coverage. The locals use these things as snake
guns. Point it in the general direction of the rattle and fire.
You'll carve out a red wedge of dirt about six feet long, assuming you don't shoot your own feet off. Dispersion is im-

mediate. There's no safety, and the noise is truly impressive, especially from the front. Aim at the dirt and never at a rock. And if it's a bad guy, aim at his teeth."

She'd had no permit for her derringer at the time of the incident, so unless Jake Cullen worked something out, she didn't expect to get it back. If they tried to hassle her about it, she'd tell them who had gotten it for her, which should stifle any further movement down that line of inquiry. But this thing was just what she wanted. She only wished that they made double-barrel ones, but the gunsmith was right—pop a cap in this beauty and entire windows would blow out. The gunsmith had also sold her a box of signal flares in case she got caught with it. It wouldn't fool any of the county law, but it might serve as an excuse in the city. "Tell 'em it's for your boat," he'd told her.

Either way, she felt better having it on the seat beside her. Not that she expected trouble up here in the hills. She'd checked her rearview mirror several times once she cleared out of the traffic of Washington, but no one seemed to be following her. She let the Shelby out a little as she rolled down the big hill where Route 7 lined up to cross the Shenandoah River. She hit ninety before she reined it back in, remembering that the state cops liked to set up shop right at the base of the bridge to catch city people coasting down the mountain at high speed. She pushed the big flare gun down into the crack between the front seats, dropped a jacket over it, and crossed the river. Sure enough, there was a state trooper's cruiser parked nose-out on the access ramp on this side of the river. She waved as she went by, and the cop actually waved back. From there, it was not quite an hour up to Garrison Gap and the lodge. She already felt better.

At noon, Swamp was helping Ben Hardee replace a cracked window in the front parlor of the Jackson Inn, when Lila appeared with the portable phone. "Busy day," she said, handing Swamp the phone.

"Morgan," Swamp said, clearing his throat.

"Jake Cullen. We have developments."

"Developments. Oh, goodie." Ben, sensing business, put down his tools and left to give Swamp some privacy.

"First, Ms. Wall ditched our cops this morning at a classic-car shop and has blown town. Any ideas?"

"She in the Shelby?"

"Yeah, so I think we can find her. The shop people said Annapolis."

"I'd bet the other way—out here in West Virginia maybe."

"There's more," Cullen said. "The shop people said there was this foreign—possibly German—dude in the shop the day before, asking about the Shelby."

"Really. And?"

"Big-haired missy there says she just might have mentioned that the Shelby was going to be retrieved at nine this morning. Now tell me something: You sure your guys aren't tailing our nurse friend even as we speak?"

"Come again? No. What gives?"

"We sent out a BOLO to the Virginia and Maryland State cops. Got a hit an hour ago, from a radar trap set up where Route Seven crosses the Shenandoah River. Red Shelby GT crossed the bridge at eleven-oh-five, westbound. Single occupant, white female. Who waved at the trooper, by the way."

"Sounds like Wall. He wave back?"

"Didn't say. But here's the interesting bit. Two minutes behind her comes this black Suburban with an emergency light rack, tinted windows, DC plates, a coupla whip antennas. State guys are asking why we have a do-not-apprehend BOLO on a vehicle that the feds are already tailing."

"Not this fed," Swamp said, wondering what might be going on. "You want me to make some calls, see what I can find out?"

"I'd appreciate it. I know it's Saturday and all, but we've

got a dead cop. Guys are all still here, leaning forward. Some of 'em aren't on safe."

"I'll give it a shot, Jake. I'll get back to you."

"You think it could be Secret Service? You know, black Suburban, tinted windows, whips, lights. That sounds like Secret Service wheels."

"Hell, I guess it could be, but they're the ones who turned me off. I even have a p memo from the PRU director. Message: It's a firefly. Drop it and then go back to your sandbox."

"Okay. It's just—"

"Yeah, I know. Right hand, left hand. Wouldn't be the first time. Let me pull some strings."

"Appreciate it, Special Agent."

"Swamp. Call me Swamp. I'm definitely not special anymore."

Swamp took the portable phone back to the kitchen area, where he replaced it on the base station.

"Such a gloomy face," Lila said. "It's the weekend. Time for some fun in the sun. Wild and wonderful West Virginia and all that."

"Washington's calling," he muttered, looking in the refrigerator.

"Tell them to go away. Or better yet, let me talk to them. I'll tell them a thing or two."

"That's what worries me," he said. There was nothing that looked like lunch.

"Then just go outside. It's a beautiful day."

"Where?" he said, pointing with his chin to the window. The sun had been out before, but now sodden gray clouds were blowing in from the west and beginning to obscure the end of South Mountain over on the Maryland side. It looked like snow to him.

"Here now, you quit pawing through the commissary," she said as Ben joined them in the kitchen. "That food is all .

for dinner patrons tonight. I'll make you a fried-egg sandwich if you're hungry. You go on. I'll bring it upstairs."

Swamp shut the refrigerator door and headed for the
stairs. Lila's brother, Ben, was about six inches shorter and
ten years older than his sister, with graying hair, a mustache, and an expression of eternal patience on his face. He
had tried his hand at running two restaurants and a motel in
his time, but had never been able to earn enough money to
make both a living and the mortgage payments, much less
take on a wife. The Jackson Inn situation was perfect for
him. All he had to do was be the innkeeper, at which he was
entirely satisfactory. Lila acted as hostess, chef for the two
nights they offered dinner, and provided the necessary female ambience to make the inn more than just another ho-
tel/motel. They lived together in their parents' house next
door. It might have seemed strange to outsiders, but in
Harpers Ferry, people either escaped at an early age or never
left at all.

He climbed the stairs back up to his rooms, passing some
tourists in the lobby who were looking through the inn's
brochure. He wondered if he shouldn't go back to town, but
then he reminded himself that it was the weekend. Anyone
he might contact would be home for the weekend. With their
families. Which was why they still *had* families, because
they managed to let go of business for two days out of every
seven on a regular basis, unlike him.

Still. What Jake had described sure as hell did sound like
a Secret Service vehicle. He had his duty-officer roster in the
briefcase upstairs. Then he wondered if he ought not call
Lucy VanMetre to make sure that Hallory hadn't put something in motion after all.

Connie parked the Shelby on the road side of the Garrison
Lodge's circular check-in lane and got out. The air up here
was frosty, courtesy of a foot of snow that blanketed the

lodge grounds and surrounding landscape. The twin lumps of Barrows Mountain and Cobb's Hump were also snow-covered, with only the vertical rock faces that created the actual Gap clear of snow and ice. The sky was overcast, with a low scud drifting uncertainly through the nearby mountains. To the north and west, a darkening sky over the distant Alleghenies promised more snow. She was glad she'd brought her cold-weather gear, but she hurried into the lobby nonetheless.

The rooms here were clean and well appointed, just as she remembered them. She had stayed at many of the state's resort spots in her years of coming up here, and this one was one of the best. She took a shower, put on her swimsuit, piled into the oversized terry-cloth bathrobe hanging in the bathroom, and went down to the spa. The Garrison Lodge did not have a ski facility; instead, it offered a faux hot-springs spa, to which many of the neighboring ski resorts sent their rattle-boned, tendon-challenged guests at the end of the day, which meant that this lodge enjoyed the bounty of the ski crowd without the hassle of maintaining, operating, and insuring a ski resort. She'd once asked if they sold stock in the place.

Her plan for the rest of the day was uncomplicated: go get a sandwich in the grotto bar next to the spa, enjoy a soak in the warm-spring pools, get a massage, have a nap, dinner, and maybe, if she felt like it, and only if she felt like it, put on some war paint and a little black dress, and go check out the lounge lizards. She'd reserve a snowmobile for tomorrow and get the kitchen staff to make her a bag lunch. Take that and her camera gear up to the higher elevations behind the town, 3,800 feet above sea level and almost a thousand feet above the town itself. Put the clinic mess out of sight and out of mind.

She reminded herself to retrieve the snake gun before she went back to her room. But then she realized she couldn't go out in the snow-covered parking lot in her bathrobe and slippers. She'd have to go back up there and get dressed first. Screw it, she thought. I'll get it when I go up to bed for the night.

It took Heismann all of ten minutes to find the Shelby, which was parked in the rear lot of the Garrison Lodge. He'd tried two ski resorts first, then remembered that he'd seen no ski paraphernalia in her house. He'd stopped in a gas station, asked which was the biggest non-ski hotel in town, and found the car immediately.

He never slowed down when he spotted the car, driving instead in a lazy loop around the lodge parking lots and then back out the main entrance. He turned left and headed back the way he had come, aiming for that cheap-looking motel he'd seen on the outskirts of Garrison Gap. He'd get a room there and then rest. In the late afternoon, he would make the requisite changes, then go to dinner at the Garrison Lodge. After that, he'd just need to find her room number. Or perhaps stage a diversion with that antique automobile; get her to come out into the parking lot. There were many ways to do it. It was simply a matter of picking the right one. And since tonight he would be a woman, he figured he should be able to move with impunity. He'd make it a test of his ability to change shape. Perhaps get right in front of his target. Remembering that savage kick to his genitals, he was looking forward to this.

Swamp struck out all across town with calls to various duty officers at Justice, the counterterrorism task force, the Bureau, the Agency, and the Secret Service. He'd had to make three calls to penetrate to the FBI duty officer, whose gatekeepers didn't believe Swamp was who he said he was, even after the OSI duty officer interceded. But no one owned up to having any sort of surveillance on a Ms. Connie Wall. He called Cullen back at 5:30 P.M., almost hoping the detective would have gone home. But he had not.

"Nada," he said. "Or at least nobody on my end is fessing up to tailing the Shelby or the pretty nurse."

"Then who the hell *is* following her in a black Suburban with red emergency lights?"

"Maybe nobody?" Swamp said. "Maybe total coincidence. I mean, it wasn't like he was actually on her tail. It was—what, five, ten minutes later that this guy came down the hill?"

"Two or so, according to the cop," Cullen said. "But that's probably a guesstimate."

"Did they get a plate number on the Suburban?"

"Shit no. He just said it looked like a D.C. plate. Actually, he said he *thought* it was a D.C. plate. That's what the report actually says."

"Well, there you are," Swamp said. "Now, it's possible someone's shining me on here, but I can't figure out why. There's one woman I need to reach. She's the deputy at the Secret Service Protective Research Unit. But she's in New York, apparently, at some weekend conference about vetting the UN people for the inauguration."

"Why her, if the duty office said no?"

Swamp hesitated. "Well, let's just say she might know shit the duty officer doesn't. I admit, she's probably a dry hole."

"She wouldn't thank you for that label," Cullen said.

Swamp laughed. "You'd need to meet her, then decide. So, you guys locate Ms. Wall?"

"Yeah. She's at the Garrison Lodge in Garrison Gap, West Virginia. Staties found the car in the parking lot. Verified she checked in there."

"Okay, so she's taking the weekend off. Going into the hills for what West Virginia does best—some gorgeous scenery, reasonable prices, and a chance to read one of our four-page phone books."

Cullen started laughing.

"You working tomorrow?" Swamp asked.

"I don't know about work," Cullen said with a sigh. "But I'll be here. We got all these guys tearing up the weeds for the cutter who did Ballard. And we don't even know what his ass looks like. Except maybe he's a German. Maybe real old, or real good at disguises. Carries a liquid Taser, so we're rousting every source of Tasers on the planet. He talked to the big-hair type at Steve's Vintage Motors, so we're canvassing the whole neighborhood around his place. Shit like that."

"Gotcha," Swamp said. "Motion, if not movement. Hey, I know it's late, but did anybody talk to that Chevy dealership across the street from the garage? If by some chance this Suburban is our guy, maybe he bought the damn thing right across the street."

"A foreigner?"

"If he's got cash money and a valid passport, a car dealer'd sell him his mother."

"Son of a bitch."

"Well."

"It's getting late. They may be closed. But I'll send some of these guys out. Get 'em out of my hair so I can get some chow anyway."

"You know where to reach me," Swamp said.

Heismann stepped back from the full-length mirror on the back of the bathroom door to admire his handiwork. Looking back at him, wearing a simple lace-bodiced knee-length black dress, stood a slim Hispanic-looking woman. The transformation had taken a full two hours. He'd begun by reshaving his head and then pasting on the hairpiece pad, to which he pinned a shiny jet black Liza Minelli shag-style hairpiece. Then the eyebrows, colored to match the wig. A small flesh-colored rubber prosthesis, stuck like a suction cup along the bridge of his nose and smoothed in with makeup base, relieved the pronounced hook shape of his new nose. A very careful and detailed shave of his face, visible sideburns, and neck to achieve an expanse of smooth, lightly olive-stained skin, followed by foundation for the coming makeup. Then he had shaved his chest, arms, armpits, and legs all the way to his groin, which always took a surprisingly long time.

The breasts had also taken longer than he'd anticipated. He first had to sterilize the pump tubing and his nipples, massage the loose folds of skin to shape them properly, and then pump each one up with saline solution through the stoma in the nipples to achieve the desired shape and size. His nipples stung after he was done, and he wondered if he'd done the sterilization procedure correctly or if it was just the saline solution. But the surgeons had performed their work beautifully: The breasts were just what he wanted—round, saucerlike, and balanced in size and shape, the nipples perhaps being a bit too large in proportion to the rest. But they were real enough: Any man seeing his naked torso would know he was looking at a woman. He finished shaping his upper half with a lightweight nylon bustier for support instead of a bra. It also helped to narrow him at the waist. He had a slim athletic build anyway, with almost no abdominal fat, so he needed the bustier to create the illusion of female hips. It also had a special compartment down against the small of his back to accommodate the flat five-inch-long Smith & Wesson stainless-steel throwing knife.

He'd spent some time over the past few months visiting Washington's surprisingly extensive transvestite shopping scene, where friendly large black ladies had taken him through all the paraphernalia available for whatever illusion he wanted to achieve. He had thought about telling them it was all for some play or act, then realized they'd heard every such lie under the sun and assumed he was just one of "the girls," as they put it, so he'd simply gone along. It was all amazingly private and discreet, requiring only lots of money to get everything he needed with absolutely no questions asked. The tight spandex bikini underwear effectively rerouted his genitals up into a surgically expanded groin pouch, so that even a suspicious grope between the legs would find correct "female" anatomy. He wished he'd had them on the night that woman kicked him. He wore a pair of black nylon briefs over the spandex; they were lightly augmented with padding across the buttocks to make up for his own relatively flat posterior.

Panty hose, simple black patent-leather pumps cleverly designed for a male foot, a half hour's worth of final makeup work, a touch of perfume, and the effect was complete. He'd practiced elements of this transformation many times once the breast work had been completed, and he'd even indulged in walking lessons at an acting studio that specialized in teaching men how to move like a woman. Standing in the motel room, he felt faintly ridiculous. If his old Stasi comrades could see him now! He had to admit that there was something mildly erotic about it, this wearing of women's clothing. But the truth was, he felt hot with his body encased in all this nylon and spandex. He shook his head. The things a woman had to put up with to attract a man. Amazing.

He looked at his watch. Almost 9:00 P.M. He'd called the Garrison Lodge and asked about the lounge. They'd told him the bar scene got going after nine. His plan was to go there, scout the lobby and the registration desk, check out the lounge, have a drink, and then find some way to get her room number. If he was lucky, she might even show up in the lounge herself. If so, he would do it directly—follow her to the ladies' room, slice her spinal cord, and stuff her body into a toilet stall.

He peered out through the curtain and saw light snow blowing across the parking lot. Not enough to coat the cars and trucks yet, but given time, it might. He made sure the bean-shaped Coach handbag he was going to carry had the hooded lightweight nylon tracksuit rolled into it, along with some trainers. He'd taken down the emergency light rack from the luggage rack on the hood of the Suburban and put it in the back, along with the two whip antennas. Now it would be just another dark-colored SUV among dozens of others in the lodge's parking lot.

He tugged at the hem of the dress and smoothed down the fabric around his hips and across his bust. So strange, having a real bust. He'd never been a breast man, really, but even so, it was interesting to touch them. To touch himself. What would it feel like to press these beauties up against another man and feel *his* reaction? He felt himself flushing red. If he kept this up, he'd soon be—what did the British call them? Nancy boys. That was it. Then he grinned a very unfeminine grin. Wait till these *Ammies* see what this nancy boy is going to do to them. Soon. Very soon. But he was going to have to rethink his movements right after the attack. This had taken much too long.

So he needed to get going. Time to take his lovely breasts out for a trial run. He patted the cold steel lump in the small of his back with his fingertips and felt the flattened eight-centimeter arrow-shaped blade. First-class, probably German, surgical steel for the surgical nurse. She'd appreciate the compliment, but not for long.

Swamp was finishing dinner at his usual corner table when Lila brought him the portable phone again. It was Cullen.

"No joy on the dealership angle," he reported. "Place closed at five, won't be open again until Monday."

"Can't you locate the owner? Get him down there?"

"Yeah, we could, but my boss says that this line of inquiry is pretty improbable. I mean, that this guy could go in and buy an expensive vehicle just like that. He'd need all sorts of ID, and it would mean letting people get a look at him, something he's avoided pretty well so far. And the boss also said what you said—that the Suburban might just have been on the road, nothing to do with Ms. Wall. Two minutes behind at sixty-five—that's about two miles. Pretty loose tail."

"He's probably right," Swamp said. "We're snatching at straws here. But I'm a little concerned that Ms. Wall is all by herself out in Garrison Gap."

"No way *he* could know that."

Swamp thought about that. "You got a name and home number for the girl at the classic-car place?"

Cullen told him to hold on while he found his notebook. Then he came back and gave Swamp the name and number. "You gonna call her?"

"Yeah, I think I will. Assuming she's home on a Saturday night. Maybe walk her back through what she told the German guy."

"She said it was all about that car."

"Let me drop the entire weight and majesty of the United States Secret Service on her, see if she may have revealed anything else. If by some chance she told Herman the German *where* Wall was going, he wouldn't have to tail her. He'd just have to go there. And probably not in some conspicuous Suburban."

"And find her how?"

"Same way you guys did—find that muscle car."

It was Cullen's turn to be silent for a moment. "Okay, fine, what the hell. You get a hit, call me back?"

"Absolutely."

Swamp looked at his watch. It was 9:15. He finished his glass of wine, glanced around at the other people dining at the inn that night. The standard mix of weekend couples, thinned out a little by the snow. No one seemed to be interested in what he was doing at his corner table. He called the girl's number.

A young man answered, his voice loud in order to make himself heard over the noise of a party going on in the background. Swamp asked for Dorie. The man told him to hold on, and then Dorie got on the phone. She sounded as if she was out of breath. From dancing, Swamp hoped. He identified himself. She said she couldn't hear him, told him to hold on. There was some banging around of telephones, and then she came back on in a much quieter setting.

"Who is this is, again?" she asked. He could hear her drinking something. The party sounds remained at full blast in the background.

"This is Special Agent Lee Morgan, United States Secret Service," he announced in his best federal voice. "Detective Cullen of the District police gave me your name and number. I need to ask you some questions about the foreigner who came into your shop asking about Connie Wall's Shelby."

"Oh, that," she said, finally getting her breath back under control. "I told the detective. Like you said, some foreign dude. Wanted to buy the Shelby, wanted—"

"Dorie? We know that part. Here's the thing. We think that guy was BS'ing you. About the car, I mean. We think he's after Connie." Connie, our mutual good friend, he thought.

"But why? I mean, he didn't even know her."

"Remember that cop getting killed out in Cleveland Park Tuesday?"

"Uh, yeah, I guess."

"Well, that happened at Ms. Wall's house, Dorie. That cop was a friend of hers. A close friend."

"Oh shit," she said in a small voice.

"And the guy you talked to? We think he might be the killer. So it's very important you think back. Did you by any chance tell him she was going to Garrison Gap this weekend?"

There was a long silence on the phone.

"Dorie, you still there?"

"You said you were what? Secret Service?"

"That's right, Dorie. We're working with the District police to find this guy."

"Well, like, I mean, how do I know you're not him? The foreign guy?"

"You don't, but listen to my voice. It's not the same, is it? Didn't he have an accent?"

"Sorta."

"This is very important, Dorie. Very important. Did you mention anything about Garrison Gap?"

Another moment's pause. "Um. I might have. I mean, I thought she said Garrison *Cap*. Like, she'd mentioned the Garrison Cap Lodge, you know? I told him she did wildlife photography. But, man, I had no idea . . ."

"There was no way you could know any of this," Swamp said soothingly. "But that's what I needed. Here's Detective Cullen's phone number. Please call him, tell him what you told me. Ask him to call me back when you're done, okay?"

"Am I in trouble here?" she asked.

Cullen was back to him in five minutes.

"Now what the hell do we do? That guy could be out there in Garrison whatever. And we still don't even know what he looks like! Other than he's maybe in a Suburban."

"I say forget the Suburban—that's a red herring. First, call that lodge. Get word to Ms. Wall that this guy may have followed her out there. Then contact local law, see if they can put somebody on her until I get there."

"*You*?"

"You wanna do it? I'm an hour from Garrison Gap. Hour and a half, if this snow keeps up."

"Shit, I don't even know where West Virginia is. You got four-wheel drive?"

Swamp laughed. "Better. I've got the original SUV—an old Land Rover. Before they Yuppied them up. I'll go up, get her out of there. I can put her up here at the inn in Harpers Ferry."

"Then what?"

"One thing at a time, Jake. The game now is to keep her alive."

Cullen agreed and hung up. Swamp went into the kitchen

and asked Lila to make him up a thermos of coffee. Outside, the wind picked up, as if to let him know it was waiting.

Connie chose a table for two down near the fireplace end of the lounge, away from the main bar. It was snowing in earnest outside, which appeared to have cut down on the size of the after-hours crowd. Or, more likely, it was simply too early.

She'd checked on the Shelby from a corridor window and found that it was slowly morphing into a red-and-white lump in the parking lot. Where the Shelby was concerned, though, anonymity was a useful condition. She thought about going out to get the snake gun, but her shoes weren't exactly Bean boots. She could hear Cat telling her the whole reason Annie got her gun was because someone was trying to gun Annie. Well, maybe. But there was no way she was going to walk out there in three inches of snow right now and then live with wet shoes and stockings all evening. Maybe later. Maybe never.

A bar waitress brought her a glass of white wine and started a tab without asking. Figures, Connie thought. Lady in her little black dress all alone in the lounge, she's going to stay for a little while at least. Although, now that she was here, she was beginning to regret coming down. It all seemed so pointless. She missed Cat and felt increasingly bad about what had happened to him. Maybe just have one drink and then pretend that she had something better to do up in her room.

The lounge area was shaped like a large U, with windows along the two sides overlooking the lighted grounds and adjoining tree-covered slopes. The bottom of the U contained the main bar, and the open end featured an enormous stone fireplace, right in front of a long dance floor. There were about fifty tables throughout the lounge, arranged in two rows, with the window row being two steps up from the inner, dance-floor row. The walls were paneled in different kinds of wood veneer, each highlighting pictures of an alpine scene framed in the individual panels. Connie found it refreshingly peaceful, and she eased her shoes off to catch some of the warmth coming from the fireplace.

Over the next half hour, she watched the place slowly fill up, mostly couples or foursomes, with only the very occasional single male easing his way to the bar, getting his drink, lighting up a cigarette or cigar, and then turning in the swiveling bar chair to scan the room. She was careful to return no appraising looks from across the room, because all of the men so far looked like professional lounge lizards. A couple of the more presentable men had given her the once-over, unfortunately while looking over the shoulders of their dates. When she realized that she was the only female sitting alone in the entire lounge, she decided she should cash out and leave. Just then, a striking Hispanic-looking woman in a black dress almost identical to her own came in and sat down at a deuce about midway up the dance floor, on the other side of the room. She ordered a drink and then looked around, saw Connie, gave a small smile, and then looked away. Okay, so what was that? Connie wondered. A sign of recognition from another lonely hunter, or a tentative hit from the Sapphic sisterhood?

Connie stood up and started walking toward the bar, but then the Hispanic woman motioned to the empty chair at her table. Connie hesitated. She didn't know this woman, and she sure as hell wasn't here to meet other women. But it was a gracious gesture, and to ignore it would be rude. So she changed course and went over.

"Hi. I'm Carla," the woman said. "You do not have to join me if you do not want to."

Connie smiled and hoped her discomfort wasn't too obvious. "I'm Connie. Thanks for the offer. I just came down for a drink."

"So? You are not here for sport? There are so many beautiful men in this place."

"There are?" Connie said, looking to see what had changed. "Where, exactly?" Then she saw that the other woman was kidding her. "Oh, yeah. Right. Beautiful men. Not."

Carla laughed—a throaty sound. She was porcelain-pretty, and Connie, the surgical nurse, suddenly wondered if Carla had had work. If so, they'd screwed up on her lumpy nose. Her dramatic front, on the other hand, was another story, because only made-to-order movie stars were that perfect. From across the room, she'd looked to be in her twenties, but now, up close, definitely thirties. Maybe cosmetically thirties, but actually older than that. Intense dark eyes. And makeup—lots of makeup.

Carla reached into her large bean-shaped purse for some cigarettes. "Do you mind?"

Connie didn't. Cat had been a smoker, and so had she, a long time ago, until she'd seen one too many blackened, cancer-ridden lungs flopped out into bloody stainless-steel bowls in the OR. "Feel free," she said. "It's a bar."

"Yes, it is," Carla said. "In America, smoking is almost everywhere a crime, yes?"

"Almost," Connie said as Carla blew a blue stream skyward. Definitely work, Connie thought, seeing the tiny scars under Carla's chin. But not at our clinic. Whoever'd done this had made her look almost mannish. "I used to smoke," she said. "But I quit. Where are you from, Carla?"

"Germany, actually," Carla said. "I work for a German business in Washington, D.C."

"Really," Connie said. "I would have made you out to be Hispanic, not German."

"Only in the movies are all Germans fair-haired and blue-eyed," Carla said with a laugh. "Especially German women. I am a Berliner."

I'll bet you are, Connie thought, remembering some posters she'd seen once at a photography exhibition—depictions of the ladies of the Berlin cabaret scene. Carla baby here would have fit right in, with that slicked-down skullcap hairdo and the plaster-and-lathe makeup. She could imagine Carla in an SS uniform, with some wicked spike-heeled boots. "That's fascinating. What do you think of the States?"

The waitress swept by and shot Connie an inquiring look, but she shook her head and passed her the tab and a twenty. "It is so-o interesting," Carla began, scanning the room while she talked. The waitress came back with Connie's change. Connie passed her a fiver and gathered her things. "It's been a long day," she said, getting up. To her surprise, Carla reached out to take her hand. Stronger grip than Connie would have expected. "Ladies'?" she inquired. "Do you know where?"

Connie flipped her head in a "Come with me" gesture. "I'll show you."

Swamp crunched down the country road at a steady thirty miles an hour, the Land Rover's four-wheel drive handling the snow with ease. Fortunately, it hadn't sleeted first, so it was all just snow. The boxy vehicle's air conditioner wasn't anything to write home about, but the heater worked fine, and he had taken off his coat. His cell phone screen was reporting that he was definitely on his own for the moment, so he'd had no word from Cullen as to whether or not they'd found Connie Wall and had her covered. He'd passed only one other vehicle west of Interstate 81. The road was typical of the hill country, one switchback after another and a steady climb. Coming back down would be more interesting. The deer were all bedded down out in the woods, and he'd seen only one coyote in his headlights in the past hour.

If Cullen had managed to get through, he should be able to go directly to the local sheriff's office in Garrison Gap and find out where she was. Probably at her room in the lodge. He knew the lodge, having stayed there himself on one of his occasional weekend trips. He wasn't a skier, but sometimes he'd get in the Rover and head west, if only to escape Harpers Ferry. Much like Connie Wall, he thought. Sometimes it was necessary to hit the road, just to make sure you still could. He looked at his watch. This was going to take longer than he'd thought, and that was beginning to bother him.

Headlights flared in his mirrors from a mile back, then were blocked out by a curve. Then back again, much closer. Brights, too. He flipped his rearview mirror down to negate the sudden glare, and then whoever it was came right up behind him and flashed his brights! What did this idiot expect him to do—go faster? Drive off the road into a snowbank? The lights flicked again, but Swamp couldn't see what was back there because Shit for Brains left them on high beam. He began to slow, his standard cure for tailgaters. The car closed in close enough that Swamp could finally see that it was some kind of sports car, with a low humped shape and round lights. Two silhouettes in it.

He slowed some more, and this time he got a double beep from the guy's horn. Horn works. Try your brakes, asshole. He grinned. Good. Pretty soon the guy would become extremely impatient and come roaring around him. He slowed some more and saw brake lights flaring behind him, and then the car finally dropped back. For the next five minutes, Swamp resumed what he considered safe road speed in the blowing snow but as he came around another curve, he saw the beam of the headlights swing out into the other lane. There was a fairly straight section ahead, maybe two hundred yards long, so Swamp put on the brakes. The sports car obligingly came zooming around him in a whine of accelerating machinery. A Porsche, from the looks of it, although Swamp wasn't up on model numbers. He caught a brief glimpse of a mop of platinum blond hair in the passenger seat and then, as the little car fishtailed ahead, one gloved hand flipping him the bird out the open window on the driver's side. Then it was gone around the next curve.

He wondered if Connie Wall would agree to return to

Harpers Ferry with him. She might not, and he had no legal
authority to make her leave the lodge. He checked the cell
phone again. One bar of signal. Getting closer to something,
he thought. Then the single bar disappeared and he dropped
the phone back into its hook in the center console. Swamp
realized he was going too fast, so he let the big beast slow
down as he went into a deep turn over a stone bridge. The
creek below appeared as a black crack between fluffy snow-
banks on either side. A pair of gleaming eyes flashed briefly
from the woods as he steered left and up the next climb. He
dropped the Rover into second, realizing there might be
some ice out here, and was rewarded with a minor skid and
then renewed traction. He climbed the next hill and then
eased through a steep cut, passing several car-size boulders
down along the side of the road, one of which was lying on
top of the FALLING ROCKS sign. Got that right, he thought as
he let the Rover coast down the hill in second. It made for a
noisy ride, but he had seen the ice this time. At the bottom of
the half-mile-long hill, the road bent to the right, and he almost missed the two tire tracks leading straight off the road
on the left side and disappearing into a stand of tall spruce.
He sighed, dropped into first, and then stopped in the middle
of the road.

He reached for his coat, hat, and gloves, then retrieved
the yellow emergency beacon he carried in a box in the rear
seat. He had a blue one back there, too, but this was Good
Samaritan business, not police business. Not yet anyway.

He was really going to be delayed now. He put the yellow
beacon up on the roof of the Rover and went down into the
snow.

Connie led Carla into the ladies' room, which was down a
short hall from the entrance lobby to the lounge itself. There
was an outer and an inner door, and when Connie, going
first, entered the bathroom, she saw a lone woman at the
sinks. The woman, who was in her forties and definitely not

made for little black dresses anymore, if ever, turned to look at the two of them as they came in. She turned off the faucet, grabbed a handful of paper towels, and then openly stared at Carla as Connie headed for a stall.

"What the hell are you?" she said in a surprisingly authoritative voice.

"I beg your pardon?" Carla said, walking toward the sinks. Connie, about to shut the stall door, looked over her shoulder to see what was the matter.

"I said, *What* the hell are you? You sure as hell don't belong in the ladies' room, do you?"

Connie watched Carla stop right in front of the woman, do a little hop in place, and then, to Connie's total astonishment, kick the woman in the crotch hard enough to double her over. She hit the floor with a tremendous gasp, and then Carla was turning toward Connie, her dark eyes burning with intensity, something glinting in her hand. Connie reflexively raised her hand, but Carla grabbed it with surprising strength and spun her around in the doorway to the stall. Connie was too surprised to fight back, even as Carla put a knee in her back and pushed her face-first into the stall, cracking her head on the partially opened door. Before she could regain her balance, Connie felt a lance of white-hot pain in her back, pain so great, she would have collapsed to the floor, except for the fact that Carla was still holding her arm. It was bent painfully up behind her back, so she couldn't fall, even though her trembling legs were already giving way.

"I am sorry for this," Carla whispered. "But I will need your house."

Then there was a crash and a scream for help as the chunky woman appeared behind Carla and hit her with something. Connie couldn't see what it was, and she didn't care now that that iron grip on her arm had been released and she was free to sag down onto her knees, which landed in blood—lots of blood, running down the backs of her thighs, making the floor slippery. She grabbed for the toilet bowl, swaying sideways and bumping her head again, this time on the side of the stall, barely conscious of the noisy struggle behind her in the bathroom. She finally collapsed to one side of the bowl in time to see Carla jab the other woman's Adam's apple with the rigid fingers of her left hand while she was attempting to beat on Carla with the metal top of the bathroom trash can. The woman made a gargling noise, dropped the square metal top onto the floor with a tremendous clatter, and clutched at her throat. Carla stepped back and drove a stainless-steel knife shaped like a flattened rocket into the woman's midsection three times in rapid, grunting succession. The woman whoofed out a large breath and sat down heavily on the floor, one hand still clutching her throat, the other her midsection, her eyes crossing as blood fountained out of her mouth and cascaded over the front of her dress. By then, Connie's own vision was starting to blur from her vantage point down on the floor. She was still clutching the toilet bowl like some hungover college student, her lower back ablaze with pain. She thought she heard voices from outside the bathroom doors. Carla appeared in the doorway to the stall for an instant and stared down at her with her flashing, almost black eyes, and then she was gone. Connie tried to make a sound as a red haze began to envelop the edges of her vision.

Those eyes . . . Jesus Christ! Was Carla a man? Oh my God! Was it *him*?

Then she heard a blur of excited voices, but they were slowly swallowed up by a humming noise that filled her head, then all her senses, and then the whole world darkened mercifully.

By the time Swamp arrived in Garrison Gap and found the Crass County Sheriff's Office, pandemonium reigned inside. Deputies were sprinting past him for their cars out front, and two dispatchers were yelling at each other and into their ra-

dios, calling for backup, ambulances, and EMTs to respond
to a double homicide at the Garrison Lodge. He stood to one
side as everyone in the central operations room scrambled to
deal with the emergency. Two homicides, he thought. Even
for a West Virginia mountain town on a Saturday night, that
was a bit unusual, especially this early in the evening. That
level of cutting and gutting usually didn't start until well after midnight. Finally, a short, balding deputy who'd been
talking urgently to someone on the phone for the past five
minutes looked across the room and saw Swamp.

"You the Secret Service guy?" he called across the room,
his words turning some heads.

Swamp nodded, and the deputy held up the phone, obviously wanting Swamp to take it. Swamp crossed the room
and found Jake Cullen on the other end. "Where you been,
pardner?" Cullen asked.

"Making a nice mountain drive through the snow. And
rescuing two idiot Yuppies from themselves about seven
miles out of town. Their Porsche, contrary to popular opinion and all the ads, cannot, in fact, fly. But why—"

"You don't know?"

A cold feeling spread into Swamp's stomach. "I know
they're going nuts up here in the sheriff's office. What's happened?"

"Bastard got to her, that's what's happened. In that lodge.
Attacked her in the ladies' room, stabbed her in the back,
killed another woman who was in there."

"Judas *Priest*! When did all this happen?"

"Apparently, thirty minutes ago. I'd been talking to the
cops up there, trying to see if they'd found her yet, but they
hadn't. There'd been this three-car collision in front of one
of the ski resorts, so they had everybody out working that.
Next thing they know, Garrison Lodge security is calling in
two homicides."

"She's *dead*?"

"Well, they're not sure about Ms. Wall. First reports said two, but then the EMTs got into it and took one to the hospital. The description of the dead woman is of someone older and heavier than Connie—Ms. Wall."

"Goddamn it! Any description on the killer?"

"Nope. They're still all going bananas up there, from what I'm hearing. One story was that a woman did it. But since you're on the scene . . ."

"Yeah, okay, I'll work it. Anybody official here know why I'm here, or what this is all about?"

"Yes. I spoke to the sheriff himself. That was just before all this shit went down. His people may or may not know anything."

"Okay, I got it," Swamp said. "I'll get back to you as soon as I have something."

Swamp handed the phone back to the deputy, who listened for a moment, but Cullen was already gone. He peered up at Swamp, taking in the Stetson and Swamp's green Air Force winter jacket with the leather name tag on the left side. Trying not to stare at Swamp's face, he asked, "Got some ID?"

Swamp fished out his OSI credentials and told the deputy about the two squirrels in their Porsche. The deputy told one of the dispatchers, who rolled his eyes. Then Swamp asked where the sheriff might be.

"Sheriff McComb's at the scene, last I heard. That's the Garrison Lodge. Go right out of our lot, down the main drag, three blocks. Look for lots of blue lights."

"Okay, and where's the hospital?"

"Other way, six blocks. Go right at the Burger King, big ugly building up the hill."

"I assume you have people at the hospital. Can you contact them and tell them I'm coming over there? And if the sheriff can meet me somewhere, maybe there? I'll give him the background on this mess."

"Y'all know what's behind this?"

"Theories, Deputy, theories is what we've got at this stage. And at least one of them went wrong tonight."

As he drove over to the hospital, he wondered how he was going to explain all this to his boss. Had their German found himself some hired help? Or were there two of them? A cell? It had been his idea to use Connie Wall as bait; unfortunately, it was beginning to look like the bait had been swallowed. So far, this killer had been kicking their asses. If she died, they were truly back to square one.

He spotted the hospital building up on the hill. If she didn't die, they might have one more chance to break their losing streak. If she could give any kind of description, maybe the thing to do would be to announce that Wall had died of her injuries, then try something else. They still had nearly a month to go before the speech to the joint session. Surely they could improve on this mess. He made a mental note to call McNamara in the morning, but now he steeled himself to go inside and face what might be really bad news. And if it turned out that a woman had done this, he would have the double pleasure of informing his bosses that they were now dealing with a terrorist cell, not just some lone wolf. Good deal.

Heismann's escape from the lodge had been a combination of quick thinking and good luck. "Carla" had bolted from the bathroom as soon as the fat woman went down for the last time, but not before making sure the damned nurse was done for. Based on the amount of blood and the glazed look in her eyes, she was as good as dead. He'd taken ten seconds to wash his hands and stow the knife. Coming out of the ladies' room, he'd seen a manager and a security man with a radio hurrying down the hall toward the ladies' room. He'd backed out of their way, put both hands to his face in mock horror, and gibbered incomprehensibly in really bad Spanish while pointing with his chin at the door to the bathroom.

They pushed right past him and dashed into the ladies' room, while he backed up to the door of the men's room, made sure there was no one watching, and then slipped inside.

Fortunately, it had been empty, so he hadn't needed to knife anyone else. Unslinging the purse from his shoulder, he stepped into a stall and locked the door. There he stripped off the dress, his wig, and the bustier, then pulled on the one-piece black nylon running suit and flat shoes. He wadded the dress, wig, and knife into the bag. He came out of the stall and opened the bathroom window long enough to drop the bag into the snow outside. The commotion out in the hallway was growing. Keeping an eye on the door, he washed his face and hands vigorously in the sink and quickly toweled off all the makeup. When he was done, he wiped the sink and then flushed the paper towels down one of the toilets, almost choking it. He went to the inner bathroom door and listened. It sounded like there was a growing crowd out there, and he heard at least two security radios going. So, the window. He went out feetfirst, dropping eight feet into the snow-covered bushes with ease after first closing the window behind him and then hanging by his hands before letting go.

Ultimately, a good forensics team would be able to trace his exit route, but he didn't care. Pulling the tracksuit's flimsy hood over the hairpiece net, he retrieved the bag and then trotted through the falling snow to the parking lot where the Suburban waited. He got in, then casually drove back to his motel, watching in his rearview mirror as the cluster of blue strobe lights began to grow in front of the lodge. That damned fat woman had almost ruined everything, coming at him like that. He wondered how she had seen through his disguise so quickly, because obviously she had. And that kick should have done the job, but no, she had to get up and, instead of running, attack him again. Well, she and that nurse could compare notes now, wherever they were. But he should have been more prepared, should have expected there might be someone in the bathroom. Should have had a contingency plan in place. He thumped the steering wheel. Too many mistakes. He was losing his touch.

As he pulled into the parking lot at his motel, he decided to wait out the night, since the police might throw up roadblocks immediately. Any vehicle leaving town at this hour would be conspicuous, especially in a snowstorm, and according to the map, there were only two roads in and out of this town. Yes. He'd wait until late morning, when there would be city-bound weekender traffic, then join it. No one had seen *him* go into that bathroom, and the police should be looking for a slick-haired Hispanic-looking woman, not a man. He'd watch the local television stations to see what they would report in the morning. His nose itched, and he unstuck the prosthesis.

He felt both relief and apprehension. Relief that this damned woman was out of his way, apprehension at the sheer scale of the thing he was going to do very soon. But given the score so far, he didn't think he had much to worry about from the police, city or federal. Even the nurse had managed to evade them, despite the fact that they were probably trying to protect her. To her extreme cost, one had to admit. And now, if he couldn't get out of the city, he had somewhere to go to ground once the attack had been executed.

He'd go to her house. Somebody might as well make use of it.

By the time Swamp penetrated both the hospital's official wall of ignorance and the police barrier in the lobby, all he had learned was that the woman they'd brought in was in surgery, and that surgery was going to take awhile. There was neither a status nor an official prognosis available from anyone. Defeated, he punched a cup of coffee out of a vending machine and headed back out to his Rover. As he was exiting through the front door of the hospital, a county cruiser pulled up and a tall, lanky man in uniform got out of the front passenger's seat. As soon as he saw Swamp, he motioned him over.

"Sheriff McComb?" Swamp asked, getting out his credentials as he walked down the steps. He noticed that the snow was thinning out and that there were patches of cold, clear sky showing through the low-flying clouds.

"And you must be Special Agent Morgan," the sheriff said. He was tall enough to look down on Swamp's face. He had a weathered look about him, iron gray hair, and a huge Pinkerton-style mustache. "Detective Cullen said we'd recognize you when we saw you."

"Most people can," Swamp said. "I was just inside, but nobody seems to know much, except that she's still in surgery."

McComb nodded thoughtfully. "I'm sorry we didn't get to her sooner," he said. "But that's the same word my people are gettin'. You want to go get a better cup of coffee than that? Those hospital vendin' machines are hard-piped to the pathology lab, I'm told."

"Yes, sir, I'd love one," Swamp said, pouring the ugly coffee out into the snow.

He rode in the back of the cruiser, still holding his empty paper coffee cup. The driver, a deputy, had to open the door for him when they got to the Waffle House diner down the street, as there were no door handles inside the backseat area. They went in and the sheriff led Swamp to a corner booth. A waitress produced two fresh coffees and a handful of creamer cups without being asked, then left them alone. The sheriff's deputy came in and took a nearby stool at the counter, parking his tactical radio on the counter, where it faced him like a waiting gnome. The sheriff poured a creamer into his coffee, lighted a cigarette, and shot a cloud of blue smoke toward the air vent in the ceiling.

"Okay, Special Agent, what in the hay-ull is goin' on here?"

The diner was noisy, with waitresses calling in orders in

Waffle House code and the clatter of crockery being dropped into the busing sinks. "Did Detective Cullen give you any background?" Swamp asked.

"He said they had a cop killer down there in D.C. and had lost a Homicide lieutenant. That it happened at the home of one Connie Wall, R.N., and that said Connie Wall was up here at the Garrison Lodge. Told me to please put some protective surveillance on her until one Special Agent Lee Morgan of the Department of Homeland Security arrived on the scene. Said there was a chance the cop killer was up here in Garrison Gap, intent on takin' out the only witness to the lieutenant's homicide. That's it." He sipped some coffee and then poured one more creamer into his mug, almost causing it to overflow. He raised his bushy eyebrows. "Sorta begs the obvious question, huh?"

In other words, Swamp thought, why are you involved, Mr. Secret Service Agent? He explained his own assignment in OSI, the background on the two cases, and how they had merged into what was rapidly turning out to be a perfect tar baby.

"A 'firefly' is what you called it?" asked the sheriff. "Right now, it seems more like an all too typical Washington cluster fuck to me. No offense."

Swamp grinned. "None taken," he said. "Although the police lieutenant getting killed added a certain exciting dimension to what I thought would be a fairly dull plod. Not to minimize that, but the government's interest here is still focused on that threat to 'bomb, bomb, bomb.' " He explained their assumption that the patient had been talking about the speech to the joint session in February, and his hope that Ms. Wall might yet give them a better description.

The sheriff wasn't optimistic. "The ER doc told me they were pumpin' her up with as much blood as possible, but he thought she was gonna scratch. Somethin' about some big vein takin' a direct hit. Strange thing is, there was a witness in the lobby, says he saw a woman, not a man, mind you, go into the *men's* room at the same time the lodge security people were runnin' into the ladies' to find the victims."

"Any description?"

"Witness was at the end of the hallway. All he got was dark-haired, pretty face, nice rack."

"Terrific," Swamp said.

"But a woman," the sheriff said. "And the lodge security guy backs that up. Said *he* collided with a pretty woman who came out of the ladies' room, actin' hysterical. He couldn't understand anythin' she was sayin'. On reflection, thinks she was Spanish. They were focused on what was goin' on inside the bathroom, tried to find her later, but she was long gone. Here's the best part: A lounge waitress said Ms. Wall and some Spanish-lookin' woman left the lounge together. She remembers them because they were wearin' the same style and color dress. She wondered at the time if they were gonna have a catfight."

Swamp shook his head in wonder. "Who was the other victim?"

"A Montgomery County lady probation officer, from down there in your neck of the woods. Lived in Bladensburg, Maryland. Up here for the weekend. She and her husband. Got herself stabbed three times in the gullet, bled right out."

"Damn. Wrong place, wrong time."

"More'n likely," McComb said. "Our detectives say it looks like there'd been a scuffle in the bathroom. Metal trash can cover was in one corner, had some blood and hairs on it. But by then, so did most of the bathroom. Until and unless this nurse talks, we'll probably never know. She got any kin you know of?"

"Don't think so. Parents are deceased. Her brother was a cop, got killed in some drug deal in southwest D.C. several years ago. She came from a cop family, dated cops, hung out with this Lieutenant Ballard, the one who was just killed.

They were probably closer friends than they should have been, seeing as he was a married man."

"Oh boy. Maybe the D.C. cops would know about next of kin."

"I'll ask Detective Cullen, whom I have to call pretty soon. I drove up from my place in Harpers Ferry. There somewhere I can get a room up here tonight?"

McComb smiled. "Thought I heard some West Virginia. But Saturday night, ski season? Rooms are scarcer'n hen's teeth. Although I guess Ms. Wall's room is free."

Swamp shook his head at McComb's black humor. "I assume you'll have some people in there pretty quick."

"Already have. Only thing of significance there was that she had a grand in her makeup kit. So maybe she was off on more than just a weekend?"

"Maybe," Swamp said. "How about her car?"

"We had a quick look. She had a Very pistol in there— you know, a World War Two flare pistol? Boys up here sometimes use 'em for snake guns."

"Snake guns?"

The sheriff shrugged. "Eight-inch barrel, twelve-gauge? You get snakeburger, long as you keep the muzzle out beyond your own knees. Takes all the hiss right out of 'em."

"That car is probably valuable."

"My deputies were fallin' all over themselves to get into that thing. They'd been talkin' about it before any of this shit went down. Got it down at impound, so's it doesn't get boosted."

Swamp nodded. "Well, the government will help your investigation any way it can, Sheriff. Although I've already told you the gist of what we know. We have a name, too, but we made a big damn assumption pegging that name to this guy. Especially if he's acquired some female help, although that would be out of profile."

The sheriff got out a small notebook and pen and looked

expectantly at Swamp, who gave him Heismann's name and some of the details from the CIA fax. He also explained about how PRU at Secret Service headquarters did not agree that there was even a threat.

McComb nodded. "I used to work for the Bureau," he said. "Long, long time ago. That's why I left—had to get some damn committee to agree to every step of the process. Couldn't do good police work."

"It's supposed to be better now, with this Homeland Security Department." He described the fusion committee.

"Law enforcement by committee, like I was sayin'," the sheriff said, unconvinced.

"It's a good idea, in theory," Swamp said, "But at the working level, everyone's still worried about their job and their budget. Anyway, this Heismann's the best candidate we got right now, so I'm continuing to work it."

"Prove it out, one way or the other?"

"If I can. But if he's had a year and a half of plastic surgery, I don't know how the hell we'll find him."

"The nurse cooperatin' before this?"

"She was, actually. At least I think so. It's just that there were so many patients. I think the second time he came after her, she would have been glad to tell us, if she knew."

"Why'd she rabbit, then?"

"Maybe because we were using her as bait, to suck the bad guy in?"

"Ah."

"We did tell her, and she agreed to it."

"Some people forget that when you're bait, your ass is necessarily on a hook."

Swamp nodded. Tonight's disaster was a perfect example of that little axiom. "I was thinking earlier about how to salvage something useful out of this mess," he said. "Assuming she pulls through, we might want to announce that Wall did *not* make it, even if she does. Get her off that hook."

"So to speak," the sheriff said with a wry grin. The deputy at the counter was bending forward and talking into his radio. One of the waitresses was watching, fascinated.

The sheriff explained the probable media reaction. "A situation like this will make state news for sure," he said. "We can start by sayin' that she's not expected to survive. That's the God's honest truth. Then next, maybe do a coma bit. TV news in this state has the attention span of a gnat. Ya have her go mamba for a few days, the vultures will usually move on to the next roadkill."

"That would help, I think. Assuming we understand the first goddamn thing about this mess."

"Comin' from the federal law-enforcement machine, that's quite an admission," the sheriff said.

"The older I get, Sheriff, the less I understand very much of anything about this world. But one thing is clear: If some squirming-brain terrorist is setting up evil shit in the capital, I feel it's my duty to accept help from wherever we can get it. And in my book, that's a two-way street."

"So Detective Cullen said," the sheriff replied. The deputy was standing by their booth. "Yeah, Tommy?"

"Larry over at the hospital says the nurse is out of surgery, but she's still unconscious and in a—" He glanced at his notebook. "In an induced coma."

McComb looked over at Swamp. "See?" he said. "That wasn't hard." Then his face sobered. "But what is hard is that I have to go interview the Bladensburg lady's husband. And I suppose you don't want me to tell him anythin' about what you've been tellin' me."

"No, I don't. Maybe you could just say two barflies got into a fight and his wife somehow got tangled up in it?"

"I'll think of somethin'," the sheriff said.

Connie Wall was dream-flying down the Potomac River. It was a cold moonlit night, and she was skimming soundlessly just a few feet off the surface, the winter air streaming past her face and numbing her cheeks. She was close enough to the surface to be able to see the flat ledges and deep pools lurking in the river. Crusts of ice winked at her from along the shores, where bare trees watched her pass in silent amazement. She swept down past the palisades below McLean, where darkened, many-windowed mansions surveyed the river below with quiet authority. Past Chain Bridge, past the spires of Georgetown University and under the arches of Key Bridge, past the graceful marble monuments of the Mall and the Tidal Basin, past the Memorial Bridge and the Fourteenth Street bridges, past the squat, baleful Pentagon building and one of its principal products, the thousands of white headstones dotting the Arlington heights in front of Robert E. Lee's old home. She saw commercial jets prowling the ramps and taxiways of Reagan National Airport, but she couldn't hear them, only the sound of her own wraithlike body slicing smoothly through the night, past the row of generals' quarters at Fort McNair, where the Potomac River was joined by the stinking Anacostia River, past Bolling Field and the ghostly white satellite dishes of the Naval Research Lab, then down past Old Town in Alexandria and under the notorious Woodrow Wilson Bridge, where semis sometimes punched through its rotting decks. And then past the marinas below Old Town, Belle Haven, and finally past George Washington's stately home up on its expanse of dormant lawns, down to where the river began to widen in earnest.

She shivered in the cold and then realized she was wearing almost nothing, some filmy gown that trailed out behind her, a rippling fabric tail streaming almost as far as she could see. This wasn't right. She shouldn't be out here like this. She should go back. She stretched out her arms and started a wide banking turn to the left, to go back up the river to wherever she had come from. But it was difficult. She encountered real resistance to the turn. She had to work at it, pushing one arm down, the other up, forcing herself to twist and bank, and now she could see that diaphanous gown trailing behind her like a wedding train, the back half still streaming down the river even as she passed it going the other way, back up the river. But she finally managed it, and this time she was soaring way above the river and the sleeping city with all its lights and monuments, and now she knew somehow that everything was going to be better, maybe even all right. But first she had to get back to West Virginia, back to Garrison Gap, back to the hospital, back to the ICU, where there were people calling out her name. Even from way down here, miles downstream, she could hear them.

7

ON HIS WAY BACK TO WASHINGTON ON SUNDAY, SWAMP PUT a call in to Lucy VanMetre. "This thing of yours is bothering me," she said. "I gave it the *Washington Post* test, and it failed."

"Ah," he said. So, she had written down the bald facts as they might be reported in the capital's newspaper after some disaster. A litany of what PRU had known, with the clarity of perfect hindsight, of course, and what they'd done about it. Which at this stage of events was nothing. "So you're having the same problem with it that I am."

"Not quite—you're still free to work it. I have this inauguration monster on my back, and it's growing apace."

"You're right. My threat, if it is a threat, is still weeks away."

"Plus, I've signed out a memo saying to ignore it. Now I'm not so sure."

"Want it back?" Swamp asked.

She laughed. "What will that cost?"

"An open mind, and some help if I can surface some real evidence."

"Let's have dinner. My treat. The Queen Bee, say in an hour?"

"They'll be open on a Sunday?"

The Vietnamese restaurant was nearly full, but Swamp

saw that Lucy had a table for four all by herself in a front corner, proof that she was a regular. She was dressed in a gray wool suit, a single strand of pearls at her throat. She raised one hand to attract his attention and he joined her at the table. He'd forgotten how blue her eyes were, and the pearls seemed to reflect the color of her hair. Unfamiliar with Vietnamese cuisine, he let her order for the both of them, got a glass of wine, and sat back in his chair. "So how goes the *big deal*?"

She sighed. "Like a giant whirlpool. Except people are trying to jump in instead of out. Hallory's going crazy. We're all going crazy. I may go back tonight."

He shook his head. "I remember that syndrome," he said. "Where you feel the whole thing will fall apart if you're not on it twenty-four/seven. It's an illusion."

"Illusion? I don't know about that. When I don't go in, things happen. Bad things."

"The solution to that is intensive training of your supervisory agents. They do their job and a little bit of yours; you get to step back, see where the serious holes are."

She smiled. "My problem is the sheer scale of what we're going to do. Like lock down the entire Capitol Hill area—Metro, city streets, airspace, every house within gunshot range of the Capitol. Everything within three blocks. And then, of course, the detailed work. There's the parade, for instance. Three hours of potential shooters walking right in front of the new president. Many of them military units or drill teams carrying rifles. Each of which has to be inspected. And physically plugged."

"Anwar Sadat got it that way," he said, remembering the video of that chaotic assassination. The first course arrived, and by mutual agreement, they put business aside to enjoy the food, which was as colorful as the names on the menu. When they were finished, Swamp walked her through the summary report he had worked on all afternoon for his boss. She was quiet, stirring her coffee when he was finished.

"The crux of it is that we believe some guy who'd been at that clinic for treatment started the fire that killed everyone except Ms. Wall. And he's been after her ever since, and last night it looks like he sent in a woman to finish the job."

"Has there been any improvement?"

"My contact in the D.C. police says she surfaced once but has gone back down again. Basically, no change."

"And you have a name for this subject?"

"We've made a tenuous connection between that clinic patient and a known, albeit low-level, German terrorist associate. And we've connected that same patient to statements recorded under residual anesthetic about bombing the Capitol during the speech to the joint session."

"Connected how?"

"Logical assumption?"

"That good," she said, a faint hint of sarcasm in her voice.

Swamp shrugged. "Well, I did say it was tenuous. I think I've admitted all along that we are basing this more on conjecture than evidence."

"All right, now what?" she asked.

"Now we pray that Wall can give us an up-close description of this unknown female subject in Garrison Gap. Something better than 'pretty woman with a nice rack.' We're leading the press into thinking Wall is dead or almost so, hoping to deflect any further attempts on her life. Much as I hate the idea, I'm beginning to think my original idea—a total screen of all the record fragments from that clinic—is going to be necessary after all. We must get *his* description."

Lucy rubbed her temples. She looked tired and not quite as perfectly composed as the last time he'd seen her. "And when exactly is this speech?" she asked.

"February fifteenth, which is the only plus factor in this equation."

"Next steps?" she asked.

"Brief McNamara as soon as I can get on his calendar. And the District cops are going to interview the salesmen at a Chevy dealership across from Steve's Vintage Motors, the garage from which Wall took off. It's a long shot." He told her about the Suburban and the fact that a man with a German-sounding accent had come into Steve's, inquiring about Wall's car.

"Description on him?"

"Useless. Airhead witness. We may get lucky at the dealership. *If* he was there."

When the waiter came to clear the table, Lucy slipped him a credit card. "All very tenuous indeed, Mr. Morgan," she said. "Hallory would transfer an agent out of PRU for cotton candy like this."

Swamp sighed. "I guess it's just systemic. Always say no, make the agent batter his way to yes, as they say in the Bureau."

Lucy shrugged. "I play the cards I get, Mr. Morgan. I suspect you did, too."

"For a while, until I became a DAD. At which point, I thought it might be time to make a difference."

"And you were a DAD for how long?"

He laughed. "Twenty-two months and seven days, but who's counting? You think I got stuck in the system's throat?"

"That's one version."

He looked away for a moment. One version? That was exactly what had happened. He nodded finally. "At that level, deputy assistant director, you're expected to be a total team player. They took a chance, promoting me. I tended to go into the terrier mode, just like Hallory said."

"And?"

"And some of the barons who had voted no on my promotion sent some really thorny issues my way. I ran with them in my own front-line style, and then stepped in some political traps."

"They let you do yourself in, you mean?"

"When you run with the wolves, don't ever trip," Swamp said. "I tripped."

"That might explain some of Hallory's antagonism," she said. "I think it's the messenger more than this firefly that's got him worried."

"Doesn't want to get any on him, huh?" he asked.

"Doesn't want to trip," she said. "So, next steps?"

"I'm going to try to get McNamara to authorize the FBI evidence screen himself," Swamp said. "He said he knew somebody, guy who owed him a favor. But he won't do it if PRU formally objects." He remembered what Sheriff Mc-Comb had said about doing police work through committees.

"See where you get tomorrow," she said. "See if the nurse can ID her attacker, or if this car thing pans out. You still have time. We don't. We're right down to the wire with our little circus. I'll get one chance to resurrect this thing, and, like you said, I'll need real evidence when I do it."

He nodded as the waiter came back with the charge slip. She was right. They waited until they were outside before continuing. It was dark now, with only the streetlights illuminating the empty streets. The temperature had dropped into the low forties, and they both buttoned their coats. "Okay," he said. "That was useful. I'll be in touch. Thanks for dinner—it was very good. And I was serious about that memo."

She gave him a tired smile. "I wasn't," she said. "The original, the one we kept, has Hallory's signature."

He started to laugh. La Mamba indeed. "I was going to walk back to the Ballston area," he said. "It's only a couple miles. But maybe I should ride with you back to your apartment building or office. Metro stations get spooky at this hour on a weekend."

"Thank you, but I think I can take care of myself," she said, patting her purse. He'd forgotten she was technically a

Secret Service agent. "You are the one who needs to be careful," she said. "If you're right and we're all wrong, some powerful people won't thank you for it. You know that, don't you?"

"That's a career perspective talking. I don't have one anymore. And career damage is meaningless compared to what this guy might be planning."

"Agreed, Mr. Morgan. But PRU's just about overwhelmed right now. Your threat isn't the only one we're working, and our threat window is in five days."

"I understand," he said. "I'll try to be patient."

"Not too patient," she said as she turned to walk away. "Forget the record search. Concentrate on tracking this German." She walked down the street toward the Metro station. He watched her go, that golden hair shimmering in the amber streetlight. The January wind blew some trash around his ankles. He saw some of the customers looking his way through the front curtains of the restaurant. One of the men gave him a sympathetic look. Tough luck, buddy, looks like she got away.

He turned in the opposite direction and began walking back to his apartment building.

Heismann sat in darkness in the tiny kitchen of the town house and sipped a beer. The lights were off throughout the house, but the darkness suited him. Enough light came though the windows for him to move about. He could hear the woman next door in her kitchen, clattering some plates in the sink. Tomorrow, he would enter her apartment and begin his preparations. She left for work promptly at eight o'clock, then walked to her job in the Library of Congress. If she owned a car, it wasn't parked in her half of the garage. Perhaps it was parked out front. He'd noticed that some cars appeared to have been parked there for a long time.

He had cut over to Route 50 from Route 7 when he got

down to Berryville, Virginia, that morning, in order not to retrace his track of the day before. He had seen the state police car lying in wait for speeders at the foot of the mountain, and he hadn't particularly wanted to see him again, or be seen. He'd lost some time dawdling behind that ancient Land Rover back up in the hills of West Virginia, but then he had made it back to Capitol Hill in under two hours. He'd noticed stacks of yellow sawhorses on some of the major intersections; the city traffic managers were beginning preparations to close down this part of the city. The newspaper had been full of details of all the restrictions, and he had kept all the notices. Not that he needed to move much before the attack, but he certainly would right afterward.

He'd overheard a waitress in the diner where he'd had breakfast that morning talking about the double murders at the Garrison Lodge the night before and the novelty of the killer being a woman. If they were calling it a double murder, then both women were dead, which was a relief. He had heard no news reports about the incident on his car radio, so he had decided to concentrate entirely on the attack. Now that it was dark, he would switch the Suburban and the minivan so that the larger vehicle was out of sight in the garage for a few days. But right now, he needed the woman next door to go to bed. So far, he had seen her, but he didn't think she had seen him.

All things considered, his little foray into the mountains had been well worth while. The nurse was finally out of the way. The police were searching for a woman killer. What did the *Ammies* say? A piece of cake? Yes indeed. But now he had much to do, and not much time to finish it all. It was almost amusing: all this work, all this time, for an attack that would take forty seconds at most. But those were the best kind. Strike like the cobra and then disappear. Watch the instant replay on their television later. The *Ammies* weren't much at security, but television? *That* they could do. So well, in fact, that he was going to use a television to ensure the accuracy of the attack.

Connie Wall finally got a real drink of water down, and it felt wonderful, although the steel tube made her front teeth hurt.

"There's someone here to see you," the nurse said. "He's been waiting awhile."

Connie frowned, trying to concentrate through the haze of painkillers. "Who?" she mumbled.

"Detective Cullen? He's a policeman. He came up from Washington when he heard what'd happened. He's been here all day. You mustn't talk too much. Just a few minutes, okay?"

"Um," Connie managed.

Jake came in a minute later and sat down by her bed. He was wearing plastic gloves and had a gauze mask over his nose and the lower parts of his face, which made him look ridiculous in the subdued lighting of the ICU. One of the nurses hovered just outside the curtain surrounding her bed.

"Hey, Connie," he said, reaching for her fingers on the side of the bed. The gloves felt warm. "They treating you okay here?"

She just looked at him, unable to put words together. Cullen. Oh, yeah. Jake Cullen. Right.

"We're looking for the woman who did this to you, Connie. As soon as you're able, we'll come back, talk about what she looks like, and what happened over there at that hotel."

She blinked her eyes, trying to keep his face in focus. Something she needed to tell Jake, but she couldn't make it come. He brushed a lock of her hair gently off her forehead with his other hand and his eyes were smiling at her. She squeezed his fingers and then drifted back off. On the way down to the nice warm place, she remembered what it was she needed to tell him.

It wasn't a woman, Jake.

It was *him*.

She thought she felt him stroking her fingers. That was nice.

8

At eleven o'clock on Monday morning, Jake Cullen, driving an unmarked Crown Vic, picked up Swamp at the Eighteenth Street entrance of the OEOB, while Gary White got into the car behind Cullen's, driven by Detective Howell. The snowstorm that had blanketed the West Virginia mountains had changed to sleet down along the Potomac River basin, fatally snarling the Monday-morning commute. As of noon, it had turned to just cold rain, making January in Washington live up to its miserable reputation.

"Great day for ducks," Swamp said, getting in and taking off his dripping hat. "You know where this bank is?"

"Yeah," Jake said. "Up on Fifteenth and P Street. A couple of blocks away from the Saudi embassy. I called. We're gonna see the managing director, a Mr. Mutaib."

"Not a prince," Swamp said. "How unique."

Jake stopped at a yellow light so as not to lose Howell. "His real title is Emir Mutaib abd Allah, supposedly, but he goes by Mr. Mutaib here in the land of the free and the home of the brave. Appreciate your coming along."

"Wouldn't miss it. So that may *have* been our guy, the one driving that black Suburban?"

"It's possible. Salesman remembers him being interested in Connie's Shelby."

"Description?"

"Medium build, dark oversized sunglasses, hat, gloves, Jewish nose—our politically correct salesman's term for it—oh, and a European accent. Never took the sunglasses off, not even inside."

"Essentially faceless, then."

"Guy had a preauthorized bank draft on the Royal Kingdom Bank—that's one of the Saudi banks here in Washington. Dealership called the bank, got immediate verification, and that was that. Gave his name as Erich Hodler."

"Damn, I was hoping for Heismann."

"Nope, Hodler. Had an international driver's license, passport, work visa, and the equivalent of cold cash. Keys and half a tank of gas, and—boom—like a rock, he's an owner."

"This dealership know they have to report cash transactions from a foreigner like that to the IRS?"

"Yep, and they say they did. By mail, naturally."

Swamp thought about it. The dealer hadn't done anything illegal, as long as the individual's papers were in order. "Address?"

"Well, that was interesting—title *and* registration to be sent to said bank."

"Oh?"

"Well, bank fronts the money, bank gets the title. The registration would normally go to the buyer. At his address. Which he gave as the bank."

"Which is why we're going to the bank."

"Yeah. Hell, right now, it's all we've got."

"How's Ms. Wall?"

Construction in the next block had even the sparse traffic gridlocked. "Cut three ways, as they say in certain quarters—long, deep, and often. Actually, it was a single stab wound, but deep and in a bad area for that kind of wound. I made contact with her twice. One time for a finger squeeze.

The second time, she opened her eyes, recognized me. At least I think so. The ICU docs said she'd be like that for a while. They've got her on morphine, so I came back down to Fun City here. The other reason was that Cat Ballard's funeral is this afternoon."

Behind them, Howell plopped a bubblegum light on the roof of his car and honked at Jake, who looked in the mirror, reached under the seat, and put his own light up top. Blooping his siren, he eased out into the other lane of traffic and they circumvented the traffic jam. "Does Ballard's wife know the real deal?" Swamp asked.

"If she does, she's not letting on. There has been a line-of-duty determination. He was on a call in connection with an 'ongoing investigation.' "

"Right."

"Well, she did call him, after all," Jake said, rolling his eyes. "We told Lynn that the woman left town and then got herself knifed in West Virginia. Adds a little depth and color to the fable, I guess. Tough scene all around, though. Two kids and all."

"You gonna go?"

"Oh, yes. Whole crew's going, plus a lot of bosses. Which is why I want to face up Ahab the Ay-rab here, see what he can tell us. I desperately need something to report back. Oh, and did I mention that the milk container contained a nerve agent?"

Swamp drew a blank, so Jake refreshed his memory about Wall's cat.

"A lot?" Swamp asked.

"Enough to have paralyzed anyone who drank that milk."

"Nice. So this guy comes packing bio?"

"Lab says it was probably ant poison, which in soluble powder form is based on a cholinesterase inhibitor. Nerve agent, in English. Get it at any home-supply store."

"Wouldn't you taste or smell that shit?"

"Not, apparently, if you boil it first."

"Our boy's been to some interesting schools, then," Swamp said. "So how do you want to play this at the bank?"

"We're on the Ballard homicide. I'll tell him you're along because it's international. Mention of the Secret Service tends to make foreigners straighten right up. Plus, in Saudi Arabia, that term has a totally different connotation, if you follow me."

Swamp smiled. It surely did. "More like gestapo," he said. "And above all, we want a description, plus anything they can tell us about who this guy is and why they gave him money?"

"Right," Jake said. "This looks like the place."

They pulled up in front of an elegant stone building with a circular driveway. A pair of security types were sitting in a large Mercedes parked at one end of the arc. Jake turned into the driveway, followed by Howell. The security guards were out of their car to meet them as soon as the cops got out of their respective cars. Swamp halfway expected some guff, but the guards, large men who looked like Germans to him, told them in excellent English that the managing director was expecting them. One of them began mumbling into a small radio.

Inside, the lobby was unlike any bank Swamp had ever been in. It looked more like someone's gracious town house, with gorgeous carpets on marble floors and a huge vaulted ceiling. There were three service desks at one end of the lobby, all manned by men. Two very handsome young men in glistening Armani suits appeared to escort them back through ten-foot-high rosewood double doors to Emir Mutaib's office. When the four of them were seated on sofas in an anteroom, two servants dressed in white uniforms brought out a coffee service on a silver tray. Once everyone had coffee, the servants withdrew, the doors to the inner office opened, and Mutaib made his grand entrance. Swamp had been expecting a dark-skinned, bearded, beefy individual in white robes and headdress, but instead, a slim man of

medium height with professionally styled dark hair appeared. His face was long and narrow, with delicately arched
eyebrows, dark brown eyes, bright white teeth, and taut olive
skin descending into a carefully groomed pointed black
beard. He was wearing an elegant double-breasted tweed
suit, a white shirt with a regimental tie and a tie pin, and
dark cordovan wing tips. He greeted them in what Swamp
recognized as an upper-class British accent, Oxbridge-
anointed, complete with a hint of the softened *r*'s affecta-
tion. Mutaib sat down in a large chair, shot his French cuffs,
crossed his legs, and beamed at them expectantly. The two
young men, one of them holding a small folder, hovered at-
tentively just behind him.

Jake made introductions, and Mutaib formally recognized each man there, repeating their names but not shaking
hands. He gave Swamp's face an extra second of inspection
when he heard mention of the Secret Service. Or maybe it's
just my lovely mug, Swamp thought. People often looked
twice, or even three times, furtively, though, as if afraid of
being turned to stone.

"Gentlemen. How may the Royal Kingdom Bank be of
assistance to you today?" he asked.

Jake took the lead, explaining the circumstances of the
investigation in very broad terms, then described the pur-
chasing of the Suburban. "Basically, as I said on the phone,
we want to know who this individual is, and we're curious
why the Royal Kingdom Bank would cut him a preauthorized check like that."

Mutaib raised his right hand, and one of the young men
sprang forward to deliver the slim folder to his outstretched
hand. He opened it and read for one or two seconds.

"This individual was named Erich Hodler," Mutaib began, still reading from the folder. "He is a German national
with a valid passport. He came into the bank with twenty
thousand Euros in cash and requested a preauthorized bank

draft, made out to the automobile merchant in question. He said he had found the automobile he wanted to buy, and he requested that we send the bank draft via messenger service to the merchant."

"And you just did it?"

"Well, of course, Detective Sergeant. Why not? His identity papers were in order. The Euros were genuine. He was willing to pay our fee for such services."

"But he's a foreigner," Howell said.

"And so are we, Detective Sergeant," Mutaib said with a faintly patronizing smile. "We reported the transaction to the appropriate authorities here in Washington, of course, because of the cash, but I must say it was an entirely routine transaction. Has this individual done something wrong? Is he a criminal?"

"We don't know," Swamp said, speaking for the first time. "But we want to speak to him. Can anyone here give a description of this man?"

"A description?" Mutaib looked perplexed for a moment.

"Yes," Jake said. "What'd he look like?"

Mutaib looked pained. He turned his head in the direction of one of his attendants and muttered something in Arabic. The young man left the room immediately, punching numbers into a tiny cell phone as he hurried through a door.

"We shall see if anyone remembers," Mutaib announced. "Although it's hardly likely."

"Are there security tapes? A video system for your service desks?"

Mutaib nodded. "Yes, of course. But they are—what is the term? Ah, yes, they are 'looped,' I'm told. One day's recording is made right over the top of the previous day's recording, unless, of course, the nightly audit surfaces a problem of some kind. Bad check, a forgery. Then we would keep them. The tapes, I mean."

"Do you have the tapes from the day all this happened?"

Mutaib consulted the folder. "Thursday last. The twelfth. Yes. The transaction in question occurred on the twelfth. But no, we would not have kept that day's tape. There were simply no incidents." He beamed at them. "There rarely are, you see. We have excellent and visible security."

The young man came back in and shook his head once. "I am so sorry, gentlemen, but we do not have a description for Herr Hodler. We do have his passport number and your American visa numbers, of course, and we have the serial numbers of the Euros."

"So you do not know this individual, Mr. Mutaib?" Jake asked.

"Me? Of course not."

"Because he asked that both the title and the registration for this vehicle be sent here to the bank. Now we can understand the title—that's your collateral. But the registration?"

Mutaib was shaking his head. "There is no collateral, Detective Cullen. This was not a loan. It was currency conversion. Euros for dollars, the dollars being in the form of a preauthorized bank draft. Any balance after price, taxes, and fees to be refunded by the dealer to the buyer in dollars."

"So why would he have the papers sent here?"

"I have no idea, sir. I assume he means to come back here to pick them up. P'raps he does not yet have a permanent address in this country." Mutaib looked back at his assistants for ideas, but they were equally baffled.

Jake looked at Swamp, but Swamp couldn't think of anything but the obvious. "Well, if he does come back to pick them up," he said, "we would still like to talk to him. He left no address on any of your bank forms? No way to contact him?"

Mutaib shook his head. "None at all. The only address we needed was that of the automobile merchant. He brought in cash, you see. Now, if he had brought in a letter of credit, or another bank draft . . . well, that would have been quite different. But cash?" He shrugged elaborately.

"And you have no other information on this individual?"

"None at all, sir. But didn't your government issue this man a visa? Surely the appropriate department would have information."

And that would be the Immigration and Naturalization Service, in my very own Department of Homeland Security, Swamp thought, his face flushing slightly. The original bureaucratic black hole. "It was a travel visa," he said, lying. "A list of destinations, but no addresses."

Mutaib shrugged again. Obviously not his problem. He raised his eyebrows, as if to ask, Is there anything else?

Swamp realized they were stymied. The bank had been nothing more than a fancy money changer in this little deal. He was a little suspicious of that story about the security tapes, but then, why would they keep them if there'd been no trouble? He shot Jake a look, stood up, and everyone else did, too. "Thank you for seeing us, Mr. Mutaib," Swamp said. "If we have follow-up questions, may we call you?"

Mutaib got up gracefully and handed Jake the folder. One of the assistants raced to open the door. "But of course, my dear fellow," Mutaib said. "Anything at all, to be sure."

Heismann stood in the woman's kitchen and listened. He had heard and watched her leave for work earlier that morning, bustling down the sidewalk with a large fabric bag full of books and papers, a clear plastic trash bag wrapped over the top to keep out the icy rain. As soon as she was gone, he'd begun smashing down the wall between the two town houses. He'd first gone into the basement, but the foundation was made of limestone, which would take much too long to penetrate. There was a hall closet just outside the upstairs master bathroom. He knew its twin should be on the other side of the fire wall. He'd gone in there, ripped the plaster and lathe down to expose the brick, and then, using a small sledgehammer, knocked out all the brickwork on his side of the fire wall. Then he punched a four-foot-high, three-foot-wide hole through the partition, exposing the brickwork on her side of the fire wall. He'd battered through that until he had the plaster wall exposed. He then made a hole low in the plaster and shined a flashlight through. There appeared to be a stack of cardboard boxes in the totally dark space on the other side. He'd then used a handsaw to cut a duplicate square hole in her plaster wall, pulling that ragged square of plaster and lathe through into his closet.

Moving some of the boxes to one side, he'd squeezed through the hole and opened the closet door, its position in front of the bathroom the mirror image of his closet. The closet being full of boxes was good—it wasn't likely that she would be moving them. Then he went through her entire house, taking care to pull shades down so he could not be seen from the street while he examined the place. He spent a half hour going through her clothes, slipping a couple of dresses over his head to see how close the fit was. The dresses, all below the knee in length, were too large, but not too long, so they would do, depending on which costume he chose. Her underwear drawer had a collection of slips, so he was set in that department as well, although he still had the nurse's. His best find was a box of wigs. He had seen his neighbor emptying a bag of trash into the alley containers, and her dark hair had been quite short. But this morning, it had been of medium length. He patted his own stubbled bald head and smiled. This would be perfect. He'd come back the night before the attack to get what he needed. He made a mental note to acquire some more gasoline containers, so that he could get a fire going in this half of the duplex at the same time as his half.

He went back through the house, adjusting shades to their original positions, turning off any lights he'd turned on, and ensuring drawers and closet doors were all as he had found them. He made a mental note of where floorboards squeaked. He took a bottle of cooking oil and went around the house, putting a drop or two on the hinges on every interior door in the house. Then he reset the stack of boxes to present a blank cardboard wall to her closet door, while still allowing enough room for him to get into and through her closet without making noise. He crawled around them, then stepped back across the two holes. He retrieved the square of plaster and lathe and positioned it back into its hole on her side. He knew it wouldn't bear close inspection, but the stack of boxes would hide most of it, and he'd unscrewed the closet's lightbulb just in case she happened to open the closet to look for something. It had to stand up for just three more days.

As he stepped back out into his own hallway, he saw the white footprints his shoes had left on the rug. He swore at himself. Plaster dust. Were there white footprints over there, too? He took the square of plaster back down and laboriously retraced his route. And there were indeed two faint white footprints out on the rug in front of the closet. He took off his shoes and then went through the house a second time, finding a couple of white smears here and there on her bedroom rug. He cleaned them all up before returning to his house again.

Details, he reminded himself. As the attack draws near, details will increasingly matter. He went back down to his kitchen and consulted his lists. Lumber supplies to reinforce the bedroom floor. Gasoline for starting the fire. He added a note to get extra gasoline containers. The television—no, he had that. The materials to modify the skylight. He felt a moment of panic—was there enough time to do all this? The newspaper was full of the preparations for the inauguration and all the constraints on local movement that were coming. Streets physically blocked with something called Jersey barriers. Dense police patrols. Dogs. Helicopters. Television and all other media coverage of the Capitol area and the ceremonies restricted to four networks, one being CNN. Airports closed. Union Station closed. No Metro trains running. "The vacuum-sealed inauguration," as one newspaper called it.

He looked at his watch. Three and a half days left to prepare. He decided to call Lady Mutaib and get some logistical help. He wondered if the poncey princeling had his own collection of female clothes, or if all those robes did it for him.

The cops dropped Swamp and Gary off near the OEOB, and they stopped in a sandwich shop for lunch before going back to the office. Afterward, Swamp went straight to McNamara's office, but the boss was at a departmental briefing in preparation for an upcoming National Intelligence Committee meeting. When he returned to his cubicle, at 1:30, Gary was waiting for him.

"Check this out," he said, handing Swamp a classified communiqué. "It's from Interpol—their file on Heismann. Look at the alias list."

Swamp scanned down the message until he found it. "Hodler. Erich Hodler. I'll be damned. We should relay this to Jake Cullen." And now I need to call Lucy, he thought. The rest of the report paralleled what they'd received from his friend Bertie. He wondered aloud why the CIA report did not have the list of aliases.

"No idea, sir," Gary said. "No mention of that. The Interpol photo's pretty close to what we got from the Agency, though. And I talked to Immigration—they did issue E. Hodler a visa, but it was eighteen months ago."

"For God's sake!" Swamp exclaimed. "Who gets an eighteen-month visa when he's in the Interpol database?"

"Anyone who asks?" Gary said. "Anyway, I faxed them Interpol's photo, and they say it's a match from his passport scan. I think we can say Hodler is Heismann."

"They fax back their file on Hodler?"

"Negative. Said they couldn't do that without a court order."

"Goddamn it," Swamp said. "I thought we were past all that crap. We're in the same damned department!" He studied the photograph. A Hollywood Nazi. Plastered blond hair.

Pronounced cheekbones. Long, straight Nordic-looking nose over flat, sneering lips. Ice blue eyes, approving the latest oven improvements in his death camp, no doubt. "But what's he look like now? I wonder," Swamp said.

"Second item," Gary said. "Remember the warrants you wanted so we could search the Pakistani doctors' homes?"

"Yeah?"

"I took a call for you from your friend Mr. Walker. Wanted to know how it was going."

"Yeah, I was supposed to keep him in the loop. I need to call him."

"Well, I took the liberty of filling him in, but then I asked him why they didn't have the same alias list for Heismann that Interpol had. He sorta waffled on that, but he had a useful suggestion—that I should check with our own Immigration people in DHS, because foreigners running a business in this country have to register yearly. And foreign doctors also have to requalify their medical licenses with HHS once a year."

"And?"

"The visa people sent me to Immigration's business records section. And guess what? Those doctors did not entirely own that business. A certain foreign bank had a major piece of their action." He raised his eyebrows dramatically.

"You're shitting me."

"Not a pound, boss. The Royal Kingdom Bank owned a stake in that clinic. That Pakistani doc ran it, but the RKB held some major purse strings. The American docs did own their piece of it and the building."

"Well, now we have something. Can you find out from Cullen if Ms. Wall is back among the living?"

After Gary went off to contact Cullen, Swamp sat down at his desk and reorganized his notes for his brief to McNamara. Gary came back almost immediately. "I forgot—the cops're all at the funeral. I'll try that hospital up in Garrison Gap."

Swamp put a call in to Lucy. He would have preferred to wait until he'd had time to brief his own boss, but now that they had a second link between the Interpol name and the likely pursuer of Connie Wall, *and* probable killer of Lieutenant Ballard, he really wanted some Bureau resources put on to the problem of reconstructing a working physical description. If nothing else, Heismann/Hodler had some questions to answer about the death of the police lieutenant, even if their own theories about a bomb plot were all wrong.

In the event, Lucy VanMetre was not available. When Swamp tried to pursue it, the PRU receptionist stonewalled him. She told him Ms. VanMetre was not available, then asked if he wanted her voice mail. When he said no, she told him he could leave name and phone number. No idea when she would be available.

Defeated, he gave up. Previously, they would have told him that she was in a meeting, out of the office, at lunch, whatever, but this was as if he'd been put on an "I don't want to talk to this guy ever" list. Had she gone in to see Hallory prematurely? He thought about sending her an E-mail, then wondered where their "agreement" stood just now.

Gary came by and told him that Connie Wall was still not "consistently conscious."

"What the hell does that mean?" Swamp asked.

"She drifts in and out. Doesn't say anything, recognizes a couple of the nurses, and then submerges again. The ICU supervisor did say they're purposefully keeping her down to facilitate the healing process."

"Anything from the Crass County sheriff's office?"

Gary looked at his notebook. "No signs of the woman who did the cutting. They did a forensics sweep of both bathrooms, but they're public bathrooms and it was a busy hotel on Saturday night. . . . Possible indications of someone going out the men's room window, but their forensics unit isn't exactly equipped like the big city units."

"So they got a ton of stuff that means nothing."

Gary shrugged. "We get a female suspect in custody, I guess they could do a match comparison. But what with the snowstorm that night, other accidents to contend with, they never even got an effective roadblock set up. According to Sheriff McComb, the cutter had plenty of time to make her creep."

Swamp shook his head in frustration. "We've got a German guy going to that garage, asking questions about Wall and her car, and being told she was going to Garrison Gap. We've got what sounds like the same German buying a black Suburban with tinted windows for cash, right across the street, and noticing the car. The next day, we've got a black Suburban with tinted windows two minutes behind her on the same road. That night, she is once again attacked and almost killed."

"We don't know for a *fact* that the guy who bought the Suburban was the same guy following her," Gary said. "I've seen three black Suburbans go by my office window this morning."

Swamp nodded. "True, we don't. Hell, there was one on my tail coming out of—"

"What?" Gary said, seeing Swamp's expression.

"When I left Garrison Gap Sunday morning, there was a black Suburban right behind me all the way to Route Eighty-one. With tinted windows."

"Wow."

"Except the state cop said he had a light bar and whip antennas. The one following Wall, I mean. This one was a plain Jane."

"You can get a light bar at just about any auto-parts store. You know, all the volunteer firemen and EMTs get 'em there. This Suburban have a luggage rack?"

"I'm not sure. I wasn't paying any attention to him, and he passed me on the first straightaway we came to, near the interstate." Swamp shut his eyes and concentrated. "Yes, I think it did."

"Well, it'd be no big deal to bolt and unbolt a light bar if there's a luggage rack. And a Suburban's plenty big enough to throw the damn thing in the back when you don't want it up there."

"Or it could have been just another damn black Suburban, up in ski country for the weekend."

Gary nodded. Swamp's phone rang. It was Mary, McNamara's secretary. The boss wanted to see him—alone. In other words, Don't bring your sidekick.

He asked Gary to assemble some data on the scope of the record screen—how much stuff someone would have to paw through, and some guesstimate of how long it would take for one person to do it by himself. Then he asked him to update that dossier on Heismann/Hodler with what they had now from Immigration. "And see if you can find someone who could build you a list of surgical procedures that would be involved in a total makeover of this guy's face."

Gary gave him a look. "And when I'm done with all that?"

Swamp waited.

"Right," Gary said, "I can take the rest of the day off. I knew that."

Heismann made the call to Mutaib from a phone booth down in the Air and Space Museum on Independence Avenue. Fifty feet from where he stood, there was a German V-2 rocket from World War II standing on its steel nozzle ring next to a scale model of the first successful American satellite-launching rocket, which was strikingly similar. In the afternoon light, he could just make out the swastika showing through the paint on the V-2's now age-dimpled side. Apparently, someone in the museum had decided to paint over the symbol of Nazi Germany so as not to offend any visitors. Heismann was willing to bet he knew what group of visitors they'd had in mind. Lots more of them over here than there are in Germany these days, he reflected with satisfaction. Mutaib came on the line.

"I have a list of materials, and I do not want to take that large vehicle out on the streets just now," Heismann announced.

"Very well, wait one moment, please."

Heismann waited, then heard one of the assistants pick up an extension. He read the list aloud, trying to keep his voice low. The list, which included heavy timbers, some sheets of plywood, fasteners, curtain material, power tools, extension cords, and gasoline cans, might have sounded a bit strange to any tourists standing nearby. When he was finished, Mutaib had news.

"We had callers today," he said. He described the visit from the Secret Service and the local police. He said the Secret Service agent in charge looked like a bloody Neanderthal."

"And this was about the purchase of the vehicle?"

"Yes. It was about the money. I explained it as a money-changing transaction, nothing more. Euros to dollars."

"Did they believe it?"

"I'm not sure. From some of the things they said, I think Interpol has been queried," he said. "We will check that, but I think the Americans have connected the Heismann name *and* the Hodler name."

Heismann blinked. Hodler? Interpol had Hodler? This was a surprise. He really had believed that Interpol did not have that name; he had paid some good money to get it out of their database.

"And of course you used Hodler to purchase that automobile."

"Yes, I did," Heismann snapped, looking around the crowded lobby of the museum to see if anyone was watching him. "What of it?"

"Well, I'm not sure about the local police, but the federal

police might put a flag on that name here in the city. The vehicle registration will be in that name."

"But no address—I had all the paperwork sent to the bank, as you directed. Besides, they told me that will take weeks—the salesman warned me about this. How slowly such things are done in this city."

"Even so. They were curious about that, too."

"Well then, this is about the bait," Heismann said. "Which was your idea."

Mutaib didn't say anything.

"What is the matter?" Heismann asked.

"Nothing. I was just surprised that Interpol had the Hodler name. You told us they did not."

Not as surprised as I am, he thought, but you are right to be concerned, princess. Because now that vehicle ties the name Hodler to you and your Saudi money. "As long as you did not use that name or the Heismann name in the apartment lease," Heismann said, "we will be fine. I will be in Hong Kong by the time those automobile papers come through."

"It's not in the lease, but there was some discussion about the famous artist," Mutaib said. "Let's hope no one remembers. I will have the materials sent around this afternoon. The neighbor is no problem?"

"No problem at all," Heismann said. "In fact, she is going to be part of the final solution. We've been getting acquainted. Or I have anyway."

"Do I want to know anything about that 'final solution'?"

"You do not," Heismann said.

"That's a rather precarious choice of words you're using," Mutaib said.

"It is just an expression, no matter what some people think," Heismann said. "It speaks to efficiency, nothing more."

"Come in, Swamp, and shut the door," McNamara said. "I have about ten minutes, and then I've got to go back and murder-board the revised NIC briefing. God, I hate these eternal committees!"

Swamp entered the office, shutting the door behind him, and sat down. He'd brought a legal pad filled with his notes, but McNamara waved him off. "Look," he said. "Mary said you wanted to brief me on this PRU firefly. But given PRU's position, why do we still want to pursue it?"

Hell, Swamp thought, he's forgotten already. "Uh, you'll remember that I subsequently talked to Lucy VanMetre and—"

"Yes, yes, I remember, but this memo apparently came in this morning."

Swamp drew a blank. Based on his conversation with Lucy last night, they were still collaborating, albeit on a loose leash. Was this a new memo? McNamara caught his surprise. "Your interlocutor over there in PRU lead you astray?"

Swamp shook his head. "I don't know what's going on here. We spoke as recently as last night. But now that you mention it, I tried to call her earlier, got stonewalled big-time. Is this a second memo?"

McNamara nodded and then read it aloud. "He references the previous memo. Then this is what he says: 'With regard to the matter of the transcript recovered from the fire at the cosmetic surgery clinic, the Secret Service/PRU wishes to reiterate that a determination has been made that no threat to presidential security exists and that no further official action is contemplated in regard to this matter. It is further and strongly recommended that no further action should be taken on this matter by any *other* office within the national security system.' Love and kisses, C. Hallory, Director, et cetera."

"That's clear as a bell," Swamp said. "But hear me out— let me tell you what's happened since we last spoke, because I think there is a very definite threat to presidential security."

"Can you do it in five minutes?" McNamara asked.

When Swamp was finished, it was McNamara's turn to be baffled. "Something's sure as hell going on," he said. "There has to be a reason why some guy is so determined to kill the last surviving member of that clinic team. But maybe—"

"What?" Swamp said, but McNamara was already shaking his head.

"No, that doesn't work. I was about to say maybe he's trying to kill her because she can ID him from the cop killing. But you say it's the other way around, that the lieutenant got whacked just because he was there."

Swamp nodded. "And the killer came back, remember? Tasered those patrol cops and shot at the house to spook her. Which worked. Now she's hanging on a morphine drip out in West Virginia."

"And the Royal Kingdom Bank provided the money for this guy to buy a Suburban?"

"Sort of, yes, sir. He brought in the Euros. But don't forget that they owned a piece of that clinic business."

"Yeah. Shit. What a can of worms."

"Now we're definitely making some assumptions here," Swamp said. "I'm hardly ready for court. But bottom line? I'm hearing 'bomb, bomb, bomb,' an identity-change shop, a German's version of 'State of the Union,' Saudi money, a determined effort to kill a potential witness, one face with at least two names from the German terrorist underground. I mean, shit, think of that laundry list appearing after the fact in the *Washington Post*."

"Be a shit storm. 'You mean you guys had all this and you did *nothing*?' "

"Exactly. Can you give Hallory a WTF call?"

"I guess I'm going to have to," McNamara said, looking at his watch.

"Or—" Swamp said, then stopped and looked at his boss.

"Or?"

"Or we haven't had this discussion. I just keep trucking. The Secret Service doesn't drive OSI. Committee of equals and all that. This outfit can still make its own decisions, can't it?"

"Yes and no," McNamara said with a sigh. "It's partly a budget issue: Our director might challenge any additional resources in light of this love note from PRU."

"How's about this: I work for you, not Hallory. I'll keep going here until *you* tell me unequivocally to shut it off. Make no decisions now. That way, I'm the runaway train if they call you out on it."

McNamara smiled. "Old habits die hard, huh?"

Swamp shrugged. "I've got my teeth in this one, boss."

"And we all know what that means," McNamara said. "Okay—I'm going to exercise some executive oversight. Meaning, because of some oversight, this executive never saw this memo." He waved Hallory's new memo. "But pretty soon, we'll have to sort this out. Hallory may be getting some guidance we don't know about." He looked at his watch again and stood up.

Swamp got up, too. "Thanks, boss. With your permission, I'll work my old web, see if I can get some help for that forensic screen I need on all those clinic records. If we can get a new face on this guy, even a composite, it will help a lot in finding him."

McNamara was already headed out the door. "What guy?" he said over his shoulder.

Heismann had the delivery people put all the building materials right in the front rooms of the town house. He wore a minimal facial disguise, because the deliverymen could have cared less what he looked like. He set to work as soon as they left.

The first order of business was to reinforce the floor under the "studio." He got up on a ladder in the dining room and began tapping finishing nails into the ceiling plaster to locate the floor joists in the center of the ceiling. When he'd found three adjacent joists, he chiseled out the plaster to re-

veal the actual wood. Then, leaving the rug in place, he cut
out eight one-foot squares of three-quarter-inch plywood.
He measured the distance between the first floor and the bottom of the exposed joists, then cut four of the four-by-four
timbers to that length. He tacked the plywood plates on each
end and then erected the timbers to form four closely spaced
columns. The rug provided the necessary clearance to
squeeze the timbers into vertical position. Then he screwed
the upper and lower plywood plates into the ceiling joists
and the floor itself to keep the four-by-fours from moving.
Right now, they just sat there. Once the weapon was brought
in, they would support almost all of its dead weight.

Then he had to reinforce the upstairs floor so it could support a dynamic load. For this, he used four more four-by-
fours, braced at a sixty-degree angle and meeting at the top
of the column arrangement he'd built earlier. After tacking
on some more plywood plates along the baseboards, he
jammed the bottom of these four-by-fours up against the
first-floor walls. He stepped back to examine his handiwork.
From the front entrance, it looked like he had the beginnings
of an oil-drilling rig erected. The air was full of plaster dust
and the floor was covered in it. Then he began hauling materials upstairs.

The location for the weapon would be determined by the
trajectory angle between the floor and that skylight in the
master bedroom. He had acquired a handheld GPS navigation device at a marina down on the Washington waterfront.
The GPS device gave him the grid coordinates of this room
in the house. Now what he needed was the grid coordinates
of the target. For that, he was going to have to take a walk,
probably in broad daylight. He'd go tomorrow, during the
lunch hour, when there would be more people wandering the
Mall and the Capitol grounds. He didn't think he'd be able to
get up to the West Portico itself, not this close to the inauguration. But he could extrapolate from a map showing the grid

coordinates and thereby refine the azimuth of fire. Mutaib
had promised him precise coordinates in time for the attack.

The master bedroom was empty, and the rugs had been
taken up, as well. The old tongue-and-groove pine floors
were in good condition, considering their age. Once he had
his materials upstairs, he went downstairs and measured the
center of the column structure from the side and back walls
of the house. Translating those measurements to the floor of
the master bedroom, he located the center of the column
support and marked it. He cut three more sheets of three-
quarter-inch plywood in half and then began screwing these
four-by-four-foot sections down onto the floor, centered on
his mark, one on top of the other. When he had six sections
stacked and screwed down, he located the center of the stack
and marked that. Getting on a ladder, he climbed up into the
ceiling dormer, which contained the skylight structure. The
skylight was rectangular, with the long axis running parallel
to the slope of the roof. The window aperture was six feet
long by four feet wide. He had thought the grillwork in the
glass contained individual panes of glass, but he found that
the grillwork had been glued on to one solid piece of glass.
He snorted in contempt. In Germany, of course, they would
have been individual panes. The day's dreary rain ran down
the outside of the glass in cold-looking rivulets. He checked
the edges of the glass to make sure there were no hinges, but
it was all set down into heavy putty of some kind.

He could do no more until he had the coordinates and
could work out the fire-control problem. He needed to remind Mutaib to get him the precise target coordinates. Tomorrow, he would take his walk, once again a Washington
office worker out for a noonday stroll. He would get as close
as he could, feigning interest in the preparations up at the
Capitol, record the readings, and then compute a preliminary solution. With that, he could make absolutely sure the
skylight was going to provide the necessary firing aperture,

because if it didn't, he might have to do some surgery on the roof itself. The marble would arrive tomorrow, so he had to be back in time for that. Which reminded him: He had to construct the ramp over the stairs so that the heavy blocks and ultimately the weapon itself could be moved upstairs. He looked at his watch. Much to do in the three days remaining.

Swamp spent the rest of the afternoon making phone calls to his old contacts in the Forensics divisions of the FBI and BATF, as well as the one out at NIH. In every case, the people he'd known had either been reassigned or had retired. Just for the hell of it, he put a call into Cullen's office a little after five o'clock, but a lonely-sounding desk officer told him everyone was still out. That funeral has to be over by now, he thought, but then he remembered that there would be a racket going on somewhere. He left a message for Cullen to call him in the morning, as there'd be no point in talking to anyone in Homicide tonight. He called Gary over and took a look at the preliminary dossier on Heismann/Hodler.

"The Interpol report says he was a tank gunner in the East German army," Gary said. "And then served as the sergeant of a mortar crew. Went from army conscript directly into the Stasi."

"Makes sense. In those days, the Soviets, the military, and the secret police ran East Germany. And he would have gotten some good operational and field training from the Soviets if he stayed in East Berlin."

"They list English as a second language."

"Right. Germans take English almost from day one in school. The Eastern Germans had to learn Russian, as well. Smart bastards. You get any better physical description?"

"Yes, sir. Not a big guy, actually. Five eight, one forty. Blond and blue-eyed. You saw the picture."

"Right. I was looking for the SS insignia."

Gary nodded and flipped to the second page of the report. "If the Nazis came back, he'd definitely be there for them. Supposedly collects Hitler memorabilia. Big on racial purity. His father was in the Hitler Youth and his grandfather was a member of something called an Einsatzgruppe, whatever that is."

"Really," Swamp murmured. He looked outside. The rain had become heavier as the tail end of the storm stalled over Washington. The streetlights were amber blurs through their window.

"What is that?" Gary asked.

"World War Two death squads. They went into the eastern front in 1942, right behind the regular Wehrmacht units. Did what today we'd call 'ethnic cleansing.' Jews, so-called Gypsies, and a hell of a lot of Russian civilians. Take 'em out behind the farmhouse and machine-gun the whole family. I take back what I said about the Soviets training this guy."

"Unless they didn't know about those connections."

Swamp nodded. "That's possible. It might explain this Heismann/Hodler business. Although the hard-core Stasi guys were typically ready and willing to revisit the eastern front. Remember, the Soviets were an occupying power until the Berlin Wall came down."

"Well, so were we."

"Not like the Russians, who lost a million civilians in that war. They crushed the Germans at the end, especially in Berlin, and then sat on the wreckage for forty years. You should see the Soviet war memorial in East Berlin. It's right out of Roman times. Their theory was that a divided Germany let everyone breathe easier for almost forty years."

"What was our theory?"

"Not too different from theirs, I suspect. Okay—I'm nowhere with getting help with that record screen. We're going to have to go through channels after all."

"I've got the dossier as up-to-date as I can get it. I also put a page in there on his weapons use—arson, Taser, a Walther nine, nerve agent, and the fact that he could hire some woman to knife Connie Wall."

"A hitter for all seasons," Swamp said. "And well funded."

"Yes, sir."

A burst of rain drummed against the windows as the wind shifted more to the north. Swamp could see a cluster of blue strobe lights three blocks away at an intersection. The traffic tonight was going to be horrendous. Gary was eyeing the weather, too.

"I need some time to think," Swamp said finally. "Keep that dossier file going. Maybe contact the Bureau in the morning, go talk to one of their reconstruction wizards. You know, the ones who can take skull fragments and produce a mannequin head?"

"But we have his picture."

"Right. You take that, and ask them if it's possible to go the other way—first get them to build a computer model of that head and face from the picture, then, as we discover surgical procedures, get them to modify their model. Surgical record says they took two centimeters off his nose. What would that look like now?"

Gary made some notes. "Will they do it if we ask?"

"You go establish liaison with the appropriate office. I'll see what I can do."

Connie was jolted awake by a lance of pain deep inside her back, as if something had torn loose. She tried to sit up but couldn't, and she couldn't cry out because her mouth was as dry as cotton. She moaned a couple of times, and that brought the ICU nurse. When she saw the tears in Connie's eyes, she gave her some water, rubbed a little Vaseline on her lips, and then checked the pain meds.

"They've backed you off morphine, dear," the nurse said. "That's why it hurts."

"Put it back," Connie mumbled. Her breath was coming in hot little spurts, each inhalation a little bit harder. Something was trying to smother her. She wanted to sit up but still couldn't. She felt panic rising.

The nurse checked the chart, looking for orders, which apparently weren't there. She looked at Connie's face. "I'll call the doctor right away," she said. "We'll get something going PDQ. Just hang in there."

Connie closed her eyes as the waves of pain washed up inside her chest in time with her heartbeat. She felt the first twinges of nausea, and realized that if she vomited, she'd tear her insides apart. She tried deep breathing, and that helped a little. A very little. How could they forget the order for the pain meds. Idiots. Or maybe the attending was one of those guys who was freaked-out about addiction. Screw that. This *hurt*.

The pain delivered one advantage: Her brain was much clearer. She could remember Carla. Who she was pretty sure was not a Carla at all, but maybe a Carl. She knew she'd seen those eyes before, just once, flashing at her through her dining room window, illuminated by a flashlight. Cat Ballard's killer, dressing up as a woman, and doing a fine job of it. She recalled the face and knew now that it had been painted on. The only jarring feature had been her nose, which had been too long for her face. What am I saying here? *His* face. And I, a surgical nurse in a plastic surgeon's office, flat-*assed missed* it.

The nurse came back with a clear plastic bag, which she proceeded to hang on the IV stand. "Here now, this will help," she said as she connected the tubes.

"Need to talk to Cullen," Connie whispered. "Detective. Washington."

"Yes, yes, I remember him. Nice man, for a policeman. We'll make sure he knows. Now, how's that? Better?"

Connie took a deep breath, and this time her insides didn't demand revenge for it.

"Yes, better. When . . . Oh well. Never mind."

And then she felt the plane of her existence once again tilt forward and down. She was feeling slightly guilty for not talking to Jake first, but then she simply didn't care. Whoever was driving this plane was doing much better.

"There now, dear," the nurse said. "There now. Lazy damned doctors."

Mario got up from the waiter's table and escorted Swamp to a corner booth in the empty restaurant. Caruso's was on the second floor of a residential hotel, which was why it was open even on a rainy Monday night. Swamp could hear the sounds of an argument coming from the kitchen, which was at the other end of the room. Mario took his dripping raincoat.

Twenty minutes later, Mario produced a platter of sausages, peppers, eggplant, and onions in a marinara sauce over perciatelli. I'm gonna die, Swamp thought as he tucked a large napkin into his shirt collar and dug in. He was just finishing up when he sensed there was someone standing next to his shoulder. He looked up to find Lucy VanMetre.

"May I join you?" she asked. She was wearing a stylish full-length black raincoat, but he noticed it was not wet at all.

"By all means," he replied, starting to get up. She put a hand on his shoulder for a moment before sliding into the booth. Her hair was once again coiled in an elaborate coif, and it, too, bore no sign of the weather outside. So tonight she had a driver, Swamp realized. He took the napkin out of his shirt. Mario appeared and she asked for a glass of Lacrima Cristi.

"I was just finishing," Swamp said. "Mario can—"

"That's all right," she said. "I had a late lunch today. It's been a total Monday."

Swamp nodded. "I remember those. Your own minders had the shields up pretty high today."

"By direction," she said. Mario brought her wine, and raised his eyebrows questioningly, but she shook her head, so he took Swamp's plates and went away. "Did you know you are becoming radioactive?"

"*Moi?* What have I done?"

"Persist?" she said. "Mr. Hallory is increasingly annoyed."

"Well, Tad McNamara showed me the latest hate mail, but after I briefed him, he decided we're going ahead, whether PRU likes it or not." Or words to that effect, he told himself, feeling a slight twinge of guilt.

"Have you spoken to Mr. McNamara since he got back from the murder board for the NIC briefing?" She sipped some wine and regarded him with those blue eyes.

"No. I left before he got back. Why?"

"Because Mr. Hallory went over there to the briefing room, called him out of the board, and—how shall I put this?—shared his thinking with him."

Swamp finished his own wine and Mario appeared with his coffee. "What's Hallory getting so spun up about?" he asked. "If OSI wants to waste time on a firefly, what's it to him?"

"Because he sees OSI's decision to proceed with it as a direct criticism of PRU. This isn't about the firefly anymore. It's all about an infringement of PRU's charter within DHS, which is the protection of the presidents—plural in this case—from external threats. If OSI says there is a threat and PRU says there isn't, it makes PRU look bad."

"Lotta alphabet soup showing there, Lucy," Swamp replied. "OSI hasn't *said* anything critical of anybody. We're continuing an internal investigation, that's all. And as I've said before, if we find a bad guy in the shadows, we call in the United States Secret Service."

"But why are *you* going on with this? Are you any closer to your 'bad guy in the shadows'?"

"Did you know we've identified a Saudi connection?" Swamp asked.

"Connection to what?"

"To the guy we're hunting. He got the money to buy a vehicle from the Saudi bank here in town."

"Really!"

"Well, let me qualify that," Swamp said. He described the transaction, noting that all the documents were to be sent to the Royal Kingdom Bank.

She dismissed it immediately. "That's not funding; that was a money-changing transaction. It's a bank."

"Then why send the registration papers back to the bank?"

"Because he didn't have an address here in the city yet?"

"He's been in this country for over eighteen months," Swamp said, and then told her about the purchaser's name being Hodler, and that a Mr. Hodler had come across the street and found out where Connie Wall was going, after which a female hitter had appeared out of nowhere out in West Virginia. That Heismann, the original name, was linked to the alias Hodler by Interpol.

"This all sounds very circumstantial to me, Mr. Morgan. You *think* all these things are true, but you cannot prove any one connecting element. Can you?"

"McNamara and I gave it the *Washington Post* test this morning. We'd be fools not to pursue it."

"And has Ms. Wall spoken yet?"

"Nope."

"So you're no closer with a description. There's no way to find this 'bad guy' of yours, is there?"

"Certainly not if we don't look," Swamp said impatiently.

She started to answer but then sipped some wine. "You

cannot appreciate," she said slowly, "the degree of stress PRU is under right now."

"Sure I can. You've got the inauguration. The ultimate terrorist target in the United States."

"Yes, it is. The old president and the new one. The outgoing government and the incoming one. The entire executive and policy base of the United States, all assembled in one public place. So, yes, we're taking extraordinary measures. Did you know, for instance, that all cell and landline phone service in Washington will be turned off for the entire workday on Friday?"

"What? Why?"

"So no one can trigger a preplanted bomb with a phone call, as they've been doing in Israel for the last four years. In case you've forgotten, cell phones are radios."

"Okay, I can see that, but—"

"There will be four—count them—just four television channels allowed within the security zone. Each cameraman will have a Secret Service agent standing behind him with a gun. We will have direct control of all their transmission facilities. Every image you see on television that day will be thirty seconds behind real time. So no one can give a signal or send out an 'initiate' message. There's more."

"Do tell."

"We will have control over all radio frequencies, police, fire, EMT units, data, radar-link, microwave, you name it. We will own the entire spectrum."

"That'll put a crimp in business all right."

"There won't be any business. The markets in New York will be shut down. All government workers furloughed with pay for the day. Airports and train stations closed until Friday night."

"The vacuum-packed inauguration," Swamp said. "The First Amendment wienies must be going snakeshit."

"Yes, I know that's what they're calling it. And as you say, there is the teeniest bit of opposition. The media corporations are already suing. The Congress is very unhappy, because they have this quaint notion that the Capitol is *their* building. And the District Police Department is . . . well, there aren't really words for it. They're completely overwhelmed, and the lockdown hasn't even begun yet."

"So why worry about one recalled retiree chasing after a firefly, maybe even a phantom firefly? This doesn't affect the inauguration. This deal's about something that's almost a month away."

"As I told you, it's being seen by Hallory and people senior to him as a direct challenge to PRU's exclusive purview in these matters."

"Well hell, Lucy, tell him to get over it. It's not like we're going out to the press and throwing stones."

"You made calls all over Washington today, looking for help with your records screen. That got back to Hallory. Along with the 'why.'"

Oops, Swamp thought. "But it was still all inside federal LE. We're both in the same department. Individual offices disagree within cabinet departments all the time. And, by the way, I got zilch in the way of help."

"You got nowhere because I made some calls after you first called in to the Bureau."

"Oh," he said, surprised. "So you're saying we're on our own with this one?"

She gave him a long look. "I'm saying you need to cease and desist, or you're probably going back to your little bed-and-breakfast or whatever it is out there in Harpers Ferry."

Lucy wasn't smiling now, and for the first time in his conversations with La Mamba, Swamp felt anger. "Now that sounds like a threat, Lucy," he said evenly. "And it also sounds like perfect fodder for a quick little spot on the *Today Show.*"

"You even try to do that, and you'll join some well-known guests of the government down in Guantánamo Bay," she said, leaning forward. "Are you aware that we've already picked up over three hundred individuals right here in Washington, D.C., for protective custody?"

"*Protective* custody? Protective of whom?"

"You figure it out, Mr. Morgan. But I strongly suggest you stop this little crusade of yours, and now would be nice."

Swamp pushed back from the table and stood up. "You know, Lucy, I think it's time we stopped having these little meetings. I'll talk to my boss; you talk to yours. That's what they get paid for." As he reached into the pocket of his suit jacket for his wallet, two men in suits stepped into view in the restaurant's main doorway. Both of them were staring at him and had their hands in the draw position under their suit jackets. Swamp recognized them as Secret Service agents. He stopped moving.

"*What the fuck?*" he growled. Then he took out his wallet—slowly.

Lucy stood up and looked at him. "PRU will brook no interference in the security arrangements for this inauguration," she said firmly. "By all means, talk to your boss in the morning. I suspect he will have been properly calibrated by then. Good night, Mr. Morgan."

Lucy strode out of the dining room, her blond hair flashing in the subdued light, followed by the two agents. Mario, who had been watching all this from his waiter's station, came over to Swamp's table and asked if he was okay.

"You need a gun?" he asked. "Those guys, they had guns, no?"

Swamp smiled. He had a quick vision of Mario producing a Sicilian *lupara* from the restaurant's linen closet. "Thanks, Mario, but I don't think so. Maybe just the check for right now."

"Watch out for the beautiful woman," Mario warned. "They are always the dangerous ones."

Got that right, Swamp thought.

• • •

Heismann had walked three blocks to the little pizza shop as soon as real darkness fell over Capitol Hill. Now he was walking back up Fifth Street, which paralleled First Street four blocks over from the Capitol itself. The rain was steady, but he was well bundled up in the loden overcoat and hat, and he carried a large umbrella over his head. He had plastered on a dark beard, thick eyebrows, and the Coke-bottle eyeglasses.

Fifth Street was apparently outside of the security zone for the inauguration, because the Jersey barriers began on Third Street, which ran north-south behind and to the east of the Folger Library. Right now, the concrete sections were stacked on either side of the street, but the newspaper said they would start being assembled as barriers on Wednesday night. Thursday would be used to sort out any residual traffic problems and stranded vehicles until noon, and from then until Friday evening, no civilian vehicle would be allowed to approach or move inside the security zone. The southern boundary of the zone would be D Street, between Second Street, SW and Third Street, SE. The northern boundary was a triangle consisting of Louisiana Avenue, Union Station, and the tail end of Massachusetts Avenue.

Fortunately, his own town house was three blocks outside the zone. There was little traffic at this hour, and only an occasional police car came swishing by in the rain. He was careful not to go near the security zone, because he had seen some television cameras being installed on streetlights and telephone poles that afternoon. When he got to Independence Avenue, he turned around and started back toward his own town house. He paused for a moment under a tree on the corner, read the street signs, looked both ways for oncoming traffic, and then pulled the lapel of his coat aside and examined the tiny glowing square of the GPS unit. It displayed the streets on a scale that contained three city blocks, and showed him standing right where the signs said he was. The image was clear one moment and then it would fade. So, he thought, this works, even in the rain. Tomorrow, he would make his noontime walk. Then he needed to acquire a smaller-scale touring map of the downtown area and record his calculations on it.

He'd talked to Mutaib at 6:00 P.M., using a pay phone in the Eastern Market Metro station. The marble blocks were coming at 3:00 P.M. tomorrow. Mutaib had promised the refined coordinates would be delivered by courier on Wednesday. The weapon would be delivered sometime on Thursday morning, and the warheads sometime after that. Heismann had questioned so many deliveries so close to the period of intense security awareness in the area, but Mutaib had told him the truck shipments were being assembled in Baltimore and that the timing was deliberately being kept vague for security purposes. In his view, multiple deliveries would make them seem more routine to the police, and, in any event, the arrangements could not be changed now.

Heismann pulled the umbrella closer to his face as another police car went by, then resumed walking back toward his town house. The one remaining element of the plan he had to focus on was his escape. He'd picked a route on the map, but now he needed to walk the route a few times to make sure it wasn't going to be blocked. And then he needed to walk through the time and motion requirements of the final identity change, setting the fires, and getting away from the house. He also had to position the big Suburban in a likely location, and dispose of the minivan. He'd seen a Catholic church parking lot three blocks away that ought to work for that purpose.

The rain rattled steadily on the umbrella. It had better not rain on *der Tag*, he thought, or they'll all be inside and this thing won't work. He had three full days to do all the walk-throughs. And he still had to figure out how to get to the bank after the attack. He smiled at the thought of what was going to happen there.

• • •

At 9:00 P.M., Swamp, who'd been pacing in his apartment ever since getting back, decided to call Bertie. He'd been stewing about the confrontation with Lucy, and he badly wanted a second opinion. Swamp told him about the developments in his own investigation, the general outline of his previous understanding with Lucy VanMetre, and what had happened in the restaurant.

"Like I told you, Swamp," Bertie said, "dangerous serpent."

"But why would she do that?" Swamp asked. "Everything up to that moment had been cooperation: I fed her information on what I was doing, and she . . . she—"

"She pocketed all that and kept you in the mushroom mode, didn't she?" Bertie said.

"Well, I guess, but I wasn't asking anything from her except some support when our own investigation coughed up something solid. If it did."

"I also told you Lucy runs her own agenda, all the time," Bertie said. "I'm guessing she may have been sincere right up to the point where Hallory told her to quit playing games with you or he'd shitcan her. Grab our Lucy by the career, you'll get a handful of teeth every time."

Swamp shook his head as a blast of wind and rain shook his windows. On the fourteenth floor, the weather was often more vigorous than down in the street. "And that's another thing I don't get—why in the hell would Hallory care what I'm doing? He has to know OSI isn't really challenging PRU."

Swamp heard some ice cubes clinking in a glass. "Hallory's close to losing it, from what my people are telling me," Bertie said. "In over his head from the git-go, and the way they're trying to seal up this inauguration, he's sinking deeper and deeper every day. I've pulled my people out of their counterintelligence effort. We feed him intel reports, but the director has told me to get out to arm's length and stay there."

"Be that as it may, I'm gonna talk to Tad McNamara to-morrow morning. Tell him what happened. Something's not right here."

"You be careful, Swamp Morgan," Bertie said. "Don't get too visible this close to the *big deal.* She threatened to send your ass to GitMo, she can probably make that happen in this threat climate. And they have their reasons, which I can't discuss on a clear phone."

"I suppose," Swamp said. He thought he heard something click on the line, and he glanced outside to see if there was lightning. There wasn't. "But I'm going to keep looking for this Heismann, or Hodler, or whatever he's calling himself."

"Just make it an office exercise for the rest of this week, okay? No nighttime excursions to Capitol Hill. No canvassing of all the realty offices in town to see if the Royal Kingdom Bank's been renting places. No late-afternoon social calls on the director of the Secret Service. Just cool it for this week."

"And then?"

"And then a new crew's gonna work security for the joint session, and *they* might care about your firefly. Right now, in Hallory's view, you're crank-dancing. You're retired, re-member?"

Swamp gave up. "All right, Bertie, and thanks for listen-ing."

"No problem, buddy. But Swamp?"

"Yeah?"

"My phone's a lot different from yours. Even here in this apartment. And right now, mine's telling me I might not have been the only one listening."

Bertie hung up. Swamp kept the receiver to his ear, but he heard only silence, and then the dial tone. He hung up and sat back in his chair.

What the hell is going on here? he wondered. Had Lucy gotten a wiretap order on his home phone? That quickly? And then he realized she might have done it a long time ago. *Shit.*

He got up, went out into the hallway, and looked out a front window. There was a semicircular drive out front, where parking was supposedly reserved for short-term evolutions, such as loading and unloading, taxis, or prospective tenants. At this time of night, there were rarely any cars out there, but tonight there was a large dark Suburban with a light rack and some whip antennas parked right out front. Because of the building's front spots, he could see two whitish blurs shimmering through the rain-swept windshield. Then what looked like a hand came up and waved at him once. Swamp just stared for a moment, resisting an impulse to give whoever it was the finger.

He went back into his apartment. This had to be Lucy's doing. Okay, let them play their games. Bertie had, perhaps unwittingly, given him an idea—canvass realty offices in the city. See if any of them had done any business with that Royal Kingdom Bank. And better yet, he'd say he was calling from the U.S. Secret Service.

Capitol grounds.

9

HEISMANN SAT DOWN ON A PARK BENCH FOR A MOMENT BE-
fore walking the final few blocks to the Botanic Garden
Conservatory. He was at the Capitol end of the Mall, wearing some of the same disguise elements he'd used the night
he'd Tasered the patrol officers, only not looking quite so
old. No cane this time, and graying hair under the homburg,
instead of white. Two blocks away were the empty reflecting
pools between the Mall and the Conservatory, drained now
due to the frigid January weather. There were a few others
out for midday walks, but not many. The wind blew steadily
out of the northwest, and the rime on the puddles was not
melting, even in the bright sunlight.

He carried a rectangular leather briefcase, in which the
GPS unit was taped to the bottom. He also had a *Washington
Post* and a deli sandwich in a white bag. His goal was to get
as close to the Capitol grounds as the security arrangements
allowed, walk to the northwest corner of the circular walks
on the Capitol lawns, and take a reading. He'd obtained a
current tourist map of the federal monuments area, which
he'd taped to the wall in the master bedroom. He'd drawn a
straight line on it between his town house and the west portico of the Capitol. Extending that line in the northwest direction bisected the corner of the lawns. The straight line
gave him his firing azimuth in relation to true north. What he

was trying to calculate was the actual range, which, in turn, would determine the elevation angle for firing. Ideally, he would walk up to the west portico steps and take a reading, but the entire western lawn area had been blocked off with barriers, and there were visible police patrols all around the Capitol grounds.

Which meant he would have to triangulate the problem. He'd take a reading at the northwest corner, then walk east on Constitution Avenue, which was still open to public access, and take another reading when the west facade of the Capitol lined up on a north-south axis. Then he would walk all the way around the Capitol, going behind the Supreme Court and the Library of Congress buildings, and do the same thing on the south side of the Capitol grounds. Draw a line between those two points, and where that line intersected the firing azimuth would be the target coordinates. He had a handheld calculator, which would give him the firing range once he entered the target coordinates and those for his townhouse. He would then check this solution against what Mutaib sent him.

He opened the briefcase, checked to make sure the GPS unit was turned on and in sync with its satellites, and then took out his newspaper and sandwich. Over the next fifteen minutes, he saw two police units making a continuous car patrol along the streets that boxed the Capitol complex: First Street, SW, First Street, SE, Constitution Avenue, and Independence Avenue. The police cars were simply driving in a big revolution around and around the Capitol square. He looked hard for video cameras, but he couldn't see any in his immediate vicinity, although he knew there had to be some up nearer the Conservatory. Anticipating that he would not be able to stop on the street, open the briefcase, and take GPS readings in full view of the security forces, he'd broken a pencil into two pieces. He'd taped the eraser end to the button that commanded the GPS unit to enter a way point. He'd cut a small hole in the narrow top of the briefcase, under the handle, and jammed the other end of the pencil into that hole. Now when he wanted to enter a way point, he simply had to push on the pencil at the top to make contact, once for each entry. If anyone stopped him and asked to inspect the briefcase, he might be in trouble, although there was space for him to push the pencil all the way through into the briefcase if he had to. This little excursion was dangerous. But he wasn't willing to depend entirely on the Arab for the most crucial bit of targeting information.

He finished the sandwich and then pretended to read his paper for another ten minutes. No one seemed the least bit interested in him, although he could barely make out the blur of faces in the patrol cars two blocks away. Time to go. He stuffed the newspaper sections loosely into the briefcase, placing them on top of the taped-down GPS unit, put the sandwich wrappings on top of that, made sure the pencil stub was in position, and closed it up.

The first two way points went in without a hitch. He stopped for just a second to push on the pencil, heard the tiny beep from inside the case, and then continued walking. A passing police car slowed momentarily as he stood on the corner of Constitution and First Street, NE, but then it made a right turn and headed down in front of the Capitol. He actually nodded at the policewoman, who was looking at him, and she smiled and nodded back. He crossed First Street and then walked two more blocks east before turning south to get behind the Supreme Court and Library of Congress buildings. He knew he had a decision to make: That woman had seen him on the corner. If she saw him again down on Independence, would she and her partner stop? Search him? Should he wait a half hour, then continue his circle of the Capitol? Or perhaps come back in two or three hours to get the bottom half of the coordinates? By that time, they might have ended their tour of duty. But no, the marble delivery was scheduled for today. He had to finish it now and get back.

He continued walking, pulling his coat tighter as he finally turned west onto Independence Avenue and faced into the wind. There were more barriers down here on this side, and a collection of telephone company trucks with jib cranes mounted on the back were parked on the little street between the two House office buildings. Four police cars were parked together behind the line of trucks, and he could see a knot of cops huddling against the back of one of the trucks. He walked a little faster now, head down into the wind, his homburg pulled low over his forehead, while he kept an eye out for police cars. He'd spotted half a dozen security cameras mounted on telephone poles.

As he drew abreast of his line, one-third of the way along the Rayburn House Office Building, he saw a police car approaching from the west on the other side of Independence Avenue, cruising slowly. Same one, or the second one? He dared not look at them. He came up on his line and pushed the pencil, not stopping this time, and then stepped up the pace a little as he went down the sidewalk toward the Mall. But that passing police car had flipped on its blue lights and was making a deliberate U-turn in the middle of Independence, scattering traffic. He swore but kept walking, pretending to be oblivious as he pushed the pencil all the way through to the inside, evoking several beeps from the GPS unit. He had the Walther in his waistband, but he couldn't use it here, not with all these police. The cruiser drew abreast of him along the curb, pointed the wrong way in traffic, and stopped. He kept walking, and the car started up again while the driver rolled down his window.

"Excuse me, sir?" the driver called.

Mouth dry, Heismann stopped and cupped his hand behind his ear, but he did not approach the car. The driver put the car in park and started to get out, as did his partner. His heart sank: It was the same woman who'd nodded at him on the other side of the Capitol. She had to wait for passing cars before opening her door.

"Sir, may I ask what you're doing down here this afternoon?"

Heismann made a snap decision and answered in heavily accented English. "A valk, *mein Herr*," he said in his best old-man voice. "The office, much too hot, *ya*?"

"Kinda cold for a walk, isn't it?" the driver asked. He was young, his uniform didn't fit very well at all, and he didn't have his coat on. A probationer perhaps? The woman officer was standing behind the unit, in a position to react if Heismann did something unexpected. A veteran's move.

"In Chermany, dis is *eine* nice spring day, *Herr Offizier*," Heismann said, still smiling. He pointed up toward the Capitol. "Dis is vhere zey vill make ze new president, *ya*?"

"Uh, yes, sir, it is. What you got in the briefcase?"

"*Ein Zeitung.* Ze newspaper only." He partially opened the briefcase to show them, clutching at the sandwich wrappings and newspaper sections, which immediately began to ruffle in the wind. He could feel the small lump of the GPS unit beneath his gloved hand. He saw the woman put her hand on the butt of her service revolver when he opened the case, but then she relaxed. The sandwich wrapping slipped out of his fingers and blew into the street. He clucked in dismay and then closed the briefcase to prevent any more litter from escaping.

"ID," the woman prompted in a bored voice from behind the car.

"Oh, yeah," the rookie said. "Sir, could we see some ID, please?"

"Ya, ya," Heismann said quickly. He put the briefcase down on the sidewalk, extracted his Hodler passport, and stepped over to the curb to hand it to the young policeman. The cop looked it over, then got out his notebook and wrote down the name and the number of the passport before handing it back.

"*Ist verboten?*" Heismann asked, gesturing to include the street. "One cannot valk *hier*?"

"Not yet, but pretty soon, sir," said the rookie, putting away his notebook. He was shivering in the icy wind, his white shirt offering no protection. The woman sauntered back to her side of the car, waited for more traffic to pass, and got back in.

"Well, you have a nice day, sir," the rookie said. "Enjoy your stay here in Washington."

Heismann bobbed his head deferentially and then picked up the briefcase as the cop car made another U-turn, turned off its blue strobe lights, and resumed what had to be the most boring patrol in the city.

Heismann drew a very deep breath and started walking again. A nice day, he thought. I will show you a nice day. Soon, very soon. He had planned to turn south when he got to the Mall proper, to slant back toward his town house. But now he decided to keep walking west, out onto the Mall, until he was completely out of sight of all the police surrounding Capitol Hill. He could take the Metro back to Eastern Market. No more nice walks at noon.

So, the city police now had his name and passport number. There would be a report, of course, but probably one of many as the city police clamped down the Capitol Hill area. He'd had the impression that the woman officer had made the stop more in order to train the younger officer than because she was truly suspicious of the old man and his briefcase. And this disguise had helped. If he'd come out with no disguise at all, one of their tactical squads would have had him on the ground the first time he walked in front of a video camera. The question now was, What would they do about the report? One report among many, yet another foreigner gawking at the Capitol. Surely there were thousands of such people. Had a briefcase, but there was nothing in it but his newspaper and his lunch bag. A non-event, to use the *Ammie* vernacular.

But still . . . He had used the name Hodler to purchase the vehicle. Interpol had reported the name Hodler to the federal

police. And now there was a Hodler walking around the
Capitol. Was there any one central organization collating all
these reports? There was one department that was supposed
to be doing that, but Mutaib had assured him that it was absorbed in sorting out the important things, such as budgets,
committee prerogatives, parking and office space.

Still . . .

He frowned, pulled his coat tighter around him, and
walked faster. Perhaps a complication, but not fatal. And he
had his targeting data.

Swamp had talked to twenty-seven realtors by the time Mary
called and said that Mr. McNamara had just come from a
meeting and wanted to see him. Uh-oh, Swamp thought. He
told her he'd be right down, and then he walked over to
Gary's cubicle. It was 2:30.

"McNamara wants to see me. Here's the list. I guess you
can make some calls, if you feel like it. Most people were
quite cooperative, but they all wanted some time to take a
look through their records. I took the liberty of giving them
your extension."

"No problem," Gary said.

Swamp went down to McNamara's office.

"I'll get right to it," McNamara said with a pained expression.

"Let me guess: Somebody senior told you to send my ass
back to West Virginia."

"Good guess," McNamara said. "Really good guess. I
think it was all the phone calls you made around town that
did it for Hallory, and then for the director."

"Theirs or ours?"

"I think both, actually." He sat back in his chair, closed
his eyes, and rubbed his temples. "You might say that I
wasn't invited to say much of anything." He opened his eyes.
"But it kinda pissed me off anyway."

Swamp shook his head in resignation. "I thought the

whole point of this Homeland Security Department was to beat down this kind of turf shit."

"It's Washington, Swamp. Turf battles are never going to go away, because if anyone ever took a really hard look, they'd realize we don't need half the people we have working in government. That's why the bureaucracy's like that gazillion-ton supertanker—each new administration tries to put the rudder over, but nothing happens for two years."

"Okay, so what's the deal?"

"They want you gone. Deactivated. *De*called instead of *re*called. But like I said, the whole time I was coming back to the office, I was thinking, This pisses me off, and I want to go up our chain of command. In the meantime, I think you should just fold your tents and steal away into the desert night for a little while."

"In what capacity?"

"For starters, just leave town for twenty-four hours. Because I know I'm going to get some calls tomorrow, and they're gonna say, 'Is he gone?' And I want to be able to say, 'West Virginia.'"

"And then?"

McNamara leaned forward, lowering his voice. "And then I want you to do what you do best: Close this thing. Because, on balance, *I* think you're right. *I* think there's something going on, and *I* think that's our frigging job, even if it looks like a firefly."

"Our job is OSI. Special Investigations. Intelligence."

"Well then, let's fucking generate some intelligence, shall we? You go off the grid. Go find out what this crap's all about. Cozy up to some of the spiders on your old web, but do it on a personal basis. Hell, Swamp, you know how to do this."

Swamp nodded. "Yes, I do. And I appreciate the hell out of what you're saying, and doing. But I don't want to get you across the breakers with agency directors."

McNamara smiled, his eyes gleaming. "We're all here for

a second run, Swamp Morgan. You *and* me. Only this time, we should at least try to do it right. I'd like nothing better than to hand both of those directors *and* Mr. Hallory a plate of shit, but preferably before somebody throws that plate of shit at the president. You go get some evidence. I'll back you up as long as I can."

Swamp stood up. He hesitated, suddenly overcome by an emotion he couldn't name. "I think anything I say right now would be mawkish," he began.

"Then get your ass out of here so I can make them think you're fired."

Swamp grinned. "Can I use Gary as my line into the building?"

"Does he understand he could get burned? He is Secret Service, after all."

"I think so. He should know how this goes. But I'll warn him."

"Yeah, do that. But right now, get out of Dodge."

Swamp got back to his cube and called Gary over. He told him what was going down, then asked Gary to requisition a weapon for him. "I'm going to leave town, as instructed," he said. "But not for long. I'll call in, see what those realtors come up with, if anything."

"I'll finish the list. And you're going where?"

"For public consumption? I'm going home, as ordered. For a day anyway. Then I might go up to see if I can talk to Ms. Wall, assuming she's still with us."

"And that would *not* be for public consumption."

"Right. Everything to do with this little firefly is now off the books. Especially where PRU is concerned. I want to protect McNamara, as well as you. I'll get that weapon from you tomorrow."

Swamp's phone rang. He'd almost decided not to pick it up, but then he saw the caller ID number in the phone's display window. Jake Cullen.

"Morgan," he said.

"Not so loud, please," Cullen said. His voice sounded a bit raspy.

"Successful wake?"

"Oh man. Irish whiskey. Don't ever mess with Irish whiskey. So where are we with this thing?"

"It's complicated," Swamp said. "How you feel about a little road trip?"

An hour and a half later, they were gunning it out the Dulles-access toll road, right on the bow wave of the serious afternoon commuter traffic. Jake Cullen had met Swamp at the Ballston station with his overnight bag, then walked the three blocks over to the gas station to pick up the Land Rover. There'd been no sign of tails when Swamp left the office, nor at his apartment building. Apparently, they'd been called off, or a more sophisticated team was working him. Swamp had briefed the detective on what had transpired since they'd gone to the Royal Kingdom Bank. Jake whistled in surprise when he heard about the business with Lucy at the restaurant and the subsequent fallout.

"Our people are getting some of the same vibes," he said. "Secret Service going medium apeshit with this lockdown operation. You know about the cell phones—how they're gonna kill all the transmitting towers in the city for this deal? On both sides of the river?"

"Yeah, she told me," Swamp said. "Good day to stay home and watch it on TV."

"Stay home my ass," Jake said. "Every swingin' dick on the force below the rank of lieutenant's going into the bag for street duty. You watch—it'll snow."

Swamp reached the Route 7 bypass around Leesburg and turned west. "My plan is to go straight up to Garrison Gap. See if we can talk to Connie Wall."

"Last time I called, they weren't that encouraging about big conversations."

"I couldn't get any real status," Swamp said. "The sheriff may still have the shields up. I think we have to go there."

"So, are you suspended or what?"

"I think that's what my boss is trying to convey to the higher-ups. They didn't tell him to suspend me. Just to make me 'go away.' They check back tonight or tomorrow morning, I'll be gone."

Jake shook his head. "You guys in the G take some shit entirely too seriously."

"Tell me about it." Swamp laughed. "But hell, they may yet be right. If Connie Wall fails on us, and the realtors all turn up empty, I'm probably done."

Jake had his notebook out. Swamp hadn't realized the detective had been taking notes as he explained the situation. Cullen started reading from his notes. "Guy named Hodler buys a black Suburban with cash money from a Saudi bank. The papers go back to said Saudi bank. Same guy learns where Wall is going. A cop on the road spots a black Suburban traveling behind Connie Wall. That night, she gets knifed in Garrison Gap. *You* saw a black Suburban leaving Garrison Gap the morning after she was knifed. Interpol says Hodler is an alias for Heismann, which is a name mentioned in a transcript where some guy's talking about blowing shit up next month. A transcript we get from the remains of a burned-out medical clinic, where Connie Wall worked. Where all hands got dead in nonlinear circumstances." He looked up. "Lots and lots of coincidences?"

"I know," Swamp said, shaking his head. "I pitched all this to the Secret Service, in the person of Ms. VanMetre. She responds by having agents throw down on me—and put me under surveillance. Let's see what Connie Wall can do for us."

They got up to Garrison Gap around 7:00 P.M. The ICU supervisor gave them a five-minute window, but not before first making them wash their hands and faces, don gauze face masks and latex gloves, and then pull scrub tops over their shirts. "She's deep into the postop-infection window," he told them. "Don't touch her or even get that close."

"Is she conscious?"

"Sometimes," the doc said, already turning his attention to a set of orders a nurse had just brought him. "But not very." He read the orders, signed them, and hustled out of the ICU. A waiting nurse took them down to the curtained bed.

Connie looked severely diminished behind the stainless-steel frames of the ICU bed. Her face was as white as a death mask. The nurse did a quick scan of monitoring instruments and tubes, then stepped back, but she did not leave.

"Connie," Jake called, bending closer to the bed. He called her name again, and her eyelids fluttered, then opened. The nurse stepped forward, wet Connie's lips with a Q-Tip, and gave her one tiny sip of water from a stainless-steel bottle, then another.

"Connie, it's Jake Cullen. And Special Agent Morgan, Secret Service."

The nurse's eyes grew larger when she heard that, but Connie was just staring at both of them. Swamp was trying to think of how to ask her a question, when he saw her eyes cross and then one eyelid droop shut.

"Shit," he muttered, glancing over at Jake, who sighed. The nurse had an "I told you so" look on her face. She glanced pointedly down at her watch. Connie's other eye closed and she made a noise in her throat.

"What?" Jake asked, leaning forward again, but Swamp thought this was hopeless. Poor damned woman. He didn't think she was going to make it. He signaled Jake with his head that they should back out. They had only reached the curtain when they heard Connie gasp out a single word behind them: "*Him!*"

They turned around and went back. Connie's eyes were still shut, but there were lines on her forehead now, as if she were concentrating. Lines and a fine sheen of sweat.

"'Him,' Connie? Him who?" Jake asked.

"*Him*," she said again, a whisper this time. "Not . . . a . . . woman."

"Him," Swamp repeated. "You mean the guy who got Ballard did this? The guy who tried to kill you down in D.C.?"

The nurse looked positively alarmed now, and the monitors were coming alive. "That's enough," she said, motioning for them to move back.

Swamp and Jake straightened up and moved back. Connie's eyes were still closed, but there was a ghost of a smile on her face.

"Okay, Connie, we got it," Jake called. "You rest. Get better. We got it, okay? We got it."

They backed out of the room and walked down to the ICU station. The first nurse had stayed with Connie. There were two other nurses there and a new doctor. Jake showed his badge and police ID. "Listen to me," he said in a voice that made them all pay attention. "She's to have no visitors other than Special Agent Morgan here and me. And if anybody asks, you must—*must*—say that she's as good as dead. On life support, but the prognosis is grave beyond telling. Can you guys do that?"

Semi-shocked nods all around.

"Okay. Please write that down in your pass-down logs. She's safe—and you're safe—as long as she's a dying woman. Here's my card. Anybody here on staff has questions, they can call me."

More worried nods. Swamp suddenly wondered if this was going to boomerang somehow. "And thank you for keeping her alive," he added with a smile, trying to pour a little oil on the waters. Then they left the ICU and went back out to the parking lot. They got into the Rover and Jake fished out a pack of cigarettes while Swamp got the engine and the heater running. He opened Jake's window so he could blow out a hefty column of smoke into the pristine mountain air.

"So he dresses up as a woman, gets close to her, goes into

the can with her, and then knifes her," Jake said. "Just like that."

"And dresses up good enough to fool Connie Wall, and she's a nurse, for Chrissakes."

"Yeah. This is spooky. But it makes more sense. There were wits who saw a woman in that hallway. One even said he saw a woman going into the men's room, remember?"

"Yeah."

"And I never could see some foreigner being able to just call Rent-a-Hitter and get something going that fast."

"But it means we're looking for a goddamned chameleon," Swamp said. "Some guy who's had plastic surgery and who can transform himself into a woman well enough to fool a surgical nurse? This is getting to be a bitch."

"Did you see her face?" Jake said. "I don't think she's gonna make it." He blew another draft of blue smoke out the window and then tossed the glowing butt into the remains of a snowbank in the parking lot.

"Well, maybe," Swamp said. "But she fought to tell us that. She'd been saving it up. Got it out. She's a scrapper."

Jake was shaking his head as Swamp backed out of their parking space. "You really think the Saudis are getting behind another nine eleven? Right there in Washington?"

"Remember who flew the planes on nine eleven?" Swamp said, pulling into traffic on the main drag. "That said, there are Saudis and there are Saudis. I've had some valuable help from that part of the world over the past few years."

"Still," Jake said.

"And those guys on nine eleven weren't exactly members of the royal family. And changing Euros to dollars isn't a crime. I've been reaching all along on that element."

"But the vehicle's papers going back to the bank like that—makes my ass wonder."

"I'm pulling a separate string on that," Swamp said. He told Jake about his queries to realtors in the city.

"You get a hit on that question, I'll personally take in a SWAT team," Jake growled. Then his cell phone rang.

"Detective Cullen," he answered. Swamp kept driving as Jake listened. Two blocks down the road, Jake put his hand over the phone's mouthpiece and told Swamp to pull over. He said, "Yes, sir" into the phone three times, snapped it shut, and swore.

"Now what?" Swamp asked.

"Apparently, my little speech to the ICU crew got the hospital all spun up," Jake said. "They called District headquarters, demanding we move her out of there and back down to D.C., where *we* can protect her."

"Shit, I was afraid of this. Can she be moved?"

"They say yes, and that was my boss's boss. He said since I started this little shit storm, would I be so kind as to 'manage' it?"

"In those exact words?" Swamp asked with a grin.

"Not exactly. I guess we have to go back."

"*We?*"

"Yeah, yeah, I know. I'll ride down in the meat wagon with her. You go on home to Harpers Ferry. Have a drink for me. Hell, have two."

Heismann surveyed the collection of gleaming white marble blocks lining three walls of the master bedroom. The delivery had come right at three o'clock that afternoon and consisted of five pieces altogether. Four of them were three feet high and one foot square, sitting on two-foot-square wooden pallets with steel bands on four sides. There was one larger piece, five and a half feet high and eighteen inches on a side. It sat right out in the middle of the empty room now, centered on the plywood stack. There was also a flat crate, made of heavy cardboard and reinforced with wooden battens. The crate measured three feet on a side and was marked TOOLS. It was leaning up against the wall by the bedroom window.

He'd had the deliverymen place the bulk of the marble

blocks along the walls to minimize the stress on the floor's center. He'd turned off the heat in the house an hour before the delivery, opened the windows, and had met the delivery-men dressed in jeans, winter boots, a bulky turtleneck sweater, a knit watch cap that covered most of his head, and those oversized square glasses. The cold house accomplished two things: It allowed him to cover himself up and it expedited the delivery crew, who wanted nothing more than to unload the marble, haul it upstairs, and get the hell out of there. The truck had come and gone by the time he heard his neighbor climbing the steps to her front door.

He stood in the middle of the room, next to the taller piece of marble, and read the delivery manifest in the failing light of late afternoon. He was pretty sure Mutaib had changed the delivery sequence, and these papers would tell him. Each piece of marble was listed, along with its provenance, metric dimensions, and weight. The largest piece, the one out in the middle of the room, had one additional dimension, expressed in centimeters; this looked like a typo on the line of regular dimensions. Ten centimeters. That was it.

Then he went over to the flat crate, and, using a large kitchen knife, opened one end of the outer cardboard box. He slid out a flat package of sculptor's tools—hammers, chisels, other steel cutting tools, and a plastic bag filled with small wooden wedges. He found a measuring tape delineated in metric units in the package and put one end right in the center of the top face of the marble piece. Draping the tape down one side, he measured off the distance in centimeters and then made a mark with a pencil on the side of the block. He repeated this measurement on the remaining three sides of the block.

He dumped the tool package out on the floor. Taking a hammer and a pointed steel chisel, he returned to the block in the center and began tapping the point on the marks he'd made earlier. When he got to the third side, his tapping bore results: Bits of white plaster fell out onto the floor. Plaster, not marble. Moving the chisel up the side of the block about two inches, he tapped again and produced more plaster. He nodded to himself again and put the tools away. When the time came, he would tap an entire vertical line of plaster-filled holes out of the side, then use the wedges to split the block from end to end. But he'd found out what he needed to know: The weapon had arrived.

Just to make sure, he put the tools to one side and looked into the box. He pulled out a smaller cardboard box, opened one end, and saw the cell phone. He set that down and felt around in the cushioning material. His fingers encountered a steel plate, which felt as if it was about eighteen inches on a side. Only the edge of the plate was visible, but it was clearly almost an inch thick. He nodded and closed the flaps of the cardboard box.

Connie Wall awakened in the dimly lighted hospital room. She took a couple of deep breaths and realized there was no more oxygen tube parked in front of her nose. She actually felt better for the first time since . . . since that night. She could hear the typical sounds of a busy hospital ward in the corridor outside, sounds she recognized from years of trudging through similar corridors. This place felt different, sounded different, and then she remembered she'd been transported, a long ambulance ride down toward Washington, although she'd gone back to sleep during the trip. And Jake Cullen had been in the back with her, holding her hand. Wearing latex gloves. He'd tried to explain what was going on, but she hadn't really cared. They'd given her a good-bye dose of something wonderful intravenously and she'd concentrated instead on the warmth of his hand.

Now she tested her toes and fingers, and everything still responded. Her back felt as if it were padded with an infant's crib mattress, and there was a new IV patch on her right hand. The one on her left hand was gone, but the back of her left hand was sore and felt inflamed. She remembered the old expression, When the IV stick hurts more than what they did to you, you're healing.

But she was better. Her lungs weren't half-full of narco-fog anymore, and she felt the first pangs of actual hunger. Tough way to lose a couple of pounds, she thought. Keeping her right hand immobile, she moved her left and patted various parts of her body to see if everything was still there. She felt a monitoring patch above her left breast and heard the regular beep from a machine above her head. She moved her head, provoking a sudden lancing headache, so she found the call button and hit it. A nurse appeared in less than a minute, and Connie asked where she was.

"GWU Medical Center," the nurse replied. She was quite young, but she did an automatic scan of the IV stand and the monitors. "They brought you in from West Virginia about four hours ago."

"What time is it?"

"Midnight. Shift just changed. You were a nurse?"

"Still am, I think," Connie said with a crooked smile. It hurt her cracked lips.

The young nurse put her hand to her mouth in embarrassment. "I'm sorry. I didn't mean—"

Connie shook her head gently. Not a wonderful idea, she discovered. "Can I have some water, and maybe some saltines?" she asked. "I have a headache and I think I'm hungry."

"Oh, sure," the girl said brightly. "But let me ask you—do you drink coffee?"

"Yes, sure."

"That headache may be caffeine withdrawal, you know? How about maybe a Coke with those saltines?"

"Great idea," Connie said, realizing the girl was probably right.

"And there's a cop outside. He asked to be notified when you woke up."

"Sergeant Cullen?"

"Uh, no. I think his name is Butts, or something like that." She suppressed a quick grin. "He's in uniform. He just came on."

"What's my prog?" Connie asked.

"Upgraded to satisfactory about two hours ago," the nurse recited. "They've taken you off the heavy-duty pain meds and switched you to Vicodin. No sign of infection, knock on wood. Vitals seem stable. We're hydrating with that IV, and they'll bring in a pain pump in the morning. Do you remember what happened?"

"Vividly," Connie said. Her eyelids suddenly felt heavy. "But I'm actually feeling better. Although it's hard to talk. Mouth's dry."

"I'll get you some shaved ice and a little Coke syrup."

"And the crackers. Don't forget the crackers."

"The crackers," the nurse said. "Right." But Connie was already back asleep.

The nurse went to tell the cop that Connie Wall had surfaced for a few minutes but had gone back down again. But she said the patient did confirm that she remembered what happened. The officer thanked her and popped a cell phone to put a call in to Detective Sergeant Cullen at his home number.

At midnight, Heismann made a trial run through the holes he had cut into the common walls between the town houses. He was dressed in a dark sweatsuit, sneakers, black leather gloves, and a black stretch-nylon hood that looked like a ski mask. He crawled silently through the boxes and reached the closet's hallway door, where he stopped to listen for a few minutes. He opened the door and stepped out into the darkened hallway. Both the bathroom door and her bedroom door were shut. The only illumination came from a streetlight out in front of the house; it shined up the stairwell from the windows in the front room. He took some tentative steps out into the upstairs hallway to see if the floorboards creaked, but the rug apparently absorbed the pressure of his feet. He slid his feet as quietly as he could along the edge of the rug until he reached her bedroom door. He could hear her snoring.

Should he take care of her now? He put a gloved hand on the bedroom's door handle and began to twist it to the right. Once he had the bolt retracted, he pushed very gently, but the door did not move. What is this? he wondered. He tried to sense what was holding the door shut, but he couldn't tell. Had he missed something here? A dead bolt, perhaps? He released the door handle and ran his hand up the side panel of the door, feeling for screws or other fasteners, but there was nothing. Maybe it wasn't a real dead bolt, just one of those bolt-and-hasp arrangements. He slid over to the bathroom door and tried that one, and it opened. But the door connecting the master bath with her bedroom also refused to open. She was still snoring away in there, so at least she was a sound sleeper. And there was no damned little dog to yap out an alarm, thank God.

So, come back tomorrow in the daylight and see what the hell was locking the doors. If it was a real dead bolt, he must find a key. People usually kept spare keys around for those things. If a bolt and hasp, he'd back out all but two of the screws on the hasp. Then when he needed to get in Thursday night, he'd crash right through it. By the time she realized he was in the room, she'd be dead. He backed out of the bathroom and closed the hallway door. Then he went back through his secret passage.

Nothing beats personal reconnaissance, he thought. But you should have noticed those locks, he chided himself. He stopped for a moment in his own darkened hallway. First the damned nurse taking forever. Then the Hodler name surprise from Interpol. Then being stopped on the street. Hodler again. Now this business with the locks. Omens? He felt a twinge of fear. He knew that he was no mastermind. He'd come from nothing, and the Stasi would never have given him a second look if he hadn't been able to pass for an American teenager back before the Wall came down and the Cold War was lost. That was a long time ago. Now he considered himself to be a competent, if somewhat mechanical, criminal, yes, but this entire business was a huge departure from his usual jobs. It was also a main chance for a second life. The money. The totally new body and face. Only the Arabs could have funded something like this, and, as they were constantly reminding him, it was war, not crime this time. A new kind of war, to be sure, but war. And in war, the Americans will never see someone like you coming, he told himself. They're totally focused on people who look like us. You will be next to invisible.

Exactly.

10

GARY WAS WAITING FOR SWAMP WHEN HE ARRIVED AT THE office at 10:10 the next morning. He produced a fat brief-case and invited Swamp to go down the hall with him to an empty conference room. Once there, he locked the door before opening the briefcase and showing Swamp a nylon-web harness for a shoulder holster, a .357-caliber Sig Sauer semiautomatic pistol, a spare magazine, and a box of am-munition. Since Gary had checked out the weapon, he had Swamp check the serial number and then sign a subcustody card for the gear. Swamp left it all in the briefcase and they went back to the office.

"Any word from the head shed?" he asked.

"McNamara's been in meetings this morning since eight," Gary said. "I talked to Mary when I went down to get a copy of his calendar for the day, and she said there was an-other message in from PRU. Concerning you."

"Great. She say what it was?"

"No, sir. She kinda hinted that it might spoil both our days."

"Probably asking if I've been suspended yet."

"Can they just do that shit without a hearing?" Gary asked as they reached Swamp's cubicle.

"Sure. I'm on a 'serve at the pleasure of' contract. As long as they don't screw around with my pension or take any adverse personnel action, I can be sent home in a day. For that matter, so can McNamara."

"Damn."

"Technically, I am retired. None of us expects to stay forever. Any hits from those realtors?"

Gary shook his head. "Twelve called back; no recent contracts with a Mr. Hodler or any Royal Kingdom Bank."

"Well, it always was a long shot," Swamp said. "I need to talk to Cullen. Maybe try calling some of the real estate offices that haven't answered. Push a little bit. And you keep your ears to the ground on that message from PRU."

"Yes, sir."

"And Gary? Start thinking about where you want to go in case I really do get the ax. I'll get McNamara to run interference for you."

"Yes, sir," Gary said somberly.

Gary left to go back to his own cubicle and Swamp decided to check in with Mary before seeing McNamara. He raised his eyebrows at her. She looked around at the other agents in their cubes, then passed him a bootleg copy of the PRU message. "Himself is back and would like to see you," she said. "And there's a lady you know in his office with him. Maybe read that before you go down there, and then shred it. Oh, and I don't think she's your friend."

"Thanks, Mary," Swamp said. "I owe you one. As usual."

"Dark chocolates are good," she said with a smile, and wished him good luck.

He sat back in his chair. Everyone was wishing him good luck this morning, as if they knew he had suddenly run out of that commodity. He scanned the two-paragraph memo, which was from the director of the U.S. Secret Service, addressed to the undersecretary for information analysis and infrastructure protection, DHS, copy to McNamara, OSI. The memo stated that retired annuitant T. Lee Morgan, Senior Executive Service (retired), had improperly invoked the name of the U.S. Secret Service in an attempt to obtain information from civilian businesses concerning a figmentary foreign agent by the name of Erich Hodler. It further stated that Mr. Morgan had also been emphatically directed to cease and desist from any and all efforts to locate said Erich Hodler, and to conduct no further investigations into a purported and totally unsubstantiated plot to bomb the U.S. Capitol concurrent with the president's upcoming address to a special joint session of the U.S. Congress.

Then came the killer words: "In my opinion, as the director of the Secret Service, Mr. Morgan has become obsessed with a plot that exists largely in his own mind, and that Mr. Morgan's obsessive nature springs from an incident of personal misfortune in his domestic life that has, sadly, unbalanced his judgment, diminished his fitness for further government service, and led to behavior that continues to cause unnecessary and distracting strains on the current effort to complete the security shield for the upcoming inauguration."

Then the clever part: "It is with great regret and some sympathy that the director of the Secret Service must now conclude that Mr. Morgan's usefulness to the government is at an end. Since Mr. Morgan is a retired Secret Service agent, on temporary recalled annuitant status within the Department of Homeland Security, it is strongly recommended that the secretary terminate Mr. Morgan from further active duty in said department in order to avoid any further embarrassment to the U.S. Secret Service. A replacement asset will be made available to DHS-OSI as soon as the presidential inauguration has been completed."

Swamp put the memo down on the table and exhaled a long breath. Hallory certainly knew what he was doing by getting the director to sign this out. Everyone who was still anyone in the senior ranks of the Secret Service in Washington knew about what had happened the day he retired. Instead of a frontal attack, like trying to bring charges or generate a reprimand, Hallory was acting "sympathetically" in recommending that this annoying nutcase be sent back out to pasture. The poor guy's lost it. He's getting too old for this stuff, desperately doesn't want to let go, and is interfering with security preparations for the inauguration.

His telephone began to ring on the intercom line. Mary, no doubt, calling to say time was up and to get down there.

He did not shred the bootleg copy. He folded it into a government franked envelope, addressed it to himself at the Jackson Inn, and dropped it into the outgoing mailbox as he went down the hall to McNamara's office. Old habits, such as keeping a meticulous paper trail, indeed died hard. He was going to fight this, but if he lost, he'd ram that little love note right up Carlton Hallory's tight ass on the front page of the *Washington Post* if anything ever did go "bomb, bomb, bomb" downtown.

Heismann stood in his kitchen, examining the paper delivered by FedEx a moment ago. It was a plain white piece of printer paper, with no identifying letterhead or return address. The FedEx air bill indicated that an art gallery in New York City had sent the envelope. On the piece of paper were two addresses. The first was the address for the town house. The second was an address on First Street, SW. Beneath each address was a set of latitude and longitude coordinates, each expressed in degrees, minutes, and seconds, followed by a second set of Universal Transverse Mercator grid coordinates, each expressed in six-digit numbers.

Heismann retrieved the GPS unit from its carrying case and switched it on. He set the display for lat-lon and then waited for the unit to initialize and then lock on to the satellite constellation and display his present location. It agreed with what was on the paper down to the second in longitude, and it was only one second off in latitude. Good. He walked upstairs, carrying the GPS unit, and took a second reading in the room with all the marble blocks. Same agreement, a small difference in elevation. Very good. He switched it over to display UTM coordinates, and the six numbers for each coordinate agreed. So the firing point was properly established.

He switched the unit off and went back down to the kitchen, where he retrieved the numbers derived from his walk around the Capitol. The target circle was centered on the west portico of the building, a point he could not have reached even in normal times. In theory, the numbers on the courier sheet represented the center of that circle. If those numbers were accurate, the center should lie on a straight line drawn between the town house and the corner of Constitution and First Street, NW, where he had taken his own readings. He had already computed what that azimuth was in true degrees.

He broke out the small handheld Army calculator that had come in the box of sculptor's tools. Mutaib had explained that it was preprogrammed to compute a fire-control solution, expressed as a firing azimuth and range between two GPS coordinate positions for the weapon. He entered the coordinates, using UTM grid numbers for firing point and aiming point. Then he entered air temperature, a notional wind vector, expressed as coming from the northwest at ten, barometric pressure from this morning's television weather, and then pressed the calculate button. The device displayed the range as 2,660 meters, and the firing azimuth as 342 degrees true. He frowned. The GPS unit, in the navigation mode, had computed 2,580 meters. That was pretty close. But the azimuth of the line of fire was off by four whole degrees.

He sat down at the kitchen table and thought about that. He'd drawn the line from the center of the house to the corner of the street intersection. On the map, that line passed right through the west portico of the Capitol. Assuming the map was reasonably accurate and oriented to true north, as it said it was, he had, using a large plastic protractor, come up with 338 degrees true. Being an old gunner, he knew that four degrees of error at 2,660 meters could mean a miss distance of almost 200 meters, especially when you were talking about azimuth.

He swore softly. Mutaib had told him they were getting the Capitol target coordinates from an ordnance survey map of Washington, D.C. Heismann had often wondered how many hikers and campers knew that the real purpose of an ordnance survey map was precisely what he was doing now, calculating an artillery fire-control solution. The big question now was which numbers he should use to set the weapon: his own admittedly crude estimate, the GPS, or the ones supposedly coming from an ordnance survey map created for this very purpose? And yet his numbers should be right, or very close. He had visually lined up the west portico from that intersection. But then he saw the flaw: He had not been able to see his town house. The city tourist map might have been drawn or printed in sections, and thus objects that lined up on the printed map might not actually line up on the ground.

The GPS and Mutaib agreed within one degree of azimuth. All right. That was good enough. He exhaled in relief. He would use the surveyed coordinates.

He went back upstairs and wrote both sets of the coordinates in pencil on the white plaster wall nearest the master bedroom's door, then took the paper and its envelope down to the kitchen, where he burned them in the sink. He could hear the big trucks going by out on his street as the city's road department began to set up the Jersey barriers a few blocks over. He was going to go get the minivan and position it this evening. He'd position the Suburban, with the emergency light rack back in place, late tomorrow evening. There had been police cars everywhere this morning when he walked down to the corner store to get coffee and a pastry, but the police did not appear to be doing anything but establishing a presence. None of them had been staring at pedestrians or pulling over cars in the neighborhood. The television news this morning had been full of reports about the security preparations and further announcements of traffic restrictions around the whole Capitol Hill area and, indeed, in other parts of the city. There had been footage of Air Force fighters in the air above Washington and Army helicopters staging at Andrews Air Force Base. Strangely, there had been other footage of waves of huge Air Force transports descending on bases along the East Coast, with the thinly veiled implication that there would even be troops deployed around the capital city. The *Ammies* were going a little crazy, in his opinion. You'd think the government was expecting a coup.

He looked at his watch. Almost eleven o'clock. Forty-nine hours and they'd have a reason to go crazy. And every measure of security they were putting in place had already been penetrated.

Swamp gave Mary a wink as he walked past her desk and into McNamara's office. McNamara was sitting behind his desk, looking worried. Lucy was sitting in one of the two chairs parked in front of the boss's desk. Swamp stood for a moment behind the other and looked down at her. She was poised and polished, as usual, and had her hands folded neatly in her lap. She nodded at him but did not say anything in greeting.

"If this meeting has to do with my assignment here in OSI," Swamp announced, "then I would appreciate it if Mr. Hallory's pet snake here is not part of it."

McNamara flushed. "Uh, unfortunately—" he began, but Swamp cut him off.

"Personnel matters are privileged and management personnel from other departments may not take part in meetings that have to do with personnel actions unless it is a formal hearing. Is this a formal hearing?"

McNamara, no expert on personnel procedures, obviously didn't know what to say. And Swamp was using the tone of voice he had used when wearing the mantle of the

Senior Executive Service, a rank to which neither McNamara nor Lucy had risen. "Um, no, it is not, but—"

"Then she goes. Or we're done here."

"That's the whole idea, Mr. Morgan," Lucy said. "I'm assuming you've seen Mr. Hallory's latest memo?"

"I have," Swamp said, working hard to keep his temper. He had wrapped both his hands around the top of the chair, and when he turned to address Lucy, the chair moved. Lucy saw it and sat up straighter, no longer affecting that supremely casual pose.

"Well then, you know it was addressed to the undersecretary of this department. Surely you're not expecting *him*"— she nodded her chin at McNamara— "to put up a fight on your behalf, are you?"

Swamp looked at McNamara, who flushed and shook his head ever so slightly.

"So why not make it easier on everybody, Mr. Morgan?" Lucy said. "Don't get fired. Don't put your pension for life at risk. Don't drag everyone into a quagmire of civil service hearings and lawsuits."

Swamp glared at her, really wanting to pick up that chair and swat her right out the window. She swallowed but stood her ground. "Just go home, Mr. Morgan," she said. "Come the first of the month, your direct-deposit check will go in right on time and you can go back to enjoying life out there in Harpers Ferry."

"Did you know that Connie Wall identified the 'woman' who attacked her as the man who's been after her since the clinic fire?" Swamp asked.

Lucy waved her hand. "We don't *care*, Mr. Morgan. Okay? That's a Washington police matter now. In forty-eight hours, we'll have a change of government here in Washington. That's the only thing we care about right now. The *only* thing. Can't you understand that?" Her cheeks were getting red and those blue eyes were snapping in righteous anger. "You're obsessed with this . . . this goddamned firefly. I think you've lost your professional perspective. So does the director. So before you get into real trouble, go home, Mr. Morgan. Just go home."

Swamp took a deep breath and tried to think of something clever to say. The wood in the top of the chair creaked audibly under the strain of his hands. McNamara stood up behind his desk and cleared his throat. "Ms. VanMetre, thanks for coming over today. Why don't you let me take it from here, okay? Give my regards to Mr. Hallory, will you?"

Lucy looked from Swamp to McNamara and back again to Swamp as she stood up. "Thank you, Mr. McNamara," she said formally. She walked past Swamp to the door and then turned around.

"Home means home, Mr. Morgan. Don't even think about going solo on this phantom conspiracy of yours. If nothing else, keep in mind that your firefly is a month away. Play it straight and maybe—just maybe—we'll come back to you. Once the inauguration's over and you've had some time to regain your balance."

With that, she walked out the door and closed it behind her. Swamp sat down in the chair he'd been abusing, hunched his shoulders, and gave McNamara a look that used to make the center on the opposing team seriously consider tennis.

"Don't look at me that way, goddamnit," McNamara said, fingering his collar. "You brought this on yourself when you invoked the fucking Secret Service in your phone calls all over the city. I told you to lay low. What were you thinking?"

Swamp sat back in the chair and exhaled. "Force of habit, I guess," he said. "What's all this mean, practically speaking?"

"It means just what La Mamba said. You get to go home. You don't work here anymore. You turn in your creds and your building pass, you read out of all your clearances, and then you take the train back to Harpers Ferry and get on with your life."

"Upstairs has already decided this?"

"The Under handed his copy of that memo to me this morning at the briefing and told me to 'handle it' by COB today. So, yeah, I think it's decided."

"Can I work with the District cops? Help them catch this bastard who killed their lieutenant?"

"In what capacity?"

"I don't know—consultant?"

McNamara sighed. "We can't prevent you from doing consulting work, but I wouldn't advise it," he said. "For starters, you'd have no inside access to federal LE., and for the city cops, that's the only thing you bring to the table right now. Is that nurse gonna make it?"

"Fifty-fifty," Swamp said. "They moved her to GWU last night."

"Then she's the one who can help them. She's seen this guy a couple of times at least, up close and personal. What's this about the woman hitter being a guy?"

Swamp explained what Connie had told them. McNamara shook his head. "Plastic surgery and the ability to look like a woman? Good enough to fool a plastic surgeon's *nurse*? No chance you're going to find this guy."

"Like I've said before, there's no chance if no one's looking."

McNamara leaned forward. "Look, everything you've laid out with regard to some attack on the joint session is assumption. The cop getting killed is a fact, and they won't let go of that, not ever. The nurse getting attacked is a fact. So when they get his ass for that shit, the rest of it, all those assumptions of yours, is taken care of, right? Like the lady said, Swamp, just go home. I think it's time."

"You think this is all about what happened on my retirement day?"

"*No, no, no,*" McNamara said emphatically. "I think Hallory threw that in because it would embarrass you and all the elephants up the chain of command. Nobody would want to pull that scab. Easier just to tell me to 'handle it.' Which is exactly what the Under said. Hell's bells, Swamp, this is how it's done. You know that."

Swamp threw up his hands. "Okay," he said. "I give up. I'll turn over my stuff to Gary and then go see the personnel people." He fished out his credentials. "You want these?"

McNamara shook his head. "Personnel and Security. They get everything. Come see me when you're all checked out. I'll be here all afternoon."

"Okay," Swamp said, getting up.

"And Swamp? I'm sorry about this. I really am."

"You know what, Tad? If they can do this to me, they can do it to you, too."

"So the Undersecretary pointed out this morning, Swamp."

Connie spent the better part of an hour chasing a block of hospital Jell-O around her plastic tray before finally stabbing it long enough to get half of it down her throat. Either the meds had numbed her taste buds or the hospital kitchen could screw up even Jell-O. Her stomach threatened retribution, so she gave up and lay back on her pillows. She could hear the hustle and bustle of daily routine out in the hallway. Her back hurt in a numb sort of way, which meant that she probably would be screaming in agony without the regular ministrations of her new best friend, the trusty pain pump. But the rest of her was coming back. She had inquired about some physical therapy, much to the surprise of the attending nurses. They said they'd ask.

She opened her eyes and discovered an hour had passed, and that Jake Cullen was standing in the doorway. "Hey there, Detective," she said.

"Shot at and missed, shit at and hit," he said with a smile. He came into the room bearing a paper wedge of flowers in one hand and his coat in the other. He hooked a chair over with his foot and sat down.

"That good, huh?" she said, wanting to brush a hank of limp hair off her forehead.

"Better than you looked up in that county boneyard," he said. "So how's it coming—you feeling any stronger?"

"Yeah, I am," she said. "My lower back's still riding the magic pump here, but the rest of me is getting bored."

"There's a reason they call you a patient," he said. "Care for some interrogation?"

"Bring it on," she said with a smile. "I'll never crack."

"They sell flowers, but nothing to put the damn things in," he complained, getting up to look for a container.

"That Jell-O will hold them," she said. "That Jell-O would hold up the Washington Monument."

He found an empty plastic urine container in the bathroom, filled it with water, and brought it out. She started to laugh, and then her lower back reminded her that laughing was out of bounds for now. He saw her grimace, and then he sat back down again.

"Where's my Shelby?" she asked.

It was Jake's turn to laugh. "All those deputies up there? They were getting ready to make it into some kind of Thunder Road shrine. So you'll be pleased to know that I've had it towed back to your house. Guy's gonna drop it on the street, then drive it up into your driveway. Said he'd put the keys in the exhaust pipe."

"You're shitting me."

"West Virginia safe-deposit box," Jake said with a grin. "And your little reptile atomizer's in the trunk. You make sure you bend your elbows, you ever shoot that thing."

"That's what the dealer said," she replied. "The exhaust pipe? Which one?"

"How the hell do I know? How many are there? I think you can manage it."

"Thanks," she muttered. "I think." She used her elbows to lever herself into a more upright position and then waited until her head stopped spinning. Have to do better than this if I'm ever going to blow this pop stand, she thought. Much better.

"Don't push it," he said. "Just tell me what happened that night."

She nodded, pressed the button on her pump, and then told him the sequence of events that night. When she was done, he was nodding silently.

"The other lady in the bathroom—what happened to her?" Connie asked.

"He stabbed her three times in the upper stomach, got her aorta. Gone in sixty seconds, as the expression goes."

"Oh."

"Guy's a badass, no doubt about it," he said. "But you said *she* fooled you completely?"

"*She'd* had work. No woman comes into the world with boobs like that. There was something off about the nose, but I couldn't tell what it was. The top just sloped out of her forehead. Not natural. And I couldn't just stare like I do in the OR. Hispanic, or maybe Mediterranean. Exotic. Lots of makeup, but skillfully done. Slim legs, and some serious stockings or panty hose. Oh, and no noticeable Adam's apple."

"Say what?"

"That's how you can almost always tell a tranny—besides the husky voice, they'll have a protuberant laryngeal prominence. That's Adam's apple in English. This thing didn't, so I never suspected until I saw his eyes when he got his killer juices going. Those I remember. From the window *and* from the woods."

She subsided into the pillow, suddenly exhausted. He put his hand on her arm and rubbed gently with his fingertips from the back of her hand, where the IV had been, up to her elbow. His hand was cool from being outside, and it felt good. They sat that way for five minutes while she drifted, and then she came back.

"This guy's still out there, right?" she asked.

"We're working on it. Us and that big Secret Service guy with the pretty face."

"But there's no cop on my door anymore."

"Well, they're pulling everyone in the department into this inauguration flail. Double shifts on the big day, so they're trying to give guys some time off right before."

She closed her eyes again, worked on her breathing. Talking still seemed to take all the oxygen right out of her. "Then I want out of here," she said. "Anybody can come in here."

Jake frowned. "They've got security, just like everywhere else."

She shook her head, slowly this time. "*Anybody* can come in here. An old lady wandered in this morning before breakfast, looking for her daughter's room. She had the wrong room, wrong floor."

"I don't think you're exactly ready for prime time," Jake said. "Look at you—you can't even talk and breathe at the same time."

"Then I won't talk," she said wearily. "But I don't want to wake up and see that *thing* standing next to the bed in his Nancy Nurse uniform."

"There's no way he could know you're here," Jake protested.

"See that phone?" she asked. "I called the hospital at Garrison Gap, asked the operator where the nurse from the stabbing incident had gone. She said GWU Medical Center."

He blinked. "Just like that?"

"Just like that."

"Shit."

"Yeah. So I want to go bye-bye."

Jake got up from the chair and started pacing the room. "Putting the medical aspects aside," he said, "you can't just go home to that empty house. You'd be even more vulnerable. How're you paying for all this, by the way?"

"I'm going to sue the police department for failing to protect me after I agreed to be bait," she said.

He turned to stare at her, and she maintained a straight face for about five more seconds. He shook his head. "Don't even talk like that," he said, although he knew she probably could sue.

"I was the one who ditched her minder, remember?" she said. "Although our boy did have himself a time with those street cops, didn't he?"

Jake nodded reluctantly.

"Which is why I want out of here. He wants my ass dead, and he's nearly succeeded. A couple of times. Plus, there's something important I need to remember about him and I can't."

"You won't be any safer out there," Jake said.

"I've worked in hospitals for a long time, Jake," she said. "I'm not safe here, medically or securitywise. All hospitals are contaminated with staph, a host of infectious diseases, ERs with walking TB cases, toxic waste and biohazards in every trash can—you name it. That's why doctors want you up and out as soon as possible. It's not about money. They want to improve their own save stats."

"Okay, okay," he said. "Look, I've got a condo apartment up in Bethesda. It's actually pretty big. Two bedrooms, two baths. Plenty of privacy."

"Never been divorced, huh?" she asked.

He laughed. "Or married. The only guy on the Homicide squad who hasn't. But you could stay there. The building has a sitting service. I could get someone to come in, check on you three, four times a day. You know, to make sure you aren't tearing the joint up, entertaining gentlemen callers . . ."

She looked at him for a long moment. "That's very nice," she said. "But getting over all this may take awhile."

He sat back down and took her hand again. "I've got awhile," he said, and then he suddenly seemed embarrassed. "Anyway, you think about it. And make sure you're safe to make the trip. Talk to your docs. They may not let you out of here."

"The hospital will when I tell them I have no insurance," she said brightly. "I'm unemployed, remember?"

Gary was visibly embarrassed as he accompanied Swamp down to the lobby of the OEOB. Without a building pass, he could no longer be in the building without an escort. Swamp had tried to say good-bye to McNamara, but he'd been called away to a meeting at State, so that was that. He carried the briefcase with the tactical gear underneath the raincoat he had folded over his left arm. He'd also made a copy of the realtor list on Gary's desk, annotated as to which ones had called back. Not many more had.

Swamp had asked Gary to continue taking calls from the realtors, but he'd told him not to make any more follow-up calls. "None of this is going to rebound on you," he reassured the younger agent. "As long as you don't do anything proactive. Taking phone calls is just doing your job."

"And if we get a hit?"

"Pass it to Detective Cullen over at District headquarters. He's the only one left on point right now."

They reached the lobby, and there was a brief discussion between Gary and the security guards. If Mr. Morgan here was now technically a visitor, why hadn't Mr. Morgan signed the visitor's log? Gary handled it and then walked with Swamp to the ornate doors at the corner of the building.

"I don't know what to say," Gary said. "Except it was interesting while it lasted."

"Yeah, and you did fine. I'll remind McNamara to make sure you get a decent performance evaluation."

Gary looked through a side window. "There are two guys out there in a government vehicle, watching this entrance."

Swamp smiled. He still had his minders, and they had

been informed. "Great," he said. "Let's see what they think about a run back out to Harpers Ferry."

Gary's smile was a bit weak. "Do I have your phone numbers, sir?"

"Well, let's see. West Virginia, the apartment—you have those. Although the apartment's going to go away, I guess. And I suppose I need to go get a cell phone now that Uncle's reclaimed his."

"Call it in when you get one," Gary said. "I don't want to lose touch." He looked around to see who might be listening. "I'm beginning to think this career move of mine wasn't such a great idea. I may want some advice from time to time."

"Absolutely," Swamp said. "But this wasn't personal, Gary. I got in the way of a little man with a big mission, that's all. The Secret Service is a great outfit. You'll see." They shook hands and Swamp walked out onto Eighteenth Street, where he was met by a brisk wind. One of the Secret Service agents got out of the car and came over.

"We got the word an hour ago, direct from La Mamba," he said. "Said to keep tabs until you left for the countryside. For what it's worth, we both think it's a bum deal."

"Thanks for that," Swamp said. "I need to clear my stuff out at the apartment and then unrent that thing. I'll probably sleep over there tonight, take the train out to Harpers Ferry in the morning."

"We'd be happy to offer you a ride over there," the agent said.

Swamp just looked at him for a moment, wondering if he should be alarmed. But the expression on the agent's face seemed to be more one of genuine sympathy than hard-ass procedure. As if sensing Swamp's curiosity, he pointed out that if they went by car, one of them wouldn't be forced to get out and physically follow Swamp around in the cold. Swamp nodded and got into the backseat of the car.

As they drove downtown toward the river, the agent riding shotgun asked if he'd mind telling them what this was all about. He did. When he was finished, they rode in silence across the Fourteenth Street Bridge. The driver finally broke the silence.

"I was a rookie when you were a DAD," he said. "I sure as shit hope they're right and you're wrong."

"So do I," Swamp said. "Mostly, they hurt my feelings. Know any good bars along the way?"

"Yes," both agents responded simultaneously.

Heismann drove around for almost an hour in search of the perfect parking spot for the minivan. He wanted it to be within three blocks of the town house, but far enough away that anyone who might chase him on foot would have to be in pretty good shape. He drove through several back alleys and up and down streets and cross streets around his neighborhood. This area was all outside the security zone, so there were no barriers and only the occasional police car.

Mutaib had relayed the realtor's warning about on-street parking in the Capitol Hill area, that it was all by permit only and that permits were color-coded for various neighborhoods. He wasn't worried about a policeman ticketing the vehicle as much as some irate resident calling the police to tow off an interloper. Once he'd made his decision, he would have to find some colored acetate to convert his own street permit to the right color. Then he would spend an hour or so laying out his escape route from the town house to the minivan. He needed the first leg of it to be across the street and into an alley, because he was going to be something of a spectacle when he made his escape. He'd position the minivan tomorrow morning, after people had left for work but before the neighborhood commuters returned, so that there would be more open spaces on the street he finally chose.

Once his route had been set and the parking permit taken

care of, he would then have to move the Suburban completely out of the Capitol Hill area and away from all the avenues where the inaugural events would take place. He'd narrowed it down to two options: going deep into the southeast quadrant of the city, which he'd already discovered was something of a no-go zone for anyone who didn't live there, or finding some extremely public place where the Suburban, made up as a federal police vehicle, would blend in with the background for Inauguration Day. He had selected two possibilities for that: under the bridges where Interstate 95 and Fourteenth Street crossed Haines Point—a spit of land in the river, it was now a park—or on one of the perimeter roads near the Tidal Basin.

He planned to re-equip the Suburban with the light bar tomorrow night and drive it down to one of these two spots, then walk over to the nearest Metro station to get back to Capitol Hill. There was a direct route from Capitol Hill down to that general area, and from either location he should be able to determine how much of the downtown had been blocked off by the time he got there. His ultimate destination was in northwest Washington, after one stop at the Arab bank, but he wanted the option to cross the river if he had to. There would be pandemonium in the downtown area, and he fully expected the government to shut down the Metro and all other modes of transportation once the attack occurred, if not before then. He might just have to walk out.

He had a final teleconference with Mutaib set for tonight at midnight. He didn't expect anything in the way of new information, but he did need to find out one last thing: where the princess would be at noon on *der Tag*. Ideally, right there at the bank, along with all his pretty minions.

After dinner, using a walker, Connie made her second trip of the day from the bed to the bathroom all by herself. The first one had taken some help, but having been up once, she was determined to stay up if she could. Afternoon rounds had been encouraging. The surgical repairs seemed to be holding up well, and there were still no signs of infection. When she'd broached the subject of getting out of there, the docs had waffled a bit, coming down on the side of her staying a few more days just to make sure. She could take the pump, of course, but they'd prefer to migrate her to the next tier of pain meds before they discharged her. She'd had the feeling that they'd been a little more honest with her in deference to her own medical background, so she'd casually reminded them of the dangers inherent to the hospital environment, even at a first-rate place like GWU. That had provoked some throat clearing, watch checking, and questions for the interns, and then they moved on.

She'd gone down for a nap after lunch, and then put a call in to the business office to discuss the really important issue. The insurance nazi on duty obliged her immediately with a lecture on financial responsibility. Connie theoretically still had medical insurance, courtesy of the COBRA law, but, as she pointed out, the company had really consisted of the two docs. They were dead, their families gone, the accounts closed, which left the question of premium payments kind of up in the air, which in turn might make the claims process "interesting." She made a bet with herself after hanging up that there'd be a wholly different take on her prospects for discharge by morning rounds.

The offer from Jake was tempting on several levels. She was growing to like him a lot, more than Cat, in fact, who'd been focused entirely on the physical side. She had no illusions about what long-term recovery was going to be like, especially if there were any setbacks, which were more likely than not, given her injuries. If she was going to get something going with Jake, she wanted it to be on a whole and handsome woman basis, with no memories of bedpans and vomiting episodes in the night to get in the way later.

Besides, she really did want to go home. She didn't care
much for that business of the car keys in the Shelby's
tailpipe. And home should be the last place that bastard
would expect her to show up.

She let herself lie back down in the bed and murmured a
prayer of thanks for articulating hospital beds. She'd have to
get one into the house, and the idea of a nursing service
seemed attractive, too. She had the money for that, even if
the insurance fell through. But for now, a night's sleep
looked pretty good.

She smiled to herself as she thought about the memo being put out on the hospital intranet right about now: "The
billing department notes with concern . . ."

Swamp finished his solitary dinner at Caruso's and settled
up with Mario, probably for the last time, he realized. He
left a generous tip and told the old man he'd be away for a
while; then he walked back to his apartment building. There
were two new faces peering at him from the watch car out
front, and he nodded to them as he walked up to the entrance
to the building. He'd told them where he was going and
when he'd be back, and they'd taken him at his word. Apparently, his conversation with the two agents who'd picked
him up at OEOB had been percolating through the
grapevine.

Back in the apartment, he got out his newly acquired cell
phone and skimmed through the instruction booklet. He saw
his wallet sitting on the living room table, next to the empty
credentials holder. He felt naked without his government
phone, credentials, building passes on chains, and the whole
infrastructure of police powers they represented. Poor me,
he thought. Just a plain vanilla civilian now.

He made himself a short drink and went out onto the balcony, which faced three other high-rise apartment buildings
across the alley. Looking to his right, he could see the amber

glow of Washington on the horizon, and the twinkle of air-craft warning lights on cell towers and television antennas all over northern Virginia. A jetliner passed overhead with a crisp engine sound as it descended into Reagan National, leading the formation of landing lights that was shaping up in the western sky.

He would miss it. Washington pulsed with the energy of the center of empire, twenty-four/seven. Everything was al-ways urgent, even the nominally routine, because a boss was always worried about being caught off base by a bigger boss. "Did you know about this?" was the one question that could spin up an entire department. If you had to stand up at the morning briefing and admit that you didn't, and the issue lay in your area of responsibility, the backroom gossip would have you on that infamous slippery slope. He heard the phone ringing and went back inside the sliding glass doors to get it. It was Bertie.

"A ripple of news came under my door," he said crypti-cally.

"That ripple started out as a wave of shit," Swamp replied, sitting down on the couch.

"Are you now officially a nonperson?" Bertie asked.

"If you have to ask . . ."

Bertie was laughing softly. "So whatever happened with your firefly?"

Swamp told him, aware that any listeners might be hear-ing all this for the first time. Good, he thought. The more working stiffs in the Secret Service who knew about this now, the better if it blew up in their faces. Bertie said noth-ing for almost thirty seconds. Then Swamp heard him light a cigarette. "And they're just going to let all this—what, *compost* until after the inauguration?"

"Hallory's certainly not going to work it," Swamp said. "I think the District cops will keep trying to find this guy, but, you know, they're all being folded into the inauguration se-

P. T. Deutermann

curity effort, too. They've got detectives going back into uniform starting late tomorrow night."

"But it sounds so damned plausible," Bertie said.

"Unless you've got your hands full and thirty-six hours until showtime. Hell, Bertie, it wasn't like they didn't warn me off."

"So what's next? I was depending on you being here to show me some decent watering holes."

Swamp laughed. "Next is, I'm going back to Harpers Ferry. Let someone else carry the Entire Free World on their shoulders for a while. Come next month, I'll go to Acapulco, watch CNN the night of the joint session address, and hope they were all right and I was all wrong."

"Yeah, that's what worries me. You weren't exactly famous for being wrong all that much. Pain in the gump stump, yes, but wrong? Not often. Hang on a minute—I've got another call."

Swamp finished his drink while he waited. Then Bertie was back. "Just checking something. Your line's clean tonight. Look, would you consider maybe going solo on this thing?"

"La Mamba was pretty explicit about my not doing that."

"How about if you were working for us?"

"Me? Work for the Agency?"

"Why not? We hire 'consultants' all the time. We pay better than your dear old Secret Service, too."

"Would I get a secret decoder ring?"

Bertie laughed but then grew serious. "If there is some evil shit afoot, I would love to surface it. *We* would love to surface it, if you catch my drift."

"Ah. And stick it up DHS's ass in some memorable interagency meeting."

"Why, yes, I suppose that's possible."

"You suppose. Actually, you're *supposed* to be cooperating and collaborating with all the working stiffs across the

river these days, Bertie. I can't believe you'd let a little bureaucratic one-upmanship guide Agency policy."

"Are you all through?" Bertie said. It was Swamp's turn
to laugh.

"Because I'm not retired, remember?" Bertie continued.
"If there's even a chance you're right, it would be positively
delicious to break Hallory's balls with it. And to step on La
Mamba's pretty neck. She was the one who called to tell me
you were being sent home, by the way. Sounded very
pleased with herself."

"And did she also tell you they'd warned me *not* to go
solo?"

"Where do you think I got this idea, old buddy?" Bertie
replied softly.

"They find out I'm still beating these bushes, they're
gonna shit, Bertie."

"If you're right and they're wrong, they're really gonna
shit," Bertie said. "So call me in the morning. Early's good."

Swamp shook his head after he hung up the phone. What
the hell, he might just do it. And not tell McNamara or anyone else. Except maybe Jake Cullen.

Heismann called Mutaib's private number at the bank from a
phone station in the lobby of the Sheraton Capitol Hill at
midnight. It was picked up by one of the whispering minions, who put him on hold. A minute later, the emir came on
the line.

"Everything is in readiness," Heismann announced.

"Very well."

He paused while two men walked by in the lobby. "And
you still wish me to proceed?"

"We do."

"You will not forget the second payment?"

"My dear fellow, it will be deposited to the agreed-upon
account one minute after we hear the, um, appropriate

noises. One minute. I will do it right from here unless they cut off all the telephone lines in the city."

And that's what I needed to know, Heismann thought. "All right. What time do you wish me to turn on the special phone?"

"Turn it on fifteen minutes prior to midnight tomorrow. When it rings, hit the talk button, but do not speak. It will be a text message only."

"Ah. A code?"

"No. Plain English. You will understand it. After midnight, put the phone outside in the sink. There is an acid destructor inside that will melt its circuits when it receives the execution-order string."

"And if your people change their minds at the last minute?"

"Midnight tomorrow *is* the last minute. We think communications in the city will become difficult, if not impossible, as the event approaches."

"What will be the cancellation code?"

"No code. Plain English. And if that happens, leave the house. And leave the city at once. And if you do run, don't use that Suburban."

The lobby was starting to fill up with formally dressed people as a banquet came to an end. A couple walked by Heismann, a man and a woman this time. The woman was a little drunk and laughing noisily. "Where in the world are you?" Mutaib asked.

"A safe place," Heismann said, and then he asked Mutaib the question he'd been wanting to ask ever since this thing began. He had all the money he really expected to get, so he risked nothing by asking it. "Do your people have any idea of what the *Ammies* will do if they tie this thing to the Saudis?"

"I don't think they can, my dear fellow. Besides, if they do, it's going to look a lot like Al Qaeda, not the Saudis. The Kingdom will be suitably apologetic, just like last time."

"But if this succeeds, and it should, and all the civilians die, it will be the generals in charge this time."

"In Russia, that might be a problem, but not here, Herr Hodler. That's why they call it the Department of *Defense*. They'll buzz around for a while, but until there's a president, they won't *do* anything."

"I hope you are right about that," Heismann said. "I would hate to find out that your bank had been atomized before that check clears."

Mutaib laughed. "You just tend to your business and we will tend to ours."

Heismann couldn't say what he was thinking, so he hung up. He felt suddenly exposed in the brightly lighted lobby area, and he was anxious to be out of there.

Once he was back out on the street, he decided to take an oblique route back to the town house. He had little doubt but that Mutaib was not only going to cheat him of any second payment but would try to have him killed soon after the attack took place. Mutaib could never allow the single person who could tie the Royal Kingdom Bank to the attack to survive the incident. And the obvious way to do that would be to create some difficulty with the second payment that would require Heismann to meet Mutaib or one of his security men somewhere. Like claim the city's telephone system had been shut down, tell him they'd pay him in cash instead.

He crossed the avenue in front of the hotel and then kept going east, walking toward the Anacostia River. Or, he thought, they could have marksmen waiting somewhere in my street on *der Tag*. Well, he had a plan for that. When he burst out of that house right after the attack took place, he was going to look very, very different, which should distract any of Mutaib's shooters long enough for him to get into the alley across the street to begin his run to the minivan. By the time they figured it out, there would be other distractions going on in that street.

Two blocks farther east, he turned north onto Fourth

Street, SW, then reversed course suddenly to see if anyone
was following him, either on foot or in a car. When he didn't
see anyone, he resumed walking toward his town house. The
row houses along here ran the gamut from expensively re-
furbished buildings all the way to some decidedly derelict
burned-out shells. The furtive shapes of Washington's nocturnal drug trade melted back into nearby alleys as he came
walking purposefully up the street, looking like a man on a
mission. There was a car at the curb, its parking lights on
and its engine running. As soon as the clockers began to fade
into the shadows, the car pulled out into the street and then
executed a lazy turn around the corner. Even so, Heismann
kept a grip on the Walther in his coat pocket until he approached his own block.

He walked past his front steps without so much as glancing sideways at his neighbor's house. Then he continued
around the corner and into the alley behind the row of
houses. He'd been as quiet as he could opening the back gate
and making his way across the narrow yard, not wanting to
attract any attention from his neighbor. But when he stepped
into the kitchen and reached for the light switch, he stopped,
his hand in midair.

What's this? Something is different.

He scanned the semidarkened kitchen, where he could
see fairly well because of the alley streetlight. Nothing
seemed to be out of place. And certainly no place here for
someone to hide. The door to the front hall was open, and
there was light coming from the front streetlights there, too.
He listened, but all he heard were normal sounds: the next-
door neighbor's heater running down in the basement; the
ticking of a small clock on the electric oven, the night wind
stirring halfheartedly across the back porch, pushing a small
draft of cold air through the partially open kitchen door.

Then he had it. Not a sound. A smell. The smell of food.

He had neither cooked nor eaten cooked food in the
house since he'd been there. But he could definitely smell

food, and it was an exotic scent. He finally recognized it: the same scent that had permeated the apartments of the Arab underground in Hamburg and, later, Berlin. Middle Eastern spices. That's what he was smelling. And since it wasn't likely to be coming from his neighbor's kitchen, it meant that someone who stank of Middle Eastern food had been in his house, and maybe was still there. He lowered his hand and felt for his pistol, easing it out of the pocket. Then, one-handed, he shed his overcoat, hat, and shoes as soundlessly as possible while still standing just inside the back door. He slipped the safety off the gun and nudged the slide back to make sure a round was chambered. He nudged the kitchen door shut with his heel.

He'd made no effort to keep quiet when entering the house, so if someone was waiting, they'd know he was inside. They. More than one? But where? He could see down the hall. He moved to his left in stocking feet, sliding across the linoleum until he was standing partially in the dining room and could see into the living room. The brace structure was still in place, and the living room furniture all looked right. Nothing visibly disturbed. Sliding his feet across the floor again, he went around the brace and into the living room, crouching slightly, gun ready, until he reached the front door. He checked the locks, but everything was in order. He peered up into the darkened stairwell.

Upstairs, then.

No, wait. The basement.

He stepped into the hall, staying close to the wall to avoid creaking boards, listening carefully for any signs of movement upstairs, but still he heard nothing. The door to the basement was under the stairs. He reached for the knob but then stopped. He knelt down and sniffed the door handle. The stink of Middle Eastern spices was on the doorknob itself.

All right.

The light switch for the basement stairs was right next to the door. He flipped it on, not opening the door.

If you're down there, he thought, now you know I've found you.

He peered back around the corner of the stairs to make sure there wasn't someone coming down the hall behind him, but there were no looming silhouettes—only the rectangles of amber light from outside flanking the front door. He recalled the layout of the basement: open-backed steps going down ten feet to the dirt floor, whitewashed rough stone walls, a concrete pad where the oil-fired heater and its service tank stood. Duct work and cast-iron bathroom drainpipe spidering across the ceiling. The old coal scuttle at sidewalk level in the front wall. An ancient but apparently serviceable submersible pump sitting in a shallow well in the middle of the floor. A single-bulb light fixture hanging from the floor joists.

No place to hide at all once that light was on. Plus, anyone lurking down there could be so easily trapped. So, it was not likely anyone was down there. Not now anyway.

There was a latch bolt on the hallway side of the door. He slid the bolt into the closed position, then went upstairs, turning on lights as he went, making no effort to be quiet now. He was sure that someone had been in the house. Had been in the basement and was now gone. It just felt that way, and he'd learned to trust his instincts when it came to an ambush. The upstairs was clear, the marble blocks, the tools, everything just as he'd left it. He left the light on in the hall bathroom and in the room he was using as a bedroom, then went back downstairs. He thought he knew what was going on now.

He confirmed that the front and back doors were locked, and then he looked in all the downstairs closets and behind the furniture. Then he grabbed a flashlight and unlocked the basement door. He went halfway down the steps and looked around. The dirt floor was too hard-packed to show footprints, but the smell of food was present even down there, just barely discernible over the smells of heating oil and old plaster dust. He went over and examined the coal scuttle, which was big enough for a large man to get through, if he was then willing to drop seven feet from the sidewalk level onto the hard-packed dirt floor. But all along its sides, there were spiderwebs that obviously had not been disturbed in years, and the whitewashed stone walls bore no scuff marks.

So, the heating system. He went over to the heater, which contained the oil burner itself and the fan chamber, all attached to a large square metal duct that rose into the ceiling and then began branching out into feeder and return lines between the floor joists. He checked the cover of the heater control panel, which was attached by four small Phillips-head screws to the base of the heater. He pointed the flashlight at them and each one showed bright metal.

Suspicions confirmed.

He went back upstairs to the kitchen and peered out the back windows. Then he rooted around in the drawer that contained small household tools and found a screwdriver. Back in the basement, he unscrewed the cover plate and lifted it off. He found a maze of old fuzz-covered wiring, some switches, metal contacts, plastic splice caps, and one brand-new white wire that led to a small plastic cigarette pack–size box taped into an empty corner of the control unit. A second wire, this one black, came out of that box and went up through the connector fitting that transmitted power to the control panel. Tracing that wire, he found that it led across the back of the heater itself and over to the fuel tank. A tiny hole had been drilled high on the back of the fuel tank to admit that wire into the tank.

There were two fill fittings and one air vent on top of the tank. One of the fill fittings was hard-piped to a two-inch-diameter metal pipe leading to the fill valve out on the street. The other had a screw cap, which, upon close inspection, revealed a wafer-thin band of metal with what looked like a printed circuit engraved on it. This was wrapped tightly around the threads and made contact with the cap. He stood there for a moment. If he opened that cap, he might activate an antitampering circuit or other booby-trap device. But he knew what had to be in the tank. The electronics pack stuck into the controller box was probably a timer, set to go off a few minutes after noon on Friday.

Mutaib's solution to *his* loose-end problem.

He would have to think about how to disable this bomb, because he would need a full minute, perhaps two, once the attack had been completed. Not much more, but definitely a better escape window than the mere seconds this device would probably allow. He'd planted some bombs of his own before, and he knew that cutting a wire could lead to uncertain and often adverse consequences. And since he didn't know anything about the control or timing circuitry, he didn't dare risk it. He knelt down on one knee and looked at the bottom of the fuel tank. Then he smiled. There was a drain valve, untouched, from the look of it. He looked over at the sump pump. That pump should move oil just as well as water.

Early Friday morning, he would drain the fuel tank and pump the heating oil into the city's sewer system with the sump pump. The actual bomb couldn't be very big, because it had to fit through that two-inch-diameter fill tube. Mutaib's explosives man was probably counting on a two-stage fuel-air explosion: a low-impulse explosive that would burst the tank and vaporize three hundred liters of heating oil into an explosive cloud that would fill every cubic centimeter of the basement, with ignition following in milliseconds by the much higher energy of the second-stage explosive. An entire basement full of fuel vapor would be quite sufficient to blow the entire duplex, both sides, into next week. But if he drained the fuel, not that much would happen. A fire perhaps, but he would have already started some of those by then.

And now he didn't feel quite so bad about what he was going to do to Mutaib. He smiled again. As if he ever had.

11

SWAMP BALANCED A PAPER CUP OF COFFEE IN HIS LAP AS Bertie steered his Volvo sedan through the gate complex of the CIA headquarters building in Langley, Virginia. He had no government identification to show the gate guards, but Bertie was apparently senior enough to overcome that problem. Swamp was able to produce his retired Secret Service agent ID card when it came time to be badged into the building itself. The security guards had given that token offering a patronizing smile.

He was surprised when he saw Bertie's office up on the fifth floor. "I didn't know spooks had real corner offices," he said. "I thought it was all secret handshakes in dark hotel rooms."

"Most of us in the Agency are just bureaucrats with really expensive phones," Bertie replied. There were three telephone consoles on his desk, one of which was set up for video teleconferencing. "Here's the paperwork."

Swamp was surprised, and showed it.

"Yeah, well, I thought you'd bite, so I took the liberty of having the Personnel Department write up the contract last night. Your security clearances were gapped for less than twenty-four hours, so we figured you hadn't had time to go over to the Commies. That basically says you're working exclusively for us as a contract consultant, one whose duties will be specified by competent authority in the due course of time, et cetera, et cetera. Here's your walking-around paper."

Bertie passed over a leather credentials folder that had Swamp's photograph already laminated into the identification papers. Bertie smiled when he saw Swamp blink.

"This *is* the counterintelligence directorate," he said. "We have a photograph of every federal law-enforcement officer in the country in our databanks. Plus your fingerprints and, of course, all your personal history, based on the Bureau's background investigation. Those creds took fifteen minutes. Here's your building pass, good for six months. I assume you have your own weapon?"

Swamp was almost too surprised to answer. "Uh, yeah, I had one issued on a subcustody basis yesterday morning. But that was before, uh—"

"Before they canned you for living up to your reputation. What were your plans for today, before DHS began behaving badly?"

"I had a canvass going of all the major realtors in town to see if any of them had done any business recently for the Royal Kingdom Bank. Your idea, actually."

Bertie nodded, remembering. "When I was telling you to back off, wasn't it? But that was then. This is now. Do you have any allies left?"

"Detective Cullen over in the District. And I can touch base with Gary White to see if he's had any further responses from the realtors I called. I left them my OSI office telephone numbers. My previous office, that is. Otherwise, no. Now ask me about enemies."

"Enemies are the people who still want your hide even after you're gone. You don't have any enemies." He took back the contract, which Swamp had signed. "We'll set you up with a virtual office here. Two numbers. One will always go to an innocuous-sounding voice mail. The other will go to a human operator who will make like you're some kind of big deal. You know, 'Mr. Morgan is not available. I can put you through to one of his executive assistant's voice mail.' And both are programmable, okay?"

"So if I tell some fibs about who I am . . ."

"Right, as long as you also tell your assigned operator, preferably in advance, although those people are pretty fast on their feet. Here's what *we* want: Find this guy Hodler, Heismann, whatever his name is. Don't apprehend. Locate him; then let us take it from there. We'll probably give the arrest to the Bureau, given their long-standing love affair with the Secret Service. Plus, we all know how busy Hallory and company are just now."

"I feel faintly disloyal," Swamp said.

"Swamp, if you're right, this would be a strike against the entire American government. All of which goes to hear the address to the joint session. Which law-enforcement outfit saves the day is of no consequence, right?"

"I guess," Swamp said. Then nodded his head. "Yes, right, of course."

"Okay. There's nothing more for me to tell you. I'll get one of my staffers in here to take you to your car."

"My car?"

"It's equipped with satellite tags so we know where it is at all times, so no cathouse visits on government time. It has a dash-mounted cell phone, which should operate even when Hallory shuts down commercial service all over town Friday. If you're stopped by cops or involved in an accident, it has license plates that will come up 'Back off and call your supervisor' on any law-enforcement computer. It has a panic button, which will alert the operations directorate that you are in real trouble. To be used only when you're in *real* trouble, obviously."

"These wheels have an operating manual, I hope? I mean, I normally drive an extremely low-tech ten-year-old Land Rover."

"Is it green, with a dented right rear fender?" Bertie asked with a grin. "Like the one down in our garage?"

Connie won her bet with herself. Morning rounds brought a bright-eyed staff physician who wanted to do a comprehensive exam and case review, with an eye toward possible early discharge. Connie kept a straight face and displayed the appropriate reverence while he poked, prodded, watched her make a Pilgrim's Progress to the bathroom and back, discussed pain-management modalities, and then asked her if she had somewhere to go. She asked him to get Patient Affairs to help set up home health-care services and get a hospital bed, making it clear that she would be able to pay for said services outside of insurance channels. A rep from Patient Affairs showed up an hour later and put all of that in train for that very afternoon, including transport from the hospital at three o'clock, assuming that was all right with her. She also showed Connie some paperwork that should get her hospitalization insurance to work even though her parent company was defunct.

Connie then decided to devote the rest of the day to getting an assisted shower, lunch, and then a long nap. Jake called in at ten o'clock and asked how she was getting on, and she told him that she was better and stronger. He asked if they were going to let her go yet and she told him that they were working on it, and that she hadn't forgotten his kind offer. The longer the day went on, the more she wanted to just go home, and she didn't need Jake or anyone else getting in the way just now. If they could turn on the nursing service today, she'd take a shot.

A different delivery company brought the rest of the marble at nine o'clock on Thursday morning. There were ten pieces in the truck, each wrapped, banded, and individually palleted in the back of a large step van. Heismann asked what the total load weight was, and the driver told him fourteen hundred pounds. Each piece was two feet long and roughly ten inches square. They'd brought a large hand truck that could be used to cart the pieces up the front steps and into the house. Heismann told them to bring it all inside and to put the pieces again at extended intervals along the living room wall to spread out the weight.

Now, for *his* remaining loose end. He gathered up all the faked documentation that had come along with both loads of marble and packaged it up in one bulky envelope. He addressed it to the U.S. Secret Service at the headquarters address listed in the Washington phone book. He included one of Mutaib's business cards, on the back of which he wrote in English, "Proceed with the attack." He walked back out to the street and put the envelope in the corner mailbox. Yes, the *Ammies* could trace the rental of the town house back to the bank, but this would make it—what was the word?— personal. The police might even check the mailbox after the attack. That would make it very personal—and quick. He still had every intention of going to the bank after the attack, but this would be insurance in case he couldn't manage it.

At 10:15, Swamp parked his Land Rover in the commercial parking lot across from the District police headquarters. Bertie's staffer had shown him all the new bells and whistles, and then how to get out of the CIA compound without getting shot. He'd used the cell phone to call Lila back at the inn, and she didn't even know the Rover had been taken. This wasn't his father's CIA, he concluded; these guys were good.

He met with Jake Cullen and Shad Howell in the Homicide office, where the coat trees were all sporting police uniforms hanging in dry-cleaning bags. Swamp suggested they go to an interview room, which they did, and there he brought the two detectives up-to-date on where he was with the Hodler matter, and also his new status as an Agency contractor.

"They do that shit?" Shad asked. "Thought they had their own operatives."

"For real operational intelligence work, yes, those are Company people. But they hire all sorts of folks to do odd jobs—language people, technical experts, journalists, ex-cops."

"And your people *fired* you?"

"Sort of," Swamp said. "Officially I'd been recalled for the national emergency. They mostly just unrecalled me, but, yeah, you wouldn't confuse it with a promotion. Jake, what's the news on Connie Wall?"

"Getting stronger. Walking on her own to the bathroom. We've got a picture of what happened that night, but still no description of this dude as a guy. She keeps saying there's something else she remembers, but she can't surface it. You know, pain meds."

"She going to make a full recovery?"

"As long as she doesn't pop an infection. Which is one of the reasons she wants out of that hospital as soon as possible."

"And the other?"

"This guy's still loose. And we had to pull our door cop off because of this goddamned inauguration."

"Where would she go? Not back to her house?"

Jake fingered his collar. "Um, I told her she could stay at my place for a little while. Until we get this guy."

Swamp glanced at Shad, who rolled his eyes. "I told him," Shad said. "She's a wit. They hook up, it could compromise any court case."

"We catch up with this mutt," Jake growled, "there won't be any court case. Righteous-shooting hearing maybe, but no court case."

"I didn't hear that," Swamp said, looking up at the video camera to make sure the red light wasn't on. "As of yesterday afternoon, Gary said we'd heard from about two-thirds of those realty offices. It's all I've got right now, so that's where I'm going to concentrate. Can you guys run a similar screen?"

"On what?" Jake asked.

"On the name Erich or Eric Hodler. And also that Suburban. You know, DMV, moving violations, parking tickets, the tax office, telephone company, PEPCO, traffic stops. Go back to that Saudi bank and ask if those papers have come over from the car dealer, and if anybody's been in to pick them up. They call you when and if he comes in. Like that."

"Yeah, sure," Jake said. "Actually, I had some of that done right after the car thing, but I guess it wouldn't hurt to run it again."

"Gary has flags up in the national credit bureaus and, of course, NCIC."

"If he's what you think he is, you won't see him there."

"True," Swamp said. "So maybe you guys need to keep running it, right up until that speech goes down next month. The federal systems won't comb those sources near as well as yours will."

"Okay, we're done here, I guess," Jake said, getting up. "We'll keep stroking it. You call us if your guy gets a hit."

As they left the interview room, Swamp asked if all the uniforms meant what he thought.

"The whole force is back in the bag as of seventeen hundred tonight," Jake said. "Inspection, would you believe. Then shifts starting midnight tonight. The feds have the Capitol Hill perimeter and inside; we flood the lockdown zone outside the perimeter. Everyone below the rank of lieutenant. The whole department's gonna basically shut down for this thing."

"If I surface an address, will you guys need a warrant?"

The two detectives looked at each other. "Yeah," Jake said. "We probably would. Better hope you don't turn up anything until after the inauguration, though. All those parties, there won't be a sober judge in town."

"Who wants a sober judge for a search-warrant hearing?" Swamp said.

It took three hours to get Connie out of the hospital, transported to her house, and set up on the ground floor in the dining room. The visiting nurse hadn't been too happy with the piece of plywood over the dining room window, but otherwise it was a fairly workable setup. The kitchen was right there, and there was a lavatory in the front hallway. Connie had asked the transport driver to retrieve her keys and personal effects from the Shelby, and the hospital-supply company had shown up with the bed and a wheelchair thirty minutes after Connie arrived.

The nurse had left her with a small Thermos of soup, some saltines, several bottles of water, and a number to call if she got into trouble. They'd done a practice movement to the bathroom, with Connie walking to it and then gratefully using the wheelchair to return to the hospital bed. But she was home, the heater was working just fine, the doors were locked and the alarm set, and she had that handy-dandy twelve-gauge snake gun within arm's reach. The nurse would return at eight o'clock the next morning and use the key Connie had given her to get back into the house. The West Virginia tow truck operator had parked the Shelby as far up in the drive as he could, apparently aware of how valuable it was. Someday she'd clean out that garage and get it totally out of sight.

Her innards were in that curious state of sensation where she couldn't be sure everything was all right or not. The trip across town, the new bed, all the activity, a new pain medication, and the need to be awake for most of the afternoon were all conspiring to make her feel uneasy. She felt as if her plumbing system was only loosely suspended inside, which had her taking constant inventory of every twinge and gurgle. She fell asleep at dusk with all the lights on and her right hand on the pain pump's control button.

That thing she was supposed to remember drifted tantalizingly close to her conscious mind, then wafted away again each time she reached for it. She could almost visualize it, and a part of her brain knew that it was important. Something that bastard had said.

At 5:00 P.M. Heismann drew the venetian blinds on the ground-floor windows and turned on some lights in the living room. He'd walked over to a local bar and grill for a beer and a sandwich. It was already dark outside, and the streetlights were wearing amber halos, which promised fog and mist later. He had the heater going in the house, although warily mindful of what was lurking in that fuel tank. He'd even gone back down this morning to look again at that new wiring, but his training convinced him to leave it alone. Mutaib wasn't doing anything that he, Heismann, wasn't also planning to do. It was just that Mutaib was going to take a direct hand, while he was going to get the *Ammies* to solve his problem for him.

He heard noises from next door, and then the sound of his neighbor's back door opening and closing. He quickly turned out the kitchen light and peered through the blinds. The librarian was going down the steps, carrying an overnight bag. She went into her garage, and a moment later, a car he hadn't seen before was backing out of the garage. She got out, secured the garage door, and then got back in and drove off down the alley.

So she does have a car, he thought. Well, this is perfect; she's probably going to stay with a friend or relative until all this security nonsense had been lifted. Now he wouldn't have to kill her. Unless, of course, she came back tomorrow before noon. But that overnight bag indicated otherwise. And, of course, there'd be nothing to come back to as of Friday afternoon. He hoped she had fire insurance.

Now to the real business: the weapon.

Swamp went back to his apartment after talking to the two detectives. His home voice mail had one message from Gary, which said simply "No hits." He changed into jeans and a sweater, put on some music, and began collating his own list of realtors before realizing his list of calls to return had to be incomplete. He called Gary at the office and asked him to fax a marked-up list to the Kinko's across the street. He then asked him what the scuttlebutt around the office was regarding his sudden disappearance.

"Not a word," Gary said. "It's like you were never here. Mr. McNamara had the department heads in for a meeting this morning, and now everybody's radio-silent. Plus, lots of people have been drafted to help with the security detail up at the Capitol tomorrow. Me included."

"There's a good deal. Great day for some sick leave."

"Not an option," Gary said. "There's only like fifteen of those realtors who haven't answered."

"I'll take it from here. If I get a hit, I'll pass it on to the District cops." He thanked Gary and hung up. He had decided not to tell anyone in his old office about his new job. He trusted Gary, but what Gary didn't know, Gary couldn't blurt out.

Twenty minutes later, with the faxed list in hand, he started making his calls. Some of the offices came up with only voice mail, and those he put down on a recall list. By five o'clock, he was down to four offices. On the third of these, a harried-sounding woman picked up. Swamp could hear voices arguing in the background.

"Crown Realty, can I help you?"

"Yes, ma'am. This is Special Agent Lee Morgan, U.S. Secret Service. We called a few days ago, asking if you'd had any recent transactions with the Royal Kingdom Bank here in D.C.?"

"Wait a minute," she said. The background noises became muffled as she put a hand over the phone and joined the argument. Then she was back. "Do you know what you're asking? We have over two hundred and fifty local listing files, and then there's all the MLS stuff we work. It would take—"

"Ma'am?" Swamp interjected. "Could you perhaps just run quickly through your bookkeeping program? Do a global search for Royal Kingdom Bank? That would do it, wouldn't it? I'm not looking for listings, just completed transactions—rentals, sales. Like that."

There was a moment of silence, and then the woman said, "Okay, hang on while I check."

Swamp heard some keyboard clicking, and then she was back. "Good call, Mr. Special Agent. We closed a rental last week on Capitol Hill. The tenant is a Mr. Erich Hodler, some kind of artist. Sculptor, I think. He's doing lobby art for the Royal Kingdom Bank, and they're the leasee. Prepaid it for six months, in fact. How's that?"

"That is perfect," Swamp said, excited now. "What's the address?"

"Um, I'm a little uncomfortable about doing all this on the phone. Is there a way I can reach you?"

"Sure," Swamp said. "Fax it to me at the Old Executive Office Building." He read off Gary's fax number, which showed up at the top of the faxed list of realtors. "That way, you'll see who you're connecting to."

"Okay, that works for me. It'll be a few minutes, though—some people are coming in."

"As soon as you can, and thanks very much," Swamp said. "You've been a big help."

Swamp hung up and quickly called Gary. He told him about the hit and asked him to intercept that fax when it came in and then call him with the address. Gary said he'd try, but that there was an unscheduled briefing for all hands regarding tomorrow's security-detail assignments going

down in five minutes. All Swamp could do was ask him to
wait as long as he could for the fax. Then he called Jake
Cullen, but once again, everyone was in a meeting about the
inauguration preparations. He asked to be plugged in to
Jake's voice mail, then left a message about making a hit
with the realtor screen. Then he hung up. He wanted to bang
his head against the wall in frustration. Right when he almost had locating data on their quarry, everybody in town
was looking at something else.

He went into the kitchen, fixed a drink, and took it to the
balcony window. It was almost fully dark outside, with a visible mist blowing by the windows. He looked at his watch.
Ten minutes had passed since he'd spoken to Gary, who was
now probably being dragged down the hall by his boss to attend the security-detail briefing. He tried to think of anyone
else he might call. Mary. She wouldn't be at the briefing. But
then he looked at his watch again and saw that it was 5:30.
Mary, experienced civil serpent that she was, would be long
gone. He swore out loud.

He couldn't do anything until he got that address and then
talked to the District cops. And Bertie. Don't forget your
new boss, there, sunshine, he told himself. But this was a
significant development, and at least the District cops would
be all over it, even if the feds elected not to care. He decided
to go out and get some dinner, rather than sitting in the
apartment and going crazy.

Heismann went upstairs and retrieved his tools and the small
bag of wedges. Starting at the topmost mark on the biggest
piece of marble, he cleared out a two-inch-long hatchet-
shaped hole in the supposedly solid marble. Then he tapped
one wedge into the hole until it just stuck. He repeated this
procedure all the way down the line of holes, then began tapping the wedges in random order. After a few minutes, there
was a loud click as a vertical crack appeared in the marble
surface. He kept hitting the wedges, top, bottom, center,

widening the opening until there was another cracking sound, and then the two halves of the block split open and fell onto the floor with a thump that shook the house. Good thing she left, he thought as he grabbed the weapon to keep it from toppling over. Then he sat back on his haunches and admired it, a dull green-colored 120-mm mortar. Soviet-born and bred, the tube was sixty-six inches long and weighed 130 pounds. With the standard base, it would weigh almost 350 pounds, but for what he was going to do, the modified wooden base he'd assembled would be quite good enough.

Mutaib's people had wanted a bomb or bombs, or even a missile, but Heismann had talked them out of that. A mortar was perfect for this kind of attack. The target was heavily defended but stationary, and a mortar required no human penetration of the building or security zone by the bomber. There were no electronic emitters to warn of an impending attack. No fancy radar guidance system to be spoofed by defensive jammers. No heat source on which defensive infrared missiles could home. The mortar rounds, themselves weighing forty-four pounds, almost all of which was high explosive, could not be diverted once fired—they were essentially dumb and blind high-explosive rocks, obeying only the immutable laws of physics. And while it was true that the American Army had a radar that could see the incoming rounds and compute the reverse trajectory to locate the firing position, that wouldn't save anyone in the target area. Downstairs were ten rounds, similarly encased in marble blocks. Five were general-purpose high-explosive rounds; the other five were fragmentation warheads, which would go off eighty feet above the grounds and shred the entire kill zone with white-hot hypersonic shrapnel.

Standing up, he dragged the tube across the floor to the wooden platform he'd built in the center of the room. The base of the tube had a projection on the bottom that was meant to fit into the receiving groove in a heavy steel base plate. Inside the crate was a much smaller version of the real base plate. It had holes drilled around its perimeter, which would allow him to bolt the plate to the plywood stack and then set the mortar down in its groove. Attached to the tube was a single tubular metal leg that could swing out and support the tube at the correct firing angle and also set the firing azimuth.

Many people considered a mortar to be a crude device, but it was actually capable of precise artillery work. The barrel, or tube, was almost five inches in diameter, and the weapon's mobility, with only a three-man crew, meant that a lot of high-explosive rounds could be rained down on a target without having to move an entire artillery company into the field. Its accuracy was a function of how precisely two sets of coordinates were known: the location of the mortar and the location of the target. He had both of those, expressed in units of accuracy of less that ten feet. Wind, atmospheric pressure and temperature, humidity, and differences in elevation between the firing point and the target point could all affect accuracy and became more important the longer the distance to the target. But this weapon could shoot effectively four miles, and his target, at a range of 2,600 meters, was just over one mile away. Given the two main coordinates, his handheld calculator would tell him the elevation angle for firing and the line of fire, expressed in degrees true. All he had to do now was establish the direction of true north in the room.

He found the magnetic compass he'd bought earlier and set it down on the floor by the north-facing bedroom window, well away from the heavy steel tube in the middle of the room. Marking magnetic north, he scratched a line in the finish of the floorboard, then repeated the process on the other side of the room. He drove a nail into each scratch and tied a string between the nails to establish a straight line that ran across the room, very near the tube. The next part would take some estimating. Consulting the GPS unit, he was able to get the correction to account for variation for the geographic position of the town house, which turned out to be a six-degree easterly difference between what a magnetic compass would read and true north. Using a protractor, he established the actual true-north line with a second string and nail set, making sure this string touched the bottom center of the tube, then removed the original string.

He again consulted the GPS unit and determined the firing azimuth, which was 342 degrees true. Then he set up the calculator and entered the range. The calculator gave him the firing solution for full-charge rounds: seventy-two degrees of elevation. He bolted the truncated base plate down onto the plywood stack and then wrestled the heavy tube onto its notch. Then, using the monopod leg, he set the tube at the required angle of elevation and locked the leg. Using a string once again, he scribed an arc in the floorboards; the origin was the tube's center notch, and the arc had a range of ninety degrees, starting on the true-north string and extending to the left, or west, of that line. Then he measured out eighteen degrees of arc, which was true north minus 342 degrees, and made a mark. Maintaining the tube's elevation angle, he swung the base of the leg to match up with that final mark. Then he looked up to see if the rounds were going to clear the skylight.

He frowned. The trajectory was going to be too close to the left edge of the skylight.

Now he had a decision to make: He could offset the entire stack of plywood and support boards and thereby move the firing trajectory closer to the center of the skylight, or he could widen the skylight. Given that his neighbor was out for the night, he elected to widen the skylight. It took an hour and a half of awkward work, because he was trying to be very quiet about the fact that he was tearing a hole in the roof of the building. It was harder than he thought it would be to get through the rafters, plywood decking, the tar paper, and finally the shingles. When he thought he had enough room, he took a break, pasted on a beard and a mustache, and went out for a coffee at the nearby all-night convenience store. He saw several police cars prowling the neighborhood streets closer to the Capitol complex, but his own street remained empty. He watched for any signs of interest in his duplex, but there was no one about and only the normal evening lights showing along the street.

The air was misty, with an underlying layer of cold air. The skylight was on the back side of the roof, so he continued past his house, turned the corner, and came back to it via the alley. He'd left the light on in the master bedroom and could see light through the skylight, but not the fact that there was now a three-foot-square hole along one side of the skylight's frame. Everything was as he had left it. But when he got back into the house through the back door, he was surprised to hear a cell phone chirping somewhere in the house.

When Swamp got back up to the apartment, there were two messages on his voice mail. One was from a rather harried-sounding Gary, with the address on Capitol Hill. Finally! The other was from Bertie, asking if there were any developments. He called Bertie but couldn't get through the counterintelligence directorate's operator: Mr. Walker was currently unavailable, but he could leave a message. As patiently as he could, Swamp identified himself and said simply that the German had been located. He gave the operator the number for his apartment phone.

He went down to his Rover and found his city map. By the beam of the dome light, he located the address. He tried to remember what the perimeter for the security zone was, but he wasn't sure he had it right. Even so, the address looked to be about a mile from the Capitol. Very close to his target. He took the map back upstairs, only to find he'd missed Bertie's return call. He went through the drill again with the Agency operator, waited five minutes, and then Bertie called back.

"Where is he?" Bertie asked without preamble.

"Right up on Capitol Hill," Swamp said, and read out the address. "About a mile from the Capitol itself."

"Son of a bitch," Bertie muttered. "Good damn work here, Mr. Consultant. What do you want to do now?"

"I'm waiting for the District cops to call back. They want this guy for a cop killing. They're more than ready to move."

"Is the German likely to survive the arrest?"

"Depends, especially if he does something dumb. But there's another problem. They'll need a warrant."

"Don't they already have one?"

"They would, except for all this inauguration security. Every cop in town's getting dragged into that. Plus, this would be a tough night to get a warrant, and the courts are probably closed down by now. So we're probably looking at a twenty-four-hour delay, maybe more."

"Yeah, you're probably right," Bertie said. "You up to doing a little recon first, though? Make sure there's someone actually there?"

"Thought about that, but let me talk to the Homicide cops first," Swamp said. "That address is very close to the security zone. Not a place for Lone Rangers tonight, as nervous as everyone is up there."

"True," Bertie said. "Keep us informed. I need to brief my bosses that we may have him located."

Swamp hung up and then checked his voice mail again, but there were no new messages. He looked at his watch. It was seven o'clock. The Metro ran until 1:00 A.M., although there might be schedule changes due to the security plan. He flipped the TV on and watched the evening news, which was giving extensive coverage of the inauguration preparations. A graphic of the lockdown zone came up, and he was able to verify that the address was outside of the perimeter, although not by much.

He also learned that at midnight tonight, the Metro system would stop running on the line that went by the Capitol.

Reagan National would be shut down all day tomorrow, and the entire city would become a TFR zone until Saturday at noon, which meant that no airplanes could come or go into Washington's airspace except for military top cover. In a related report, the newscaster said that there had been rumors of large Air Force transport movements for the past twenty-four hours along the East Coast but that the Pentagon wasn't responding to questions about this. Then there were quick clips of the various police and National Guard units that were being mobilized around the city tonight.

Just as Swamp was wondering if Cullen and Howell would ever be available, the phone rang. It was Jake.

"You found him?" Jake asked.

"Found an address rented by the Royal Kingdom Bank on behalf of an E. Hodler, German sculptor."

"Hot damn! Although we can't work it tonight. No one's available, including Shad and me. But give it to me and then I'll trade you."

Swamp read out the address and then said, "Trade me?"

"Yeah. My ops center people got a hit, too, while the rest of us were doing a goddamned uniform inspection. They plugged into all those things you suggested, plus our own patrol incident logs. Something Shad suggested. Guess what? A Capitol Hill patrol car stopped an elderly foreigner who was walking around Capitol Hill at noon Tuesday. German passport, name of E. Hodler. A current work visa. Well dressed, carrying a briefcase, which had a newspaper and his lunch in it. Strong accent. Said he was out for some fresh air. He seemed harmless, so they let him go. Suggest anything to you?"

Swamp felt a sinking sensation in his gut. Oh shit. This guy wasn't targeting the joint session. He was targeting the inauguration.

They didn't have a month. They had less than twenty-four hours. Fuck me, he thought, because Hallory and his people will never believe this.

"You still there?" Jake asked.

"I was just swallowing my heart," Swamp said. "We've got to get this to the Secret Service."

"Um."

"Yeah, I know," Swamp said. "Can you guys get free to work?"

"I explored that, got shut down. I'd already told my boss what had happened to you, and so—"

"And so if it wasn't good enough for the Secret Service, it wasn't good enough to get you out of the bag."

"More like the chief of D's not wanting what happened to you happening to him. So we're all locked in until tomorrow, after all this bullshit is over. And even then, half the department's gonna be detailed to inauguration parties."

"Let me get back to my new boss at the Agency. I'll try to convince *him* to call in the Secret Service. They've got tons of people up there already."

"Sure they won't just blow you off again?"

"They might," Swamp said. "Especially when they hear the source. But I think it's my duty to try."

"*Duty?*" Jake said. "To the guys who shit on you? Then do it by phone, man. That way, they won't be tempted to bag your ass up and put you in a rubber room out in Saint Elizabeth's until it's all over."

"Good point," Swamp said. "Although that's not likely."

"You didn't see the agent who came to brief us. Talk about having your hair on fire. Stay away from those people tonight. Let your new bosses drop the dime."

Swamp nodded. "Goddamn, Jake. I know this whole thing has been an evidentiary house of cards all along, but what if there *is* some gomer up there getting ready to do something like that?"

"He's gonna be getting a hell of time getting at the Capitol, I'll tell you that," Jake said. "The feds have that whole area shrink-wrapped. The District cops are the middle barrier. None of our people allowed in or near the building."

"Could he do it with a truck bomb? Hezbollah-style?"

"No way. No vehicles anywhere. The building scrubbed once an hour for explosives. No way to get something in there."

"Unless the bomb is already in there. Down deep. In the congressional subway tunnels or—"

"You know they've checked all that," Jake said. "And sealed it. Besides, what bomb? What freaking guy? Nobody believes us!"

"Yeah, I know, I know. Lemme go. I got a call to make."

Swamp confirmed he had the number for Jake's cell phone, and then he called Bertie, hit the usual wall, and hung up to wait for a call back. But it wasn't Bertie who called back; it was the same operator he'd been dealing with. Mr. Walker was in conference and was not to be disturbed. "Is there a message?" she asked.

Swamp identified himself and said, "You need to break him out of that meeting. This is urgent. Really urgent."

"You're a consultant?"

"Yes?"

"Doesn't work that way for consultants, Mr. Morgan. Message?"

Swamp hesitated, trying for some oblique wording. "Tell him . . . tell him, um . . . Shit."

"'Shit'?"

"No, no—tell him that I think the party's Friday, not a month from now, and I'm going to go have a look. Tonight."

There was a moment of silence as the operator wrote it down. "'Having a look tonight.' That it?"

"Yeah, that's it. He'll know what that means. I hope."

"Okay, got it."

"He can reach me on the cell number he issued me."

The operator, obviously used to oblique messages, acknowledged and hung up. Swamp put down the phone with another sinking feeling in his gut and sighed. Jake was right. If he tried to get to Hallory or even McNamara tonight, one or both of them would detonate and then send a psych team to pick him up. Find a judge at home. Recalled pensioner, Your Honor, just dying to stay on active duty, conjures up this wild-ass theory about a bomb plot. Keeps banging on about it even though there's no solid evidence and everybody tells him it's a firefly. Guy gets sent home but won't go, and now he's truly delusional, claiming his phantom German assassin is going to bomb the inauguration instead of his other crazy-ass speculation about the speech to the joint session. We need a committal order, please.

And at the moment, he had to admit he didn't know if this Hodler was even there. Just as Bertie had suggested, he ought to go see. *Then* cry wolf and take his chances.

He looked out the window and tried to imagine the network of edgy federal agents roaming the security zone around the Capitol. Even though he was working for the Agency, just claiming to be a consultant for the Agency to any of the Secret Service guys would bring an instant rolling of eyes. Sure you are, mate. He picked up the Agency credential folder and looked at the identification documents inside. He'd never seen a real CIA identification card. Would this thing convince a Secret Service agent? Should he even take it along? If a local cop stopped him up there, it might be useful. But if the Secret Service even saw his name, there was probably an order out from Hallory's office to bag his ass.

Screw it, he'd leave it. He'd just be a citizen tonight. All he was going to do was have a look at the house. See if it was occupied, lighted, or what. Then get the hell out of there. If anybody asked, he was out for a walk. It's a free country, right? Used to be, anyway.

He took his new cell phone anyway, even though it probably wasn't fully charged. Better than nothing. Then he went to get the Rover. He'd have preferred taking the Metro, but he wanted that panic button handy.

A telephone? Heismann thought. What telephone? Then he remembered—the cell phone in the box. But he hadn't turned it on yet. It wasn't time. So what is this? How could it be ringing?

He hurried upstairs and located the phone, still in its case by the box of tools. Remembering Mutaib's instructions, he hit the talk button but did not speak. He put the phone to his ear but heard nothing. Then he looked in the phone's illuminated text screen. Two words appeared: *Warning. Intruders.*

He hit the button to end the call and the light went out in the text window. From all appearances, the phone had gone back to sleep. He put the phone down on a small table in the corner of the room. Then he remembered what Mutaib had said about the thing self-destructing. But that was supposed to happen after the midnight call. What the hell was going on here? He moved the phone over to where the split blocks of marble were stacked and put it down on top of some marble. If it melted, then nothing would be damaged.

Intruders. Assuming Mutaib had sent the warning, it must mean that someone was coming here to the house. Surely Mutaib was not warning him about his own people and their deadly little present in the fuel tank. He became aware of all the lights that were on in the house, and he began turning them off, upstairs and downstairs, leaving only one small light on in the kitchen. Then he went to the bedroom and got his gun and a flashlight. No, no guns. Not tonight, with the streets crawling with security people. The Taser. He got the rig out of his closet, stripped off his coat, and put on the power pack. He checked all the connections and then put his coat back on. He found his watch cap and went out the back door. If police or security people were coming, he didn't dare get trapped inside the house. He would check his perimeter, then wait outside in the dark for a while, see what happened.

Forty minutes later, Swamp walked out of the parking lot of the Capitol South Metro station, through the concourse area, and into a foggy yet surprisingly nippy January night. He was stopped by two uniformed police officers and asked for identification. He showed his West Virginia driver's license and said that he was going to visit a friend, then gave them the address of the town house. The cops nodded him through, reminding him that the last train going back over to Virginia would be through this station at 11:30. They were obviously assuming he had taken a train.

He walked east on D Street, intent on not bumping up against the security cordon around the Capitol and its grounds. This was one night he didn't need to run into any of Hallory's people out here on the street. He was wearing woolen pants and a long-sleeved shirt under a dark woolen parka. He had his government-issue weapon in one pocket of the parka and a small flashlight and his personal cell phone, set to vibrate, not ring, in the other. He'd had some second thoughts about leaving his Agency identification credentials back at the apartment, but he finally figured that if he did get picked up, he didn't want to involve the Agency, since Bertie had not actually ordered him to do this. Sounded good anyway.

He had rented a row house up here in the Capitol Hill area a long time ago, when he first came to Washington, so he knew the general layout of the neighborhood, with its interior alleys and double garages. His plan was to scout the house from the street and then go down the alley behind it to see what he could see. If he could confirm that someone was in the house, he'd back out and call Cullen. If he couldn't raise the District cops, he'd call Bertie again. And if that didn't work, he'd call Hallory's office. No, he wouldn't. He'd wait for Bertie. Let him do it.

He thought he could count on the District cops being a lot more responsive than the feds. Rather than risk another embarrassing confrontation with Hallory and his people, get the Homicide cops, who had a personal reason to grab this guy, to come take him into custody tonight. Let the inauguration happen, and then they'd sort it all out the following day. If Swamp's final leap of logic was right, they'd prevent a terrorist attack during the inauguration. And if he had been wrong all along, Mr. Hodler would be free to go as soon as he convinced the District Homicide squad he hadn't been involved in Cat Ballard's killing or the attack on Connie Wall. They had some hair and fiber samples from both crime scenes, so they could develop tangible evidence if it was there. Or they could always deport him under the antiterrorism statutes, which would solve the problem just as well. And as for the Saudi money angle, there were people at DHS who could work that problem.

One thing Swamp was not going to do was to try to enter the town house. Take a quick look, front and rear, see if it looked lived in, back out, and then call for the cavalry.

Heismann climbed the wooden partition that divided his part of the back porch from that of his next-door neighbor. He then crept along the middle fence to her side of the garage. If she was like him, the alley door would be locked but not the yard door, and it wasn't. Her garage was exactly like his, only with more cardboard boxes stored along the walls. She'd been driving a small Japanese import tonight, so there was plenty of room for car and storage. From her part of the garage, he could watch the back of his house through the small window in the yard door, although he still couldn't see out into the alley. Unless . . .

He went to her garage door, tripped the inside latch, and raised the door as quietly as he could. Light from the alley flooded in. Too much light, and besides, in this neighborhood, no one would leave a garage door cracked open at night. Any police car cruising the alley would investigate that. Then he had an idea: He could pull the door back down but leave it cracked at the bottom. Then rearrange the cardboard boxes to create a hiding place in her half of the garage. He could watch the house through the window, but if he heard someone in the alley, he'd get behind the boxes and

wait for the prowler to discover that the garage door was unlocked.

Yes. That would work. He pulled the door down again,
doing it slowly to mask the rattling sound, and then set about
building a hide. In the back of his mind, he kept wondering:
Who will the "intruders" be, and how did Mutaib know they
were coming? He had the uneasy sense that he was misun-
derstanding something here.

Swamp slowed his pace as he entered the block where the
house ought to be. Checking the house numbers, he crossed
the street so that he would be on the opposite side from his
target. Most of the houses had lights on, and every one of
them had shades fully drawn on the street-level windows.
Cars were parked close together, and he wondered how
some of them would ever get out. There was no traffic about,
nor any other pedestrians. Given the foggy, chilly weather,
he wasn't too surprised, but he was worried that he might be
conspicuous on the empty street.

As he drew abreast of the house, he stopped and bent
down to retie his shoelaces. The house was a duplex, and the
only light showing was through the vertical windows flanking the front doors. The duplex appeared to have been restored recently, and the facade was freshly painted and
neatly trimmed. He didn't see any signs of the Suburban, but
there was always the alley garage. He kept walking, passing
the midblock alley to his right, and then turned left at the
corner, crossed the street, and went halfway down the block
to the alley. He paused before entering the alley, looking
around to see if anyone was obviously watching him, but
there was no one about. The houses all seemed to be settling
into a normal workday-evening routine. A dog started barking in the next block, and he could just barely hear the hum
of traffic out on the broad ceremonial boulevards beyond the
Capitol, whose upper dome glowed in floodlights about a
mile away.

The alley was narrow and cambered to move rainwater, but still big enough to admit a trash truck, based on the big plastic containers lining the wooden privacy fences along its length. Each duplex had a detached double garage at the back. There was one light on a telephone pole midway down the alley, which illuminated almost the entire alley. Halfway down, there was a short T-connection alley leading out to the front street.

Swamp turned into the alley and walked slowly down toward the other end, counting houses until he saw that the trash containers had the house street numbers on them. When he got to the one he wanted, he stepped to the other side of the alley so he could see over the fence. The back of the house was dark except for one small light on one side, in what was probably the kitchen. A covered back porch was divided by a privacy partition, and the yard was similarly divided by a privacy fence. The garage looked too small to house a Suburban, but he walked up to it and tried to look through the row of dusty windows across the garage door. He couldn't be sure, but he didn't think there was a vehicle in there.

He stepped back from the windows and scanned the windows of the surrounding houses. If anyone saw him back here peering into windows, there'd be cop cars turning into the alley very soon. He'd promised himself that he wouldn't do any B and E work, not that he'd really know how. He thought about throwing a rock through a window to see if the lights came on, but then he thought better of it. How could he be sure there was someone there? He lifted the trash receptacle's lid, but the bin was empty. Go knock on the door? Flash his retired ID card, tell some fairy tale, and then beat feet? Hardly. And anyway, if his man was what he thought he was, he might rabbit. The cold night air was beginning to penetrate his coat as he stood there, and then he saw that the door on the other half of the garage was cracked open at the bottom. Suppose he lifted it enough to get in there, and then—what? Wrong yard, wrong house. But still, if he could get to a window at the back of the house . . .

He put both hands under the crack and lifted, and sure enough, the door came up. He raised it three feet, far enough for the top section to roll into the horizontal track, and then stopped. He had no warrant and zero authority to be doing this. But he had to know if there was someone in that house. At that moment, a police car went by on the cross street, cruising slowly. Swamp saw it out of the corner of his eye and then saw a flare of brake lights reflected in the windows of the cars parked next to the alley entrance. Oops, he thought. He got down, slipped under the door, and then lowered it back to the ground. Sure enough, headlights illuminated the alley outside and he heard the cruiser's tires crunching down the alley. He stood up and plastered himself against the wall.

The cop car stopped outside the garage, and he heard a door open. Footsteps approached the garage door on the other side and then he heard the rattle of the door handle. He quickly put a foot on the inside handle and shifted his entire weight to it just as the cop outside bent down and tried the door. Swamp hunched himself over as the cop shined a flashlight through the windows. The garage was empty except for a pile of cardboard boxes in one corner. He heard the cop say something to his partner, then more footsteps. And after that, the car door closed again and the cruiser continued on down the alley. He exhaled, turned around, and saw a figure silhouetted in the dim light coming through the windows. A man was standing in front of him with what looked like a toy gun in his hand. Before he had a chance to say anything or even focus on the man's face, an electric hammer jolted his whole body and he went down into a huge dark hole. As he struggled to climb back out, a second hammer descended, and this time he lost consciousness.

It took Heismann twenty minutes to drag the intruder from the neighbor's garage out into the alley, lock everything up again, and then drag him through his own back gate, across the yard, and up the steps into the kitchen. He almost didn't make it up the steps, because the man was big—220 pounds or more of dead weight. Once in the kitchen, he rested for a few minutes, puffing. He studied his captive's face. An older man—late fifties, perhaps—with coarse features. And big, which is why he had fired twice. Then he remembered Mutaib telling him about the Secret Service and the Washington police coming to see him at the bank. His description of the big homely man who seemed to be in charge of the questions. He closed his eyes and concentrated—he was forgetting something. Then he had it: He'd seen this man before. That day when he was watching the nurse's house to see if she'd survived the poison. The two federal policemen. This man had been one of them.

He bound the man's hands together with tape. Then he lifted the man's joined arms over his head and taped them behind his head with a swath of tape that went over his forehead, under his chin, and also over his eyes. Then he laid him back down on the kitchen floor, where he looked like someone who had decided to take a nap on his back, with his hands behind his head. He went through the intruder's coat pockets and found the flashlight, the cell phone, and a gun. He then dug deeper and extracted the man's wallet and keys. Driver's license: T. Lee Morgan, West Virginia. The same state where he had knifed that bothersome nurse. Then he found the ID card. U.S. Secret Service—retired.

What was this "retired"? He searched his English vocabulary. Retired? Ah, yes, a pensioner.

He sat back on his heels. The identification card with its notation "retired" puzzled him. He knew what the Secret Service was—they protected the president. He had read in the *Washington Post* about how they were in charge of the security cordon for the inauguration tomorrow. Well and good. But a pensioner? With a gun? Were they so desperate that they had recalled their pensioners to walk the streets the night before the big event? No. No. No. Pensioner or not, this man was connected to the nurse and to Mutaib. An investigator. And now he was here?

The big man stirred and then groaned. He didn't look all that old, although there was plenty of gray in his hair. Heismann stood up and backed away from him. He pulled a kitchen chair over and sat down. Why was this man, especially *this* man, sneaking around his back gate, and why was this happening right after he had received a warning from Mutaib about intruders? He couldn't be positive about the face, but it certainly resembled the man he'd seen from the park. The same thick brows, bent nose, coarse features.

He rested his face in his hands and watched the man work his way painfully back toward consciousness. Then he reread the man's driver's license and ID card. Both showed an address in Harpers Ferry, West Virginia. He had seen that place on his map when he went to that Garrison Gap resort in pursuit of the nurse. Perhaps this was not about the big event tomorrow. It might be about what he had done in West Virginia. Perhaps the state police there had connected him somehow to that killing, alerted Interpol, and then Mutaib's spies in Europe had warned him. But why tonight, of all nights? And on a phone that wasn't even supposed to be turned on.

The big man opened his mouth, licked his lips, grunted, and then tried to get up. He tried to roll, but his own elbows prevented it. Then he raised his knees, which is when Heismann knelt down beside him and put Herr Pensioner Morgan's own gun against his left ear, racked the slide, ejecting one round onto the floor, and said, "Stay." The man stopped moving at once. Heismann got back up and returned to his chair. He waited for the man to say something, but he did not. He was breathing deeply, as if gathering his strength to do something. Heismann kicked the bullet on the floor into a corner and considered his options.

One of them was to run. Right now. Abort the entire mission. He had half his money, and he could disappear a lot more quickly than Mutaib might imagine because of his new physical appearance. He could become a woman, take his pick of the woman's clothes next door, walk, not run, to the minivan, and simply drive away. Leave Herr Pensioner Morgan right here on the floor, perhaps with one more tap from the Taser. Let him get loose finally. Let him find the weapon upstairs, sound the alarm. Let the *Ammies* see how close they had come. And then leave some more evidence implicating Mutaib and his Saudi clan, something besides the shipping documents.

He examined the man's cell phone. He could use that, call Mutaib directly, tell him he had this man tied up in his kitchen and ask what he should do. He smiled. The Arab would positively panic if he received a direct call, especially from here. Especially on a cell phone. This was Washington. They could probably triangulate any cell phone in the city, especially one of their own. And they were undoubtedly listening, on this night of all nights.

He looked at his watch. Almost ten o'clock. Fourteen hours.

He was probably making too much of this thing. Perhaps what Mutaib had meant was simply that there would be all sorts of police saturating the neighborhood around the Capitol Hill area. The message had said "intruders," plural, not a specific intruder. And here was the proof: They'd enlisted the help of pensioners to increase their presence on the street. This one had seen the cracked garage door and come to check. The man's backup had been outside in the alley in that car, but he'd sent them away. And down behind the boxes, it had been impossible to see what happened when the policeman outside tried the door. So, the pensioner wanted to show them he could still do the job. And when he didn't report in? Would they even notice? The old fellow probably just went home and didn't even check out.

He snorted in contempt. They were using *pensioners*? Even if this was the same man who'd been at the nurse's house, or even at the bank, asking all those questions, his being a pensioner clearly meant that they didn't believe there was any kind of real threat.

To hell with it, he decided. I am going to do this thing. Show these arrogant bastards what a real threat looks like. And right under their noses, too.

He stood up and gathered up the pensioner's stuff. He'd take it along when he made his run. The driver's license and ID card might be useful later.

Pensioners! Truly incredible.

Swamp heard the man get up and start moving some furniture around. It felt like he was lying on linoleum, so he was probably in the kitchen. On his back, with his hands taped together and some kind of tape lash-up holding his arms behind his head. His one attempt to move had confirmed that every joint in his body now felt like it was harboring full-blown arthritis. Even his fillings hurt. Had to have been a Taser. His eyes were taped over, but not his nose and mouth, for which he was grateful—he had a fear of suffocation. Then he felt the legs of a chair dropping over his body, followed by the sounds of kitchen utensils being piled on the chair. He kept still, and was rewarded with the feel of that gun pressing against his ear again. No, not the gun—something else. Something plastic, blocky. Then he heard the hum, felt the hair rising along the side of his head. The Taser.

"Stay," the man whispered again, as if he were addressing a dog.

Swamp said nothing. The message was clear enough. And the chair on top of him piled with kitchen utensils meant that if he moved, there'd be a clatter, and then he'd get to find out how serious this guy was about him remaining still. One thing he knew with perfect clarity: He did *not* want to be hit with that Taser again. Some of his larger muscles were still cramping, and his heartbeat hadn't stabilized.

He stayed quiet, desperately trying to think of a way out
of this mess. He could almost hear Bertie's voice: Smooth
move, Ex-Lax. At least you were right about his being a bad
guy. And tell me again why you didn't call for backup? On
the cell phone right there in your pocket?

That said, there was a man here with a Taser. The cops
outside Connie Wall's house had been hit with a Taser. The
big question was, Did he have weeks or hours until whatever
this guy was planning went down? Or maybe *up* was a better
word.

Hell with it, he thought. It's him. It's the inauguration, not
the speech to the joint session. And right now, I need to figure out how to get loose.

Heismann went upstairs and checked the cell phone. It did
not appear to have melted down on its marble bed. He
checked for any further messages, but the phone was dark.
But it was early—midnight was the commit point. He looked
at his watch. Another ninety minutes. He had some more
preparations to make, beginning with final verification that
the mortar rounds would clear the hole in the roof. He took a
flashlight and taped it down inside the mortar tube, attaching
it to the side of the tube nearest the extended hole in the
roof. Then he switched it on and looked for a spot of light
anywhere on the ceiling. There wasn't one. He could almost
see the beam of light shining up into the blowing mist outside. Definitely clear. Good. He removed the flashlight and
went back downstairs to begin hauling up the ten mortar
rounds. He checked on his prisoner, whom he found still lying beneath the chair, looking for all the world as if he were
taking an extended nap. And soon he might, Heismann
thought. Very soon.

Each mortar round came with six yellow packets of propellant explosive in clear plastic pouches the size of fast-
food condiment packages. These were taped to the
projectile's cylindrical tail fin assembly. Once he had the

rounds all upstairs, he consulted the handheld calculator
again, this time entering the range to the target, the elevation
angle of the weapon's monopod leg, the air temperature, and
the barometric pressure. The answer came out two, which
meant that only two, not six, packets of additional explosive
propellant were needed for the range and conditions of the
firing. He went to each round and pulled off all but two of
the yellow packets, making sure they were distributed on opposite sides of the tail fin tube. He put all the rest of them
into a plastic bag and put the bag in his backpack. Never
know when something like that might come in handy. Then
he recomputed the firing azimuth and range problem and
checked the physical lineup of the tube with his true-north
reference lines. Everything matched his original computa-
tions, but he still had this niggling worry that he'd forgotten
something elementary.

He stood back and examined the setup. Then he had it:
level. He hadn't checked the level of the floor. And even if
he had, all that extra weight had probably disturbed the level
of the base. He swore.

He retrieved the bubble level from the pile of carpentry
tools and checked the base. Level on a line running from
the alley to the street. *Not* level on the line running across the
duplex from side to side. Off a half a bubble. He swore
again. Now he would have to move the mortar, and do
the entire damn thing again.

Idiot! You know better. A half-bubble error could throw
the aim point off a hundred meters at this range. That was
the length of one of the *Ammies'* football fields. He felt like
hitting something, then thought immediately of the pensioner trussed up on his kitchen floor. It would be satisfying
to go down there and stomp his face in.

His face.

He sat there, suddenly mesmerized by an exciting idea.
Here was the perfect way to take care of Mutaib once and for
all. If this was the same man who had questioned Mutaib,

and also the nurse, then he could be used to *ensure* that Mutaib was taken for this huge crime. Even if he was a pensioner, he had to have been investigating the clinic fire and the killing of the nurse. Yes, yes, yes! This was much better than what he had originally planned. Yes, perfect. Absolutely perfect!

Then he set about correcting the level problem while he waited for midnight and the Arabs' final decision.

As soon as Swamp heard the man working on something upstairs, he went to work on getting out from under the booby-trapped chair. He couldn't see anything and could barely blink to wet his eyes under the tape. His arms were useless and beginning to cramp, and he could not move his head without pulling on his eyelids. He could feel the four legs of the chair wedged firmly alongside his body. But he was on his back. If he could turn on his side, he would probably be narrow enough to be able to slide free of the chair. After that, he'd find a way to get up. And then work on all this damned tape.

It took him fifteen minutes to get all the way over on his side without moving the chair, mostly because the way his arms were pinned behind his head made rotation almost impossible. Holding his body in a full twist, he began to inch his way past the chair legs until he couldn't feel them anymore. Then he ran into what felt like the refrigerator, and he couldn't go any farther. But were his feet clear? He tried to visualize it, but he hadn't had a decent look at the kitchen before being taped up. He stopped to listen, but the man was still doing something on the floor above him. Moving something heavy, from the sound of it. He decided to arch his back and try to turn to the left to get that extra two or three feet of clearance for his feet. When he felt he'd moved far enough, he relaxed his arched back and then the twist above his hips and took a breather. So far so good. No clatter of kitchen spoons to alert his captor.

He began to draw up his knees preparatory to getting himself upright. He thought he felt one of his boots touch something, so he stopped, squirming to reposition his foot to make damned sure he wasn't going to hit that chair. Then he pulled his knees up into his stomach and once again twisted his body to get his knees underneath. But now his arms got in the way. This wouldn't work.

He stopped to listen again, still heard the noises upstairs. No, he would have to do a sit-up while lying on his side, then roll onto his knees and—what, forehead? He knew he was running out of time. He had to get his arms and his eyes free or all this was for nothing. He decided to just go for it, and he pulled himself up with great effort into a position where his posterior was in the air and his torso looked like he was praying to some awful god. And then he felt himself rolling on over, losing his balance entirely and thumping down onto the floor again while falling directly into the second chair, which he didn't know about, the one filled with pots and pans, all of which came crashing down onto the floor with him.

He sighed and lay still. No point in even trying to get up again. He might be vertical, but he'd still be trussed up like a roaster, and blind to boot. He heard the man's footsteps as he came down the stairs and into the kitchen. They stopped for a moment. He heard a door open, and smelled a whiff of basement air. Then there came that deadly humming sound.

"Hey, don't hit me again," he said. "I'll be good."

"Oh, ya, you will," the man whispered, and then Swamp felt himself being dragged and then dumped headfirst onto the top few steps of what was probably the basement stairs. The man was silent, and Swamp held his breath. He wondered if he was supposed to start crawling down the stairs, but then the electric trip-hammer came again, whaling both of his shins so hard that he lurched forward in a huge spasm of contracting leg muscles and then slid all the way down the stairs for what seemed like forever, banging every protrud-

ing edge of his body several times on the way down. He
fetched up on what felt like hard-packed dirt, his bruised
right cheek pressed against a stone wall. He could hardly
feel all the bumps and bruises through the haze of cramping
leg muscles and jangling nerves.

He stopped fighting the program and just went limp instead. He heard a door close up above him, followed by the
sounds of someone coming down the steps. At least no one
expected him to get up and do it again just now. He barely
felt the man wrapping his lower legs in tape, nor did he
much care. What was a little more tape at this juncture? He
was well and truly screwed.

Heismann went back upstairs after locking the cellar door. It
was twenty minutes to midnight, and he wanted to be right
next to that mysterious cell phone, the one that turned itself
on. The mortar was perfectly level now, although he had had
to reset the elevation angle to compensate for the newly level
platform. He was still uneasy about the discrepancy in target
coordinates, but had to assume Mutaib had access to ground-
truth data. And he had the television, which would provide
spotting data.

He would fire two rounds and then stop. If the television
covering the inauguration proceedings showed direct hits,
he'd drop in the other eight rounds and then make his run. If
they were off, he would adjust the mortar one time and then
fire the eight rounds. He had to assume there would be air-
borne surveillance over the city, and if by chance they had
one of those reverse-trajectory radars, there'd be F-15's
rolling in on the town house as soon as the rounds stopped
falling. Even if he was off in his aim point, those big projec-
tiles would still be devastating, going off above the packed
west portico at eighty feet in the air and blasting hundred-
foot-wide cones of shredded steel all over the exterior of the
building. A total decapitation strike: all the important outgoing government officials, the incoming government, the

Supreme Court, the congressional leadership, both presidents and vice presidents. And all this using a weapon that had been around since the late Middle Ages. Give the Arabs credit: They had seen the beauty of it at once. And as everyone knew, the Arabs held a certain fondness for the Middle Ages.

Eleven-forty-five. He turned on the phone. The text screen lighted up but remained blank. He set the phone down on the windowsill and sat down to wait. He would have to find a way to get the big man in the basement up here for the attack. His prisoner would now have a vital role to play as the witness, so he needed to leave some way for the pensioner to escape before the house burned down around him. And if the Arabs decided to abort the mission, he'd leave all the fuel in the tank and his uninvited guest in the basement. Let Mutaib's bomb take care of business. What was one pensioner? He kept looking out the windows to make sure there wasn't a search on for the man, but with all those police out on the streets tonight, he would most likely not be missed until morning. By then, it would be much too late.

The phone trilled from the windowsill. He picked it up and read the text: "Execute."

He felt a cold chill spread through his stomach. They were going through with it. He shook his head in wonder. Did they have *any* idea of what would happen next? He was reminded of a sick joke he'd heard circulating after the Arabs attacked the World Trade Center in 2001. A father takes his young son to view the memorial at the site in lower Manhattan. The son asks what happened there. The father tells him that Arabs attacked the World Trade Center and killed three thousand people. The son asks, "Daddy? What's an Arab?"

Very well. He felt the bottom of the phone getting suddenly hot and dropped it on the floor, where it indeed proceeded to melt itself.

Time now to double-check the structure supporting the

floor, attend to the fuel tank, and then get both his body and his escape wardrobe ready. He shut off the single table lamp in the bedroom and looked out the back window at the distant Capitol dome, all lighted up for the festivities. Even from here, he could see reflections of blue strobe lights from the street in front of the Capitol, the lights playing across the towering white marble facade. There must be a thousand security people over there, he thought. He wondered if they'd get much sleep tonight. They were probably still poking around in hall closets and looking under vehicles for bombs.

He wondered if *he'd* get any sleep tonight. But why not? He was ready. *Alles ist in Ordnung.*

12

SWAMP AWOKE TO THE SOUND OF THE TASER HUMMING
nearby and flinched. He lay partially on his side on the cold
floor, his arms still hoisted above his head. His shoulders
were numb and his back and sides ached so much that he
could barely move. He had no idea of what time it was or
how long he'd been out on the basement floor. He seemed to
remember the man coming back down the stairs last night
and doing something that produced a stink of fuel oil, which
he could still smell. Now the man was doing something at
his feet, and suddenly his legs were free. Kick him hard, his
brain said, but his leg muscles just laughed at him. They
were far more interested in the restoration of normal blood
circulation than in launching any surprise attacks. A wave of
pins and needles flooded through his feet.

"Up," the man ordered. Swamp thought the guy was trying to disguise his voice, because the word came out sounding more like "op" than "up."

"Can't move," Swamp said as he tried to raise his knees.

"Up," the man said again from behind his head, and then
he emphasized the point with the hum of the Taser. Up it is,
Swamp thought.

It took him a full minute of bending, twisting, and gasping as his body resisted the maneuver. One of the problems
of being a big guy, he thought. Lots of muscle mass to un-

kink. He got on his side, then to his knees and then, using the wall, pushed himself relatively upright, although off balance because his arms were pinned in the air like that. The man closed in again with the Taser and attached something around his neck. It felt like a rope. He could see dim light through the tape but not much else. He leaned on the stone wall for a moment, but then the rope was pulling and he had to follow it or fall down. Getting up had been much too hard, so he followed the pull.

"Stairs," the man said after Swamp had taken four painful steps. He felt with his right foot and encountered the lowest tread. The rope tugged again and up he went, leaning against the wall all the way up to make sure he didn't fall off the outer edge. He didn't know whether or not there was a railing and didn't want to find out the hard way. He concentrated on remembering what he was doing as they went up the stairs, the man in front of him; then they reached the top and turned left and left again. Hallway? His head collided with something and he bounced back, lost his balance, and slipped sideways up against what felt like a plaster wall.

"Up," the man said again, impatient this time. He reinforced the order with an ugly jerk on the rope. Swamp went through the whole process again, his arms and shoulders complaining now as he tried to use them for balance. Once vertical again, he resumed his forced march, going down the hallway, then right and up more stairs. He could see light through the duct tape, so he knew it must be morning. This time, he felt the presence of a railing and climbed with a bit more confidence. The man took a right at the top of the stairs and then tugged Swamp through a doorway, which scraped both his extended elbows. As he regained strength and flexibility, he began to think of what he should be doing to escape, but then the man ordered him to sit and pushed him back against a wall. He slid down obediently, grateful for the sudden support the wall provided for his arms and shoulders. It was much colder up here on the second floor, and Swamp thought he could hear tree branches moving around, as if the room was open to the outside air. His feet and legs were free, and now he needed to get this tape away from his eyes.

The man left the rope around his neck and went out of the room, coming back in again after a minute. He came over to where Swamp was sitting with his back to the wall and then put a foot on Swamp's knees and forced them flat to the floor. With the humming sound of the ever-ready Taser in his ears, Swamp just had to sit there as his feet were rewrapped in tape. So much for some sudden karate moves, Swamp thought, as if he remembered any. Then the man moved to Swamp's right side, and the humming noise got louder. He felt steel on his cheek and the sharp point of a knife working its way beneath the duct tape over his eyes. He froze, not wanting his captor to make any mistakes just now, and then the man began sawing at the tape. Then he was working his fingers under the edge, and Swamp squinted his eyes shut as hard as he could, knowing what was coming. The man ripped the tape off in one sudden move and Swamp grunted with the pain of it as his eyelids tried hard to go with the tape. He struggled to open his eyes, but there was enough mastic from the tape on his eyelids to stick them together. The man dropped the knife with a clatter on the floor and then pried Swamp's right eye open with his fingers. The sudden exposure to daylight made him blink furiously, which opened his other eye, and then both his eyes filled involuntarily with tears and he couldn't see a thing.

The man got up and backed away from him, waiting for Swamp's vision to adjust. Then he stepped right around in front of him. Swamp blinked several times again and looked up. He was stunned by what he saw when his eyes finally cleared.

"*You!*" he exclaimed as he looked into the dark eyes and

hawk-nosed face of Emir Mutaib abd Allah, managing director of the Royal Kingdom Bank.

"Hello, old chap," the Arab said. "Remember me?"

The Arab straightened up and walked out of Swamp's sight before he could reply. My God! Swamp thought. *This* was Erich Hodler? As he was trying to assimilate the idea, he saw the giant mortar poised out in the middle of the room. He looked up and saw the skylight, with the big bite taken out of the roof structure to its right. He looked left out the window and saw the Capitol dome bathed in noontime sunlight.

Son of a bitch! Could that thing reach the Capitol? There were ten rounds clustered around the mortar, looking like olive green demon spawn clustered around their mother. He looked back out the window. It was a huge mortar, nothing like the 60-mm Army weapon he'd seen demonstrated at agent school. And those things could go a mile, so what could this monster do? Then he understood precisely what it could do. There was a small television behind the mortar, on which coverage of the inauguration ceremony was in full progress. Ten rounds, properly aimed, fired right at noon, fragmentation warheads, and they'd get the whole government. Correction: the old and the new governments. He remembered every picture he'd ever seen of an inauguration, with all those people packed in like sardines all over the Capitol steps. It would be a massacre. Then the man was back, and so was the duct tape around his eyes. He tried to lunge forward, to do *something*, but he got absolutely nowhere as the Arab grabbed that rope and pulled hard, toppling Swamp over on his side and cracking his head against one of those pieces of marble littering the room. He fought to stay conscious, but it was very, very difficult. So much easier to just give into the beckoning red haze.

Heismann checked his prisoner's pulse and found it strong. He hadn't meant to knock him out, but the man was truly large and he'd startled him with that sudden move. But he would still remember that face. And with luck, this man would escape and tell the world who had been in the room with the mortar. Nothing like an eyewitness who was also a federal agent. Even if he was a pensioner. Mutaib was a dead man, and he, Heismann, wouldn't have to go to the bank after all.

He got up and kicked the knife away from the prostrate pensioner and then made sure the man's arms were still firmly pinned. He tied the end of the rope to a radiator and tightened the noose. He'd go make his transformation, then come back and cut through enough of the tape that the pensioner would be able to get free once the attack was completed. And, of course, he'd let him watch, as long as he remained compliant. He'd leave him with one good chance to get free. Or not, as the case might be, he thought with a shrug. Pinning all this on Mutaib was a nicely satisfying wrinkle, but not vital to his own escape or the success of the attack. But still . . .

He looked at his watch: 11:20. Forty minutes to go. The television camera was panning over the crowd on the Capitol steps, stopping to zoom in each time the announcer identified an important official. Time to reincarnate himself as the lady next door. He pulled the curtains, being careful to remain out of sight, and checked the street outside. More cars than usual were parked along the street because most people had stayed home from work today. The morning news had reported that most of the country was as shut down as the capital, with all government offices closed, as well as the banks and all the major stock markets.

He'd not been able to detect any lurking shooters sent from Mutaib parked out in the street, but that didn't mean they hadn't rented *two* town houses on this block. He could just imagine telescopic sights focused on his front door, and probably his back door, too, for that matter. But they would have to be circumspect. Looking through the crack in his curtain, he saw a police car cruise slowly down the street, the cops visibly scanning the parked cars and house fronts. Mutaib's people would wait for that bomb in the basement to do its work, but if it didn't—and it wouldn't, not now—that's when he'd expect long guns to begin poking out of windows.

But Mutaib's assassins, if they were there, wouldn't see what they expected to see. Instead of Jäger Heismann slipping out a door or a window, what they would see was the beginning of a house fire and then an almost naked *woman* come screaming hysterically out of the house next door and run right across the street and into that mid-block alley.

He checked on the pensioner once more, but he was still down. Then he left the room and crawled through the hole in the middle wall. He pushed the boxes aside in the closet and went into the woman's bathroom, where his makeup, clothes, wig, and the breast pump were all laid out on the counter. He checked his watch again. He had thirty-seven minutes. He stripped off all his clothes, sat naked on the chair he'd pulled up to the bathroom countertop, and went to work.

Connie propped herself up in the hospital bed to watch the inauguration. She had muted the sound, tired of the newscasters' lame attempts to fill the time until the proceedings began. The visiting nurse had come, then left after arranging a few more things to her satisfaction. She had inspected the wound, changed the bandages, and adjusted the settings on the pain pump. She'd warned Connie that she was beginning the weaning process on the pain meds and that she would have to evaluate her tolerance for the new settings. Connie had a chart and the appropriate instruments for measuring her vitals, as well as water and food, books, the TV remote, and a telephone, all within reach.

None of it probably would have been possible if Connie hadn't been a nurse. But as it was, she thought she was medically safer here at home than she would have been in any hospital. She'd tried to reach Jake, but the headquarters operator had told her that everyone was on the street today to handle the inauguration. Connie had declined to leave a message on his voice mail, unsure of who might have access to it. She dreaded all the upcoming paperwork and legal documents that would be necessary because of Cat's murder and also the Bladensburg woman's death in Garrison Gap. Jake had promised to help her through all that, but she was probably going to need a lawyer.

She finally saw the two presidents, the new and the outgoing, along with their wives, step out of the ornate Capitol doorway and approach the dais. The cameras did enough of a close-up to contain both men, and Connie thought they looked a little different, until she realized they were probably wearing makeup, which in the cold light of day subtly altered their features. They both wore long, bulky overcoats, made even bigger by their bullet-resistant vests. Her cable system had gone dark this morning, so she could only receive the three major networks via her rooftop antenna, and the quality of her picture was definitely diminished. She unmuted the set and sat back to watch.

Swamp came to with a painful headache and a sense of total dread. He halfheartedly tested his bonds and confirmed that he had been trussed up again and was completely immobile. He thought about his options. Muster the strength to roll across the room and knock that damned mortar over? Or dislodge it enough to throw off the aiming point? But where was his captor? He listened carefully but could hear only the wind outside. The television—why couldn't he hear the television? Had it been on mute before? There was tape over his ears, which might explain it.

He tried to move—nothing major, just an inching movement with his hips and upper legs. He was almost getting used to this business of having his arms lashed up over and behind his head, and except for the cramp in his neck, he found he could move his upper body along the floor on the points of his elbows. But then the rope noose tightened about his neck, cutting off his air. Okay, so much for that idea, he thought, swallowing as he felt the sudden constriction, then easing back toward his original position.

The knife. The guy had dropped a knife not too far away. He remembered hearing it hit the floor. Maybe he could pivot on his upper body and find that knife with his feet, maybe kick it back this way, get his fingers on it and—what? His headache was getting worse, and it felt like his scalp was bleeding a little. What time is it? he wondered. And what's going to happen in this room when this crazy bastard fires that mortar? The noise is going to be incredible, even with that big hole in the ceiling and roof. And won't the recoil from that thing damage the floor? He'd gotten a quick glimpse of plywood where the base plate ought to be, but surely that wouldn't resist the impact of a five-inch mortar firing multiple times. He heard a noise and relaxed his body, trying to feign unconsciousness. But then a stream of cold water hit him right in the face and he spluttered as he tried to catch his breath.

He felt the man move behind him, heard that familiar humming sound. He tensed, expecting the hammer, and tried not to whimper. Instead, the man did something with the rope, and then he felt himself being pulled by the rope across the floor. He could either help by pushing with his feet or strangle, so he helped. The man dragged him for several feet and then did something with the rope. Probably securing it again, Swamp thought.

"Stay," the man said, quickly passing the Taser by Swamp's right ear. Swamp didn't move. Then he heard the man kick the knife across the floor, grunt in irritation, and then walk across the room to retrieve it. He felt the man approach again, and then his feet were free as the knife sliced through the tape. He definitely heard the knife drop, close by this time, and the man was back at his head. He felt the cold plastic snout of the Taser come to rest against his temple.

"The knife," the man said, his British accent less pronounced than it had been at the bank. "A meter from your feet. Once the mortar stops firing, the house is going to burn. You may go for the knife once the shooting stops. Not before, or I will hit you with this"—the Taser pressed hard into his forehead for emphasis—"set on *full* power this time."

Shit, Swamp thought, what was it set on before? He heard a strange swishing sound as the man stood up, but he couldn't fathom it. He actually thought he could smell perfume. Then the man was moving around the room, positioning some kind of cans and moving some heavy objects. He waited, frantically trying to think of some way to prevent this, but the man had rendered him helpless. Where the hell were Bertie's people? They knew where he'd been going. Or did they—had that message ever gotten through?

And the cops. Where were Jake and the cops? They had this address, didn't they? Surely Jake would have sent someone to take a look, especially since Jake had figured out that the real target might be the inauguration. But then he remembered why they hadn't come. By now, Jake, Shad, and a thousand of their professional brethren were schlepping around town in their blue uniforms, probably directing traffic.

He tried his bonds again, but the tape did not yield. His heart sank. There was no way to stop this thing. Well, he'd tried. He hadn't felt so hopeless since that day at the Tidal Basin.

Then the mortar went off.

Heismann had put his fingers in his ears after he dropped in the first round, but he'd forgotten to bend away from the blast. His fingers weren't nearly enough protection against the reverberation and the noise. He was actually knocked backward, as much by surprise as by the actual concussion.

He scrambled back to load the second round, this time bending way over and clapping both hands over his ears, but the monster muzzle blast still boomed hard enough to make him squeeze his eyelids shut. He grabbed up the third round, positioned it over the smoking muzzle, and then focused on the muted television. The new president was taking his oath of office. The robed chief justice was reading the words out and the new president was dutifully repeating them, when suddenly a bright light flooded the picture frame and the camera jumped off its focus point and panned crazily across the ground, getting a fuzzy picture of several dozen legs and feet. Then another flash, and more jumping camera shots. He waited a couple more seconds to see if the camera would zoom out and show the whole scene, but the cameraman had apparently hit the ground, leaving the camera to its own devices. He dropped the third round in, saw it slide out of sight, bent over again, and pressed his hands against his head as tightly as he could. A third tremendous blast, only this time a large part of the ceiling fell in, raining plaster and lathe wire all over the place.

Squinting through all the hot smoke, he grabbed the fourth round and tried to see the television, but the plaster dust and smoke were too thick. Then he caught a glimpse of the picture, in black and white now, where a different camera was panning across the portico, revealing a scene of total pandemonium. Another brilliant pulse of glaring light, and this time he actually saw the spray of white-hot shrapnel flatten the crowd of scrambling bodies, knocking over metal folding chairs as if they were made of paper.

It was perfect: The rounds were landing exactly on target! He dropped in the fourth round, followed quickly by the fifth. By now, there was so much dust and smoke in the room, he couldn't see very much at all, but he knew right where the rounds were, each cradled in its marble nest in a semicircle surrounding the mortar. He dropped in the sixth round, and then the seventh. He was dimly aware that there was fire now in addition to the smoke, and he was having real trouble breathing. He caught a quick glimpse of the television screen through the smoke, and he saw that the screen was alternating between black-and-white test patterns and fuzzy, jerking pictures. There was another flare of whiteness across the screen as one of the rounds slammed directly into the portico area.

Quickly, finish it.

The eighth round brought down the whole skylight and its frame, showering him with broken glass, but he kept right on loading and firing. The ninth round went in, followed at last by the tenth and final round. The last two seemed to cause less damage to the ceiling. He glanced up and saw why: The ceiling and a good part of the roof were totally gone, which probably accounted for the huge pile of debris that now trapped his feet. The pensioner was a white lump over in the corner of the room, but he was struggling to get loose. Good.

He wiped the dust and glass out of his own face, took a deep breath, choked on it, and then pushed through all the debris out to the hallway, where he grabbed one of the one-gallon cans of gasoline, popped the top off the spout, and threw it down the stairwell. He could hear flames crackling in the bedroom walls behind him. The pensioner better move quickly, he thought.

He ducked through the hole between the buildings and popped out of the closet on the other side, where he could finally get a clear breath. There he took the second can of gasoline and splashed it all over the closet and the upstairs hallway of the neighbor's house, being careful not to spill any on himself. He threw the partially empty can back through the hole and into his own upstairs hallway. At that instant, he felt and then heard the bomb in the basement next door, a heavy double thump that shook even the walls in the woman's apartment. But it did not blow the building to pieces. Success there, too. He grinned.

He'd been right again: a fond farewell from Mutaib. Now he *really* hoped the pensioner would get out.

He unwrapped the bath towel from around his head, stripped off her bathrobe, which was now covered in plaster dust, and dashed down the stairs. Despite the turbanned bath towel, he had a couple of small cuts on his head, and they were bleeding out of all proportion to their size. He smeared some blood across his face and forehead. He peered carefully out the front windows at the houses across the way. No open windows, but there were people standing in their doorways, gaping in the direction of the house. There was a whumping sound from upstairs as some of the gasoline caught fire. Then a police car was skidding to a stop right in front of the duplex, the cop on the passenger side opening his door before the car had even stopped, his gun drawn and a wild, horrified look on his face.

Now. Go!

He kicked over the third can of gasoline onto the living room rug, adjusted his neighbor's now-rumpled black wig on his head, made sure his genitals were firmly pressed back into the groin pouch, and snatched open the door. He burst out onto the front steps, screaming hysterically in his best impression of a female voice. He stumbled down the front steps, bare from the waist up, breasts bouncing everywhere. He was wearing a plain white half-slip, white nylon briefs, one beige knee-high stocking, and flat leather slippers that he'd taped to the bottoms of his feet. The blood on his face and cheeks had conveniently smeared all the makeup. He ran right past the astonished cop, screaming and gesturing that there was a man up there in the other house, and that there was fire everywhere. The policeman on the driver's side had started to open his door but then stopped, gaping at those naked bobbling breasts. Heismann tore away from the reaching hands of the first policeman and bolted across the street and into the alley, still screaming. And still running.

He heard a second and then a third police car come

screeching into the street behind him, just as there was another thumping explosion from the house. Some flaming debris shot right out into the street. He could hear the parked
cars being hit by some of the debris, which meant that the
police were all flat behind their cars. But by then, he was
through the connecting middle alley and had dodged left
into the back alley. He ran a hundred more feet to the oversized green trash can that held his clothes. Squatting down in
a corner between the nearest privacy fence and its garage, he
kicked off the shoes and stripped off the wig and the slip. He
then jumped into suit pants, a white shirt, and a matching
suit coat. Buttoning only the top button, he clipped on a tie,
then put on black socks and brown leather loafers. Just then,
he heard the first fire engine come blatting down the street
out in front. There was another thumping explosion from inside the house, this one propelling some debris over the
rooftops and into the alley, twenty feet away from him. He
took a quick look up the alley, but there was no one pursuing
him—yet.

Clear. *Go*.

He stood up and quickly pulled on a hat and a London
Fog–style raincoat, picked up the briefcase, which contained
the pensioner's papers, and the transformation was complete. Using the slip, he wiped as much of the blood and
makeup off his face as he could and then shoved it and the
shoes under a stinking garbage bag in the adjacent trash can.
After one more quick look around, he trotted down the alley
to the next side street, wiping his face again with the sleeves
of the raincoat. At the street, he slowed, turned right, and began walking east, away from the growing commotion behind
him. He walked with his shoulders hunched forward to mask
the breasts.

He walked two more blocks as calmly as he could, heading to where he'd parked the minivan. Seemingly oblivious
to the excited people running past him to see what had happened, he continued to wipe as much makeup and soot off

his face as he could. Looking over his shoulder, he saw a thick cloud of black smoke rising above the row houses and trees and heard several more emergency vehicles converging on his street. There was an even bigger smoke cloud hovering over the Capitol precincts in the distance. Two police cars came roaring past him on the street, but the policemen inside paid him no attention. He was just a nondescript office worker, complete with briefcase, walking down the street. They saw thousands of them every day. He was invisible. And he was certainly not a hysterical naked woman.

Five minutes later, he was driving out of the area. The column of smoke in his rearview mirror was getting bigger, not smaller. The third can of gasoline must have gone off. He surely hoped the pensioner had made it out. Roasting alive was such a hard way to go.

Swamp was almost totally deaf by the time all ten rounds had been fired. He'd had nothing to protect his ears other than his own arms and the duct tape that was already taped around his head, and the muzzle blast from the huge five-inch mortar bounced him around like a dog under a bus. A large piece of ceiling fell on him halfway through the firing, and in his frantic attempts to seek cover, he tore off the duct tape that had been pinning his hands and arms. Still blind, he'd begun scraping at the tape on his face, but as more ceiling fragments rained down on him, he had to curl up into a ball to protect his head and face. It wasn't until the firing stopped that he realized his arms and hands were actually free, and then he smelled fire, overlaid with the rich stink of gasoline.

He stripped the rest of the tape off, pried open his sticky eyelids, and saw the smoking mortar still pointed up at the huge hole in the ceiling. The hole was now framed in crackling flames. He climbed painfully out of the pile of wreckage that covered the entire floor, took a deep breath, and promptly inhaled a lungful of heavy smoke, which doubled

him over in a paroxysm of coughing. While he was still
down, he sensed a flare of overpressure out in the hall and
then felt the hot breath of a fireball flash into the room over
his head and billow out the hole in the roof. A distant rum-
bling, crackling noise followed the fireball, and he knew he
had to get out of there quickly. He couldn't understand why
the fire didn't sound louder, until he realized what the problem was: He'd been deafened by the mortar.

Gasping for air, he started crawling over the piles of
smoldering rafters and ceiling debris, making his way toward the front window of the bedroom, which faced the
street. All the glass was gone, so he poked his head out, conscious of the soundless boiling cloud of black smoke that
was streaming out around his head and shoulders. He pulled
his head back in. He had seen the roof of the front porch below. It was tiny, but it looked like salvation to him. He put his
head through the window, took another deep breath of clean
air, and then jerked his head back as the windowsill next to
his cheek exploded into a shocking blur of splinters. He sat
down heavily and then bounced right back up again when he
realized there was no breathable air left in the room. He
staggered sideways to get to the other side of the window,
just in time to see another bullet come blasting in, tearing
out the bottom of the windowsill and stinging his face with
brick dust.

Okay, not this window, he thought, and, ducking low, he
scrambled through all the wreckage once more, kicking
burning wood and debris out of the way before tripping over
the mortar's support foot and sprawling up against the back
window, which had also been blown out by the muzzle blast.
Most of the smoke was going up through the hole in the
roof, so back here he could at least breathe without sticking
his head out the window.

Who were the shooters? And *why* were there shooters?
Cops? He felt the floor lift and then begin to sag as something blew up downstairs. There was a much stronger stink

of gasoline again. He spied a plate-size patch of plaster at his feet and reached down to pick it up as the volume of smoke grew exponentially, enough to start it boiling out the window. Holding the plaster by its edge, he slid it out into the window aperture and waited. He was hoping that in all the smoke, it would look like a face. But nobody shot at it. Either they weren't fooled or they weren't there. He realized he was having to hold his breath, so he dropped the plaster and risked a quick look over the lower sill. The long expanse of the back porch roof beckoned, even as he felt the floor sag behind him again and saw a ragged edge of fire come up through the center of the floor and envelop the mortar. The sagging floor was again threatening to suck him down into the fire on the floor below.

No more time, he thought. He thrust his legs out the window, rolled over onto his stomach, winced when a wall of flame lunged at his face, and launched himself feetfirst over the sill and down onto the back porch roof. He landed hard on the metal roof, dimly aware that there were cops in the alley and still others running into the backyard. He managed to grab hold of a metal protrusion and stop his slide toward the ground, but then a gout of fire billowed out from a crack in the wall, singeing the tops of his hands. He let go involuntarily, sliding down and then dropping heavily into the yard. He landed on his feet and staggered backward, right into the arms of two uniformed policemen. They slammed him down to the ground and stuck a variety of guns into his neck and back, screaming soundlessly at him to get down, wild-eyed blood lust on all their faces.

He went limp and closed his eyes, momentarily grateful for the fact that he couldn't hear them. He felt his arms being pulled roughly behind him and the cuffs going on, and then he was jerked upright, frog-marched out into the alley, and thrown into the back of a cruiser. He felt a moment of panic as the door was slammed in his face, but then he realized that, even cuffed and surrounded by hostile police, he was probably safer than he had been for several hours. They obviously thought that he was their Capitol bomber.

Two men who looked like federal agents appeared at the windows, followed by several others, all brandishing machine pistols and staring in at him with the same furious expressions that the cops had, until one of them blinked, grabbed another agent's arm, and pointed excitedly at Swamp, saying something Swamp couldn't hear.

But he knew what it meant: The man was probably Secret Service, and he'd been recognized. Now the real fun would begin.

Connie, along with millions of viewers around the world, had watched in complete horror as an obviously unmanned television camera recorded the carnage on the west portico. The audio had been cut off right after that first flash of reddish white light, and then it had come back on for thirty seconds, filling her dining room with the screams of the dying and wounded, who were visible but out of focus in the skewed picture. Then the sound cut out again as the picture turned black and white. At one point, a black river of what had to be blood had appeared on one side of the picture, spilling down the white marble steps. Within a minute, it had grown large enough to cover all the visible steps. There was smoke boiling across the scene, and blurred figures moving in and out of the picture. Without sound, it looked like some kind of horrible documentary from World War II. Then there was a test pattern, which came up momentarily in color. But that soon disappeared and the transmission continued in black and white. The bottom half of two policemen appeared in the picture, dragging a body across the scene. As they did, the body's right hand dropped off and lay right in the center of the picture, at which point Connie looked for the remote, her fingers scrambling for the off button.

Before she could press it, the carnage disappeared and in its place the United States seal appeared on the screen. The audio signal returned. A calm, sonorous voice announced that a state of grave national emergency existed. All citizens within the Washington metropolitan area were directed to remain at home and off the city streets. Those citizens who were at work were told to go home and stay home until further notice. Then a caption began crawling across the screen, indicating that all highways, major thoroughfares, bridges, airports, and Metro trains into the city were closed and that only outbound traffic would be allowed to move within the city.

A human face from the Federal Emergency Management Agency appeared on the screen and a news bulletin of sorts was issued. It stated only that there had been a terrorist attack on the inauguration proceedings, that there were many casualties, that all lines of communication within the city were being shut down, and that military Defense Condition One was being set within the continental United States. Then the government seal reappeared, along with the tape loop about everyone being requested to remain at home. The message along the bottom of the screen requested that emergency medical personnel report to their respective hospitals throughout the city, and that they should make sure they were carrying proper identification, as anyone attempting to evade or interfere with police were liable to be shot on sight. Then a pause, and a new message began unfolding at the bottom of the screen. It stated simply that the president and the vice president were unharmed and moving to a safe, undisclosed location.

Connie felt her pulse racing. No mention of which president, old or new. Or what kind of attack had been mounted. But surely it had been a pretty huge deal, based on those grainy, slightly out-of-focus pictures she'd seen before somebody had gotten to the camera. She knew that most federal government offices would have been shut down because of the inauguration, but there were still a lot of nongovernmental people downtown, including the thousands of families who would have begun mustering along Constitution Avenue to see the parade later that afternoon. She suddenly felt glad to be sitting at home in bed, despite how she'd ended up here. And then she remembered that Secret Service agent telling her about a possible terrorist plot.

Good God! Had he been talking about *this*?

Then it hit her—what it was that she needed to tell someone. Jake, or the Secret Service. What her would-be killer had said in the bathroom as he was stabbing her in the back. She grabbed for the telephone, only to discover that it didn't work. All communications sealed. She looked across the room for her purse and cell phone, but that system would be shut down, too.

She felt a cold chill ripple through her. If she was right about this, the bastard who had just executed the unspeakable crime she'd seen on the television was coming right here.

"But I will need your house," he'd said.

Heismann had made it all the way down to the bridges area and was actually driving down the ramp when a policeman stepped out in the road with his hand up. In a split second, Heismann saw the police car. There was no partner, no other police cars. He made a decision to run smack into the man, knocking him sideways into the grass. Heismann got the minivan stopped fifty feet past the bottom of the down ramp and quickly backed up, his right front wheel protesting as it rubbed against the smashed-in grille. The policeman, a black man in his late forties or early fifties, was sprawled on the grass embankment, his cap, one shoe, and his flashlight lying nearby.

Heismann jumped out and ran over to the man. The policeman was still breathing, but there was a trickle of blood coming out of his mouth and his right knee was bent at an odd angle. Heismann looked around, but there was still no one in sight, so he got back in the minivan, drove to where he'd parked the Suburban, and changed vehicles. He then drove back to the ramp, put the Suburban's emergency lights on, got out, and opened up the back doors.

He dropped the second seat and then went over to the injured policeman. He threw the flashlight and the shoe into some bushes and then hauled him into the back of the Suburban. He knew he was probably doing some more damage, but the man was still unconscious, and he would serve his purposes, dead or alive. Once he had him secured in the back, he fished out the policeman's handcuffs and cuffed his hands across his belly. He removed the officer's gun and stuffed it under the driver's side of the front seat. He retrieved the officer's cap and put it on his chest. Then he took off his raincoat, folded it into a rolled pillow, and put it under the officer's head. He covered the man's supine form with his own suit coat and then got back into the driver's seat. He drove under the bridge and stopped to take stock.

He'd tried to find news of the attack on Capitol Hill on the minivan's radio, but all the stations were off the air. He finally found something calling itself the civil defense station on the AM band. It was announcing that a state of emergency existed in the national capital area and that martial law was being imposed. All citizens were directed to go home and stay there. This message was in the form of a continuous tape loop.

He examined his face in the mirror, wiped a few more traces of makeup off, and centered his hat. He then drove east one block before turning down Seventh Street, SW, and heading for the Washington Navy Yard on the Anacostia River. From there, he turned back west and drove all the way to Maine Avenue, going right past the spot where he'd parked the Suburban. All he could see of the Capitol was that cloud of grayish smoke and a host of twinkling blue and red strobe lights. He had been passed by several police cars and three ambulances, all headed back toward the Capitol precincts.

He pulled over for a moment and fished out his city map. He'd already seen blue lights on the other side of the river, so he knew that within minutes they would be locking down all the bridges over the Potomac. His only option was to drive back into town from the river. The injured policeman was going to be his passport through any roadblocks, as long as he made enough noise and could convince the officers posted there that he was rushing to get their comrade to a hospital, preferably one in the city's northwest quadrant, in the direction of the nurse's house. He quickly consulted his city map and saw that Georgetown University Hospital would be a plausible destination. He heard sirens up on the bridge above him, emergency vehicles headed across the bridge toward Virginia. No more time for thinking; he must move, and fast.

He drove out from under the bridge, did a U-turn, and drove back toward the Jefferson Memorial and the Tidal Basin. He turned on his high beams, buttoned the rest of his shirt, and straightened his clip-on tie. The policeman gave a low groan as they roared down the narrow road surrounding the Tidal Basin, but then he went silent. Heismann ran into the first roadblock as soon as he turned out onto Twenty-third Street and headed up toward Constitution Avenue. He got the pensioner's identification out of the briefcase, snapped on his seat belt, put on dark glasses, and drove right at the cluster of police cars blocking the intersection, laying on the horn.

He screeched to a stop with the nose of the Suburban pointed between two police cars wedged in the middle of the intersection. There was traffic on Constitution, but it was creeping as a crowd of police went from car to car, looking inside each one. He lowered his window and the back window on the left side as three cops came running over, hands on their gun butts.

"Secret Service," he yelled, flipping open the pensioner's wallet, waving his ID at them, and pointing with his thumb into the back. "Georgetown Hospital. Let me through!"

All three cops tried to stick their heads into the back window at the same time, but then they backed out, swearing, and one, a sergeant, yelled for another cop to open the roadblock. The sergeant came up to the driver's window, staring at the mask of smeared blood, soot, and grime on Heismann's shirt collar.

"How bad?"

Heismann shrugged and then shook his head.

"Shit! *Shit!*" the sergeant exclaimed, and then waved him through as one of the blocking cop cars backed out, creating a space. Heismann hit the gas and roared right through it and up Twenty-third Street. He saw a constellation of emergency lights to his right, on the major avenues, and Army helicopters circling the downtown area. The pall of smoke farther down Constitution seemed to have thickened. He drove at high speed on the nearly empty street, passing some more roadblocks, which were placed across the intersecting streets. The police were making cursory checks of vehicles, but they seemed mostly interested in getting the downtown streets cleared out. At Washington Circle, he headed west toward the Whitehurst Freeway and Georgetown. Once on the freeway, he went a quarter of a mile and then cut off onto the stub connection, which became Wisconsin Avenue. From there, he had a clear shot into northwest Washington and his safe haven. He turned off the emergency lights and his headlights and slowed down to normal in-town speed.

He passed several more emergency vehicles headed into town, but there were no more roadblocks. He tried the radio again, but there was still nothing but that annoying tape, with the rest of the stations reduced to a hiss of static. He had expected much more traffic, but with the federal holiday, the

lanes headed out of town had been practically empty, as
were the sidewalks. Then finally, halfway up Wisconsin Avenue, he ran into a traffic jam as he caught up with the general exodus. Everyone who'd been home watching the
inauguration, which was probably everyone in the city who
had a television, was staying put.

He began looking for a parking lot on a side street, anywhere that he could get off the main avenue for an hour or so
while the traffic sorted itself out and the streets opened up
again. Ideally, he would approach the nurse's house at dusk.
The sky was becoming increasingly overcast, which meant
that darkness would come early.

All good omens, he thought. Very good omens. He wondered if the pensioner had gotten out. If he had, and he was
the man Heismann thought he was, darling Mutaib was in
for some interesting times.

Swamp closed his eyes and sat back against the smelly rear
seat of the police cruiser, giving in to the waves of pain that
were sallying back and forth through his body. Getting much
too old for this shit, he thought with a sigh. Outside, there
was a growing crowd of local cops and federal agents, with
everyone seemingly trying to talk on a radio at the same
time. A fire engine had come down the alley and parked immediately in front of the police car where Swamp sat in
splendid isolation. Firemen in full gear gave him interested
looks as they trotted past, unrolling a fire hose. The duplex
was fully engaged now, with both sides burning fiercely. The
firemen in the alley appeared to have given up on the duplex
and were playing hoses on adjacent roofs to keep the fire
from spreading. He could barely hear the rumble of the fire
engine's pumps. He thought about asking for the cuffs to be
removed, but right now he was exhausted and he hurt in
more places than he could count. And he was heartsick
about what that goddamned Arab had managed to do.

A mortar. The original artillery. The ancient Chinese had

used them. Right up there with catapults. Perfect for a surprise attack. He'd seen those glaring white blooms on the screen before the picture had been obliterated by all the smoke, the camera being knocked this way and that. I was right all along, he thought ruefully. All except for those minor details, such as the date and the target. But would Hallory and company have paid any more attention if he had keyed the thing to the inauguration instead of to the address to the joint session? He doubted it. Still, he wondered what more he could have done. Or *should* have done. He knew he should never have opened that damned garage door. What in the hell had that bastard been doing in the garage?

He felt a rush of air as the rear door was unlocked. With difficulty, he opened his eyes, which were still sticky from the duct tape. Some smoke blew into the backseat of the car, and he could actually feel the heat from the house fire. A federal agent he didn't recognize was saying something, but Swamp could only shake his head. Then a police lieutenant appeared with cuff keys, shouldered him forward in the seat, and undid the plastic bracelets. Swamp gestured for a pen and paper, and the agent produced a notebook and a ballpoint.

"Can't hear," Swamp wrote, then showed it to the agent. The man took the pen and notebook. "Was this where the attack came from?" The agent scribbled.

Swamp nodded.

"What were you doing here?" the man wrote, and then passed back the notebook and pen.

"Chasing the bad guy," Swamp wrote. "Got caught instead. He used a mortar."

"We know," the man said, and Swamp read his lips. Then a hand appeared on the agent's shoulder and he stepped back. To Swamp's immense surprise, Lucy took the agent's place in the doorway.

"Come with me," she said, stepping back to let him get out of the car. He still couldn't hear her, but her meaning was obvious. Based on their hostile expressions, there were still lots of cops around who thought Swamp was the bad guy. They were milling around with drawn weapons and patently itchy trigger fingers. The roof of the duplex caved in with a great shower of sparks, making everyone flinch.

Swamp followed Lucy as they squeezed around the fire engine to a black Crown Vic bristling with antennas and emergency lights. A large man in Secret Service tactical gear was in the driver's seat, and Lucy indicated for Swamp to get in the back while she got in the front. The driver, who had a beefy red face to match his red hair, began backing the car down the entire length of the alley before Swamp even had a chance to close the door. Lucy turned around to look at him.

"You look like shit," she said, and once again, Swamp could read her lips. He shrugged and instantly regretted it. "Can't hear," he announced, barely able to recognize his own voice. Lucy nodded and then turned around to put on her seat belt.

"How bad is it up there? And where we going?" Swamp asked, but she didn't answer. The driver reached the end of the alley and backed straight out into the street, causing two cop cars to slam on their brakes, veer sideways, and lay on their horns. The driver, still stopped in the middle of the street, turned around to glare at Swamp and then reached into his jacket and produced his .357 Sig. "*You* shut the fuck up," the man said, pointing the weapon right at Swamp's face. Swamp still couldn't actually hear him, but that message was abundantly clear. Lucy tapped the man's arm and told him to put it away. Swamp sat back and fumbled for his own seat belt as the furious driver put his weapon down on the front seat and then began wrenching the car around. He flipped on his brights and took off down the street, scattering cops, firemen, and curious civilians alike.

They drove quickly up toward First Street and the Capitol grounds. The driver had to slow down and then stop when he

got to First, as there was a solid phalanx of federal agents
and vehicles blocking the way. A nebulous cloud of grayish
smoke still rose from behind the Capitol, but Swamp
couldn't see anything in front of them except wall-to-wall
blue lights. He did notice that the District cops were all outside the federal perimeter. He wanted to get an answer to his
questions from Lucy, but, mindful of the enraged driver and
that .357 on the front seat, he kept quiet. Lucy got out and
went to confer with a small crowd of agents inside the
perimeter, and there was another round of radio talk. The big
man up front glared at Swamp again, this time via the mirror.

Swamp was suddenly grateful that he'd left those CIA
credentials back in his apartment. That Arab banker would
have taken them when he escaped, and Swamp had a strong
feeling he wás going to need them later today. Lucy came
back to the car, got in, and said something to the driver that
Swamp couldn't hear. The driver nodded, gave Swamp another glare via the mirror, turned the car around, and drove
down toward Independence Avenue.

They negotiated another six roadblocks before getting
clear of Capitol Hill and abreast of the Mall. Swamp turned
around to look back up at the west portico, where there were
dozens of blue and red strobe lights blinking through the lin-
gering smoke. He thought he saw several small white
mounds out on the grass at the base of the portico steps, but
then the National Arboretum buildings blocked his view.
Lucy was talking on an encrypted radio as they drove down
the river side of the Mall. Whatever pedestrians were still
out on the mall were being herded toward the Metro station
by District police. Something popped in Swamp's right ear
and suddenly he could hear what Lucy was saying.

"—in custody." She paused to listen. "Yes, sir, he was
definitely *in* the house." Another pause. "Yes, sir. Right
away." She put the radio in her purse, loosened her shoulder

belt, and turned around to look at Swamp, who decided to
give no sign that he could hear again. Before she could
speak, Swamp saw a moving blur to their left as they entered
an intersection, and then the driver swerved and hit the
brakes hard enough to throw Lucy sideways against the right
side of the windshield. The car then got slammed on the left
side, spinning out in a blur of noise and screeching tires.
Swamp, who was still belted in, struggled to keep upright by
grabbing the top of Lucy's headrest, but he could no longer
see her. The car tilted onto its right-hand wheels, banged
back down onto the pavement, and then lurched to a stop
with the engine still running and the smell of radiator fluid
filling the air.

Swamp unbuckled his belt as the driver wrestled his way
out of the car and hurried around to the right front door. He
wrenched it open and pulled Lucy out from between the seat
and the dashboard. The side of her face was bloody from a
cut on her forehead, and she looked dazed. Swamp tried the
right rear door, but it was jammed. The left rear door was already partially open, so he got out and came around to look
at the front of the Crown Vic. The left front fender was
bashed in, as was the left rear wheel well. The grille and radiator assembly were protruding out of the front of the car.
He moved back to the side of the car, crunching through
glass and plastic on the pavement. A green trickle of radiator
fluid was leaking out onto the street. The other car, a District
police car, also a Crown Vic, was fifty yards away, out on the
Mall lawn, having come to a standstill at the end of two
muddy ruts. A dazed-looking cop was getting out, talking on
his radio. Steam rose from the front of his wrecked cruiser.

The redheaded driver, who had a bloody nose and the beginnings of a shiner, was kneeling by Lucy's head as he
fished out a radio and started calling someone. His seat belt
must have failed, too, Swamp thought. Then he saw that .357
down under the accelerator pedal. Seeing the gun and realiz-

ing that both of them were out of the vehicle gave him an idea. The engine was still running, the lights still flashing up top, and the left front wheel looked like it would still roll. He had no idea of where they had been taking him, but wherever it was, it wouldn't get him to the Royal Kingdom Bank and face-to-face with the bastard who'd fired the mortar. Assuming that's where he'd run back to. But either way, he knew these two would never believe him, so he decided to stop wasting time and go get the murdering bastard himself.

He slipped into the driver's seat without closing the door, got the gun out of the way of the pedals, and dropped the shift into reverse. The car backed right away from Lucy and the driver, who looked up in astonishment. Swamp popped it in drive and hit the gas, watching the agent reach for his gun, then realize that it must be in the car. Lucy, obviously still out of it, just stared at him. He drove around them, fishtailing and scattering broken glass and pieces of fender, went three blocks, and then turned off Independence at the next corner. Which is when red lights appeared all over the instrument panel and the engine made a shrieking sound just before the car shuddered to an ominous, jerking stop.

Swamp retrieved the gun from the floor and then spotted Lucy's purse, its contents spilled all over the seat. He grabbed her credentials folder and then piled out of the ruined vehicle and looked around. He saw the Capitol South Metro station one block away. His Rover should still be in the parking lot. He stuffed the gun into his waistband, covering it with his coat, and put her credentials into a pocket. Then he walked as fast as his aching legs could go toward the station, aware of the cop cars that were whizzing by on their way to and from the Capitol area. He climbed a low barrier to get into the nearly empty Metro lot and saw his Rover. He patted his pockets for keys, but they were gone, as was his wallet. He swore and then remembered he had a spare key in a magnetic box under the trailer hitch. He found the key and let himself in, then took a minute to think out his next move. He saw the fancy Agency cell phone unit and re-membered that it had a button for serious trouble. But what would happen if he pushed that button now? Had Lucy's driver managed to alert the entire federal law-enforcement apparatus that he was a fugitive? That he had been in the building from which the attack had come? Was he a suspect?

And the tags—Bertie had said they were satellite tags. He got back out and examined the license plates, but he could see nothing on them or near them. Two more cop cars went roaring by the Metro lot, lights and sirens blazing. A third, seeing the disabled federal vehicle, slowed to a stop and then backed up to have a closer look. Swamp realized he couldn't stay here, nor anywhere in plain view. Lucy and her driver would have assets coming fast. Once the car was identified, they'd all be looking for an ugly man, limping away on foot.

Okay—boogie time. He didn't know where he stood with the Secret Service, but he did know what his objective was, and that was to get to that goddamned Arab bank.

He had to push his way through the lot's flimsy ticket bar-rier, but then he got back out to Independence and blew down the empty avenue as fast as he thought he could go without attracting police attention. When he got to Thir-teenth Street, he turned right and headed north, across the Mall and across Constitution, where the District cops clus-tered around the major intersections were no longer inspect-ing cars. They waved him and a few other civilian cars through, as if anxious to get everyone out of the downtown area. There was almost no traffic higher uptown as he went left on P Street and drove the two blocks down to the Royal Kingdom Bank. As he got halfway down the block from the bank building, he pulled the Rover to the side of the street and shut it down.

He pulled the mirror over and examined his battered face. He used a packet of Kleenex from the glove compartment to clean himself up a bit. There was nothing he could do about his clothes, which were a mess of plaster dust and soot and which still stank of gasoline smoke. He could see the entrance to the bank, but the security people were not in evidence. A large black Mercedes was parked out front, but there was no other sign of activity.

He knew what he was supposed to do—hit that emergency button on the Agency's cell phone and then wait for the cavalry. If the cell phone still worked, call into Operations Control at Langley, tell them that the guy who had mortared the inauguration was the managing director of the Royal Kingdom Bank. Except he didn't know the number for the Agency's OpCon center. Okay, call the Secret Service control center, a number that every agent knew by heart. Ask for massive backup and then wait for the entire Secret Service to arrive.

Except that it wouldn't. Lucy's driver would have called in with an "agent down" report and what he would describe as the hijacking of a Secret Service vehicle by a rogue agent. In a very few minutes, if not already, the streets around the Mall would be aswarm with agents and District cops looking for him. They had already found the damaged Secret Service vehicle. His only chance was to go into that bank and hope like hell that his emirship had come back here after what he'd done. It was a reasonable possibility: This bank probably had some kind of diplomatic immunity, unless he'd run for the embassy itself. So, get in there, find out if he's there, grab the son of a bitch, try to restrain yourself from killing him, and then call into Operations Control. He patted the Sig in his waistband, zipped up the jacket, and got out of the car. Then, just to make sure, he leaned back in and smacked the panic button on the cell phone. A red light came on and stayed on. Good, he thought. Something's working.

Ignoring all his protesting joints and muscle spasms, he walked straight up to the front doors of the bank, but they were locked. A small brass sign inside one of the windows said CLOSED. He looked up and found the security camera pointed right at him, its tiny red light clearly visible. He extracted Lucy's credentials, which displayed a Secret Service badge and a picture ID, and held them up for a second where the camera could see them, but not long enough for the operator to zoom in on the actual picture.

"Secret Service," he declared in his most authoritative voice. "Open up, please."

A moment later, the door was being unlocked and one of the young men he'd seen before was backing away as Swamp pushed through the door. The two German security guards were standing at one end of the lobby, hands held tensely inside their coats. Swamp stopped and looked pointedly at those hands. The two guards straightened up and withdrew their hands from their jackets, but they didn't move.

"I want to see the managing director," Swamp announced. "Right now."

A second young assistant came out into the lobby. Four against one, Swamp thought, measuring the angles.

"May I inquire as to the purpose of your visit, sir?" the first assistant asked, taking in Swamp's disheveled clothes.

"You may not," Swamp said. "U.S. Secret Service Agent Morgan wants to talk to him. That's all he needs to know."

The second man looked again at Swamp's clothes. He appeared to be older and better dressed than the others, and he had a tiny radio or cell phone in his hand. "And the other officers, the ones who were with you the last time?" he asked. "Where might they be today?"

"On their way," Swamp said. He pushed past the first assistant and headed for Mutaib's office. One of the guards reached inside his suit jacket again, and Swamp drew the gun, a Secret Service standard-issue Sig Sauer .357. He was suddenly aware that he hadn't checked to see if it was chambered. He put his back to a counter, swept the lobby with the muzzle, and surreptitiously felt for the extractor, which protrudes slightly on a Sig .357 if it's chambered. He couldn't be sure.

The four men in the lobby froze when Swamp drew the gun. He waved them all to get in front of him and then motioned them toward Mutaib's ornate office door. The assistant with the cell phone surreptitiously began to key in numbers. Swamp saw it but didn't do anything, because, if he remembered correctly, there would be no service. Especially now. He lined himself up in front of the door and told one of the men to open it. They all just looked at him.

"Open that goddamned door," Swamp growled. His fleeting vision of uncounted injured or dead Americans under all those white sheets up on Capitol Hill put something in his voice that made the man nearest the door grab the handle and push the door open.

"Now, single file. Go in. You first. And if I can't see your hands, I'll shoot whatever part of you I *can* see."

The man with the cell phone backed into Mutaib's office, followed in turn by the two security guards and then the younger assistant, all of them holding their hands out in plain sight. The office was empty.

"Where's your boss?" Swamp asked, eyeing a single closed door in one corner of the office. He got shrugs and sideways looks all around.

"You," he said to one of the security guards, "open that door and step away from it."

"It is just the emir's private lavatory," the older assistant said. "There is no one in there."

Swamp stared at the security guard and then raised the .357. "If there's no one in there," he said, "then you won't mind if I do a little reconnaissance by fire, will you?" He aimed the gun at the wooden door, but the security guard moved quickly to open it, only to find that the door was locked.

"Tell him I will start shooting through the door if he doesn't come out right now," Swamp said, moving across the room to a position from which he could cover them and better carry out his threat. The security guard spoke softly in Arabic, and a moment later, the door swung open and Mutaib came out. He was dressed now in traditional Saudi garb, and he blanched when he saw Swamp's gun.

"I say," he began, but Swamp told him to shut up. He ordered everyone in the room to get down on their knees and put their hands behind their heads, including Mutaib. In that instant, he saw the security guards exchange glances, and he pointed the gun at the space between them and pulled the trigger. The gun produced the snapping sound of an empty chamber. The instant the security guards heard that, they both drew their weapons as Swamp racked the slide while doing a drop and roll in the direction of Mutaib's huge desk. As soon as he could focus on the security guards, he opened fire, dimly aware that they were both already shooting at him. The room was filled with the sound of gunfire, and he felt more than heard the hornet sounds of bullets around him as he let his years of annual qualification training take over. Lying prone now on the rug, part of his body protected by the desk, he maintained an iron-fisted two-handed grip while he fired in quick succession at the two blurred figures still standing on the other side of the room, not stopping until they weren't standing anymore.

He checked his gun and saw that the slide was still closed. He didn't know how many rounds he had, but there was at least one left. His face and neck were covered in mahogany splinters as he heard a wet cough come from the other side of the room. He then rolled as fast as he could toward the still-open office door. Staying down on the floor, he saw that both security guards were down, the fronts of their suits covered in dark stains. The two assistants were huddled together against the far wall, arms over their white faces, hands buried in their hair.

Mutaib had vanished, but then Swamp saw the open French door. He got up, rushed to where the filmy curtains were dancing, and looked out. Mutaib was already across the small parking lot behind the bank, opening the door to what looked like an armored, silver Mercedes. Swamp didn't hesitate. He quickly knelt down at the window, rested the gun on the sill, and took careful aim. Mutaib must have sensed it, because he looked back over his shoulder at the window. Swamp fired once, his last round, as it turned out. He aimed for Mutaib's midsection but hit him in the throat, spinning the Arab sharply back against the glistening car. Then the banker slid down onto the pavement and proceeded to generate a lake of blood, arms and hands out at his side, as if in astonished supplication.

Swamp pulled his head back in from the billowing curtains and pointed the now-empty gun at the two quivering assistants. They both still had their eyes closed, and it was obvious they were fully cowed. The breeze from the open window started to clear the air of gun smoke as Swamp picked up the telephone to call for some backup. But the phone was dead. As he was trying to figure out what to do next, he heard vehicle sounds out front and then the front doors of the bank were banging open, followed by the sounds of several people running across the lobby. He reversed his grip on the gun so that he was holding it by the barrel as the first agents rushed into the room, all pointing either handguns or submachine guns in his direction. A full dozen of them spilled through the doorway before the tactical supervisor realized Swamp was holding his gun out for someone to take. Everyone froze for a moment, and then one agent came across the room and snatched it out of his hand while three others went over and stuck guns in the faces of the assistants, one of whom was now crying. Then Lucy VanMetre and Carlton Hallory came into the room, both of them brandishing handguns, as well.

"Where's Mutaib?" Lucy asked. One side of her face was puffy and bruised, and her normally immaculate clothes were rumpled.

"He's dead," Swamp said. He pointed to the open window. "Out there."

She put a hand to her mouth and looked over at Hallory. Then she asked what had happened.

"Well, Lucy, that dead Arab out there was the son of a bitch who fired those ten rounds into the Capitol this morning."

"Not possible," Lucy said, gesturing in his direction with her gun. The other agents, sensing trouble, began to ease out of any possible lines of fire.

"Oh yes it is," Swamp said. "I was there, remember? And I physically saw him do it. From about ten feet away." He pointed to the blowing curtains, where two agents were already peering through the window. "That guy, out there. He even spoke to me. 'Hello, old chap. Remember me?' I figured he'd come back here. Foreign bank, maybe diplomatic immunity. Call the embassy, which would get him out of town. That's why I came here. To arrest his ass. Those two started the shooting, and then that bastard went out the window. But it was *him*."

All the agents in the room were just staring at him now. Hallory raised a radio to his mouth and started talking quietly. Lucy walked past him to the window, looked out, and swore. "This isn't possible," she said again.

"It was this morning. That guy was your mortar man."

"Sir," one of the assistants said in a tiny voice.

Lucy turned to look at him. It was the younger man, and he had visibly urinated in his trousers. "What?" she snapped.

"The emir? He was here all morning. He was *here*, in this room. We watched the . . . the incident on the television, but he was here. Right here."

Lucy turned to look back at Swamp, who felt the first twinge of uncertainty. "You are in such deep shit," she said to Swamp. "And you are never going to get out of it."

"I don't care what *his* minions say," Swamp replied. "I

know what I saw. It was *him* in that town house. Him or his identical twin brother."

"Get those two out of here," she ordered, pointing to the cowering assistants. "And remove the bodies. Make sure you clear the street of civilians before you bring anyone out."

Four agents grabbed the two assistants and manhandled them to the door and out into the lobby, while four more began dragging the two dead security guards across the rug. Two stepped through the French doors to see about Mutaib. The rest went out front to clear the street. Hallory finished talking on the radio, watched for a moment as the agents cleared the room, and then spoke for the first time, asking the tactical supervisor, the only agent remaining, to give them a moment. He closed the office door behind them and then dropped into one of the armchairs. Lucy exhaled noisily and leaned against a wall, looking at Hallory. She was still holding her weapon. Swamp suddenly needed to sit down, but he wasn't sure what would happen if he moved. Hell with it, he thought. He pulled Mutaib's executive chair out from behind the desk and sat down with a groan.

"Okay," Hallory said. "Now we can talk."

Lucy started to shake her head.

"No," Hallory said. "We have to tell him. This"—he pointed at the open French door—"this is really unfortunate."

"Unfortunate?" Swamp said. "*Unfortunate?* That bastard lobs mortar shells into the inauguration and kills how many people, and this is *unfortunate*?"

Hallory was looking at Lucy. "We have to tell him," he said. "He's done his part. Now we have to tell him."

"We should wait," she said. She looked at her watch. "Another five hours at least. No one outside the primary loop until midnight in Europe."

"Tell me what, for Chrissakes?" Swamp said, totally confused.

Hallory gave him a sad, tired smile. It was the first sympathetic look he had ever seen on the executive's face. "This Mutaib guy was one of ours," he said. "He didn't do the mortar attack."

"Goddamn it, I fucking saw him!" Swamp shouted.

Hallory put up a placating hand. "No, you didn't. But I think I know what's happened."

Swamp felt his face getting red. "I saw that bastard out there drop ten rounds into the world's biggest mortar. He burned the house down doing it. I was *there*! He had a fucking television in the room. I saw the rounds hit. I saw—"

"What we wanted you to see, Mr. Morgan," said Hallory interrupting Swamp and then pausing to let that sink in. "You and the rest of the world. The German fired ten rounds, but they never got there. They were BL and P rounds. That stands for blind-loaded and plugged. The 'warheads' contained plaster and a small bursting charge. When the rounds reached their apogee, they blew up into a cloud of plaster dust about four hundred feet in the air on the other side of the Capitol building."

"*What*?"

"Nobody died at the Capitol, Mr. Morgan. It was all a fake. Everyone's safe. The new government is installed." He stopped and rubbed his face with both hands. "But Lucy's right. We shouldn't talk here. I guess you'll have to come with us. We'll leave as soon as they get the mess cleaned up. In the meantime, relax. I think this is going to come out okay. You did well, actually. Except for the bank manager, perhaps."

Heismann drove to within a mile of the nurse's house and then pulled off the avenue and into the parking lot of a large church. He drove around to the back of the lot and parked the Suburban in a corner, well out of sight of any passing police cars out on Wisconsin Avenue. The injured policeman was still breathing, albeit with audible difficulty. His face was bruised and swollen, but one eye was partially open.

Heismann thought about what to do with him. He could smother the man and simply end the problem. Except the officer hadn't really seen him, and he had served a useful purpose in getting the Suburban through the immediate security cordon around the downtown area after the attack. He decided to leave him to his fate.

Although it was just midafternoon, the skies were growing dark and overcast. Rain tonight, he thought. Help them clean up the Capitol steps. He flipped on the radio, but both bands were silent except for the emergency broadcast station, which was still telling everyone to go home and stay there. Otherwise, there was only an electronic wall of static.

They had obviously shut down all the commercial stations, trying to limit knowledge of the extent of the disaster. Well, that made sense. He consulted his city map and fingered his way to the nurse's house through the nearby residential streets. He retrieved his raincoat, grabbed the briefcase, got out of the Suburban, and locked the doors. He felt like he should leave a note somewhere, but he did not dare draw attention to the vehicle until he was well clear of the area, probably in twelve hours or so, once the initial search frenzy died down. Anyway, someone would see it. Even these police would find it soon enough, once they started looking.

He walked through a side gate and turned right, still just another commuter, hurrying home a little early, as requested by his devastated government.

Forty-five minutes after the shoot-out in the bank, a government limo pulled up and Swamp, Hallory, and Lucy got in. Hallory pointed Swamp into the back left corner, so Lucy ended up in the middle. She seemed to be avoiding even looking in Swamp's direction. Her face was still puffy and she sat down carefully. He wanted to ask where they were going, but he was still trying to absorb what Hallory had told him in the bank.

They drove in silence down Seventeenth Street. Swamp observed many police cars but no pedestrians and zero civilian traffic. The city's office buildings appeared to be virtually deserted. As they got closer to the Mall and the White House, he began to see military police vehicles, Humvees and even armored personnel carriers, parked along the broad avenues. He couldn't tell if they were manned or just parked there. He could hear but not see helicopters flying low over the city. They drove into the precincts of Lafayette Park and the limo pulled over to the sidewalk.

"We walk from here," Hallory announced.

"Where?" Swamp asked.

"Crown," Hallory said, using the Secret Service code word for the White House.

They walked southwest across the park, which was surrounded by military vehicles, many with engines running. Looking through the bare trees, Swamp could see what looked like Army troops up on the roof of the White House itself, the men carrying rifles and other weapons. As they arrived at the West Executive gate, a large limo with diplomatic plates, dark-tinted windows, and headlights blazing exited past them, while another one was easing up to the gate for inspection. A single heavily armed Apache helicopter was flying a tight orbit about a thousand feet above the White House, turning slowly in a continuous 360, as if looking for something to kill. Secret Service Uniformed Division officers processed them through the gate security equipment.

Five minutes later, they were in the White House Situation Room. Swamp caught a glimpse of a video screen showing a nighttime scene of what looked like a dozen large Air Force transports at an air base somewhere, surrounded by military and civilian vehicles of every description. A second screen showed a picture of a devastated and still-smoking west portico at the Capitol. The ground was littered with the wreckage of the viewing stands and what looked like dozens of sheet-covered lumps.

The main conference table was filled with officials in their shirtsleeves, working phones or conferring with staffers. The sitroom seemed smaller than he had remembered it, and those screens were new. Swamp recognized at least three cabinet secretaries, including the secretary of defense from the outgoing administration. Or was he still the SecDef? Was there a new government or not? Hallory had said there was.

Hallory nodded at a side conference room, then led Swamp into it and closed the door. Bertie Walker was inside, talking on a secure phone. He hung up and got up to greet Swamp and shake his hand, a sly grin on his face. Lucy had remained outside to talk to a cluster of Secret Service people.

"Oka-a-y," Swamp said, grateful to sit down again. His various aches and pains were becoming more than just an annoyance. "Whiskey-tango-foxtrot, over?"

"Mutaib's dead," Hallory announced, and Bertie's grin faded.

"How?" he asked. Swamp thought his question sounded rather offhand.

"Our trusty firefly hunter here popped him when he tried to run from the bank."

"The *bank*? I thought Lucy was supposed to take him to Langley?"

Hallory shrugged. "Shit happens, I guess. Lucy's car collided with a cop car out on the Mall. Mr. Morgan here was in the backseat and seized the opportunity to commandeer the vehicle and go to the bank. And now I think we know precisely what Heismann/Hodler looks like, by the way."

Bertie sat back down, trying to digest the news. Then he understood. "Ah. He had himself recut to look like Mutaib?"

"Clever bastard, huh? And then apparently he made sure Mr. Morgan here got a look at his face, in hopes, I suspect, that he would go take care of business. Sooner or later. He was the eyewitness, after all."

"I'm going to break somebody's head, somebody doesn't tell me what's going on," Swamp said.

Hallory looked at his watch, as if trying to make up his mind. Just then, a muted cheer went up out in the Situation Room. Bertie got back up, opened the door, and looked out. Swamp heard someone say, "Almost two thousand, not six hundred. More being brought in. First C-seventeen is rolling as we speak."

"They gonna do it, Jack?" Bertie called over the general conversation out in the main room. "The whole enchilada? OPEC, too?"

Swamp couldn't hear the answer, but Bertie was closing the door, a satisfied expression spreading over his face. "It worked," he announced to no one in particular. "It fucking worked. Amazing."

"*What* fucking worked?" Swamp asked, almost shouting himself.

The door opened again and in walked Tad McNamara. He was grinning as he came over to shake Swamp's hand. Everybody wants to shake my hand, but nobody will tell me shit, Swamp thought. He repeated his question.

Bertie and McNamara sat down at one end of the conference table, flanking Hallory, who finally explained it.

"You've been the victim of a Communist plot," Hallory said.

"There aren't any more Communists," Swamp said, and Hallory grinned.

"Figure of speech, Mr. Morgan. But you've been running a script ever since we first dropped that firefly in your lap. And today is payday. As I told you earlier, the attack was a fake. The German, Heismann/Hodler, was real, and he really thinks he's done his job. But his controller worked for us."

"You're telling me you people knew where this guy was all along?" Swamp asked.

Bertie and McNamara looked down at the table. Hallory

was nodding. "More or less," he said. "His campaign to kill the nurse was not in the plan, of course, but we had to let that play out."

"Jesus Christ, you let that guy damn near kill that woman."

Hallory was shaking his head. "We didn't know he could change shape like that. We didn't really know what he looked like, because not even Mutaib knew what he looked like. The guy always wore a disguise of some kind after he went through all those surgeries."

"Is that why Immigration came back with oatmeal when we pulled the string on Heismann and Hodler?"

"They were following instructions, Swamp. A lot of people followed instructions in this op without knowing what or why they were doing it."

"And the fire at the clinic?"

Hallory looked uncomfortable for the first time. "That again was at Heismann's initiative. When we started this thing, Mutaib warned us that Heismann might wipe out his trail. The problem was that we didn't know when he would actually finish his plastic surgery program, other than it would be before the inauguration, because after that, he'd go to ground. There were admittedly some unknowns loose in this little equation."

"And what equation was that, exactly?" Swamp asked. "Anybody?"

"Did you see all those transports out there?" Hallory said. "On the screen when you came through the Situation Room?"

"Yeah. And?"

"Those transports were all staged last week at Diego Garcia, in the Indian Ocean. Now they're convened at Prince Sultan Air Base in Saudi Arabia. They began landing two hours after the 'attack' took place, coincident with an ultimatum from the United States. Right about the same time as we sealed their borders and their airspace."

"Ultimatum."

"Yeah. An ultimatum that said we had direct, incontrovertible, *eyewitness* proof that a faction of the Saudi royal family was behind a decapitation strike aimed at the inauguration proceedings. That American transports were loading up every American citizen who could get to the air base. And that unless the Saudi government handed over everyone involved in this attack, plus every swinging dick currently in the country who'd ever been associated with, a member of, a supporter of, an ally of, a relative of, a business or banking partner of—you name it, anyone, and especially Saudi government and military officials who'd ever even *thought* about or mumbled the name Al Qaeda—a dozen or so hundred-kiloton nuclear warheads would soon be arriving to turn the entire Kingdom into green glass."

"Wow."

"The Agency had a preliminary list of about six hundred people 'of interest.' The Saudi royal family has informed us they're going to hand over some two thousand sweating bastards, who apparently are on their way to Prince Sultan Air Base as we speak."

"Mutaib was dealing with the Saudi royal family?"

"He was dealing with a Saudi prince," Bertie said. "Admittedly, there are dozens of them, so one can just about always say he's dealing with the royal family."

"Was the king involved in this?"

"No. This was one faction, one of many. They owned the bank, they'd installed Mutaib, and they approached him about doing the attack. Unbeknownst to them, he'd gone infidel on them. He contacted us in Langley when he finally understood what they were contemplating. We brought it to the fusion committee, where someone came up with an interesting idea."

"Which was?"

"Which was, in essence, why not take over the plot? Let them think they'd actually executed the attack, and then, once and for all, beat the Saudi problem into complete submission. And one of the things we'd need was an eyewitness."

"Eyewitness proof," Swamp said. "And that would be *me*?"

Hallory nodded his head. "Right after this fake attack, we told them that land-based intercontinental ballistic missiles were being retargeted and readied for launch. We showed them some video of what that looks like. We told them that we would turn every horizontal habitable acre of the Kingdom into the world's biggest caldera if they didn't meet our demands. Like I said, we said we had lists. And if anyone on our lists didn't show up under guard at Prince Sultan Air Base in four hours' time, we would launch."

"And they believed it?"

"Hell yes. The whole world has been watching a very carefully and elaborately staged disaster scene play out on the Capitol steps. We've got footage of the attack. We've got footage of the terrible damage, hundreds of bodies. We've got smoke, ambulances racing through town, because ambulances did race through town. They just didn't go anywhere."

"Holy shit."

"The whole world got to see what we allowed them to see, because this is probably the only city in the country where we could pull this off. We're the feds. Mediawise, we own this town. We've got every channel—visual, data, voice, broadcast, satellite—including all the foreign embassies' comms, locked down or jammed down. We have all the major networks clamped off, with only one television channel going. And that channel is ours."

"Wouldn't they figure that out?" Swamp asked. "That all their regular sources had been shut down?"

"A total national emergency," Hallory said. "The government took over everything immediately. Foreign governments would expect that. It's what they would do. And brother Mutaib, who, as the head of one their most important banks, was de facto an important member of the Saudi establishment here in Washington, dropped a hint to the Saudi security service in Riyadh about thirty minutes before the ultimatum hit. Said there was a rumor circulating in Saudi circles here in Washington, to the effect that the attack was the responsibility of this faction. And then he, as well as their embassy, went off the air. Yeah, they believed it."

Swamp shook his head in wonder. "And the president, the president-elect? They're safe?"

"As I explained, everyone is safe. *We* fed the target coordinates to the German via Mutaib. He did do his own little reconnaissance, but there was no way he could get the exact coordinates without waltzing up to the steps of the west portico and pointing his GPS at the sky. Plus, *we* provided the Russian mortar, and the mortar rounds. The German had no way of knowing. He was totally dependent on Mutaib for logistics."

"But what about all those people? The people invited to be there?"

"All hustled inside the Capitol when the first round was fired. We took over the TV coverage and began transmitting some really good special-effects work, courtesy of our friends in Tinseltown. They do that shit pretty well, don't they?"

Swamp nodded. "I saw it. It was very realistic. Even the bit where the cameraman dropped his teeth and left the scene. But after that, it was all smoke and noise in that house. My ears are still ringing."

"Especially that," Hallory said. "They set it up to look like the one camera still going was unattended. The actual TV signal was running thirty seconds delayed, so we had time to switch over. We cut off the other networks, and we cut off all the sound. But we let it run for about three minutes before we showed a Secret Service agent, all bloody and bandaged, run up to the camera, and then it went off, too. After that, it was all government statements, official briefings, like that. But the whole world, including the Saudis, of course, got to watch what looked like unfiltered, if totally doctored, video of mass murder and mayhem. Good stuff."

"And your eyewitness?"

"That was going to be you. Which is why Lucy was right there, waiting to pick you up. When the time comes, you are going to be taken before some cameras to tell the world what you saw and that a German terrorist, hired by the Royal Kingdom Bank, did it."

Swamp finally asked the question he'd been wanting to ask for several minutes. "How did you guys know that the German wouldn't just shoot my ass the moment he caught me sneaking around there?"

Hallory looked at McNamara for a second before answering. "I guess we didn't."

"You guess you didn't."

"No, we didn't. We had the house wired, of course, so we could hear some of what he was doing in there. But we had to be very, very careful with that—if he'd tumbled to surveillance, he'd have been gone. We did know that you'd gone there, and we did know he'd taken you prisoner."

"So there was a plan B?"

"Another agent."

"An actor, actually," Hallory said.

"So the whole time—"

"The whole time you were running with the firefly, you were headed toward the second floor of that town house," Hallory said. "We knew you'd keep going on it. That's what you were famous for. Swamp Morgan, the closer. At some point, we had to kick you out of OSI, but when we thought you might be hesitating, you got a new job offer. From Bertie here."

Swamp suddenly remembered Bertie's speculation about a decapitation strike, back when he'd provided the details on Heismann. He had to admit he'd been skillfully steered—

suggestions, musings, planting the seeds of every action he took. They weren't kidding. They'd been playing him right from the beginning. Now they were playing the whole world. Bertie was watching him work it out. Bertie, who'd come out of the dark just a couple weeks back, renewing old acquaintances.

"How long do you have to keep this thing going?"

"It'll be dark here in a couple hours. Europe's quit for the day. Going on midnight over there in Arabia, of course. But everyone who was at the Capitol for the inauguration will stay there, inside the building, until the last plane leaves Prince Sultan Air Base. Probably early tomorrow morning, our time. In the meantime, we've got crews working hard to provide the appropriate visual fodder for all the foreign intelligence satellites—cleanup crews at the Capitol, emergency vehicles, signs that we're treating the wounded inside the building, smoke generators, all the appropriate infrared signals, the military at DefCon Two, warships leaving port, AWACS and F-sixteens on station—the whole bit."

"You've got both presidents held at the Capitol?"

"Their doubles anyway," Hallory said. "The real deals might have actually been here in the White House, with the real chief justice."

Another muted cheer sounded from the Situation Room. McNamara slipped out to find out what was going on.

Swamp's head was spinning with the sheer scale of it. The whole damn thing would depend on the feds being able to totally isolate Washington electronically. Landline telephones, radios, cell phones, satellite phones, microwave links. And most of all, the media sources—which depended on these means of communication. Show them pictures, cut off the sound. Hell yes, that would work. They only had to do it for about twelve hours, too. And after that . . .

McNamara came back into the room. "They've loaded and launched eight C-seventeens so far. The Saudi secret police are bringing people in by the truckload and in helicopters from places all around the country. We're talking bankers, bureaucrats, clerics, students, and not a few senior military officers. Not to mention over a thousand detainees, and that many again are expected shortly. A second wave of C-seventeens is leaving Dee-Gar right now for Sultan. And, best of all, the OPEC deal is confirmed."

"What OPEC deal?" Swamp asked.

Hallory hesitated for a moment. "This is what makes the thing really worth doing: The Saudis have agreed to opt out of OPEC. From now on, they will sell oil as an independent producer—at prices within a range acceptable to the United States, at least for a while anyway."

Swamp thought about it. "I can see us being able to force them to do that now, but when they find out the attack was a fake . . ."

"The *results* of the attack were fake," Hallory said. "But the plot to make the attack itself was not. That faction hired the German. He did fire those mortar rounds. The original plot was not a fake—that was entirely their idea. The deception today nets us the heart and brains of Al Qaeda. The fact that they started it in the first place will net us the destruction of OPEC as an effective cartel. Which is going to dampen a lot of the outrage from our Western brethren, once they understand OPEC has been gutted."

"And how does this collection of prisoners square with our own suspect lists?" Swamp asked.

Bertie smiled. "An amazing congruence of suspected Al Qaeda supporters to actual detainees has been achieved," he announced in his best PR voice. "Of course, we knew who they were all along, you understand."

"Yeah right," Swamp said.

Bertie just grinned.

"They just showed the Saudis some footage of a Trident submarine surfacing in the vicinity of Dee-Gar and opening its missile tubes," McNamara said. "Just in case any of the top-echelon princes start to lose focus now that they've been up most of the night."

"I thought those things launch from underwater," Hallory said.

"Well, yeah, but you can see the palm trees on Dee-Gar behind the sub, and British patrol boats providing security. They shot it earlier from a helicopter, and you can see down into the missile tubes. Scary shit."

"They really believe we'd nuke the oil fields, too?"

"They were told we'd use neutron bombs. High-altitude detonations that kill all living things but do almost no physical damage. No sense in losing a big chunk of the world's supply of oil just because its owners went extinct."

Swamp watched the excited confusion in the Situation Room through the open door, and he marveled at the pictures streaming in from the other, now-dark side of the world. On one screen, there was file footage rolling of two American aircraft carriers plowing through cobalt seas, pushing up house-size bow waves, their flight decks bristling with fighter-bombers. On another, three busloads of American citizens carrying bags were debarking from buses in front of a C-5 transport, obviously bound out of a country that was now square in the crosshairs of an aroused nuclear-armed state. That footage was replaced with some of an entire field of ICBM silos with their armored caps rolled aside, showing glistening ten-story high missiles connected to umbilicals and venting oxygen. A third screen showed an entire flight line of huge Air Force transports glinting dangerously in white sodium-vapor lights at the Saudi air base as streams of captives, bound and hooded, were channeled up into ominously dark aluminum wombs by American military police.

The dark side of the world, it occurred to him, in more ways than one. "How'd you get all the American businessmen and contractors out before this went down?" he asked.

"Christmas," Hallory said. "We made damn near everyone come home for Christmas home leave, or they'd lose their passports. Only a select few went back. They were all ordered to be at Sultan this morning, our time, including the diplomatic staff. Supposedly to watch the inauguration on a special American television channel. We've had people leaving for many hours."

"So where's the German?" he asked.

Hallory shook his head. "We don't know. The first responders at the duplex reported a nearly naked woman running out of the other side of the duplex, screaming hysterically about some guy being up there where the fire was."

"Sure she was a woman? Sure it wasn't Heismann dressing up again?"

"Guys swore she was real. Naked from the waist up. No Wonderbra or falsies. A full rack, and they were real. Female underwear on the bottom, and no compromising equipment in view. The neighbors reported that a middle-aged woman did live in the other half of the duplex, so now the cops're looking for her."

"Was this running woman middle-aged?"

"She was mostly naked, Swamp. That's what the cops remember. Naked and hysterical. They probably weren't looking at her face."

"So where's the German?" Swamp asked again.

"We've given that problem to the District cops," Hallory said. "And, of course, we have some of our own assets looking, too. But we almost don't care now. If they find him, he's probably not going to survive the arrest. Thanks to you, they want him for a cop killing, plus we kept the District cops, and everyone else in the city, at arm's length from the Capitol. The folks looking for the German don't know this wasn't real."

Swamp saw Lucy giving him a cool, appraising look through the partially opened door. He wasn't sure he cared for that look. "And if he does survive the arrest?" he asked.

"Then he's also an eyewitness. You make a pretty good one, but the shooter himself?"

Another pawn, Swamp thought. Just like me. Who's probably going to get dead before morning. Just like me?

Heismann retraced his original route down into Rock Creek Park, where he had begun his frustrating campaign to tie off the loose end named Connie Wall. It took him forty-five minutes to reach the stone bridge, from which he could see the bluff on which the nurse's house stood. He'd attracted some curious looks from passing cars while walking down the hill road, which had no sidewalks, toward the bridge, a man in a raincoat and suit, carrying a briefcase. But most people seemed to be intensely interested in getting home. It was getting darker as the winter sun gave up on the day. There had been no police cars. Probably all still downtown, he thought. Sometime in the next few hours or so, if they didn't already know it, the disaster would be pinned on his former employers, whether by the pensioner, if he survived, or by the documents he'd put in the mailbox. The mailbox decals said they emptied those boxes six days a week, rain or shine. Then the world might get to see some real fireworks.

No great loss, he told himself as he left the road and merged into the underbrush near the stone bridge. The Arab States had stopped evolving somewhere back in the 1500s and offered nothing but religious barbarism these days. And oil, of course. Fortunately, the precious oil was all safely thousands of feet below ground. He wondered if you could burn radioactive oil as easily as the original stuff. Probably. The hard part would be drilling through all that crusty sand.

He took a quick look in both directions along the road and then slipped deeper into the woods.

Swamp was stiffening happily in a corner chair, dozing while Bertie and Hallory worked separate phones, coordinating the cleanup at the bank and steering assets toward the growing logistics problems up on Capitol Hill. The airlift operation was about two-thirds complete on the other side of the world, and the controlling factor now was how many hours of darkness remained in Washington. The consensus in the room seemed to be that the hoax would be sustainable only until daylight returned to Washington. The major Western governments and permanent members of the UN Security Council had already been briefed secretly that both presidents were alive and well and that the American government was intact. They'd also been told that what had been shown on global television might not be entirely accurate, except for one solid fact: There had been a Saudi plot. The only place the faked attack itself had to be believed was in Riyadh, and that only until all the prisoners were out of the country.

A Uniformed Division officer pushed the side conference room door fully open and told Hallory that they were ready. Hallory terminated his phone conversation and motioned for Swamp to go with him. Swamp rubbed his eyes and then rose carefully out of the comfortable chair, checking all his major joints for full range of motion before actually trying to walk. He felt pretty scruffy compared to everyone else in the Situation Room, some of whom stared at him as he was led out of the conference room.

The officer took them past the Navy mess, the Secret Service command post, upstairs to the foyer coming off the West Wing colonnade, and into the staff office outside the Oval Office. Whoa, Swamp thought, thinking about how he looked, but Hallory was guiding him through the ornate doors. The new president was sitting behind the famous desk, and he got up to come over and shake Swamp's hand.

"Mr. Eyewitness," he said with a tired smile.

"Mr. President," Swamp croaked out. He hadn't voted for this man, but that invisible presidential mantle was fully in place, and Swamp was suitably awed. The president had them both sit down and asked if they wanted coffee. Following Hallory's lead, Swamp shook his head. It hurt when he did it, and the president noticed.

"Mr. Morgan, you've done the country a significant service. I apologize that you weren't exactly given a lot of choice in the matter."

Swamp thought for a couple of seconds. "Well, Mr. President, did we get what we wanted out of this?"

"Oh yes, I think we absolutely did. You've been down in the Situation Room, so you know what's been going on. It's a pretty amazing bag. Plus, there's the OPEC arrangement."

"As I understand it, sir, Al Qaeda is a lot more than Saudis," Swamp said. "Those bastards are everywhere."

"They are indeed, but their heart and soul, not to mention their principal funding source, has always been Saudi. We've known that for a long time. And right now, the bulk of that cancer is being transported to a special internment camp on Diego Garcia, courtesy of our British allies. More permanent facilities are being readied at an air base in Texas. I suspect my predecessor is looking forward to seeing some of them up close and personal."

"You took some big chances today, sir," Swamp said.

"So did you, from what I've been told. Again, I apologize for not giving you a vote."

"I take the king's shilling," Swamp said. "But won't there be pandemonium in the rest of the world?"

"For the most part, our real friends have been put into the picture, Mr. Morgan. And our sometime friends might prosper from a little pandemonium these days."

"And the world financial markets?"

"All the New York markets are closed, tomorrow begins the weekend, and the after-market operations are experiencing some significant communications problems. The 'disaster' will be exposed tomorrow, and the money guys will have two days to think about it. If the premarkets still seem to be unstable by Sunday night, we'll announce the new OPEC situation."

"What will happen when the Saudis find out they've been duped, if I may ask?"

"The plot to decapitate the government was real, Mr. Morgan," the president said. "Right now, the principals in the Kingdom are fairly quivering with gratitude that they're not all in low earth orbit. We had two objectives: To eviscerate Al Qaeda. We won't kill it, but we've hurt it grievously, and to achieve that, we needed blood and gore on the Capitol steps. Those pictures are what's driving them to fill those transports, before we change our minds."

"And the second objective was the OPEC concession."

"Correct." The president was looking at him with speculative eyes, and Swamp wondered if he wasn't getting out of his depth asking these questions.

"Will they hold to that OPEC agreement, sir? After they discover the hoax?"

"You mean might they get angry and slap a Persian Gulf oil embargo on the West again?"

"Yes, sir."

The president sighed. "You can't quote me on this, Mr. Morgan, but the mirror image of an embargo is a blockade. They slap an embargo on us, we'll put the fleet across the Straits of Hormuz, take out every facility that makes or pumps water over there, and then wait for the hammer of Allah to work. In the meantime, nobody will get Persian Gulf oil. Maybe some genius will find a way to drink it."

Swamp nodded, suddenly awed by this glimpse of absolute power. "I assume we're looking for Heismann or Hodler, whatever his real name is," he said, glancing at Hallory. "I wouldn't mind joining that hunt."

"First, we need you to make an appearance before the Joint Committee on Intelligence, Mr. Morgan. Up on the Hill."

"Yes, sir, I understand."

"Do you?" he asked, his eyes boring into Swamp's. "The

entire free world has a lot to gain tonight. You'll be given a briefing paper before you go before the committee. At this juncture, it's supremely important that you adhere to that paper."

Swamp frowned. He was tired and beat up after his experience in the town house. The president was trying to tell him something, but without coming right out and saying it.

"What is the official line, sir?" he asked.

"You recognized the terrorist who fired the mortar," Hallory prompted. "You pursued him to the bank, where you made a positive identification that this was the man. When he attempted to escape, with the aid of armed accomplices in the bank, you shot him and them dead."

"And that's the end of the story, Mr. Morgan," the president said.

"Ah," Swamp said.

"We didn't start this," the president said as he stood up. "They did. But you personally can go a long way toward finishing it."

"Yes, sir," Swamp said again, beginning now to understand fully what was expected of him. Both he and Hallory rose, as well.

"Thank you, Mr. President," Hallory said.

"Thank you, gentlemen," the president replied. "Thanks to the three of you, and my predecessor's huge *cojones*, America struck a real blow for freedom today. Everyone involved will be suitably recognized once the dust settles."

An officer opened the doors to the Oval Office and they went out into the secretarial area. Lucy was waiting for them there. She handed Hallory a piece of paper and then turned aside to answer her cell phone.

"Aha," he said.

"Find him?" Swamp asked.

"His trail, maybe," Hallory said. He looked at his watch. "We've got time before your briefing. Up to a little ride in the dark?"

Lucy was looking his way again as she talked on her cell phone. "Am I going to survive this one?" Swamp asked.

Hallory blinked but then smiled. "That game's over, actually," he said.

"Just checking," said Swamp.

The director of the Secret Service appeared and signaled Hallory that he wanted a word, which left Swamp standing alone with Lucy. She had cleaned herself up a bit, fixed up that golden hair, but she still looked like she'd been on the losing end of a domestic dispute. She closed the cell phone and gave Swamp her full attention.

"How are you feeling?" she asked. Her expression was fathomless.

"Like a puppet who's just had all his strings cut," Swamp said. "Now I'm supposed to walk on my own again."

"You were very lucky back there, in that bank."

"I guess so."

"Two on one at close range. Assuming they were trained security guards, one of them should have hit you."

"I did a Marco Polo. Dropped flat and looked for China. I wish I could say that was due to years of great tactical training, but the truth is, I think I was looking for China. They went rapid-fire. Which usually means high."

She nodded. "And you?" she asked. "You went rapid-fire, too?"

"Yeah. But of course for me, being down on the floor, shooting high was good."

"And the Arab? The scene report said you fired just *once*?"

"Only had one round left," he said. "Although I didn't know that at the time. I was just bound and determined that he wasn't going to get away, not after what I'd seen him do. Hitting him was pure luck." He stopped, regretting his words. "Or maybe not, as the case might be, I suppose."

She nodded thoughtfully, suddenly preoccupied again, and then Hallory was back. As they headed for the east entrance, Swamp wondered about Lucy's sudden interest in his tactical ability. And also why the president had mentioned three of them as being responsible for this amazing caper. His joints were still aching after being zapped by that Taser, and it was an effort just to keep up with them.

Connie collapsed back into the bed, her heart pounding and her breathing ragged. She'd just managed a halting tour of the entire ground floor, checking windows, pulling drapes and lowering venetian blinds, and making sure the doors were all locked. She'd used the wheelchair and the walker to get around, but it had been much harder than she'd anticipated. She had no reserve of strength. She'd thought about going upstairs, but stairs were clearly out of the question. Besides, the danger, if it came, would come from ground level.

It was almost dark outside, and she'd turned off all the lights in the house except the one in the dining room, where the hospital bed was. She wished she could raise someone on the phones, but they were still all shut off. And Jake might not even know she'd left the hospital yet. Probably did *not* know, she realized, remembering her somewhat evasive answer to his question about her leaving.

Okay, so she was on her own. She reached over to the dining room table and pulled the small oxygen bottle with its attached mask over, cracked a valve, and took some hits to get her breathing stabilized. The doors were all locked. The lights were off, all but the small bedside lamp here in the dining room. There was no way he would know from the outside that she was in the house.

The car. He'd see the car. But if he thought he'd killed her up there in Garrison Gap, then he'd have to assume someone else had brought the car back. As they had, in fact, done.

"But I will need your house," he'd said.

For what—to hide out until the hullabaloo all died down? They'd expect him to try to get as far from Washington as possible, not hide out right here in town, so it wasn't a bad move.

She looked over at the dining room curtains. They were moving around, billowing in slightly as the night wind probed the edges of the plywood. If he came around to the back of the house, he might see this light. That won't do, she thought, so she reluctantly switched it off. The room dropped into total darkness, except for a small green diode on the pain pump and the green clock numerals on the microwave in the kitchen.

The wind seemed more audible now, and she could almost hear the drapery material rustling above the noises of bushes scratching against the living room windows. She tried the phone again, but it was still dead. Were they all dead, or just hers? Was he here already? Had he cut the wires? Was he out there right now, crouching in the bushes in her backyard, figuring out how he was going to get in without setting off the alarm system? She felt around under the bedcovers for the snake gun. Had she loaded it? She couldn't remember.

With trembling hands, she cracked the awkward thing open. She put a finger in the back of the barrel and felt nothing at all.

She hadn't loaded it!

And where was that box of special twelve-gauge shells? Somewhere here in the dining room with the rest of her stuff. But where? And should she turn on a light to see? No. Seen from outside, a light coming on would mean that someone was in the house.

She lay back on the covers and thought hard. Where was the damned box of shells?

She heard a noise outside that was not the wind. She was sure of it. Something different from tree branches or the usual creaks and cracks of an old house in winter. She felt his presence, and then she held her breath when a thin white beam of light came through the crack between the edge of the sheet of plywood and the curtain. A small spot of white light began to traverse the room, starting at the door into the kitchen and moving slowly, very slowly, across the dining room–living room wall. She pulled the covers right up over her head and got as flat as she could under them, all the while keeping one edge pushed up by her face so she could watch that spot of light.

It traveled slowly but purposefully across the wall, but higher than it should have been if he wanted to see everything in the room. Then she remembered that someone on the ground outside looking in would have to have a box or a small ladder to really see, because the ground was almost six feet below the windowsill.

The beam went across the china cabinet, slowed, and then kept coming, now illuminating the serving surface of the buffet. There was all sorts of stuff up there.

Including the small green rectangular end of the box of shells.

She watched the spot of light slip across the box, go past it, and then stop.

Shit! He'd seen it.

But when the light came back, it didn't stop on the box. It stopped on the shiny scale of the sphygmomanometer, which the nurse used to take her blood pressure. The light lingered on that for a second and then moved left again, continuing its inspection of the wall.

If I slip out of the bed right now, before it gets to me, she thought, then maybe I can get to the box. And the light, if he does get it low enough, will reveal an empty bed, too.

Have to do it, she told herself. Now, right now. Before he puts a crowbar into that crack and levers the plywood out of the way. The alarm system is only on the doors, not the windows.

The tiny spot of light was illuminating the tops of the living room curtains twenty feet away, but still moving left. Pretty soon now, it would hit the headboard of the hospital bed. She dreaded making the move—it would put direct pressure on the bandaged area of her back.

You have to move now, she told herself again. Before he sees the bed. Without that gun, you are dead meat.

She stopped thinking about it and forced her bare feet to move left and out from under the covers. The floor was colder than she had expected. She hesitated, trying to figure out the best way, and then decided to slip down onto her knees at the side of the bed, as if she were saying prayers. That would allow her to hold on to the sheet so she wouldn't fall, while getting her down on the floor with the least wrenching of her back.

She rolled carefully over on her left side, clutching the covers, thankful for the traditional nurse's tight tucks at the corners, and then felt her knees slide off the edge of the mattress and then down onto the frame, and finally onto the floor with a bump that jarred her wound and caused some of the bandages to pull tautly across her skin. But she was on the floor.

She could see the beam of light coming closer, so she smoothed out the covers as best she could and began to crawl over toward the buffet on her hands and knees, each movement a little more painful than the last. She kept her head hunched down so as not to pass out, but the dizziness wouldn't go away. It hurt to move, but she had to get to the buffet.

She couldn't see the light anymore from her head-down position on the floor, but she could see the legs of the buffet, and they were right in front of her face. Her knees were stinging and the stitches around her wound felt like they were tearing, but now she had to stand up, or at least reach up, and get that damned box. She lifted her head but then put it right back down again. She was much weaker than she'd thought. She looked left, searching for the beam of light, but it wasn't there anymore.

Show time, she thought to herself. He's done looking.

Now he's coming. She grabbed one of the legs of the buffet and began to lever herself off the floor.

"Where we going now?" Swamp asked as they headed up Wisconsin Avenue in a Secret Service sedan. Lucy was in the front seat with the driver, seat belt fully on this time. Hallory and Swamp were in the backseat.

"District cops report a church warden finding what he's calling a government Suburban. There was a badly injured cop in the back. This was the same cop who's been missing from the downtown Mall area for a couple hours. And it sounds like the same Suburban that was seen going through a police checkpoint, supposedly en route to Georgetown University Hospital."

"Why do we think it's him?" Swamp asked.

"Because the VID numbers make it as the Suburban bought last Friday," Lucy said. "By a Mr. E. Hodler."

Swamp nodded his head in the darkness as the car went through another roadblock checkpoint on its way uptown. The cops examined ID cards, looked inside, and then waved them on. Swamp could just about imagine what had happened: The guy had had a vehicle prepositioned, maybe two, but he'd rigged one out as federal law-enforcement vehicle. He'd done it before, if that was the same Suburban that had been behind Wall when she fled to West Virginia. Find a cop on the way, run him down, throw the body in the back, and then get through the rest of the roadblocks with an injured cop, one of their own, in the back. Yes indeed, that would work.

"The cop alive?"

"Was when they transported him. Came to long enough to say the guy ran him down in the street near the Jefferson Memorial."

Ten minutes later, they stopped next to the entrance to the church parking lot, which was shimmering with flashing blue strobe lights. The lot was filled with vehicles and both District cops and Secret Service agents.

"We really want to go in there?" Swamp asked.

"It's the hottest part of the trail right now," Hallory said.

Swamp looked out the window, searching for a street sign. "Where are we now, exactly?"

"Quebec Street and Wisconsin," the driver announced. Swamp turned to Hallory.

Quebec Street, Swamp thought. That's her street. The nurse. Who'd been trying to tell them one more important thing. "I have a hunch," he said. "He's obviously abandoned the vehicle. He either had another one set up here or he's on foot. And if he's on foot, I think I know where he's headed."

"And the answer is?" Lucy said skeptically, turning around in her seat.

"This is Quebec Street. That nurse's house is on Quebec Street. On the other side of Connecticut. That's only— what?"

"Five, six blocks," the driver said, pointing. "That way."

"Okay. He thinks he killed her up there in West Virginia. After trying more than once. Why did he want her dead so bad?"

"Because she could ID him, of course," Lucy said wearily.

"But she couldn't. This guy had totally changed his face, not to mention the ability to grow breasts on demand and fool even Ms. Wall into thinking 'he' was a 'she.'"

"Excuse me, 'grow breasts'?" Lucy asked, exchanging glances with Hallory. The driver was listening with rapt attention.

"When I first interviewed Connie Wall, she told me that they'd done a partial sexual-reassignment procedure on one male patient. Gave him the ability to pump some kind of fluid into skin pouches on his chest that would give him totally realistic breasts. One procedure among many, but what if that patient was him? That naked lady running out of the burning duplex? I'll bet that was him. And he needed the nurse dead because he needed her house when it was all over. To go to ground, right under our noses."

Hallory looked at Lucy. She shrugged. "It's possible, I guess," she said.

"Anybody got a better idea?" Swamp asked.

Heismann swore under his breath. He hadn't been able to find anything to stand on, so he'd been able to see little through the crack between the plywood and the window frame. The problem was that antique race car. What was it doing back here at the nurse's house? Would the police have just returned it to her house, even though she was dead? The car salesman had indicated it was valuable. Wouldn't they lock it up?

He shivered in the cold night air. The neighborhood was as quiet as a graveyard. He'd seen no police vehicles anywhere since crossing Connecticut Avenue. The house was dark and locked up tight. Those security company decals on the doors and out in front of the house meant that there was an alarm system, but would it sound if all the telephone systems were still down? It might not ring in a central office, but the system could have a locally audible alarm that would bring neighbors if he smashed in a door.

So, it would have to be a window, and this one was already broken. Leaving his briefcase, he went over to the garage, but now it was padlocked. Then he saw the trash cans. There were two. He rolled them both over behind the house to the dining room window and turned them over on their sides. But when he tried to stand atop them, the plastic gave way and he sank silently down into the grass. He stepped back from the house, backed into the shadow of a tree, and examined all the windows again. Then he saw movement up on the second floor, in a window above the back porch roof. Was there someone in there? He stared hard at the window, and then saw it again: A curtain or drape moved. He finally realized it was moving in time to the occasional gusts of wind.

That upstairs window was cracked open.

He stared at it for a few more minutes before he was convinced. Then he saw that one of the tree branches above him could get him to the porch roof.

Connie heard the scuffling noise out on the back porch and held her breath. Had she imagined it? But then it came again, a sound of something heavy moving on the roof of the back porch. Then silence, then a sound from *inside* the house: a window being raised. She swore silently: She hadn't been able to check upstairs. She knew exactly which window it was, the one she cracked open to provide some cross ventilation when the house was all shut up in winter.

She heard him drop down onto the floor and then slide the window back down. The floorboards creaked above her head, although he was otherwise moving quietly. She could imagine that white flashlight beam probing the upstairs rooms and hallway. She lifted the phone again, but there was still no dial tone. She put it back as quietly as she could and lay back on the covers, gripping the snake gun between her knees.

Okay, he's going to search the house and eventually come in here. What do I do then? She tried to remember what the dealer had told her about the snake gun: It was originally a flare pistol. Twelve-gauge gun, but only an eight-inch barrel. You needed to hold it with both hands, because it would kick like a mule. Around six feet for an effective range. And you had to use only the special shells, or it would blow up.

She heard footsteps coming down the stairs. He was confident now, sure that there was no one home. Connie gripped the gun with both hands. She raised her knees under the sheets, and twisted her body slightly so that she could cover both doorways, the one to the kitchen and the one to the living room. Then she took a deep breath and waited.

Heismann stopped two steps from the bottom. His mental antennas had detected something. What, exactly, he didn't know, but his instincts were buzzing, and he drew out the Walther. He remained on the stairs for a whole minute, wondering if he was imagining something or if there was someone in the house. Because that's what it felt like—someone in the house.

All right, if there was, where would he be? The stairs gave him a view of the living room, where he'd encountered the nurse's derringer that night and nearly had his head blown right off. The chair was upright but still askew in the living room, but the drapes were drawn, admitting almost no light except across the very tops. That left the kitchen and the dining room. He tried to remember the layout. If he went through the living room and into the dining room, someone in the kitchen could get behind him by coming down that front hallway. But if he went the other way, left through the hallway, into the kitchen, and then into the dining room, anyone trying to sneak up on him would have to come down that narrow hallway, and thus present a much better target.

He listened some more, but he heard only the outside sounds of wind and shrubbery. He felt his heartbeat accelerating. He'd been on the run ever since noon, and he was tired, thirsty, and hungry. His "breasts" hurt. But he was almost safe. No one would look here for the Capitol bomber. All he had to do was wait for a few days. They couldn't keep the capital of the entire free world sealed for more than a day or so, and then he'd find a way to start that car out there and simply drive away. He'd go west and then south, sell the old race car and get himself another invisible minivan. He had two other passports, so from Florida to the islands, and from there to his money. And from there, anywhere at all.

There was no one in this house. It was just his overactive imagination. He pocketed the gun and stepped down onto the main floor and walked into the kitchen, where he turned on the light. He saw the hospital bed in the dining room out of the corner of his eye and stopped dead, one foot just off the floor. There was someone in the bed.

He turned his head and stared, amazed to see that damned nurse looking right at him, her knees raised as if she were about to give birth, the sheet pulled right up to her chin.

He turned slowly to face her, casually dropping his right hand into his pocket to grip the Walther. When he had his fingers wrapped securely around the gun, he stepped toward her, forcing a smile.

"I am impressed," he said, although his throat was dry. Where were her hands? Did she have a gun under those sheets? But then he saw that she was trembling, and that her lower forearms were visible just above the hem of the sheet, which she must be clutching. Hands trembling, too. He took another step, approaching the foot of the bed. Her face was very white, and there were pouches under her eyes.

"You should be dead," he said in German.

She just looked at him, her eyes bright with fear. He took in the pain pump's tubing, the walker, and the wheelchair. She was here, but she was gravely injured. And so helpless, those knees drawn up like a child's, as if she'd just awakened from a bad dream and found her nightmare at the foot of the bed.

He stood there for a long moment. Well, there was nothing more to say here, now, was there? He withdrew the gun, glanced at it to make sure it was ready for business, and then lifted it.

Something changed in the woman's eyes, and then the sheet billowed out toward him and the world ended in a shattering roar of noise, bright red light, and incredible pain.

Lucy got up off one knee, the edges of her mouth working, as if she were trying to contain something in her stomach. "Took his face right off," she announced unnecessarily. "And his chest . . . well . . ."

Swamp could see that Hallory was a little green around the gills, too, which wasn't surprising, given the mess on the floor. He didn't feel so great himself. Connie Wall had her head back on the pillows, her eyes shut. Her face was pale in the light from the overhead fixture. They had driven up right before the shooting, and there was still a strong smell of gun smoke in the room. And some other smells, too. They'd been getting out of their car in the driveway when they heard the truncated roar of a shotgun in the house. The driver had broken down the back door and then had to silence the alarm siren with a hammer while the other three assessed the situation in the dining room.

The blast from the snake gun had blown Heismann's body back into the doorway between the kitchen and the dining room, where it proceeded to create a large, wet, and still-spreading mess all over the kitchen linoleum. The driver was talking on his radio to the agents still gathered in the church parking lot.

"What is that thing?" Hallory asked, looking at the snake gun lying on the scorched sheet. Swamp explained it to him.

"On their way," the driver announced.

Hallory stepped delicately through all the blood. "So, is that him?" he asked Swamp.

"Who could tell?" Swamp replied.

"Open his shirt," Lucy said. "See if—"

"We shouldn't disturb the body," Hallory told her. "Technically, this is a crime scene."

Lucy made a rude noise. "You want a scene?" she said. "Go to Capitol Hill. I need to know if this is what those cops saw."

Hallory looked to Swamp as if seeking some support, but Swamp just shrugged. He wanted to know, too. They sure as hell weren't going to get anything from the wreckage of this guy's face. Lucy walked out of the dining room, going the long way around to the kitchen. She rooted through drawers until she found the cutlery. She took out a knife, then threw a pile of dish towels next to the body so she didn't have to walk in all the blood. Bending over, she cut his shirt off from neck to waist, then pulled the material aside.

Swamp looked but couldn't tell. The bottom half of the shotgun pattern had hit the man in the chest, and where any breasts would have been was now a field of tattered hamburger. It was possible. There was one rather pronounced fleshy pouch on the right side. Was that a gleam of plastic? A plastic sac? Yes, it was.

"Son of a bitch," Hallory whispered.

"Got that right," Connie croaked from the dining room. "Is he dead?"

Just before sunrise, Swamp took his seat at the folding table in the makeshift hearing room, which looked like a plain staff lunchroom. He was flanked at the table by Hallory and the director of the Secret Service. Sitting behind Swamp, their chairs against the wall, were the United States Attorney General and the Secretary of Homeland Security. Some of their staffers were standing alongside. Swamp felt uncomfortable sitting at the witness table while cabinet officers were sitting behind him like support staffers, but that was the way they had wanted it. We'll be behind you all the way, Mr. Morgan, the AG had said. Wa-a-y behind me, Swamp remembered thinking.

Seven tired and harried-looking legislators were facing him at a second folding table on the other side of the room. They were variously dressed—some in shirtsleeves, some with ties, others with no ties. Only the chairman had a suit coat on. The room was already hot and musty. Attempts to open some windows had failed as they were apparently painted shut. There were no thrones, no individual microphones, no raised dais—none of the accoutrements Swamp normally associated with a congressional hearing. Each legislator had been allowed one staffer, who had to stand right behind his principal, his back against the wall. The chairman, a white-haired senator, had a single yellow legal pad in front of him. The other legislators had a variety of folders, notebooks, coffee cups, and legal pads. Arrayed against one end wall was a bank of television cameras surrounded by portable stage lights. The reporters were trying hard not to stand on the snake's nest of thick black cables littering the floor.

The chairman knocked an empty coffee mug against the table to bring the session to order. He said good morning to the cabinet officers and then addressed the director of the Secret Service. "Mr. Director," he began, "I understand that you've brought us an eyewitness to what happened yesterday."

"Yes, sir, that's correct," the director replied. "This is Special Agent T. Lee Morgan, U.S. Secret Service, retired. He was recalled to active duty in the Department of Homeland Security after nine eleven, and he now serves in the Office of Special Investigations, DHS."

"Very well. Mr. Morgan, please stand to be sworn."

As if upon signal, the floodlights came up and Swamp had to avert his face to avoid the sudden glare. The chairman himself, apparently used to bright lights, stood and administered the oath, and Swamp stood to solemnly swear that he would tell the truth, the whole truth, and nothing but the truth, knowing already that he was about to do just the opposite. He had had one hour to read and reread his White House–prepared statement, an exercise that had required more coffee than he'd had in many months. Now his hands were jittery as he gripped the statement folder, which bore the gold seal of the Secret Service. Hallory scribbled something on his legal pad and then turned it so Swamp could read it. It said, "Relax—they think you're a hero."

"Mr. Morgan, we've not been given a copy of your statement, so if you'd like to just say what you have to say, we'll proceed from there." He paused to rub the side of his face wearily. "It's been a long day and night for everyone, and I apologize for the rather Spartan setting. But the building is very full right now, as I'm sure you know."

He proceeded to introduce the other members of the

hastily convened Joint Committee on Intelligence for the benefit of the television cameras, then signaled for Swamp to read his statement. Swamp could almost feel the cameras swiveling to focus on him. One of the attorney general's staffers got up and passed copies of the statement down the table to the legislators, while another gave some copies to the press representatives.

He read the statement, which consisted of ten pages of double-spaced fourteen-point text. The statement gave the antecedents of his original investigation, and then the sequence of events Swamp had experienced personally, up to and including the shoot-out at the bank. It ended with Swamp saying that he could unequivocally certify that the person who fired the mortar rounds was the same person he had met before during the course of his investigation: the managing director of the Royal Kingdom Bank. He closed his folder and waited for questions.

The chairman started it off. "Mr. Morgan, did you have the bank manager under surveillance after you and the District police interviewed him?"

"No, sir."

"Why not?"

"No probable cause, Senator. At the time of the interview, it appeared that their only connection to the German was essentially a money-changing operation. An entirely legal one, which they did report."

"How about after you realized they had rented the town house to this German assassin?"

Swamp hesitated. The whole truth, as much as I can, he thought. In fact, both Hallory and the director of the Secret Service had coached him to channel all the questions, if he could, toward blaming the Secret Service for not listening to him. "Congressional hearings are always about blame," the director had told him. "They'll know the attack failed, but not why yet. We need twenty-four more hours of confusion to tie off all the loose ends."

"By the time we—I—realized that there was a connection, and that the target might be the inauguration, not the speech to the joint session, I was no longer inside the system, Senator."

"You'd been fired, I understand. They thought the whole thing was a firefly."

The director raised his hands. "Special Agent Morgan wasn't fired, Senator," he said. "He was on recalled annuitant status, and he was simply relieved of his active duties."

"With all due respect, Mr. Director," the chairman said, "that's a distinction without a difference. Mr. Morgan, did you feel like you got fired?"

"Yes, sir," Swamp said, remembering his instructions.

"Yet you persisted, Mr. Morgan. You'd been a member of the SES, a high-level official at Secret Service headquarters. Surely you knew the rules."

"I judged these to be highly unusual circumstances, Mr. Chairman," Swamp said. "Just as the security precautions for the inauguration were unprecedented. It seemed to me that I had little to lose if I was all wrong, but the government had a lot to lose if this guy managed to bomb the inauguration."

"You got that goddamn right, Mr. Morgan," the Senator said. Murmurs of agreement filled the room. "I was in the Army, in Vietnam, seems like a hundred years ago. I heard that mortar thump when it started firing. I knew what that sound was. I knew that it had to be a big-ass mortar, too. And when stuff started going off in the air above the Capitol, I was looking for my trenching tool." There was some subdued laughter.

"I was in the room with him, Mr. Chairman," Swamp said. "And with the mortar. I still can't hear so well. But the main thing is, it was him. The manager of the Royal Kingdom Bank. He even taunted me. I think he wanted me to watch him do it."

"So, Mr. Morgan," the chairman said, his genial smile

fading, "if the bank manager executed the attack, where the hell was the German during all this?"

Swamp just looked at him for a second. The smile was gone, and the Senator now looked like the prosecutor he had been. Shit, Swamp thought. He knows. He knows this is all bogus. Hallory cleared his throat gently, as if to nudge Swamp to respond. "All I can surmise, Senator," Swamp said, "is that something happened right there at the end that necessitated the bank manager's direct intervention. We think the German had had a year's worth of identity changes at that clinic, which was owned in part by that bank. That may have been part of his payoff—he was known in the Interpol system as an associate of Muslim terrorist organizations. They used him to destroy his trail—to burn the clinic, to kill the one possible witness who was still alive and who might remember what he looked like when he was finished with the ID changeover. They used him to set up the town house for the attack. To receive the weapon. To set up the weapon."

"And then what, they kill him right before the attack? Why would they do that?"

"I don't know, sir. Perhaps they were cleaning up their last remaining loose end. I don't know."

"You don't know," the chairman stated, more than a hint of skepticism in his voice.

Swamp decided to just stay on message. "There's a lot we don't know here," he said. "But what I *do* know is that the man I saw firing that mortar into the Capitol was Emir Mutaib. And when I confronted him at the bank, he ran."

"And you just shot him?" This from another senator.

Swamp nodded. "That's right, Senator. His security guards opened fire on me. I returned fire. When the smoke cleared, he was in the parking lot, about to get away. At that time, I had no idea the attack had failed. In fact, I was pretty much convinced that the attack had succeeded all too well. So, yes, I shot him down."

"Was this man working for the government of Saudi Arabia?" another legislator asked.

"I don't know, sir," Swamp said.

"Does the government of Saudi Arabia own that bank?"

"I don't know, sir," said Swamp. "I would assume that the same people who run Saudi Arabia run that bank. That's the way things seem to work over there. But technically, I don't know."

The chairman leaned forward intently. "So you don't know for a fact," he said, "that this man you shot, this Mutaib, was an agent of the government of Saudi Arabia?"

"What I know, Senator, was that this was the man who fired that big-ass mortar at you yesterday noon."

There was a sudden silence in the room. But the senator then came right back at Swamp. "The fact that you were all on your own, both in that town house and, later, in that bank, indicates to me a pretty massive failure of the government's intelligence operations, Mr. Morgan. Can you explain how that happened?"

"No, sir, I cannot. I can speculate, maybe."

"Yes, by all means, speculate for us, Special Agent Morgan."

Swamp resisted an urge to wet his lips. "I think that the entire security apparatus here in the capital was totally focused on the inauguration. You also have to remember that my theory of this so-called firefly was that the attack was aimed at the joint session. Mr. Hallory here was not convinced. He thought it was a firefly, and if it wasn't, he had almost another month to deal with it. But the correct answer is, I don't know."

"There's an awful lot you don't know, Mr. Morgan," the senator said.

"I'd have to agree with that assessment, Senator," Swamp said. "I suspect there will be the mother of all investigations into this one once the smoke clears."

"You all can count on that, sir," the senator said, then sat back in his chair, his lips pressed together. Swamp didn't know what to say to that, but it was clear that some, if not all, of the legislators knew or at least suspected that they were being had. He was saved by the attorney general, who announced from behind Swamp that the Federal Bureau of Investigation, which, unfortunately, had not been brought into this matter, had already launched an in-depth investigation into all aspects of this breach of homeland security. To Swamp's surprise, the secretary of Homeland Security echoed those sentiments, choosing to ignore the AG's cheap shot. Or was he reading from his own carefully prepared script?

"This is all passing strange, Mr. Attorney General," the chairman said. "But as for me, I'm presently satisfied that the actions now being taken against the government of Saudi Arabia as a result of this incident are justified. Especially given the fact that we have an eyewitness. And, for my esteemed colleagues' information, yes, there will be a great deal of sorting out to be done in the days ahead by the new Congress. Gentlemen, I'm exhausted. I see no purpose to prolonging this little . . . exercise. Do I hear a motion?"

The representative to his right moved to adjourn, and this was seconded immediately by another senator. The television lights hissed off and the media people began a scramble to get through the door at the same time.

"Good job," the attorney general murmured as he brushed past Swamp on his way over to talk to the chairman. Hallory said the same thing, then indicated that they should leave through the room's other door to avoid any media ambushes. They succeeded in doing that and made their way down to the congressional subway, which would get them back to one of the House office buildings.

"I felt like I was standing in front of a campfire, kicking up smoke and ashes," Swamp said.

"Exactly so," Hallory replied. "Trust me, some of them knew it was Kabuki. But now the whole world knows we have an eyewitness to what they were trying to do. Consider yourself the smoking gun."

Swamp had a thought. "This was really all about the OPEC thing, wasn't it?" he asked. "The Al Qaeda prisoners—they were the bonus, not the other way around."

Hallory didn't say anything as the two-car train pulled quietly alongside the platform. "That's well above my pay grade, but I think you may be right," he said finally. "I mean, hell, what's the Persian Gulf always been about, Swamp? Bombs and oil. Bombs and oil. That's all those people seem to be good for."

"Why do I know I'll be coming back here for the entire next year?" Swamp asked as they waited for the doors to open.

"Not necessarily," Hallory said. "I will, for damn sure, and lots of folks senior to me, too, especially when the full scope of this becomes known."

"How about Lucy?"

"What about Lucy?"

"She was kind of intimately tied up in this thing, wasn't she?"

Hallory looked at him with a tired smile. "Two things you don't know about Lucy, Swamp. One, she doesn't work for me. She works for Bertie. She's his direct liaison officer to the Homeland Security fusion committee. And, two, this whole goddamned thing was her idea."

Swamp was stunned. "She works for *Bertie*? She told me she was your deputy."

Hallory shrugged. "I guess she lied," he said. "She does that, you know. All those people across the river do that."

Union Station was starting to fill up with nervous travelers at ten o'clock that morning as Swamp and Bertie sat in the Amtrak passenger lounge, having a cup of coffee. The city had been unsealed at 7:00 A.M., and there'd been a government announcement on all the television channels that the national emergency was over. The new president had come on the air to give a reassuring speech, accompanied by his principal cabinet officers. He said that details of the terrorist attack on the Capitol would be forthcoming later in the day. And then he declared the capital and all members of the government were safe and that the conspiracy, which had originated in Saudi Arabia, had failed. He hinted broadly that what people had seen on their televisions might not have been entirely accurate. Swamp had watched the news back at Secret Service headquarters, including three minutes of his own testimony before the hastily assembled Joint Intelligence Committee, and then he'd grabbed a quick nap in Hallory's office. A while later, Bertie'd showed up from Langley to announce that they were going to Union Station. Swamp had cleaned up in one of the office bathrooms.

On the drive over in the Agency limo, Bertie had explained that the government wanted their eyewitness out of sight and out of town for the next few weeks. The airlift of over two thousand Al Qaeda suspects was almost complete, and all Americans were either out of Saudi Arabia or safe at the Prince Sultan Air Base there. The Saudis, along with the rest of the world, were going to learn over the course of the weekend the full extent of the American deception. All this would be clear once the government restored the phones and the airwaves to civilian control.

"There's going to be medium chaos in the network news departments," Bertie'd said. "Not to mention some pointed questions in certain diplomatic channels. You know, why the governments were *not* given a heads-up last night at the White House."

"Pointed questions."

"Well, you know how they get," Bertie had replied with a weary smile. "This is going to be a really interesting weekend here in Fun City."

Swamp had tried to stifle a yawn but failed. "Where's Ms. Wall?"

"That cop you were working with? Detective Sergeant Cullen, was it? Word is that he's taking her in."

"Is that smart, legally speaking?"

"Not like there's going to be a court case," Bertie'd said, and Swamp had smiled, remembering what Jake had said earlier. Then they'd arrived at the station, where there were still squads of cops milling around out front and within the great hall. Bertie had ushered Swamp through the security cordon with the help of some Secret Service agents, handed Swamp a ticket to Harpers Ferry, and then suggested coffee, as they had about a half hour to kill.

"We're going to need a full-scale deposition for the classified case record," Bertie told him, lowering his voice as the passenger lounge filled up now that the station was coming back to life. "That will include input from Special Agent White, of course, and the District police and Arson officers involved."

"And your own case executive, Lucy VanMetre? Gonna depose her, too?"

Bertie's eyebrows rose. Swamp told him what Hallory had said earlier. Finally, Bertie nodded. "That's probably more than you needed to know."

" 'Liaison officer' to the fusion committee? That could mean anything at all, Bertie."

"As you should know, Swamp. Anyway, we'll have a full-scale deposition team out there later today. Get it all on tape. Then you're expendable."

"Again."

"Like you told the Man, you take the king's shilling. We're all expendable in this business."

"Back there in the Situation Room," Swamp said. "You said you people had surveillance set up in that duplex. So you guys had to know that Heismann looked like that banker."

Bertie took a sip of coffee. "Not really," he said. "We had no phone line in there. We could listen via a radio device, but video requires a much bigger pipe. Besides, we had no reason to know what he looked like."

"But you owned Mutaib from the time his German went under reconstruction. Mutaib's bank owned the Paki doctors. You could have followed every procedure done on the German."

Bertie's face hardened. "And your question is?"

"You knew I'd go after that guy."

"Yes, we suspected you might."

"The cop car, the one that crashed into Lucy's official car down on the Mall—accident?"

"Looked like one to me," Bertie said.

"And yet their seat belts failed, while mine worked."

"Government cars. What can I say? Maintenance often isn't what it's supposed to be. The front ones get a lot more use."

"And the car was hit hard enough to hurt the people in the front seat, and yet it was still drivable."

"Swamp," Bertie said patiently, "you're starting to bore me."

"Who were the shooters at the town house, Bertie? Right after the attack?"

"Shooters?"

"Yeah. Long guns. When I tried to get out of the burning building. On the front side."

"This is news. Did you report this to Lucy when she picked you up?"

Did I? Swamp asked himself. No, he had not. He'd been deaf and his adrenaline had been crashing. He said as much.

Bertie gave him an elaborate shrug. "And your real question is?"

"You knew I'd go after him, and that Mutaib might get killed in the process, especially after what *I'd* seen on television."

"Perhaps." Bertie sighed. "There was also the chance that he'd just put up his hands and surrender. He was our Arab, after all. He didn't have to admit that in front of all those people, but he could have just gone along quietly when you showed up."

"Until his security guys drew down on me. Who were they really working for, Bertie?"

"Oh, c'mon, Swamp."

"They working for you, too?"

"Listen to you."

"But if he did try to escape, there was a pretty damn good chance his ass'd be a grape. As, in fact, it turned out."

Bertie looked around to make sure no one was eavesdropping. "What's your real problem here, Swamp?"

"Two problems: One, you let your pet Arab authorize a fire that killed four innocent people. Okay, maybe two not so innocent. But two were. And second, I think you used me to take your Arab out. Something I suspect *you* were going to have to do, one way or another."

Bertie shrugged again, but he said nothing.

"I didn't sign on to be one of your executioners, Bertie."

Bertie's face settled into a cold mask. "Correct," he said. "You were *Mutaib*'s executioner. And we, of course, don't employ executioners."

"Oh right."

"We don't," Bertie insisted. He looked around for a moment. "They're all contractors."

"I was carrying Agency contractor credentials when I did that," Swamp said.

"Actually, you weren't. You left them back in your apartment, remember? Where I suspect they've since gone astray."

It was Swamp's turn to stare. "Look," Bertie said. "Okay, you were used. To very good effect, as it turns out. We've bagged the heart and soul of Al Qaeda and split OPEC right down the middle. Prices are going to fall like a stone. If your conscience is really bothering you, balance one turncoat Arab banker, two shady foreign doctors, and two—okay, three—innocent American women against all those folks in the World Trade Center back on nine eleven. That do it for you?"

"I can't believe I'm hearing this, Bertie. This is America, for God's sake."

"It's America *at war,* Swamp. Wake up and smell the body bags. War's hell, just like Sherman said." He sat back in his chair. "If it's any consolation, the German told Mutaib he was going to kill the next-door neighbor, and we did get her out of there. But that's not what you're really worried about, is it?"

Swamp stared down at his coffee cup for a moment as the first departure calls of the morning echoed through the cavernous station. "No, that's not what I'm really worried about," he said finally.

"You have to say it."

"The Arab banker's dead, which solves one of your problems. The mortar man's dead and his face is conveniently gone, which solves another problem. Which leaves me. I'm the only *outside* guy left alive who knows what actually happened here."

Bertie smiled then and patted Swamp's hand reassuringly as he got up to leave. "You just get on your train and go home, Swamp Morgan. The deposition team will be up shortly."

"How do I know it's a deposition team," Swamp said, "and not a disposition team?"

"Because you're the eyewitness. That committee tape this morning was nice, but a live agent will be better, you know, once Congress really gets rolling."

"Hallory said this morning that I wouldn't be needed on Capitol Hill."

"He was probably trying to make you feel better. Of course you're going to be going back there. We all are. You're our only inside guy."

"Would that be the case if Mutaib were still alive?"

"But he isn't, is he?"

"Hell, I don't know," Swamp said. "That body at the nurse's house had no face. Who's to say that *wasn't* the German at the bank? Who's to say you and Lucy don't have Mr. Mutaib squirreled away in a safe house somewhere?"

"So who was the guy at the nurse's house, then?"

"Some body you planted?" Swamp said. "Shit, Bertie, which guy did I kill, and which guy did she kill?"

Bertie just shook his head. "You're tired and you're getting paranoid in your old age, pardner. You'll be just fine. Just catch your train. We'll talk later, when you've had a chance to rest up a little, get your head right."

Swamp couldn't think of anything else to say, so they shook hands and Bertie left. Swamp exhaled forcefully as he watched Bertie walk across the concourse, and then he saw Bertie acknowledge the three large men who came out of nowhere to assume protective flanking positions around him. Swamp wondered how long they'd been there while he and Bertie had been having their little talk. Or who else was still in the great hall, watching him.

He got out his ticket and then looked up at the scrolling arrival and departures board for his train time. The train to Harpers Ferry always went through Baltimore, and the next train to Baltimore was boarding in eight minutes on Track 9. He finished his coffee, left a tip, and headed for the bathroom. From there, he went out to Track 9, walked up the line of cars until he finally saw some empty seats through the windows, and slipped into the lead car.

Once in his seat, he tried to reassure himself that everything was going to be all right, despite his many misgivings. This wasn't Russia. The Agency wasn't the KGB, or whatever it was called these days. Yes, there would be hell to pay from several quarters, but the timing had been pretty clever—precisely at the change of administrations. If any truly ugly stuff came out, the new people could always blame the previous people, which probably had been the original agreement. And, yes, there were still lots and lots of Muslim and other terrorists out there bent on the destruction of Western civilization in general and America in particular, but the United States had stabbed the Arab piece of the puzzle right in the heart. Take down the terrorists' brains and money, get your hands around the oil monster's neck, if only temporarily, and you'd done a good day's work.

Bertie was right: He was exhausted, and his physical exhaustion was making him paranoid. And he was not the only one who knew what had happened—everyone involved in the planning of this thing knew it. Those security guards in the bank couldn't have been working for Bertie, because that would mean the Agency had put out orders to kill him.

The train lurched into motion and began to gather speed. But something Bertie had said was still nagging at the back of his mind—some phrase. He closed his eyes and thought about it.

What had Bertie said about the deposition team? "Get it all on tape." Right. "And then we're all expendable."

No, wait—he actually said, "Then you're expendable."

And they already have me on tape. Saying the most important thing anyway. And *not* saying anything about what happened later, or why. Surely they're going to explain, or are they just going to hunker down and make inquiring minds find out?

"Get it all on tape. Then you're expendable." That's what he'd said. Right out loud.

He opened his eyes as he felt the train slowing. Why are we stopping? he wondered. And then he remembered. The commuter trains always stopped at the New Carrollton Metro station, out along the Capital Beltway, en route to Baltimore and the northeast corridor.

But wait a minute, he thought. Not going this way. Not outbound in the morning. They stop at New Carrollton on the way in, but not on the way out. They only do that at night, to pick up outbound passengers.

In fact, he thought as he looked at his watch, this can't be a commuter train to Harpers Ferry. It's too late in the morning. It might be going to Baltimore, but it sure as hell won't be going over to Harpers Ferry. He shook his head to clear the cobwebs. He knew he was still missing something important here.

And then it hit him: It wasn't a workday. This was Saturday. There weren't any commuter trains to Harpers Ferry on Saturday.

So why had Bertie put him on this particular train? Maybe he'd forgotten it was Saturday, too?

The train slid into the New Carrollton station and squealed to a stop. On impulse, Swamp got up, walked quickly to the back of the car, and got off. He saw the backs of a few people as they climbed into the train but otherwise the upper station platform appeared to be empty. The train's doors remained open.

What am I doing? he thought, even as he acknowledged a strong and certain urge to get off that train. He couldn't have put it into words, but he just knew.

Get out of here. *Move.*

He walked quickly over to the down escalator, which would take him to the tunnel leading over to the Metro side of the station. He caught a glimpse of some other men getting off at the far end of the upper platform, but right now he was unwilling to turn around and show his face.

Move. Get off this platform.

He kept his face averted and started down just as he heard the train doors close behind him. As the train began sliding out of the station, his head was just about to descend below the escalator's threshold. He chanced a look just as the sixth and last car pulled abreast. The train was accelerating, going fast enough to blur the faces visible inside the windows. Which is when, just as his head submerged below the platform, he caught one quick glimpse of a woman sitting all the way in the back, next to the very last window. A woman whose hair looked like a glowing mass of spun gold in the midmorning light.

Lucy?

He felt his pulse begin to pound and his face flush in fear. He started to trot down the descending escalator. As he stepped off at the bottom, his mind was already arguing with itself. Couldn't have been. Sure looked like her. You couldn't see her face. That hair. Had to be. Couldn't be.

He turned right and headed for the street-level tunnel that went under the tracks for the main line. There was no one else about, and he hesitated as he got to the entrance. It was a short tunnel, maybe a hundred feet, but brightly lighted, with clean white-tiled walls. Nothing in the least sinister about it. But still he hesitated. Tunnels were traps, and if that had been Lucy in the train, he needed to watch his ass here. He was physically and mentally exhausted, so he really had to concentrate.

He glanced around one more time, but there was still no one in the lower station, not even an Amtrak attendant in the ticket kiosk.

That's strange, he thought. There's always—no, not on Saturdays. On weekends, they check the tickets on the train. Right.

He started into the tunnel, already planning out his route. He'd take the Metro's Blue Line all the way over to the Rosslyn station, then transfer for Ballston. Get to his apartment. Get his Rover. No, the Agency had his Rover. Or did they? He'd left it in Arlington, hadn't he? What seemed like a hundred years ago. He was getting confused.

When he was three-quarters of the way through the tunnel, he stopped short as four large men appeared in front of him. They were all in suits and trench coats, and all wore mirrored sunglasses. Instinctively, he turned around, but a fifth man was walking into the tunnel behind him, dressed like the others, but without the sunglasses.

It was Gary White.

"Gary?" Swamp called, hearing his own voice break in nervous relief.

"Mr. Morgan, sir," Gary said as he closed the distance. "You look like hell, if I may say so."

"What—"

"Relax, Mr. Morgan. We're the good guys. We've got cars out front."

Swamp didn't know what to do. The other four had closed in from their end of the tunnel, but nobody was taking a threatening stance. A man and a woman came into the tunnel, saw the group of men in suits, and walked right by them.

Swamp and Gary ended up in the backseat of a gray Crown Vic; two of the other men sat up front. The other two were in another Crown Vic behind them. Swamp rested his head on the back of the seat as the cars pulled out.

"Okay," he said wearily. "Where to this time? And what's going on?"

"What's going on is that Carlton Hallory had some reservations about Mr. Walker sending you on a train ride. So he sent us to ride with you."

"I'm really losing my touch," Swamp said. "I never made a one of you."

"You weren't exactly looking, sir," Gary said.

"Been a year or two since I've been a street agent."

"You never really were a street agent, Mr. Morgan."

Very true. Swamp nodded. It hurt his neck. "You said *Carlton* Hallory."

Gary grinned. He still looked like a twenty-year-old to Swamp. "Nothing wrong with your hearing now," he said. "I didn't call him Mr. Hallory today because he and I are the same rank."

Swamp turned to look at him in surprise. Gary was still grinning. "That's right. I was part of it. Right from the git-go. When did you ever get an assistant so easily?"

"I'll be damned," Swamp said. "You never worked Homicide in Fairfax County?"

"Nope. Been Secret Service for a whole lot longer than my dashing good looks would indicate."

"So what's going on? Where are we going?"

"You recall when they had your apartment phone up? La Mamba set that in motion, but she ran it out of Hallory's shop. Even got a warrant, but she used the Secret Service to get it. Secret Service operators, too. Anyway, I was your intercept supervisor."

"Cute."

"Well, we were keeping it *en famiglia*. Anyway, after the big op went down, some of the equipment operators came to see me. Said they were concerned because of some things they'd heard Lucy say in Hallory's office."

"They had *her* phones up?"

Gary shrugged. "Her office, not her phones. The Agency can always detect shit on their phones. Carlton thought as long as the Agency was going to bug a Secret Service operative, it was only fair that the Secret Service bug an Agency operative in return."

"Hallory didn't trust Lucy?"

"She didn't get that nickname working with us," Gary pointed out. "It was mostly insurance. Anyway, I took their concerns to Carlton early this morning. When Bertie said he was going to get you out of sight after the hearing, Carlton felt uneasy. So did I. So here we are."

"And where are we going?"

"Home, Mr. Morgan. We're going to take you out to wild and wonderful West Virginia, see you through your front door, and then some guys are going to hang around for a while. Remember the agents who took you back to the apartment the day you were fired? Remember them asking you what was going on? They're back there in that other car. That's how the word got around headquarters."

"And you'll do this long enough for Bertie and company to get the message?" Swamp said.

"That's right. The director has approved this, by the way. Care to guess why?"

Swamp thought for a moment. "This whole thing was a very dangerous gambit," he said finally. "Even though it succeeded, Congress is going to investigate." He turned to look at Gary. "This was an Agency operation. Lucy's brainchild. The Secret Service was used. I'm living proof of that."

Gary smiled again. "Exactomundo," he said. "Emphasis on that word *living.*"

"The Secret Service, looking after its own."

"Ass," Gary added. Swamp laughed.

"This is the Agency we're talking about," Swamp said as the cars accelerated down the on-ramp to the Capital Beltway. Westbound, he noted with some relief. "They're not the goddamned KGB. I'll admit that this was a pretty daring thing for them to attempt, much less pull off. But they'd never go so far as to put a hit on another government agent, right?"

"Right," Gary said.

"Right," Swamp echoed, nodding his head. The other two agents were nodding, too.

There was a five-minute silence in the car as they drove around the top of Washington, D.C., headed for the Cabin John Bridge. The Beltway traffic was its usual swirling mass of aggressively incompetent drivers. Then Swamp couldn't stand it any longer. He turned to look Gary in the eye.

"Okay," he said. "Was that or was that not Lucy I saw on that train?"

All three answered in perfect unison: "Yes."

Swamp leaned back, exhaled, and closed his eyes.

Fireflies II

There are many species of firefly illuminating the common summer garden, and while their bioluminescent blinking appears to be completely random, it is not. Most of the blinks we see in the warm night are actually males in search of a mate, and each kind of firefly blinks out a specific code. The females watch. When they see the code of a male of their own species and it suits their purposes, they blink back the same code. The male then approaches for breeding.

Occasionally, though, the female has another need in mind—hunger. In this situation, the female will watch the night sky for a while, and she will see a male not of her own species blinking out his code as he searches for a mate. The female will then blink out the code of that alien firefly species, and when he approaches, she will kill him and eat him.

Deutermann Electrifying Action
from P. T. Deutermann

DARKSIDE
0-312-98636-X

At the United States Naval Academy, a murderer lurks in the shadows of tradition.

HUNTING SEASON
0-312-97906-1

A retired FBI agent finds himself and his daughter trapped in an elaborate game of political scandal and personal revenge.

TRAIN MAN
0-312-97370-5

A single man known as the Train Man is bringing down bridges one by one. But as more death and destruction strike, no one can guess that far greater danger is looming.

ZERO OPTION
0-312-97004-8

They call it "Wet Eye": a biological weapon that literally eats out the eyes of its victims. Now, the only person who can stop a biological nightmare is an innocent child.

Edge-of-Your-Seat Suspense
from P. T. Deutermann

SWEEPERS   0-312-96447-1

A sweeper gone rogue is about to rock the inner ring of the Pentagon—and his killings have only just begun.

OFFICIAL PRIVILEGE   0-312-95713-0

Naval Commander Dan Collins and Naval Service lawyer Grace Ellen Snow's investigation into a grisly murder leads them into Washington's highest circles and to a case of sexual misconduct that could create a national scandal.

THE EDGE OF HONOR   0-312-95396-8

It is the height of the Vietnam War, and young Lt. Brian Holcomb is aboard the guided-missile frigate USS *John Bell Hood*. As the *Hood* steams towards an explosive showdown with North Vietnam's killer MiGs, Holcomb will be forced to make the most agonizing choice of his life.

SCORPION IN THE SEA   0-312-95179-5

As skipper of an obsolete destroyer, Mike Montgomery is skeptical at first about the strange sightings and unexplained events off the coast of Florida. The East-Bloc threat has passed, and others don't have the technical capabilities to challenge the U.S.—or do they?

AVAILABLE WHEREVER BOOKS ARE SOLD
FROM ST. MARTIN'S PAPERBACKS

SOTS 09/04